COME FIND ME
IN THE
MIDNIGHT SUN

Visit us at www.boldstrokesbooks.com

COME FIND ME
IN THE
MIDNIGHT SUN

by

Bailey Bridgewater

2023

ISBN 13: 978-1-63679-566-9

This Trade Paperback Original Is Published By
Bold Strokes Books, Inc.
P.O. Box 249
Valley Falls, NY 12185

First Edition: November 2023

Credits
Editors: Anissa McIntyre and Stacia Seaman
Production Design: Stacia Seaman
Cover Design by Tammy Seidick

Acknowledgments

Thank you to the team at Chulitna Wilderness Lodge in Lake Clark, Alaska. It was during a writing residency there that I read Alex Tizon's amazing article "In the Land of Missing Persons," which inspired this novel. Thank you also to my beta readers and to Anissa at Bold Strokes. I could not have asked for a better editor. All writers should be so lucky as to find a gem on the first try.

For Natasha, who's been pulling for this book from the first draft.

Prologue

June 2009: Seward, Alaska

Some people say it was luck. Somehow my eye caught the familiar shape, dark against the base of charred spruce trunks. The gray ash settled all the way to the tree line of Mount Alice where the fire ran against hard shale and burnt itself out. Luck isn't what I call it.

The blackened skull was fragile. When I tapped it tentatively with my gloved finger, the bone at the back of the skull began to cave inward.

"Careful. It looks like the molars are still there. We can use them for ID." The tech grunted and lifted the thing roughly, then dropped it to the bottom of a large plastic sack. He was supposed to have been off this weekend, not to have been called to investigate the fire's cause. Not to recover remains where there should have been none.

If I hadn't been there, maybe he would have never noticed it. Or maybe he would have, and he would have let it be. A family would have gone on believing they'd buried their son, and a mother could have gone on hoping that one day the man she loved would return home— just walk through the door after five years, happy to be home. In early fall, the snow would have covered the skull and it would have collapsed under that weight, the teeth caught in the summer melt, flowing down to one of the waterfalls, into the fjord, out to sea. Maybe it would have been better that way.

Over two thousand people go missing in Alaska every year, most of them from the Kenai Peninsula. They go into the wild to try to survive. They go to commit suicide. They crash their cars and try to walk home, confident the land they love won't harm them. They wander the wrong trail, fall into a ravine, freeze, starve, collapse into an ice bridge, slide through a crack in a glacier—and they're gone. The animals find the remains, and the snow covers what the animals can't digest. Eventually most of them find their way to the ocean. Probably. There are no explanations and no clues. They leave families that don't know whether to hope or to grieve.

For Alaskans, it's an unspoken agreement. You move here, you work here, you raise your children here knowing that at any moment, the ground may shake, a tsunami may carry you away, an avalanche may bury you. It is the nature of the land. Which isn't to say we three hundred or so state troopers don't try with the missing persons cases. We do. But each trooper covers an area the size of smaller states, and we start a search knowing that ninety-nine times out of one hundred, the person couldn't make it more than a couple days anyway. Perhaps they wander home in a day, in a decade, after a lifetime—but often they don't. After a short time, another case presents and we quietly stop looking, especially in winter.

But then, every once in a long while, a fire, a strange item in a pile of bear scat, a piece of fabric in a stream, brings someone home.

CHAPTER ONE

October 2004: Anchorage, Alaska

The missing persons call comes in from Seward. Their troopers are occupied with a string of burglaries on a cruise ship that Carnival must want solved ASAP so the boat can leave approximately on schedule. Pretty much all of us troopers resent the cruise lines, but we do their bidding since no one can argue with the money they bring to the state. Especially not the politicians who keep their eyes on the force. So, with their officers deployed to the ship, Seward needs help for this less dire case.

There aren't divisions of labor in Alaskan policing like there are in the Lower 48, where the forces are infinitely bigger. If you're an Alaska State Trooper, you work homicide, you work missing persons, you work kidnapping, you speak with the shopkeepers mad about hoodlums on their street corners, you give tourists directions, you make notes about where the bears and moose are today. Don't get me wrong, there are things I like about it. I like the introverted shopkeepers and fishermen and the schoolkids who insist their buddy put that candy bar in their jacket as a joke. I like trudging up snow-covered mountains to post signs warning hikers about moose, though everyone else claims to hate that job. Some days my job feels meaningful. But other times, even working in such a massive state, the job feels claustrophobic. With so few of us upholding the law, it can feel as if all eyes are on us, even off-duty.

Chief Quint calls me to his office. The other officers all seem to look away from me at once. They generally pretend not to notice me. At least that's how it seems. I am a woman, and a brown woman—biracial. I've been here six months, and the jury is still deliberating whether I make the cut as an Alaska State Trooper. When the chief hired me, he was straightforward about that.

"It's my duty to let you know right off the bat that you're the only woman at this station now." He looked at the door as he spoke, as if five or six women might stroll in also looking for jobs. "Shouldn't be a problem at all, but if any of your fellow officers is anything less than accommodating, please come see me. There aren't enough for us to have officers who can't play ball for the same team."

I must have raised an eyebrow or scowled—my facial expressions always say more than I ever mean to—because he chuckled in a way that would have qualified him for a mall Santa position. "Oh, don't worry, they're a good group. A little old fashioned maybe. People around here tend to be, you know. They talk a big game sometimes, but you get out there on a case, and it's all equal. You've gotta be tough to handle a place like this." He waved a hand at the view of Anchorage's streets. "You show them you are, and they won't give you no trouble." He looked me straight in the eye and smiled. "I'd put money on you being just fine."

He's just as blunt with me now. "Linebach, we've gotten called to a case in Seward. Male, late twenties, been gone a few days. Mom has reported him missing. She's not exactly forthcoming with information. I'm thinking maybe she'll relate to you a little more."

I concentrate on not rolling my eyes. If he's assuming I have some magical feminine touch that makes difficult people want to talk to me, he's much mistaken. I've never been good at small talk, and my tendency to get straight to the point is often perceived as rude. Even by me.

Still, I don't say anything because I'm glad he thought of me first, even if it is because I'm the only female trooper in Anchorage. Besides, I like Chief Quint. He was the first person to make me feel welcome here.

I call the mother of the missing man immediately, a brand-new notebook the only thing to indicate my excitement. Through the gravel of her low voice, she explains the situation.

The missing person is Lee Stanton. He didn't show for the usual Sunday dinner at his mom's house, four miles up the road from his trailer, halfway up the Chugach Mountains outside Seward.

"Did you drive to his house?" She sighs into the receiver, but her voice remains steady when she speaks. She may be a heavy smoker; her sentences are periodically interrupted by coughs that sound wet and cavernous.

"Yeah, I drove to his place. That's the thing. I can see him missing dinner. Happens sometimes. He gets caught up playing one of his games or goes hunting and loses track of time. But…his things was boxed up. Most everything. Boxes with no lids. All them boxes had a Post-it Note on it with somebody's name written on it. *Ma*, or *Pa*, or *Johnny*—that's his cousin's boy—or *Aunt Sue,* my sister over in Primrose. That's not like him. Why'd he be giving his stuff away?" My first thought isn't a good one.

"Has he mentioned moving?" Her laugh turns into a phlegmy cough that lasts a full twenty seconds.

"Move? Where the hell'd he move to?" She laughs again but controls it. "No—no, he wouldn't move away. We've always lived here, same house even, until he moved out after high school. Don't know where he'd go otherwise. Anyway, his job is here."

"What does he do?"

"Fixes snow machines at a shop near town. Just him and a few other guys, they're the regulars."

"Has he been missing work?"

"Yeah, his boss says he's no-showed the last four days." Not a good sign. Still, if he's a suicide, a body shouldn't be too hard to recover. He probably wouldn't go hide himself. What would be the point?

"Any guesses as to where he might be?"

She exhales a long breath—or cigarette smoke. "Well, *no*, sweetheart, if I knew where he *might be*, I suppose I wouldn't have called *you*, now would I?"

I grit my teeth and try to remember fear doesn't always bring out the best in people. "All right. Can you give me the address of his place? I'll get over there this afternoon. Your address too if you would."

It's a nearly three-hour ride to the location, more if the road is blocked for a planned avalanche. I'm taking the Tank, a spacious but beat-up blue boat of an SUV we keep for long runs like this when we anticipate dealing with snow, which is pretty much always. The Tank's owner committed suicide and no relatives claimed the vehicle. Abandoned property becomes the force's property. It's a bear to drive and has several annoying quirks, but it's a better choice than my sedan.

I keep a go bag in my locker because troopers get called to so many far-flung locations, but this is my first opportunity to use it. Per my mental checklist, I have all I need: my gear, my notebook, a destination, and a case. I'm headed out. The chief yells for me before I can get to the door.

"Hey, you'll need a partner on this." I'm sure my face shows how unpleasant I find the idea. I always worked cases alone in DCS. I have major anxiety and extremely obsessive thought patterns. They help me do my job, but they're a little much for most people to understand, so I just work solo when I can. It suits me fine since I'm not one for talking much, anyway. This forced partnership with almost every case assignment is the aspect of this job I hate the most so far. I've never addressed the whole room before. It's usually just me talking to Chief Quint or whichever trooper I'm grudgingly working with on a particular case.

"Anyone want to come with me? Missing person. Road trip." The other officers stay perfectly still, side-eyeing one another. None of them will volunteer. The chief will have to assign someone. The others will make commiserating comments to the lucky guy as they punch him on the arm in solidarity. "Bad luck, brother. Hope she doesn't nag you to death." or "Watch out—you know how women drive." The usual.

In the end, it's Officer Michael Harper who's voluntold. He's younger than me, and I'm not quite thirty. He could be a lead actor in one of those childhood buddy movies, all blond hair, blue eyes, and round and pink at the cheeks. He's nice enough when he says anything, which has been about twice to me in the time I've known him.

When Chief Quint suggests to Harper he may want a break from Anchorage, Harper just nods and retrieves a granola bar and a small container of Nutella from his desk drawer before he heads to his locker. I wonder how he intends to eat the Nutella, since there are no utensils in sight. He crashes into my desk as he swings his bag over his shoulder on the way to the door. He touches the desk as if he's apologizing, then looks around as if to check whether anyone noticed. We're the only people standing, so odds are everyone did.

I look away. Other people being awkward makes me feel awkward. I hate that about myself.

I am in a hurry to get out of the station.

"Let's go." I grab the keys to the Tank and make deliberate eye contact with Harper to make it clear I'm driving. He smiles and nods. We load up, and after a few miles, it becomes obvious the Tank is having one of its good days. It works out its grinding and settles into a smooth and barely perceptible rumble. I pat the dashboard, feeling an odd fondness for the cranky vehicle, which sometimes runs so loud you can't hear yourself think. Unfortunately, Harper takes the relative silence as an opportunity to talk.

"Gotta be honest with you. I am really glad the chief put me on this one." I glance at him as he elaborates. "I don't get a lot of missing persons. I'm the chief's go-to for drug cases. Which, you know..." He shrugs. We both know drug cases are the vast majority of Anchorage crime. Even petty robberies usually end up being related to drugs. Harper clears his throat.

"I noticed you get a lot of the kid cases. That's because you're from DCS, right?"

"Yes, probably."

He whistles. "That's a job I couldn't do. No way. Kids, man. They get me right in the heart." He smacks his chest.

They can have that effect on me too. Children bring up a lot of complicated feelings since my time in DCS.

"Sounds like we've got an interesting case. What details did the caller give?" He flips open a notepad, though I'm not sure how successful notetaking will be right now. The Tank may be less vocal than usual, but it's never a smooth ride. On Highway 1, I recount the conversation with Mrs. Stanton about her missing son. Harper stops writing as he draws the obvious conclusion. "Suicide?"

"Yes. Probably."

"Easy-peasy."

"Wouldn't go that far." I talk as if I'm the veteran when my most significant experience with missing persons was with DCS.

"If he's a suicide, why didn't he just kill himself in his trailer? Guessing he had a gun."

"Right. Probably not so easy-peasy. Don't assume anything, and don't talk about him in the past tense in front of his mom."

"Right. So, what do we do when we get to his place?"

I fumble. *I don't know.*

"Take pictures?" I put the authority back in my voice. "Look for a weapon, anything like that, and without disturbing too much, I'd say. Take a walk around the trailer. If he was just out to commit suicide, I doubt he'd make a big effort to go far."

"If we don't find him right away, how long do we look?"

I can't even pretend to know the answer. "I think we focus on trying to find him today, yes?"

"Good plan." Harper opens the granola bar, and then the whole car smells like hazelnut. He dunks the bar into the jar. *Ingenious.* I watch a few crumbs fall from his mouth before I refocus on the drive.

❖

The scenery is amazing. It reminds me of the long drive to Anchorage six months ago.

Seattle had been my home for almost twenty-nine years, but I had to get away. My partner had just broken up with me. My mom had died after being sick for ages. I had no family and a job I gave way too many shits about to remain healthy. I packed a few possessions, loaded the car, and left.

I hopped around Washington and Oregon for a while and worked as a security guard for a few months in Eugene. I asked around to see if I could get into legitimate law enforcement, but it was rent-a-cop or bust. The towns had colleges with kids studying criminology, so the police departments had their pick of the litter. A woman with no training from the Department of Child Services didn't stand a chance. The men I talked to scoffed, smirked, and checked out my chest while they suggested I try a job that wasn't so tough. Finally, a woman in Corvallis pointed me in the direction of Anchorage.

"They need law enforcement," she'd said. "You've worked for DCS, so you probably have the stomach for it. All you'd need is a little basic training, and they'll pretty much teach you on the job. That is, if you can handle the snow and those crazy dark winters when everyone commits suicide."

I could, I assured her. She gave me the phone number for her brother-in-law, Chief Quint.

Of course, a trip to Anchorage means a drive through Canada, and it's a long one. For endless stretches, you don't pass anybody or anything but scenery. Sure, the mountains are majestic as hell and it's stunning—gorgeous, even—but after a few days you are immune. There's not a McDonald's in sight. I developed a taste for gas station coffee I naïvely figured would benefit me as a cop. At one point, I stopped adding powdered creamer to it. My sedan smelled like slightly burnt French roast and jerky. I embraced it and cranked up Queen on the radio, belting lyrics out my windows at the herds of livestock as I passed them.

In all that driving, waking at sleazy roadsides at six a.m. to get started, going until my eyes felt like asbestos theater curtains on the drop, I never once pictured what it would *really* be like. I had a vision in my mind of Alaska. It was a postcard with interchangeable white mountains, some moose, maybe a bear. *Alaska* always featured in navy blue font on a green background in my head. I didn't picture people, only animals and wild. I didn't picture buildings, police stations, or officers in cubicles. I just pictured me, dressed for snow, trudging up a hill. I don't even know to what destination, or for what reason.

Where I was going was an abstract dream. What I was leaving was real.

So, I stomped on the pedal.

❖

Harper is asleep when I turn off Highway 9. The road is rough, and it bounces him awake. Lee Stanton's trailer is in the middle of nowhere. We climb gradually, then at a steep incline, then over a muddy road with ruts so deep a person could go ice fishing in one, especially since they're covered in snow. I wish I'd bothered to get out of Anchorage before this—I would be a little more familiar with the ultra-rural terrain. Now I wish we'd brought something other than the Tank, which is great on powder but slides on ice—which is what the roads are covered in once the powder blows off. I work myself up to more conversation before I ask Harper how familiar he is with Seward and the surrounding area.

"Pretty familiar…Seward is where my family vacationed when I was a kid. Couldn't afford much else. It's a great town. Real quiet except in the summer. You've been?"

I shake my head. He raises his eyebrows and smiles.

"You're in for a treat. It's beautiful."

Good to know. Anchorage can be beautiful too, especially the trail that goes around the water and past the mansions. I run there when I need to clear my head. So, I run there a lot. On sunny days, you can see Denali. Still, Anchorage isn't the *Alaska* I envisioned. I wanted remote, and Anchorage is still a city. A city where all the locals know each other's businesses, which means if I'm not careful, everyone will know my business. They'll wonder why I couldn't hack it in Seattle. Maybe Seward is more what I want.

"The people in the mountains, though…they can be skeptical of Anchorage cops. Cops in general, really, but Anchorage troopers especially."

"Why?"

He shrugs. "People who live on the mountains don't want to be bothered. Not that they're doing anything wrong usually, they just like to mind their own business."

"So do I. What's wrong with that?"

He briefly looks flustered. "Oh, nothing at all. That's the Alaskan way, right? It's just, if people are a little hostile…I just thought you'd want to know that they're not—"

I take a deep breath in. I'm not off to a good start with my impromptu partner. "That it's not personal?"

He looks relieved. "Totally. I'm just really up-front. Transparent and all, so they feel like I'm not out to get them or anything."

"That's good information." He smiles and nods. "So, you've worked cases in Seward." *Maybe Harper will be helpful to have around after all.*

"In the summers they call us out for a fair amount for drug issues. The tourists move all around the state then, so we chase people around. Seward tourism is growing so much, so fast, they can't keep up."

The road narrows and I'm convinced the trees are forming into a canopy that's going to close and swallow us like bugs in a Venus flytrap.

It was pale orange October light when we left three hours ago. Now it could be seven p.m. The sky is dusky here in the forest. Moss clings to the half-dead cedar limbs, and tiny animals scurry away as the Tank comes bumping along. I check the rearview to be sure those clunking sounds aren't pieces falling off. The oppression of the trees makes me claustrophobic, so I roll my window down. My passenger immediately puts his down too. The smell of pine needles and not-too-distant sea salt fills the car, mingling with the Nutella to make something not entirely unpleasant.

The Tank doesn't want to shift up the final stretch of hill. But gradual intensity on the gas pedal, a lot of cursing by me, a hint of burnt rubber smell, and something that vaguely resembles a prayer from Harper is all it takes for us to arrive alongside the trailer.

CHAPTER TWO

The place looks like something I see on those cheaply made homicide shows I watch when I'm burnt out and can't stand to do anything that involves the use of my brain. It's white, or it used to be, with brown paneling along the sides and a door that will fall off if you push it wrong. There's dead ivy climbing the sides of it and cinder blocks piled against it. Maybe they're holding the sides on. The whole scene looks like it's been here since roughly the '70s, right down to the partially rusted pickup parked at an angle near the trees.

There's a woman leaning against the trailer, arms folded, as if she's been here for just as long as the blocks. Men's jeans hang low on her hips beneath a flannel and a barn coat. Her bleached curls look so dry they'd crack open if you touched one. She watches us watching her but doesn't approach as we exit the Tank.

"You must be Mrs. Stanton."

"I am."

I extend my hand. "I'm Officer Louisa Linebach." Her shake is firm, like mine. I let go before it becomes a contest and motion to Harper, who dusts the front of his checkered shirt. "This is my, uh... partner, Officer Michael Harper." I'm not sure we will work together beyond this case, but she doesn't need to know that.

"Pleased." He holds out his hand, and the way his arm goes kind of limp when he shakes makes me cringe.

She raises her head, looks down her nose at him. She and I may get along.

I nod toward the trailer. "Would you mind giving us the tour?"

"Sure." She swings the door open and holds it for us. The smell hits me and brings tears to my eyes before my eyes have even adjusted to the hostel-dorm look of the place. The odor is some combination of rotting potatoes and sour milk. Mrs. Stanton watches me closely.

"Yeah, sorry 'bout that. Lee left dishes in the sink with food still stuck on. Figured I probably shouldn't wash them on account of you coming. Didn't want to disturb things."

"That was smart."

Harper is headed toward a window. "Mind if we open it up a little?"

"Go ahead."

He grabs what appears to be a greasy pane and pushes outward. A cold gust of autumn wind rushes through. "Ah. Better already." He smiles a big, disarming grin. Her facial expression remains slightly skeptical. I assess the place.

It's a single trailer, maybe fifteen feet across and sixty feet long. Most of it's dominated by one of those plush, chocolate brown reclining sofas everyone had in their basement a couple decades ago. The stuffing is protruding in places and there's a smooth-worn spot on the left side where someone clearly sits routinely. A Solo cup perches on the arm and crumbs line the cushion seams as if someone rose from the seat just before we came in. There's a large television on the opposite wall with gaming consoles settled haphazardly on a table below. The video game set-up looks to be the only thing of value in the place. In the slim pathway to the kitchen, boxes are piled—almost neatly—a yellow Post-it Note stuck to each one. None of them are taped shut, and bits of contents peep from the tops.

"Your son lives alone?"

She chuckles without smiling. "Oh yeah."

"No partner?"

"No girlfriend in years."

I touch a hooded sweatshirt that hangs on a makeshift wall hook. "Does he ever have visitors?"

"You mean women?" There's something hard beneath the hoodie. Harper's head swivels between us as we speak. I expect a score to pop up on a brightly lit board somewhere like we're in a tennis match and he's the ball.

"Not necessarily. Friends? Family? Coworkers maybe?" I retrieve the end of a dog collar.

"Not that I know of. He's not…well, I can't say he's the real sociable type." I open my notepad. "Not saying he's a weirdo or anything." She checks my scrawl as if to make sure I'm not recording *weirdo* in all capital letters across the blank page. "Just sayin' he's—what's the word?"

Harper chimes in. "Introverted?"

"Sure. That."

"There's nothing wrong with that." I would know, *that* describes me too.

"Nah. He just likes time to himself. Most nights he gets home from work, comes back here, and just plays games, I think."

"Does he have a dog?" I shake the military green, tag-less collar.

"Yeah, he got a mutt about a year ago. Found it maybe, or some friend of his had it. Pretty big thing. Ain't seen it today, though, or last time I was down."

"Do you think he took it with him?"

"I'd imagine if he went somewhere he'd take it. Brings it to dinner when he comes over."

"He'd take it without a collar?"

She shrugs quickly. "Maybe. I don't think I've ever seen the dog in a collar. Nobody's about to steal a dog around here."

I make a mental note to look for dog prints. She glances at the door.

"Do you visit him often?"

"Well, maybe not as much as I could, I guess. Maybe once a week. And of course, I see him Sundays." Her eyes stray to one of the boxes labeled *Ma.*

"Sunday dinners?"

"Right. He misses once in a while, but not usually. And if he does, he'll call round to apologize once he's noticed. Usually brings food with him."

"But he didn't call this time."

"No." Her eyes go back to the boxes.

Harper breaks the silence. "When's the last time you spoke to your son?"

She shakes her head while she considers the question. "I'd say Tuesday. He would have been on his way to work. Sounded like he was in the truck."

"The one outside?"

She nods.

"Do you remember what you talked about?"

"My snow machine. He was reminding me to bring it in while the weather's still okay. Before the first serious snow."

"Was that it?"

"Pretty much."

"What did his mood sound like?"

"Same as always."

I look at her. Of course, I wouldn't know anything about his usual mood. "And that would be?"

"He's not a talkative kid. Just says what he needs to and that's it."

I share a glance with my fellow officer. I would guess he's thinking the same as I am. *Lee Stanton gets his demeanor honestly.* Harper's tone is light and conversational.

"Did it seem like anything was botherin' him? Was it just a regular ol' workday?" I note his ability to adjust his speech patterns to match hers. She shrugs.

"I'd say so. I wouldn't know. Lee don't get emotional. He's always about the same. A little sullen maybe. That's just his way."

"All right. Thank you, Mrs. Stanton."

She shifts, and her eyes go again to the boxes. "You need me to stick around?"

"No, but I should ask…have you or anyone else gone through any of these boxes?"

"No."

"Any idea what's in them?"

"Some of the things I can see. They're just things he owns that's always been here. I see one of my old pots in the box that says *Ma.* But that one marked *Pa* has got a wall clock coming out the top, you see? That's my son's. Don't know why he's trying to give it to his dad." She shifts again.

"Thank you, Mrs. Stanton. We'll give you a call if we need anything."

She rests her weight on her right hip, opens her mouth, closes it again like a catfish cleaning a tank. Starts to turn. Turns back. "You don't mind me asking, Officers, what do you think this is about?"

Officer Harper and I share another glance. I press my lips together in silent warning. I am sure she knows what we think, but I'm not ready to say it to her. I need more proof and less circumstantial evidence. Even if I was ready, how do you tell a mother you think her son has killed himself?

"It's too soon to make any guesses, Mrs. Stanton. For all we know, there could be other boxes and he's busy moving them somewhere else. But I assure you we'll do everything we can to find your son."

She looks doubtful but doesn't press. "All right. I'll be up at the house if you need me."

I nod slightly and Harper smiles. His childish face goes soft and reassuring in a way I wish I could do with mine.

"Pleasure meeting you, Mrs. Stanton."

She lifts a corner of her mouth at him and opens the door, letting more of the smell leave with her.

Harper goes straight for the boxes, but I wander a bit. I venture into the kitchen, which is covered in fake knotty pine paneling like the rest of the place. The cabinets are actual pine, which makes the whole thing visually confusing. A border featuring bear cubs playing against a navy background runs along the top of the walls, peeling at the corners. I open the cabinets and confirm Harper is focused elsewhere before I rise onto my toes to peer in. I hate being short. I don't want him to see my height adjustment, and I'm not about to call him in here so he can grab the stuff on the top shelf like we're some married couple and I'm incapable of reaching the ginger powder.

The labels I can read on the lower shelves surprise me. There's cardamom, saffron, and even a container of star anise. I've never seen the spice in person before, only on the late-night cooking shows that seem to abound during my insomnia. I twist off the metal cap and delicately pluck out one of the flower-shaped pods. It smells like licorice, which would normally make me cringe, but it temporarily overpowers the sour milk stench. There are coriander seeds and four containers of powdered cinnamon showing various levels of use, as if Lee kept forgetting he had cinnamon and bought it every time he went to the grocery. He clearly enjoys cooking. I rethink the stereotypical antisocial gamer in my mental profile, reminding myself about all the anti-stereotyping training I received in DCS.

Lee Stanton is Mrs. Stanton's son who likes video games, fixes people's snow machines, visits his mom every week, and cooks dishes with complicated spices found in specialty stores. He doesn't have a partner, and he is apparently totally okay with keeping his own company with just a trusty dog a million miles away from almost anyone. He cares enough about his family to put little trinkets they would like into boxes labeled carefully with their names before he...before he what? We should look for him. Time is passing.

"You ready to get a move on?" My voice sounds loud to my ears. It's intensely quiet this far out in the mountains. Harper's head jerks up as if I've snapped him out of deep concentration. He holds a dog bowl to his face.

"Seems he was going to give the dog to Pa."

"I wonder if it's with him."

"Only one way to find out, right?"

❖

The ground around the trailer is as uneven as a teenager's face, mounds of dirt standing like blemishes and foot-deep craters threatening to trip anyone not watching her step. The dark soil is spotted with sporadic patches of peach-fuzz soft green moss. Some boulders mark the trailhead of an old landslide, but they've been resting for a long time judging by the small tufts of grasses and succulents growing on them. Something about the gray stones and the scent of the pines reminds me of Scandinavia, though I've never been there. Ten yards or so behind the trailer, the forest forms a dense curtain we'll have to part if we want to travel up-mountain. I gaze into it, trying to make out any movement. Harper follows my gaze.

"You think?"

"I don't know." I turn back to the trailer. "We better check the immediate area first, starting with the truck."

The truck has some empty soda cans and a couple clean Tupperware containers, a little dog hair, but nothing else of interest. No documents, no weapons, no blood. I make note of the license plate. We can always come back to it, if need be, but for now I want to get out there.

"Let's make a circle around the trailer, all the way to the tree line the whole way around. I'll go left, you go right. You check under the trailer too, just in case."

He eyes the ground around the trailer.

"All those sheds and toolboxes and crates will need going through. Look for any signs of blood or a struggle, and anything missing that should be there—especially tools and weapons."

He nods and starts slowly to his right, while I angle my body to the left. I am drawn back to those trees and their light dusting of powder, but I resist their pull for now. There's what looks like an old state park outhouse straight ahead, and I need to clear that first. No need to go wandering through the woods if the guy had a heart attack on a compost toilet.

Toilet and sheds on my side checked, I slowly circle back to the front of the trailer, where I find Harper shimmying from under the home, which is raised on mismatched cinder blocks.

"No luck?"

"Nope. You?"

"Nothing interesting. No footprints, but that's not too surprising."

He dusts off the seat of his pants, then pulls a string of cobweb from his fine hair. "Now what?"

I eye the woods again, but he looks hesitant.

"You think we have time?" He's got a point. We have about two and a half hours of sun left, maybe.

"Seems like a shame to waste good light."

His face clears, and he grins. "You're already thinking like an Alaskan!"

We head toward the tree line, where the sun abruptly disappears. My boots sink into the soft pine needles as I point out a downed tree just at the end of my line of vision.

"You head out that way. I'll meet you there. Don't stray too far." I bite my lip to stop myself giving orders. I'm so used to working with children that parental-sounding reminders are second nature. Thankfully, Harper is already gone.

I head toward the tree line, head down, checking the ground for footprints, blood, clothing fragments, hair, any clues. I arc my flashlight in front of me to better spot anything out of place among the needles and moss. Harper and I head slowly away from each other for what feels like hours. I jump over some shallow waterfalls and clamber over some slick rocks. I pick my way through soft-looking Devil's club, which threatens to spear me with lengthy spikes that want nothing better than to lodge under my skin and get infected. I learned my lesson the hard way in the woods around Anchorage.

I head back toward Harper. Once the rush of the water is behind me, I can hear him singing to himself. He belts out a familiar line that mocks the semi-darkness we're searching, then falls silent. There's some rustling of branches, then the warbling baritone breaks through again. He's examining something closely, a hollowed tree trunk maybe. He doesn't call out and goes back to singing when he's moved on. I'm close enough to startle him when I speak.

"Solid choice."

"What?"

"That song. 'In the Pines.'"

"Was I singing? Oh, sorry. Being out here's got that old Nirvana song stuck in my head." He looks at me as if I'm an ice-cold pool and he's considering jumping in. "So, you like Nirvana?"

I think about the lead singer's suicide a decade before. "I do, actually." His face relaxes a little. "But that's not their song. Their version is based on the Lead Belly take, and plenty of other people recorded it before Kurt Cobain did."

Harper looks a little startled. "Well, you learn something new every day."

I freeze, my inability to engage in small talk on full display. *Best to get back to the comfort of work.*

"You find anything?"

"Nope. Some animal trails that look fresh, but nothing human from what I can tell. Hard with all these needles though."

"It is. What kind of animals?" I'd seen mink prints, but that was about it.

"Something big. Moose probably. No bear. Not a dog." Lucky he only encountered moose prints, and not the live thing. Moose are more dangerous than bears, but most people don't know or think about that.

"He could have startled a moose, maybe. Baby with it?"

"Didn't look like."

"Hmm. Well, we shouldn't rule it out."

He turns a slow circle and looks at his feet, rubbing the back of his head. "What's next?"

I can't decide. There's so much space to cover. If our missing person is out here, he could be anywhere. He's in a bar in Sitka or Fairbanks, or he's just as likely at the bottom of a fjord. I think about the other officers in Anchorage. What they would do? Where would they look? Then I remember that even the best of them rarely finds a missing person alive, and I try to push them from my mind. *This will be different.* I'm going to find Lee Stanton and get a firm solve on my first Alaskan missing persons case.

"Let's head down the mountain. If he ended up in the water, we're more likely to find evidence downstream." I pause to rethink my plan. "Actually, let's stop at the trailer on the way. I want to check something." He leans his head to the side in a silent question. "I want to look at his clothes. See what he might be wearing in case we find any fabric or anything."

"Oh. Nice one. Sounds like a plan."

We pick our way back through the trees. Small animals shake the underbrush, it sounds like sea grass in the wind. I look to see what they are, but they're always just a blur ahead of my sight.

It turns out we're looking for jeans or long underwear. Probably flannel on the top based on the three thick ones hovering over the edges of his laundry basket. He doesn't own a lot of clothes; I don't see a single pair of boxers or briefs. What clothes he does have looks like it was all bought at the same farm supply. There are two pairs of gray sweatpants with banded bottoms, three pairs of thick wool socks, two pairs of faded jeans with holes that have been patched over, four plain, pocketless T-shirts, and three flannels in various shades of blue. One of the flannels has been haphazardly patched at the elbow. Some of the clothes have short, auburn hair on them. These don't match Lee's physical profile. His mother described him as having medium brown, slightly oily hair, usually parted in the middle if at all, and heavy body hair, curly. After we've both meticulously noted these details, I drive us to town for a station stop and debrief before we head to the hotel.

Chapter Three

A s soon as I open the heavy glass door, I could be in any police station anywhere in the United States, possibly in the world. I haven't done a lot of traveling, but I'm betting they all have the same stale carpet, the same beige walls stained with a tinge of yellow from back when you could smoke inside, the same Febreze fresh air scent in the bathrooms, and the same smattering of day-old, half-full paper cups. There are only three desks visible. One is a sort of a makeshift reception desk with multiple phones. No one sits at it.

A tall man, muscular but very skinny with a dark Sam Elliott mustache, emerges from the back and shakes our hands. He's Chief Willington. He looks flustered. Harper must think similarly.

"Good to see you again, Chief. Something wrong?"

Chief Willington shakes his head and a stack of papers at Harper in response.

"These damned cruise ship robberies. So many man-hours, and we're not making a bit of progress on them. One woman's missing an emerald ring, a guy's missing a Rolex, and then I've got a report from some geezer who's going to pieces. He swears someone stole his illustrated collector's edition of *Robinson Crusoe*. Soon as people find out something's been stolen, all the junk they happen to set somewhere and forget has been stolen too!"

I try to make sympathetic noises—not my specialty—then launch into what we learned today and our plan for tomorrow. He says something vague about our good work and tells us where to find our reservation.

❖

The hotel is a single-story affair with a steeply pitched orange roof. It looks a lot like my apartment building in Anchorage, but that doesn't mean it doesn't make me think of movies where teens on vacation are serially murdered. As I get the keys from the desk, Harper pauses and turns to me.

"Would you—I mean, I'm real hungry…You must be too."

I fumble with the key card and wonder vaguely if our rooms are next door to each other, and if I'll have to hear him snore. I shrug noncommittally. "Hadn't thought about it, I guess."

"Well, I think I'll head into town. Maybe grab something. You want to come along?"

I don't feel like watching everything I say because anything even remotely personal will be repeated to everyone at the station. "No, thanks. I think I'll just order something in."

He looks away and the red of his face deepens. "Well, suit yourself. Real hard to find delivery in Seward, though, I'll warn you!"

For a moment I feel guilty. I try to make amends with what is hopefully a friendly smile. "I'll take my chances." He hasn't turned to go yet, so I add, "Should've taken some of those spices in the trailer. I could have cooked something real nice!"

He laughs. It seems forced. I've failed to make nice. I'm sure I've already double-checked, but I reconfirm. "Nine o'clock tomorrow?"

"You got it."

His room is next to mine and the walls *are* thin, so I wait a solid twenty minutes after I hear his door click shut to head out for my own dinner.

❖

Harper is already in the lobby at nine a.m., seated on the worn leather sofa with a paperback and his feet on an ottoman like it's his living room. The book is a crime novel. You'd think he'd get enough of that in real-life Anchorage. As soon as he sees me, he closes the book and gets to his feet.

"Morning!"

"Good morning."

"There's a coffee machine here if you want any." The machine is roughly three feet away from us.

"I see. I made some in my room, though, so I'm all right." It's not a complete lie; I made my now usual gasoline-consistency brew using three single-serve pods instead of one. But *all right* is a stretch since I received a call from Chief Quint this morning. I consider not telling Harper, but Chief Quint's instructions were clear, and I'm not seasoned enough to go rogue just yet.

"The chief called."

He suddenly looks worried, as if he fears we're in trouble. He steps to the coffee maker. I'd bet all three of the tiny cups in the trash can below it are his.

"There's another case close by, so he figured since we're here already…"

"Oh crud! What kind?"

"Missing person."

"Seriously?"

"Yes. Another twenty-something guy, lives a few miles from the Stantons."

He pours two full seconds of sugar into the tiny cup, then two seconds of powdered French vanilla creamer.

"Whoa. What are the odds?"

I run all the statistics I've seen in the past six months or so over in my head. "Pretty good, actually. The Kenai Peninsula's where we lose the most people. There's a couple thousand every year, most of them men—"

"I just meant…you know. Like, I guess the odds of two back-to-back that close together. Just wondered if maybe they knew each other…" He shifts his weight, downs the coffee, tosses the cup on top of the others.

I feel bad for him. That's the same remedial tone my ex used to point out. I'm correcting someone who hasn't said anything wrong. She and I had been together for long enough she would just point it out and I'd try to correct it. Then I drove her away for good. I guess I'll have to start catching it myself now.

"No, you're right. Within a week and so close together when they're living so remote…It *is* kind of weird."

He brightens and is visibly pleased. "So, do we check that out or go ahead to the Stantons'?"

"The chief wants us to check this one out first, see if it's anything obvious, then get back to the original plan of interviewing Stanton's dad and extending the search. We'll check in with the chiefs after we interview the new people."

"Roger that!" He grabs two more Styrofoam cups. "Coffee for the road?" He's already pouring creamer.

"I'll be all right."

❖

I start the Tank and we settle in to let it run through the usual round of painful metallic thumps before it settles down. The air feels tense in the vehicle, but I can't identify why.

Eventually, Harper asks, "How was dinner last night?"

"Fine?"

"I saw you walking back from downtown."

It takes me a second to suppress my instinctive snapback of *So?*, and remember I told him I was going to order delivery. *So*, I could avoid eating with him. *Shit.*

"Oh. Yes, I ended up at one of those places on the water."

"Yeah. Me too." He lets it hang but doesn't look at me. He just gazes out the window, tiny coffee cup held in both his large hands. I think it's because he doesn't ask for an explanation that I feel like I owe him one. God, I'm terrible at conversations about feelings, but I don't want our relationship strained while we try to find these men.

"Look, it's not—it's nothing personal, okay? It's just…"

He looks at me earnestly, as if he genuinely wants to understand. My ex used to wear that same open expression when I talked about my DCS cases. "It's just that most of the other guys are not exactly friendly with me, you know? It was nice of you to ask, but I didn't want to have to find something to talk about knowing that it was going to get repeated all around the station soon as we get back."

"Oh. Yeah, I've noticed that. The way they are. It sucks." He gazes into his empty coffee cup. "You know, though, I'm a little offended you think I'd repeat stuff to them."

I'm caught off-guard. I can't remember the last time I heard a man so easily express an emotion. My father would have laughed in Harper's face. Hell, if I'd said I was offended by something, he would have rapped me on the head and told me to *man up*. At least before he left.

I'm not sure what to say. *Do I apologize?* It's not like I'm wrong for assuming he'd repeat what I say to him. *Right?* He would, *wouldn't he?* He wants them to like him…*Doesn't he?* I am trying to recall every interaction I've observed between Harper and the other officers. Harper speaks into the silence.

"The other guys all think police work is a pissing contest, and they just don't like that you're always so fast to solve your cases. I'm not like that." It's as if he read my mind, and he looks me straight in my right eye when he speaks. I can feel it even though I've got my eyes on the road.

I turn my head to meet his gaze. "Okay. I'm sorry I thought you were like them. I'm just used to the guys being shitty with me."

"They are pretty crappy with you. Usually when someone's got such a good solve rate, they all try to work with them to make themselves look better. Why aren't they like that with you?"

I shrug. "I don't really know. I'm a woman? I turned a couple of them down?"

He snorts. "No way. Some of them hit on you?" He laughs hard, then turns red. "Not saying—I mean…not like they shouldn't…er…I mean not like you're unattractive or—Well, I just put my foot in it, didn't I?"

He's right, I'm not unattractive. I know that. Not a raging beauty queen or anything, but I'm subtly pretty in a vaguely foreign way. The first officer who hit on me, Boggs, was apparently into my hair. I'd noticed him staring at me from his desk but didn't put it together until an incident at the water cooler. He pretended to bump into me and grazed his hand against the end of my braid, long and thick courtesy of my Bengali mother. Then he'd sidled up to the bar next to me on one of the rare nights I went out. He lisped with alcohol when he put his hand on my loose hair. "Anybody ever tell you, you got beautiful hair?" It took me a moment to interpret his words since there were no clear enunciations of r's or t's in the compliment accompanying his assault. I started wearing my hair in a bun after that, even at the bar. I shake my head at the memory.

"You're fine, and yes, Boggs and Rippy. They are pains in the ass."

He whistles. "Yeah. Rippy's a total womanizer. I've been out drinking with him. He can be aggressive, so I don't go out with him after work anymore. I've always wanted to say something, but I've always chickened out, I guess. I feel so bad for the female bartenders. Boggs, though, I've never seen him bother women. Maybe he's really into you."

I shrug. "You wouldn't want to date him because he's a coworker."

He nods as if he completely understands. "Yeah, you are real professional. That's why I was glad the chief assigned me to work this case with you."

I consider telling him the truth, but him thinking I'm just so professional is better. I let it be.

❖

The new missing man is Branden Halifax, age twenty-seven. His girlfriend reported it. He went out a few nights ago to meet some friends at the bar, but he didn't show, and he didn't come home. The woman sounds embarrassed and very worried on the phone. She's been doing her own police work since he disappeared, calling all his friends and relatives to see if anyone's heard from him.

Their property is far up the mountain, and there's more substantial snow. The Tank handles it like a champ because it's powdery. It's that season where you're not sure if it'll melt off by the afternoon. Maybe not up this high. There's a clearing of about a half-acre where the house sits, along with a row of four to eight lopsided sheds and shacks that seem to come with many rural Alaska homes. The forest encroaches on the place gradually, dense trees give way to thick, then sparser underbrush that eventually surrenders and turns itself over to crawling moss that peters out just before the foundation. The owners don't try too hard to keep their yard a civilized oasis against the wilderness.

The house itself is nicer than most of the rural houses I've seen so far. It's a two-story wood-sided affair with no shutters and a steeply sloped metal roof so the snow will slide off. Firewood is piled high on the porch running three-fourths of the way around the house, and the fuel is protected from the elements by an overhang. It vaguely reminds me of fairy tale picture books where a thin line of white smoke trails from the chimney and the exposed gray stone of the foundation sprouts tufts of withering grass. I could see myself living somewhere like this, though I'd hope I could afford to maintain it better. The gutters are sagging, and the power lines are so low someone could clothesline themselves on them. Some of the exterior wood is starting to bow out and away from the house.

A woman comes out onto the porch when we slam the Tank's heavy doors—the only way to ensure they stay closed. She's pretty in a healthy, woodsy way, and Harper brushes his jacket though we haven't eaten anything on the ride. She's barefoot despite the crisp air, so she meets us on the bottom step. I extend my hand and she takes it but doesn't squeeze or shake. Her light eyes squint from behind her slightly puffy eyelids as I introduce myself and Harper. The wind blows the woman's light brown hair into her face. She retracts her arm to tuck it behind her ear, but it is immediately lifted again by a gust.

"I'm Marli Lei. I'm Branden's girlfriend."

"It's good to meet you, Ms. Lei." He nods his head slightly.

"You too. So…I don't really know where to start. What do you need to know?"

I glance toward the door. I'm surrounded by cold-hardy people. I don't want them to see me shiver under my jacket. "Mind if we come inside?"

"Oh. Yes, of course—I'm sorry. Sure. I'm…I'm still kind of—well, I didn't sleep."

"That's totally understandable, ma'am, under the circumstances."

She raises the corners of her mouth slightly, though somehow her eyes look sadder than they already did at Harper's words.

The house is tidy. I'd guess she and her family don't have a ton of money, but she's creative with what she has. The red and white checked curtains might be hand-sewn from flannel sheets, and the windows are spotless. There's not a single stain on the linoleum counters. A baby bottle dries on a Halloween dish towel.

"Are there kids home now?" I automatically skim the house for signs the children are properly cared for. I remind myself that I'm not here for them. She nods.

"They're asleep, finally." She drops her voice to a near whisper. "The baby cried all night again and Alicia, she's four, wanted to stay up too. She kept asking where her dad was. I didn't know what to tell her." Now I want to check on the kids and make sure they're all right. But the woman, the likely innocent woman, who sits before me is my focus right now. I drop my voice too. "Tell us about your boyfriend's plans the night he went missing."

She picks up a farm chair so it doesn't make noise dragging across the bare wood floors. She sits heavily, then motions with her head to the other chairs.

"Please feel free to sit." Something in her cadence strikes me as different, but I cannot place it. She jumps up.

"I'm sorry. Can I get you coffee or tea or anything?" Despite her fatigue, it's easy to see she's the kind of woman I've always kind of wished I was—both helpful *and* considerate.

"I'm all right."

"And I've already had so much coffee that I'll need to ask about your bathroom before too long." Harper laughs and then covers his mouth.

"Well, when you need it, it's out the front door and to the left."

"Thanks."

We both have a seat, and she sits again after we have.

"Have you and Branden always lived here in Alaska?"

"No. Well, I haven't. His family moved around the state a few times when he was a kid. I know he lived in Fairbanks, Juneau, Anchorage…around here sometimes. His dad moved around with his job. I'm from Norway, originally. My family moved to Petersburg when I was seventeen. You know, where most Scandi immigrants go. I met Branden when I was on vacation here with some friends." Ah, now I hear the light accent.

"So, he knows the Alaskan terrain."

"Oh, absolutely! Better than just about anyone. He hunts and fishes all over the state, sometimes for weeks at a time. When I first moved out here, he used to take me foraging in these woods. We'd pick berries and…" She smiles. "Well, you know. It was a way to be alone." She blushes and quiets for a time before she continues.

"He taught me which fruits could be used for pies or jams. He can find his way through the forest without a single path. He knows how to get around out here."

She looks like she can hold her own too. Aside from her height, which makes her look like some sort of statue of the goddess Athena, her biceps are strong under a layer of insulating fat. When she moves her hands back and forth across the table, then into her lap, then back onto the table, the muscles in her forearms ripple.

"So, where was he headed the night he disappeared?" Harper has his pen poised and ready. He makes a small circle at the top of the pad as proof of ink. I glance at the blank lines of the flip notebook, ready to see them filled with details.

CHAPTER FOUR

That night," Marli speaks deliberately, "he was going out with his friends. Same bar they always go to on Fridays, about six miles from here."

"They don't go down to Seward?"

She titters. "Sorry. Nothing offensive about Seward meant. Are you from there?"

We both laugh quietly.

"We're based in Anchorage."

"Oh good. Branden doesn't think much of Seward. Says they've sold out to the cruise lines. He only goes there if he has to for work. I go into town sometimes to get clothes, but he never comes with me unless he wants to visit his mom."

"So where is the bar they were headed to?"

"The Lodge? Oh, it's in Kolit's Hole."

We both look at her blankly.

"I'm so sorry. I'm talking to you like you'd know where that is. It's not even a town, I don't think. There're just five or six houses there. A man named Kolit used to own all the houses—the same Kolit that started Kolit's Landing. It was all just one family for the longest time. The bar's right there at the edge of the houses, same building as the store. Everyone who lives on the mountain goes there." She says it brightly like that should be impressive.

"Nice! Sounds like a good place."

She smiles at Harper's reaction.

"So, he goes there often?"

She scowls slightly at my question but quickly smooths her expression. "He definitely does."

Harper chimes in again. "He always go with the same people?"

"Oh, yeah." We both look at each other when she doesn't continue. "Oh, that'd be Eliyah, AJ, Tony, and Antoine. I've called all of them. Tony and Antoine are in Anchorage. AJ and Eliyah haven't seen him or heard from him."

"Do you know last names?"

"Antoine is also Halifax. That's Branden's cousin. Tony Long. The other two...I don't know. I'm sorry. Someone in town will know. Eliyah and AJ work at the hardware store. AJ lives in one of the houses in Kolit's Hole. His mom lives downstairs."

"These friends. Do you like them?" I get what I was going for with that question. I want to know if these are good men, good influences.

She looks at her hands quickly, then darts her eyes to what I assume are the bedrooms. "Yeah. I mean, they're nice guys. They like the kids and all. They're always polite to me."

I look directly at her. "Ms. Lei, we have to know what we're dealing with if we're going to find Branden."

"I know. I know. I just..." She picks at a callus on the palm of her hand. "I don't want you to think Branden's..."

Harper leans forward and folds his hands on the table next to a vase of fake sunflowers. I can almost see him shapeshifting into the least intimidating, most relatable version of himself he can be.

"Ms. Lei, we're not here to judge your boyfriend. If he was into anything illegal, he's not going to be in trouble. We just want to find him. Once we find him, we get him back home to you and those kiddos. No questions asked. That's it."

She examines Harper's hands, then looks into his face for what feels like forever. It's all there, clearly nothing hidden. "Promise?"

I cringe. We shouldn't make promises.

"I promise."

Marli twines her hands together in the lap of her long denim shirt dress. The sound of rustling blankets comes from somewhere down the hall and her eyes grow wide. A sigh from the other room, and the rustling subsides. After we take a few breaths into the renewed silence, she slowly begins to tell us more.

"Branden has...made choices...some people...some people might find...questionable."

Harper hasn't written anything yet; he doesn't move. I am frozen in place too.

Marli blinks slowly and wipes the corner of her eye. "Branden... well, he likes to...I guess you can call it *party*, maybe. It seems stupid to call it that out here. I don't know how else to say it, though."

"That's all right—"

"Do you mean he's into drugs?"

Harper winces next to me. He probably would have found a less abrupt way to ask, but my gut says she'll appreciate being able to get straight to the point on this topic. This isn't a situation where we suspect suicide and must be delicate. There's a real chance we can find this guy alive, so time and honesty are of the essence.

She sighs and then leans back in her chair. "Yeah. Yeah, he's into drugs sometimes."

She sits straight abruptly, with her hands on the table in front of her, stabilizing her body. "I don't mean...I don't want you to think he's some sort of addict. And he certainly never deals. It's just...sometimes on the weekends when he's out with the guys, he gets high."

Harper nods slowly. "He sure wouldn't be the first person to turn to drugs for entertainment in Alaska. Nothing unusual there."

I nod. "Ms. Lei, what kind of drugs does your boyfriend use?"

She turns her gaze to the exposed beams in the ceiling. There are wicker baskets hanging there with strings of ivy cascading down. As she gazes at them, I stare at her face, trying to somehow read in it exactly how worried I need to be. This woman has lived with Branden for years. She knows what drugs he's on and exactly how much he takes. She probably knows where he keeps them. They might even be in the house right now.

Should I have gotten a search warrant? What if they're somewhere the kids could get to them? I feel my pulse gain speed. Marli's answer snaps me from my train of thought.

"I'm not totally sure. I don't mess around with it. Weed..." Harper looks unmoved. "Pills sometimes." She shakes her head. "I'm not sure what they are."

"How does he act when he takes them?"

"He says they make him feel content, like things are more

interesting than they are. I don't know, though. He seems sort of hyper and anxious to me. He's normally easygoing."

"Okay. Anything else?"

"I think he does coke if someone else has it. He won't spend money on it, though. He'd *never* do that. Every bit of money he makes goes to me and the kids." *Well, except for the money he spends on marijuana and pills.*

"All right." I hope there's no skepticism in my voice as I relax back into my chair and let Harper ask the next question.

"And he drinks." She looks at a gold ring on her right pointer finger in a complicated love knot design. She rubs the surface of it with her thumb. "He drinks a lot."

"I'm sorry to ask this, Ms. Lei…but…is he ever violent when he's drinking or using?"

She looks shocked as she puts together what Harper must be thinking. "Oh no! No! No. You mean with me and the kids? No, *never.* He's…I guess you call it a functional alcoholic? His personality doesn't change with alcohol, not at all. Sometimes he'll drink enough to forget things, though. Whole evenings. Things the kids did or said. We'll wake up in the morning and he won't remember…" She flushes.

"It's all right." He's leaning forward. He's not writing anything down.

"Sometimes he won't remember we made love." She looks on the verge of tearing up and I have no idea what to say. Harper, though, chuckles like he's in on a secret.

"Now that's not a thing a man will want to forget!" She glances at me. I glance at Harper. I'm glad he's not perfect at this either. He blushes and continues. "Does *he* think his drinking is a problem?"

"No, not really. We've fought about it before. I try not to badger him—I don't want to be *that* woman, you know. It's just…I know there are little milestones he won't remember. Like—like when Alicia called him *Daddy* the first time. It was after he'd downed a third of a bottle of tequila. He was *so* happy, his face was all lit up, and he picked her up and threw her in the air and I was so terrified because I knew he was drunk. But like I said, he functions just about the same as always and it was fine, and she laughed and laughed and said *Daddy* over and again and he called his mom to tell her, and then the next morning…" I hear the catch in her voice. A tear wells at the corner of her eye.

"The next morning when I mentioned it, he didn't know what I was talking about." Her voice drops to a whisper. "He'd forgotten the whole day."

"That must have been hard." At least I know to say that much. I may not have kids yet, but even if I never get that chance, I can imagine how it must have felt to not be able to share such a good memory.

"It was. I was so upset I didn't even fight with him. I was just quiet. He didn't say anything, but I knew he was hurting. He waited for days for Alicia to say it again. He thought I didn't notice, but he kept trying to get her to say it again. And when she finally did...Well, it wasn't the same."

"Of course."

"He tried to stop drinking after that, for a while. But as soon as his buddies would come around, he'd be right back to it. He did stop keeping liquor in the house, though." She stands and walks to a small built-in pantry, opens the door. "The whole top shelf, there? That used to be hard liquor. There's the wine I use for cooking now, but that's it. I stopped even having a glass at night, so he'd know it was okay not to."

"That was thoughtful of you." I mean it. I'm not sure I could make such a big lifestyle change for a partner. Maybe that's why I'm single and Marli is not. Then again...

"I don't want it to be difficult for him."

I nod, glad to be able to refocus on her instead of my own relationship failings. I'm anxious to get back to anything that might tell us where he is right now.

"But you say when he's with his buddies, he drinks again."

"Oh yeah. Very much so. Probably even more now than before since he was only drinking a couple times a week back then."

"So, there's a good chance he was drunk when he disappeared?"

"Well, I would say yes if he'd made it to the bar, but he didn't. The guys said he never showed. So, I don't know. I guess...it depends on where he went."

I'm frustrated. Not knowing where he is or where he went is why we're here. I scowl, and I don't consider my next words. "Is there anyone else he might have visited before he went to the bar he might not have mentioned?"

She turns so deeply red the area beneath her freckles is almost purple. "No, *no*. Branden isn't like that. He wouldn't…he *loves me* and the kids."

My breath catches. I didn't mean to broach the topic, and I know how sensitive the subject of cheating can be. That's not a road I want to travel with her. Harper doesn't either—he jumps in.

"Oh, she didn't mean to imply…that's not at all what we were thinking, ma'am. Sorry, ma'am." Harper widens his eyes at me. "My partner wonders if maybe he went around to another bar, to pick up one of the guys, or to a relative's? Does he have family around? Did he maybe have to stop by the store first?"

She breathes out heavily, and the red in her face softens to pink. Marli sinks back into the chair. "He didn't go to his mom's. I talked to her." I make a mental note that we'll need to chat with his mother. "Maybe. Maybe…" Marli gets lost in thought for a full minute before her eyes light up. "Oh! It was Friday! He would have stopped to get his check and cash it!"

Harper scribbles some notes. "That's perfect. Where would he have picked up the check?"

"That would be from his boss's place, Mr. Drew's. He lives a good ten miles out in the other direction of Seward."

Harper nods. "Mr. Drew. Is that a first or a last name?"

"Last. It's Randolph Drew. He owns a construction company and Branden works on his crew usually May through October."

I nod my understanding. Almost all construction projects take place over the few months of long light. There's not much sense trying to build in December or January, where even the couple hours of low daylight don't provide adequate sun. Now that we're rolling again, I reenter the conversation.

"What does he do over the other months?"

"Sometimes he has sporadic emergency work. Roofs collapsing from the weight of the snow, holes that keep people's homes from staying warm. That sort of thing. During the winter I take in sewing projects to make a little extra money. He's here with the kids then, so I can focus." That makes sense.

"Do you happen to have Mr. Drew's number?"

"I don't, but I could give you directions to his place. Branden would have gone there, then he would have gone to the hardware store in Kolit's Hole to cash it, and that's the same building as the bar. So, since he didn't get to the bar, he probably didn't cash his check."

She's standing and speaks quickly now, albeit still quietly; she rummages through a drawer for a piece of paper and pen. She seems ready to run out the door to try to find him on her own. If it weren't for the sleeping children, she probably would.

She perches at the edge of her chair while she sketches a map. "Will you be able to go over there right from here, Officers? He's driving a white pickup, a Ford. It's got a green *Drew's Construction* sticker on the side of it. He wouldn't have taken the main road, so I'm giving you the road he would have taken. It's usually used by rangers." She finishes the crude map and slides it to me. "Will you let me know right away when you find him?"

"We will absolutely let you know right away. Promise." *Ugh.* The look she gives Harper is full of trust, and I know we need to find Branden Halifax. Most people who call in a missing person seem to know it's a formality. She honestly believes we're going to bring her children's father back to her safe and sound.

As we get to the door, I catch a glimpse of a family portrait proudly displayed right by the entrance. I turn back to her.

"I'm sorry, but would you be able to lend us a picture of Branden? We'd just make copies and get it back to you, but it would really help our search for him."

She seems confused for a second. I suppose most anyone looking in this area knows Branden and wouldn't need a picture. She turns, eyes landing only on family photos. She holds up her finger and heads to her purse, which dangles from a hook in the wall. She pulls a battered photo from her wallet. It's a picture of a grinning Branden presenting a freshly caught salmon. He's not wearing sunglasses or a hat, so his face is clear even if much of his body is hidden by his waders. She brushes the picture with her thumb as she hands it to me. I stare at it, memorizing the missing man.

I flip the picture over to see if there's a date. Close handwriting slants hard to the right. *Marli, make sure you don't walk off with the wrong guy.* There's a heart drawn, and then it's signed *Branden.* I look at Marli and cock my head to the side. She laughs.

"When we first started dating, I asked if I could have a picture of him for my wallet. He asked if I was worried I'd forget what he looked like, because he thought so many other guys were after me. It was just a joke, of course. He was the only one."

I have a hard time believing Branden was the only guy interested, though I do believe she may well have been oblivious to any others. I slide the picture into my coat jacket.

"I'll get it back, right?"

"Yes. But our hope is that the real Branden finds his way back first." My smile to her feels tight. She smiles back, but all I can see are the dark bags under her eyes.

CHAPTER FIVE

After several miles that seem as if they take two hours to travel, Harper picks out the turn-off Marli drew on the map. Good thing too. It's so overgrown I might not have noticed it otherwise. Somehow, it's an even bumpier ride over the next couple miles, which head uphill via a series of switchbacks that become increasingly covered in snow as we approach the tree line. It would be near impossible to find this place randomly. It's obvious the location was at least partially selected to protect Mr. Drew's preference for privacy. No Trespassing, Private Property, or most frequently, Trespassers Will Be Shot signs are posted every few yards. I wonder if he even tries to leave in the winter.

Eventually, a pair of iron gates block the road that is now a driveway. There's an intercom system with a sign *You Must Buzz to Enter.* The buzzer is lower than I can reach from the driver's seat, so I throw the Tank into park and jump to the ground, sloshing into a substantial pile of snow. I press the button. Nothing happens. I press it again and hold it down.

There's a click, then some static. Someone is listening, I'm pretty sure. I say nothing, waiting for the listener to speak first.

"Yeah?"

"Mr. Drew?"

"Yeah?" Mr. Drew uses the exact same inflection.

"Alaska State Troopers Linebach and Harper. We need to talk to you about one of your employees. Can we come in?"

There's a long pause.

"Which employee?"

"Branden Halifax." Another pause.

"I'll need to see some ID. There's a camera just above the speaker. Hold your badge up to it. Your partner's too." I show mine for a second, then I open the door for Harper's. He already has his badge ready. His face looks even younger in his photo. After a few seconds' display, the gate clicks open.

"Pull right up to the front door."

The trees end just behind the main house, a stone structure that's not mansion large but rivals the monsters along the water outside of Anchorage in style. It has three chimneys and a small turret as if Mr. Drew lives in some sort of modern-day vampire novel. The steep roof is dark red metal and looks deadly covered in a thin coat of ice. We are required to mount a short series of wide steps with empty planters placed along the edges to reach the front door. It's a double door made of walnut, with no window inset. I wait for Harper so we can approach together. Fancy places like this make me uncomfortable, even with the rustic Alaska vibe all houses here have, no matter how expensive. Harper strolls up the steps as if he goes into this kind of place all the time. I still have the distinct impression we're being listened to, so I bite back my observations.

Mr. Drew opens the door before we knock. He stands in the entryway and assesses us before he motions us in. He looks less tidy than his house. A scraggly beard with flecks of gray makes a messy underbrush of his chin, and he wears a flannel shirt, ill-fitting jeans, and wool socks. The hallway to the living room is understated, with only a few heavy wood pieces. They look handmade, though expertly crafted. There are no paintings on the walls, but my boots sink into a bearskin rug I am pretty sure is real.

He directs us to a modern leather sofa, and Harper and I take opposite ends. Mr. Drew sinks into an academic-looking cognac-colored armchair across from us and props his feet on a coffee table that is a massive tree trunk with a clear finish. I count the rings while he gets settled.

"So, what's this about Branden?"

I study his face, which is heavily wrinkled. "Mr. Drew, did Branden come by to get his check on Friday?"

"Well, yes, he did. Last construction pay of the season. He was anxious to get it, I'm sure."

"Do you remember what time he came by?"

"Oh, I'd say about six, maybe? Six thirty?" There's a pause while he lifts a glass from the table and sips whatever is inside. "Can I ask what this is about?"

"Mr. Halifax is missing, Mr. Drew. He didn't return home that night, or since." He scowls and sets his glass down deliberately, tracking it the whole way. "His girlfriend thought he might have come here before he went to meet some of his friends."

"Oh, down at the bar at Kolit's. Yeah, I think they go around there most every weekend. So, you think he went missing from the bar?"

"No, he never made it there. Or at least that's what his friends told Ms. Lei."

"Poor Marli. Good God, she must be worried. Is she all right?"

"She is. Officer Linebach and I just came from there. She's certainly anxious about him, though, so any information you have will help. Can you tell us about Branden stopping for his check?"

He picks up his glass again before he leans back in the chair. "Not much to tell, really. He almost always comes by on Fridays about the same time. Pulls to the gate, buzzes. I met him at the door with his check. We didn't really talk or anything. He was here maybe two minutes and on his way."

Harper's taking notes in his nice curving loops, so I follow up. "Did he seem like himself when he was here? Was there anything out of the ordinary?"

Mr. Drew strokes his beard while he reflects and twirls a hair around a jagged fingernail. "I can't say that. He seemed about the same as he always does. Energetic. Excited for the weekend."

"So, that's just his natural way?"

He presses his lips together and looks across the room at a stone fireplace. The ceiling fan, big as the propeller of a small plane, makes a steady clicking as it pulls the cold air into the ceiling's cedar. "I wonder occasionally. Can't say I'm sure…I don't drug test my employees unless they're having trouble on the job, and Branden never has. He's a consistent worker, never misses a detail. Haven't had reason to question him."

"Mr. Drew, does Branden ever talk about his home life at work, or with you?"

"Oh sometimes, sure. He talks about those two kids and Marli an awful lot. All positive, I can tell you that. Some of the crew complain about their wives and girlfriends or joke about getting away from the kids. Not Branden. He puts in an honest day, and he goes right home."

"Except on the weekends, he goes to the bar."

"That's been my understanding."

"But he didn't mention whether he was going straight there when he left your house."

"He didn't, and I didn't think to ask."

"Okay."

Harper looks up from his notes. "Mr. Drew, we didn't see the truck Branden was driving on our trip from Ms. Lei's. If he was going to go to the bar, is that the only route he could have taken?"

"Yeah. It's just this one." Mr. Drew answers promptly.

Harper reaches into his interior jacket pocket for his business cards. I produce mine too. Harper starts to speak but stops and looks at me. I am the lead here.

"Mr. Drew, will you call us if you remember anything at all helpful?"

"Absolutely. Branden's a good guy. I sure as hell hope nothing's happened to him."

He reaches for our cards, lifting from his chair to pull his wallet from his back pocket and slide them carefully inside. He hands us his business cards in return, and we shake hands.

"Can I ask what your next steps are?"

"Look for the vehicle. That's our best chance of finding him, unless of course he just wanders home." Mr. Drew looks doubtful. "It happens more than you'd think. People go on a little bender, need a little break…There's all kinds of reasons. Maybe that's just what he'll do."

Mr. Drew nods, not believing me and not trying to pretend.

❖

"Well, crud." We're back in the car with the doors closed. I look at Harper inquisitively. "Just torn, I guess. I want to get back to the Stantons', but I was hoping we'd find Halifax's vehicle, at least."

"Me too. We need to get going, though. We'll come back tomorrow to talk to the bartender at the Lodge."

He grunts. "Yeah. I guess so." He looks at his notes and flips through them with his lips pursed. I ease the Tank around the looping driveway and back onto the road. We retrace the switchbacks and eventually come to a T-junction that heads away from Lei's and toward the Stantons'.

Harper now fiddles with the radio. A preacher yells about the sins of the wicked, then a fuzzy and decidedly unsexy "Pour Some Sugar on Me" plays, then an old Johnny Cash song about a boy who's humiliated to have a girl's name tunes in. I've always hated the song, but Harper stops there. We bounce on the road; the car groans the whole way. A short distance from our destination, the radio signals mix, and the preacher's voice cuts in and out of "Black Velvet."

I jab a button and the sound clicks off abruptly. Harper turns a wide-eyed gaze to my face. He's pale.

"What?"

"Didn't it just…Didn't that feel sort of…surreal to you?" I shrug, but it *was* a little strange. He continues after a moment. "It felt like… some kind of sign, or something."

"What, like bad luck?"

"Not exactly. It doesn't matter. It's silly." I look at him. It's not like I can miss a turn. The color returns to his face.

"You superstitious?" I sound judgmental.

"No. Well. I don't know. Maybe a little."

I understand if he's cautious to admit it. I let him off the hook with a laugh. "I tell you something, promise you won't tell anyone else?"

"Sure!" Now I hear pure relief.

"When the Canucks play, I'll only turn on the game nine minutes after it should have started, and I always wear the same jersey."

He snorts. "Why nine minutes?"

"My first live game I arrived nine minutes late and they blew the other team out the water."

"Nice!" He laughs again. "I wouldn't have pegged you for a hockey fan."

"Oh?"

"Yeah, not really. I mean, I guess it makes sense and all since you lived up north. Just never pictured you watching sports."

I wonder what Harper and the other officers think I do when I'm not at work. Maybe I don't want to know. I side-eye him intentionally and lower my voice. "Tell you another secret?"

"Yeah!"

I pause for dramatic effect.

"Sometimes I even have a beer while I watch." He grins. I train my eyes back on the road just in time to catch the sun's glare on something metallic to my left. I jerk my head toward the window and stop the Tank. "What was that?"

"What?" I throw the car in reverse. The tires spin and slosh half-frozen mud from a puddle before we start to back up.

"I thought I saw—" And I was right.

Off to our left, almost hidden between a couple of massive, snow-covered pine trees, is the easily missed rear end of a white pickup truck.

❖

I'm already out of the car, mud splashing to my knees as I land. I push through the pine needles and barely notice them catching in the hairs that have come loose around my face, leaving their sticky sap behind. The front half of the truck is embedded in a muddy bank, and the side is partially obscured by thick underbrush. But there is Mr. Drew's logo. I realize Harper is right behind me when I feel his warm breath on the back of my head.

He whistles low. "Well, how about that?"

I pull the door open. The truck is empty. I look to our feet. "Shit! Hold still. He might have left prints, but there's so little room." My eyes scour the few square feet of muddy snow not covered in brush. I know Harper scans for broken branches or any other trace of Branden too.

"There!" He sees it first. A slick spot on the muddy bank in front of the truck where it looks like someone pulled himself over the incline. We both head toward it. Then I see some faint tracks that lead to the visible tree line.

"Hang on. Grab the camera from my bag and take some pictures of the truck and the surrounding area. Stay with the car. I'm just going to—"

"Hey, you shouldn't go wandering f—"

"The prints lead that way. Should be easy enough to spot the truck from the edge of the trees, and hell, you'll be able to see me once I'm past them."

"Okay. Just don't go too far, yeah? You can always come back and get me."

The prints are a heavy traction work boot, driven deep into the mud like they were made by someone heavy—or stumbling. They stop at the tree line. When I find them again, they head left along the ridge. I turn to memorize the view so I can find the truck. Then I go on. Before long, the ground levels off in a narrow plateau, the top of the mountains off to my right, a steep slope into the forest to my left. The tracks cross the plateau. I'm almost crouched to my knees looking for them. As I squint into the whiteness, I spot bright yellow paint reflected off a layer of ice.

What is this? The paint seems to be laid in a circle. It's so faded I wouldn't have seen it had I not been looking so closely at the ground. The tracks go through the yellow circle, then proceed in a straight line for a length of the flat area. I travel about three-fourths of its length before the tracks disappear, and I stop. There's still snow ahead, and still mud that should hold the distinctive shape of prints in the frozen land. I rotate my torso as I keep my feet still. Maybe the tracks circle back or head in another direction. They don't. There are at least ten yards of open snow and mud around me with no underbrush and no trees. And no more tracks. As I return to Harper, I almost crawl to check if any of the boot prints are backward. None of them are. When I'm within range of the truck, I yell. Harper appears at the tree line.

"Hey, lock the Tank and get up here. Bring the camera!"

I hear him crash through the brush, then he reappears, clutching the bank with one hand, the bulky camera clutched to his chest with the other. It's not graceful, and I hope he's not erasing tracks. I stop him as soon as he reaches me and point to one of the shoe prints.

"That's our man, Halifax. Make sure you're not walking through his prints."

"Roger that." He follows me breathing heavily and just as crouched as I am, as we follow the missing man to the plateau. Harper sees the paint earlier than I did. "What's this?"

"I hoped you could tell me."

He huffs and tries to catch his breath while he rubs the stubble on his chin. "It almost looks like a helipad."

"What?"

"I mean, they're all over the place around here for emergency evacs. And this long flat space must be an airstrip."

I try to picture one of numerous tiny planes that cruise the Alaskan mountain passes taxiing this place or landing on the packed dirt. "Seems like a weird place for an airstrip, doesn't it?"

Harper is still hunched over. "You haven't spent much time in rural Alaska yet, have you?"

I shake my head. I haven't. I've been pretty much confined to Anchorage since I got here.

"Well, out here pretty much anybody with means owns a small plane. Those that can't own know someone who does. Sometimes it's the only way to get where you need to go, especially if you need supplies that won't fit in your vehicle. You can't swing a dead fox without hitting an airstrip. People will clear out and use anywhere that's flat and long enough. I'd bet Mr. Drew's got one. Hell, this one's not too far from his place. Could be his."

"Hmm. Okay, but that still doesn't make sense—"

"What doesn't?"

I continue tracing the man's tracks. "The tracks get all the way to…here…" I stop at the last footprint. "And they just end."

"Whoa." He slowly makes the same careful circle I did. "What, did he catch a plane?"

"Well, he didn't catch a helicopter since his tracks go right over the landing pad. He could have caught a small plane, I guess. Maybe one on skis?"

"Maybe, depending on what the weather's been like here." He double-checks, but there are no obvious signs of traffic on this airstrip since the last snow. "So, he just what? Disappeared?"

"It looks like it, unless you're seeing something I don't."

"Nope." He puts his hand to his eyes, scanning the horizon. "No animal tracks, either. Out in the open like this, we'd see them. It *doesn't* make any sense. If he'd fallen in a ravine or something, we probably would have too."

"Right."

"Well, crud." That's my conclusion too. "What do we do?"

I so want to continue around the mountain, looking for other tracks. *But why would they stop and start again somewhere else?*

"Go back to the truck, I guess. Try to figure out why it's in that bank."

"Oh, I can tell you that. The tire's totally flat. My guess is it blew out and he lost control..." He puts his fist to his mouth as he releases one last slightly labored huff.

"He wasn't carrying a spare?"

"That's the thing. He was! It's still there, but it doesn't look like he made any effort to get it. Jack's still there and everything. He even left his wallet in the glove compartment. There's the check in there from Mr. Drew, and his license. Not much else."

"Why would he abandon the truck and walk up here? Unless he thought the damage to the front was so bad it wouldn't drive."

"Could be. The front end *is* pretty bad. There might've been smoke or something."

"Maybe." I look around us, unsure. "But there's nothing here. Why come up here, of all places? Why not head back toward Mr. Drew's? It would have been close to dark. Wouldn't he just stay on the road?"

"Maybe he saw something weird and wanted a closer look. Or maybe he lost track of the road. I mean, it's not like there's streetlights out here."

"But he'd know the road wasn't up this bank."

"True..."

"And the tracks head straight for this airstrip, like he came here on purpose." He nods his agreement. "Do you think the road would lead here if we kept following it?"

"Only one way to find out." With that, we return to the Tank. And it turns out it does. The road travels to the end of what we've dubbed the airstrip. There are no tracks.

Harper speaks my thoughts. "So, it's possible he meant to drive all the way here, but the tire blew, and he figured forget it, just walk."

"Maybe. But we still don't know why he came here in the first place."

"He was expecting someone, maybe? A meeting?"

I turn the idea over. Why would a man on his way to a bar meet someone at an airstrip in the middle of nowhere? He was an occasional party guy. Was this a drug exchange? Were drugs being flown in? Seems awfully elaborate for a guy who only indulges with the weekend stuff he could get cheap. Harper is shaking his head slowly. I'd bet he's working through the same thoughts.

"Lou, I don't think we're going to solve this one today."

"Lou?" I raise my eyebrows at my new nickname. He grins but doesn't answer or recant. I'm okay with that. "You're right. We'll need to come back here with a dog and a search party."

He nods and slowly turns in a circle as he snaps his last pictures of the area before we leave. "Should we let Marli know we've found the truck?" He promised her, but I'm not so sure.

"No." At his look, I explain. "I get the feeling she'd come out here to see for herself, and the last thing we or those kids need is her wandering off."

He bobs his head. "Makes sense, Chief. So, on to the Stantons'?"

"One stop on the way."

CHAPTER SIX

B ecause it's on the way to the Stantons', I want to go over to the machine shop to talk to Lee's coworkers. They're a motley mix of seasoned Alaska residents and seasonal kids just passing through. They all say the same thing. Lee was depressed.

They don't use that word; mental health is not something you talk about here. The evidence adds up, though, and I'd know. I struggled with it while I worked for DCS.

Lee Stanton had started arriving late and un-showered when that had never been his MO. He'd stopped talking, stopped joining the other guys for a cigarette at lunch. He'd retreated. They couldn't say why. They were on friendly terms, as in they'd talk about video games and surface shit, but nothing deep. They don't know if he'd been seeing anyone. They don't know anything about his family life.

Lee's supervisor's eyes are downcast when he admits he'd given Lee two warnings about his tardiness. He planned to fire him, and Lee knew it. "That's the rule," he says, "three strikes and you're out. Would have hated to do it, though."

It adds up. Kid's depressed, starts having a hard time getting out of bed in the morning, starts feeling hopeless about his life, then starts failing at his job. He knows he's about to be fired and that's the last straw. He decides to kill himself. But he still loves his family, so he also decides to leave his few possessions to them before he takes a shotgun out into the snow.

This case seems like it will come to a neat close as we get back on the road to the Stantons' home.

❖

The only word I think describes Lee Stanton's father, Pike, is *gruff*. The man's face is deep ravines the color of a desert landscape, and his broad jaw is covered in salt and pepper stubble. Despite his years, his gray eyebrows are still thick and imposing. He sits at the oval kitchen table chain-smoking. His voice sounds like it's being dragged over charcoal as he gives monosyllabic responses to my questions. I don't get the impression he's trying to be unhelpful—only that he just normally doesn't say much of anything. Especially to strangers. In the end, he doesn't tell us anything new. He's not as close with Lee as Lee's mom.

They can't help us determine where he might have gone. *Does he have any favorite places to hunt?* Probably, but they don't know where. *Is there anyone he might have gone to visit?* They don't think so, but maybe. *Does he have any favorite places to go and relax?* No answer at all, just shrugs.

Now that we're talking to the Stantons, my mind is on Branden Halifax. Ironic, given when we were on the road to Mr. Drew's to ask about Branden, my mind was on Lee. The whole time we talk, Harper has frown lines in his expression conflicting with his baby face, and he rubs his neck. After we've left Lee's parents and begin the ride down to the trailer in silence, he finally speaks.

"So, what's the plan?"

"No plan. I'm hoping something catches our eye when we get there."

When we open the door, the smell is almost pleasant; it's some sort of air freshener meant to smell like clean sheets. I sniff around for the change and find a Glade Plugins in the kitchen wall. The dishes are gone from the sink. Otherwise, the place looks untouched. Mrs. Stanton believes Lee will come home.

I plant myself in the middle of the trailer and slowly rotate.

Harper paces. Suddenly he stops and completes an about-face on his boot heel. "There's no gun in here."

"No."

"Don't you think there would be?"

"If he doesn't have it with him? Living out here? Yeah, probably. I'd sure as hell keep one with me. You'd never know what you were going to encounter when you open that door."

"Right. So, what kind of gun do you think he has with him?"

"Hard to say. I'd guess shotgun if he's thinking run-ins with wildlife. But if he went to kill himself? I don't know. A handgun? He wouldn't exactly be worried about fighting off animals. They might save him the trouble."

"There were loads of extra bullets in the sheds outside for a bunch of different guns. Did you see any in here?"

We open drawers and cabinets. I rifle through the nightstand. Nothing. "He'd have extras. So, he took them with him."

"Maybe."

This isn't going anywhere. Why does it matter how many bullets he took? I resume my rotation. My eye catches the edge of the dog bowl in a cardboard box. I open kitchen cabinets again. There it is—a bag of Purina dog food.

"What are you thinking?"

"I just want to try something." I grab the bowl and the bag and carry them outside. I shake the bag vigorously and shove my fingers in the sides of my mouth to whistle. It's the one skill my dad bothered to teach me. Harper is startled and covers his ears. He gets it, though.

"Heeeeeere, dog!" He whistles too while he walks around the trailer. I shake the bag for a bit, then pour the food from a distance so it makes a loud clang as it hits the aluminum bowl.

I hear Harper's voice as he dog-speaks brightly. "Hey there, buddy! You know that sound? It's all right! Come on!" Harper is crouched with his hand extended when I round the corner of the trailer.

"Careful. We don't know if that's the dog, or if it's friendly."

"I think this is our guy. Who else's dog would be around?" As if to confirm this thought, the dog prances right up to Harper and licks his hand. He's a big dog, maybe eighty pounds when he's not so scrawny. He's got the eyes of a boxer and the body of a shepherd with ears that flop up and down as he trots. He vigorously wags a nub where his tail should be. He's dirty, especially around the nose, as if he's been digging, but his hair is still clearly auburn, and about the right length for what we spotted on Lee's clothes.

The dog runs toward me when I shake the bowl and immediately dips his head to eat. I pet him while he devours the food, then I refill the bowl. He downs that too, then looks to me expectantly. I scratch him behind the ears and give him a little more food. When he's finished, he looks at me, then over at Harper. He barks once with his nose toward the sky, and he starts to walk away.

"No, stay, buddy!" Harper starts toward the dog. I hold out my palm to stop Harper.

"We should follow him and see where he goes. He might lead us to his owner."

Harper's eyes grow large. "Good call."

"Grab the collar and leash by the door."

Harper opens the trailer door as I follow the dog to the tree line. The dog looks back at me periodically as he high-steps through the fine snow. He's headed up the mountain at a zigzag. Harper's trotting after us.

The dog canters a good three-quarters of a mile, splashes through an ice-cold stream, and then looks at us from the other side. I've slowed to wait for Harper. The dog yowls at both of us, which I interpret as dog-speak for *Hurry!* We don't have our water gear, so we find a good crossing spot. I grab Harper as he starts to slip on moss. For an Alaskan, he's surprisingly not outdoorsy. I don't say anything, but I notice he blushes.

The foliage is denser on the other side of the stream. We've come around the mountain. At a massive boulder, the remnant of some landslide surely, the dog stops, puts his large wet black nose to the ground, and sniffs with his mouth open and foam forming around his tongue. He trots around the boulder, then army crawls under a couple downed trees. I drop to all fours and follow as I fumble in my pocket for my compact flashlight. Even with the sun out, it's dark here and I can feel the moisture of the ferns beneath me seeping through my pants. The underbrush smells of leaf rot. Harper hesitates. The hole I've squeezed through is barely wide enough for me, and there's no use in both of us getting our uniforms filthy anyway.

"I'll check it out and holler if I find anything!" I'm not sure why I'm yelling, it's so quiet here.

"All right. I'll…keep an eye out." For what is unclear.

I resume tracking the white patch of fur under the dog's truncated tail. He wiggles himself free of the downed spruce, and soon after, I emerge into a clearing with streaks of sunlight filtering in through the branches.

I get my bearings. There's a circle of pines around me, and within the circle, the remnants of what must have been a riot of purple, white, and yellow wildflowers. They're wilted now, as are the teaberries that still exude a weak fragrance. It reminds me of coming into the kitchen every morning as a kid, my mom sitting over the newspaper with her favorite mug of an hours-old beverage.

The dog is across the circle, now several yards away. His head is raised, his back straight like a pointer. He stares at me, and his nub has gone still. He turns his head toward the trees behind him, then back at me. As I slowly approach, he barks, but he doesn't move away or show signs of aggression. When I get within a few yards, he moves to the trees and starts pawing at the ground.

The smell hits me, and my entire visage goes temporarily green. My throat and nose are acidic, and I gag. Salt from my eyes falls into my mouth and I blink rapidly. When I can see again, a boot emerges from a clump of soft fern. The dog uses its nose to lift something, then drops it back to the dirt. A hand. I yell for Harper.

❖

I cautiously approach the body. The dog stops manipulating the corpse as if he knows it's not necessary now that I've seen it. A shotgun is still clasped in the right hand. Once I see what's beyond the barrel end, I have to turn away. My stomach pulls itself into my throat and I dry heave, simultaneously focusing on pinching my nose shut and keeping down bile.

The neck is a crater of torn flesh that ends in a pool of foamy dried blood and what appears to be the top of the severed spine. It's like a deformed sail mast visible from a morbid seashore. The entire corpse is so bloated it barely looks human, and it wears a moldy shade of green. Any number of birds and animals have been at it; there are holes through the clothing and skin. I hear Harper fighting with the underbrush behind me, which gives me time to pull myself together.

"What's up? Is that—"

"Don't. It's—"

"Oh hell!" He turns away so quickly he loses his balance and drops to a knee. He's as white as the snow around us, with a hint of yellow behind it. He opens his mouth, presumably to speak, and gags a little instead. It is several minutes before he manages words.

"I'm guessing that's our guy." He closes his eyes tight as if he's meditating.

The dog stands there watching us, seemingly unfazed by the horror right next to him. I force myself to approach again, bracing myself to act like the medical examiners I've seen on television. I've seen some gross shit, but a rotting decapitated corpse tops the list. There's something so brutal about the finality of headlessness. I recall *The Legend of Sleepy Hollow* and the nightmares I had for months after I selected it from my mother's shelf well before I should have. Even now I do not know if it was the visceral repulsion of the missing head that frightened me, or the possibilities for all the ways a human head could be removed.

"Some people think a person stays conscious for like, a couple minutes after they lose their head." Harper is at my shoulder, glancing back at the body as if it might stand. His comment calls to mind the wives of Henry VIII and royalty during the French Revolution, at the guillotine, the executioner holding their skull aloft after the blade fell. Were the victims aware they had been torn apart, but unable to express their horror? If it is true, I wonder what Lee Stanton might have seen, heard, smelled, or tasted in those last seconds. The smell of damp bear fur? The taste of shotgun powder and blood?

Harper steps forward with the camera but turns back around.

"I can't do it."

I take the camera and the pictures. The lens at least offers some false sense of separation. After, I dial the chief. The connection is static, and I walk around in circles until I can hear something. It's mostly mumbled garble, but a great excuse to distance from the putrid stench of decayed meat and curdled milk with a hint of metal.

"Chief?...Look, I can't really hear you. You hearing me?...Good. Hey, we've got a body up from Lee Stanton's." I give him the location as best I can. "We'll be on the lookout for a team." His next words sound like a question, and I take my best guess. "Can't tell what the cause of death is. Head's gone." I hear "Shit" before I end the call.

We've got some time while he relays it to the Seward team and they relay it to the medical examiner. I need to get away from the body even though one of us should stay. It's been here this long.

"Wanna wait for the team in the car?"

"Yes! Oh God, do I ever!"

I laugh. It's nice to have a partner who doesn't play the tough guy. I whistle for the dog. Best to make sure he doesn't bother the body any more than he already has. He trots alongside us all the way back, and as soon as I open the door to the Tank, he hops in and settles on the back seat like it's the most natural thing in the world. As if he knows it will be a while before the Seward team arrives, he dozes off.

"Guess we'll need to find a car wash before we head back to Anchorage, huh?"

I check out the muddy paw prints on the back seat. Then I look at the seat below me. It's also filthy from the mud all over my uniform. "Probably nothing the Tank hasn't seen before."

"You think that's Lee?" I suppose it's easier for Harper to talk about the body here.

"About the right height. Hard to tell weight and skin tone. Gun seems like something he'd carry based on what we saw around the trailer. Too early to say for sure, but based on the circumstantial plus the location and the description his mom gave us...That's probably our guy." I glance back at the sleeping pile of fur while its chest moves rhythmically with his breath. I put my hands on my stomach, which is finally starting to settle. Still, that's not a scene I'm going to forget, ever.

"Besides, the dog knew where he was. I'm betting that's his owner." The dog must sense I'm talking about him. He startles awake and lifts his head.

Harper reaches to pet him. "What do you think his name is?" The dog wrinkles his forehead into an oddly human sort of scowl. "What's your name, bud?" The mutt tilts his head to the side so that his ears flop over. "Rover?" A slow head tilt to the other side. "Sparky?" The dog just blinks. "Lucky. Willis? Cletus? Bill?" I smirk at Harper, baffled he can think about dog names right now, but also grateful for the distraction. "Henry? Woodhouse? Phillip?"

"What the hell kind of names does your family give to animals?"

"What? My dog as a kid was Bruce." He speaks with such earnestness I laugh again. "You got any animals?"

"Nah. Had a rabbit growing up. Wanna guess its name?"

"Ethel."

The dog and I both give him a skeptical look.

"Fluffy."

He laughs and turns back to the dog. "Is your name Fluffy?"

The dog puts its head back down as if it's offended and will now ignore us. Properly admonished, Harper turns back to me.

"When we try to hack into people's computers, we look at their possessions to see what they're into, and we guess passwords based on that stuff. We know Lee's into video games and spices. So, hmm… *Mario*?" There's no reaction from the dog, so Harper rattles off a bunch of vaguely familiar names. "Zelda. Link. Sonic. Tails." The dog jerks his head up.

"Tails," Harper repeats. The dog stands up, wagging his nub.

"Tails!" Tails barks once.

"Are you kidding me? What a cruel joke, to name a dog with no tail Tails."

My partner cheers triumphantly and twists around to grin at Tails, who lunges forward to lick Harper's face. Harper barely dodges the wet offering. Maybe this is better than working alone. I don't even want to imagine what thoughts would be going through my head right now if Harper and this dog weren't here and it was just me. I smile at Harper. He looks confused but smiles too.

"Well, Tails it is, I guess." As soon as I say his name, Tails climbs into my lap. He's not exactly a lap dog, so I'm pinned when the team finds us.

CHAPTER SEVEN

A man with a thick Canadian accent addresses me through the window of the Tank. "Brought your dog, eh?"

"No. He led us to the scene."

"All right then. I'm Stan Guffman. I'm the tech with Doc Fenway." I assume Dr. Fenway is the medical examiner. "Where's this body?"

"In a clearing up through the underbrush. It's not a pretty scene."

"That's usually true. Any ID on him?"

Shit. I don't want to admit we didn't check. "We haven't looked yet."

Harper maneuvers so he can see across the SUV to the tech on my side. "We were a little distracted trying to figure out why he's missing his head."

Guffman leans further into the window. "Thoughts on why?"

Harper punts the question to me with a nod.

"Hard to tell, but he's still holding a shotgun," I say. "Forensics will need to test the weapon. Seems like he might have shot himself and the blood attracted wildlife that...*removed* what was left."

"Any sense of how long it's been out there?"

I am vaguely disturbed that he refers to the body as *it*. "A few days at least, based on the timeline we have on his disappearance."

"All right. Wanna show us?"

"Sure thing." I open the door and Tails jumps out and wiggles his butt in my direction. Harper clambers out and follows close behind us.

There are three other people on the team, two younger men and a red-haired woman wearing a bright orange down coat with *Seward* written in white caps across the back. Once we've all crawled under the downed trees and approached the body, it's clear she's the medical examiner. She jumps in, gloves on, fingers in the hole of the neck. One of the younger men asks if she should be disturbing the body so much while it's outside.

"Oh, don't lose your head over it." She grins. "Besides, based on the smell and bloat, I'd guess he's been out here four or five days. Every animal around has been disturbing him."

She picks up his left hand—the one not holding the gun. "No wedding band." A large chunk of skin comes off in her hand. She seems undisturbed, as her chipper smile doesn't fade. She drops the hand. "I definitely want to get this guy back to the lab and do a more thorough examination, but for now I'm betting this gun has a lot to do with his death and missing head." She stands lithely and turns to the two younger men. "Bag 'im, boys!" Guffman records Dr. Fenway's verbal observations in a flip pad. "You get everything, Stan?"

"Think so!"

She approaches me, and I scent an amber perfume, a wonderfully welcome change from the stench of the body. When she's next to me, I find myself looking up into her green eyes.

"Anna Fenway, Seward ME. For most of the surrounding area too. You want to tell me about the investigation? Who is this?" Her voice is melodic and surprisingly deep.

I stammer, unsure where to start, and then I spit out a clumsy deluge. "We think this is Lee Stanton, but we don't know for sure yet. That is, we aren't certain yet. His mom reported him missing a few days ago. Lives a mile or so from here by himself, in the trailer where we are all parked. The trailer's full of boxes he packed and labeled with people's names."

She whistles low. "Suicide?"

"That's the assumption we've been working under. The dog"— Tails runs over—"led us to the body." Tails's timing is impeccable. I suppose there's nothing like knowing who, or what, you are.

She pats Tails's head, then something crosses her face.

"I'll need to give this pup a go-over. He could have blood or hair on him. Mind if I take him back to the van for a few minutes? I'll bring him back."

It's rare for me to zone out on a case, but something about Dr. Anna Fenway overwhelms all my senses at once. I'd be at a loss to say whether it's her striking good looks or the way she carries herself with natural authority. By the time I process her words, she has disappeared with Tails.

I compose myself. Harper comes over to watch operations from where I'm standing. When Dr. Fenway returns, she eyes him.

"This your partner?" She nods toward Harper, who sticks out his hand.

"Sorry I didn't think to introduce myself! I'm Officer Michael Harper. From Anchorage."

She looks down at his hand, then grabs it firmly. "Dr. Anna Fenway, I'm the ME. Nice to meet you." She turns to me. "In fact, I don't think we were introduced."

"Officer Louisa Linebach. Also from Anchorage." I offer my hand and she shakes it, then seems to hold on to it for a little longer than necessary before dropping it. "Find anything on the dog?" Tails lies between us.

"Sure did. Pulled what seems to be some dried blood off his belly, which could be good stuff for running DNA. He may turn out to be a helpful little man." She pats his head, then straightens to address me again. "Well, I'm sure glad you've found your way to Seward. We're way more fun down here!" She winks, and something in my chest heats a little. "You going to stick around town for a while?"

"Seems like it. We're also on another case just a few miles down the road." She lifts both of her eyebrows, revealing fine lines I hadn't noticed before. "Missing person. Found a vehicle, but no body yet. Sorry." I wonder why I just apologized. I'll kick myself about being awkward later, but if she notices, she doesn't let on.

"Well, I'll look forward to seeing you when one turns up!" She grins and her teeth are shiny and small. She turns. "Stan, go round and get the Snow King so we can load him out!"

"The Snow King?" I can guess what that is, but I want her to stay just a few moments longer. Being next to her is like standing in a spot of sunshine on a cold morning.

"Yup, that's our ATV. Necessary for moving bodies around here."

"Makes sense." Damn my remarkable communication skills.

"I'll give you a call as soon as we know something definite. *If* we know something definite." I must look concerned, because she grins and adds, "Don't worry, we end up knowing something definite in a good five percent of cases! Great to meet you, Linebach—and Harper!"

"Just Mikey, please!" my partner calls after her.

"Got it! And hey, if you two will be here for a while, ask the chief for a couple of these stylish coats!" She gives a tug to the hemline of her jacket. "Lots of hunters out here. You want to be visible." I nod and she waves over her shoulder as she follows her brightly attired team to their vehicles, where she removes a variety of straps and harnesses. I want to follow and watch her work, but I also *don't* want to watch the horror show as they prepare the body to move. I turn to Harper instead.

"You prefer Mikey?"

He lowers his head a little and smiles sheepishly. "It's true. I kind of hate being called by my last name."

"Well shit, you could have said something." I think about that for a second. "Never mind, I should have asked. It's not like I'm easy to talk to."

"Maybe not at first, but I think you're all right."

I'm not sure how to respond, so I glance back toward the Tank. Harper—*Mikey* nods and we're on our way. Tails happily trots alongside me.

"Do we let the Stantons know about the body?" Mikey's tone is somber. We get into the Tank.

"Not yet. There's still a chance it isn't him. No use upsetting them."

"Do you think knowing he's dead is worse than thinking their son is missing?"

"Maybe not, but as long as they think he could be out there somewhere, they'll keep hoping, and that's what we want them doing until we're sure this is our man."

He's silent for a long while. "Man," he finally mutters, "these poor people." We are both quiet for the rest of the ride.

❖

Before we head back down the mountain, we stop at Marli's to check in. The door flies open so fast it's like she was waiting for our soft knock. I wonder it doesn't come off the hinges. Her hair half tumbles from a messy bun. She wears flannel pajamas under a fluffy white bathrobe and still manages to look charming.

"Please! Come in." When she's closed the door behind us, she crosses to the table, her fur-lined leather mukluks making no sound.

"Can I get you something hot?"

Mikey sighs. "Oh, that would be amazing!"

I agree. The house is drafty and the air around my feet is especially frigid. I picture blue toes in my hiking socks.

"Tea? Coffee?"

"Coffee, please." Mikey looks at me.

"Coffee sounds great."

She preps the coffeemaker, then sits across from us, hands clasped in front of her on the table. "Have you found him?"

I look down. Her face is uncomfortably close even several feet away.

"We're afraid not." The muscles in her face relax. "But we did find the truck."

"Oh!"

"It was a couple miles out from Mr. Drew's place. He wasn't in it, and there was no indication of struggle. It looked like he drove the truck into a bank, then got out and proceeded on foot."

"To where?"

"Well, that's what we're trying to figure out. Ms. Lei, do you happen to know of an airstrip in the area? Footsteps lead to what looks like an airstrip with a helipad."

"Well, Mr. Drew has one. All the rich people around here have one." She leans back in her chair, bathrobe flopping open. She plays with her ring. "There's also…*people* talk about an abandoned airstrip too." Mikey's taking notes. The coffee starts to pour into the carafe, and Marli startles up. Her back is to us when she speaks again.

"The kids around here, they talk about a haunted airstrip nearby. Silly ghost stories. I'm not sure if it even exists, but it would make sense. Airstrips appear when people need them, then just get overgrown when someone moves or stops needing it."

"Might be our airstrip, then. This one didn't look particularly well-tended, and it's difficult to access. We'll ask Mr. Drew in case it's his, though." She places a steaming mug in front of each of us and I'm tempted to hold my face over the liquid even though it would cloud my contact lenses.

"So, you found the truck near an old airstrip? I don't understand."

"We don't quite yet either. Looks like he climbed an embankment and headed for the runway, as if he knew exactly where he was going. The tracks lead onto the strip, and then..." She leans forward, her breath catching. "Well, and then they disappear."

"Disappear?"

"Yes. They don't turn into the woods or anything. They are there in the snow, and then they just—stop."

Her face contorts as she undoubtedly runs through scenarios in her mind. "You don't think...Could he have...What if he..." Marli leans hard against the table with a hand to each cheek while she theorizes. Mikey stops her.

"No use getting yourself worked up with speculations at this point, Ms. Lei. We've got nothing to indicate Branden came to any harm. If something happened on that airstrip, there'd be signs of a struggle. For all we know, he got into an aircraft and that's why the footsteps disappear." He and I haven't had a chance to talk about that possibility, but I'm glad he's mentioned it because her face relaxes immediately. At least it's something to hang on to.

Mikey produces Branden's wallet from his pocket.

"We need to take this back, but we found it in the truck. He wouldn't have gone too far without his wallet."

Marli reaches across the table slowly, as if she's afraid to touch it. "He left his wallet." She's not speaking to us.

"The check from Mr. Drew is still in there. Not much else. Did Branden usually carry cash around?"

"No, he just keeps some pocket money and gives the rest to me for bills and the house." She's tearing through the wallet as she speaks. "Did you remove a picture?"

"No, ma'am." We haven't removed anything. The wallet will need to go into evidence.

"That's so strange. He always keeps a picture of me and the girls in his wallet. *Always*. It's all beat up. It wasn't in the truck?"

"I'm afraid not. We went through the whole vehicle. This was in the glove box. No sign of a picture. Maybe he slipped it in his pocket?"

"But not the check?" She shakes her head. "I don't know. That's not right."

We don't have an answer. As we fall silent, I remember what's planned at the airstrip.

"Ms. Lei, we've called together a search team to check the area near the runway, just in case. Some police and volunteers that the Seward police department gathered. We wanted to let you know so you wouldn't be surprised, and so you can join if you'd like. They'll be there soon after sunrise."

Mikey leans forward. "Would you like to join the search party?"

"Thank you for this. And I want to. I really want to. But..." She indicates the bedrooms where little Alicia and the baby are still asleep. "I don't want her to feel scared. Seeing all those people looking for her dad—"

"That makes perfect sense, and it's perfectly okay. So, you stay here and take care of your family, and we'll report back to you as soon as we know anything, all right?" She nods. I gather the empty mugs and place them carefully in the ceramic farm sink. I try to imagine running a household with children while my partner is missing in the Alaska wilderness. There's no way I could do what Marli is doing.

"Thank you, Ms. Lei, for your help and for the coffee. I know waiting like this is hard, but we should know more soon. Finding the truck was a good, solid start."

She shows us out into the cold civil twilight, where snow is starting to fall.

❖

It is barely dawn when Mikey and I make it to the airstrip. The team is already assembled and waiting for us. There's about a dozen people, and they're a mix of concerned—or morbidly curious—citizens and Seward officers. I record their names, hoping Branden's mother will be in the crowd. She's not. Then again, she may have wanted to ensure she wasn't the one to stumble across her dead son.

"All right, everyone, listen up. We're looking for a white male, age twenty-seven, name is Branden Halifax. Officer Harper is handing out a recent picture of him. He was last seen at his employer's home a couple miles from here. His vehicle was found abandoned just over there." I indicate the truck, which is still wedged in the embankment. "The snow has covered most of what we believe are Branden's footsteps, but when my partner and I tracked them yesterday, they led up the embankment, to an airstrip. Is anyone familiar with this airstrip?"

"This is the old Burger strip. It's been abandoned for a while now." We about-face to find Mr. Drew walking toward us wearing a leather bomber jacket and jeans. Mikey and I look at each other, and then back to Mr. Drew.

"How long has it been abandoned, Mr. Drew? Do you know?"

"I'd say around a decade or so."

"Do you know anything else about it?"

"Kids hang out here sometimes. The kids that live around the mountain. I know they come on Halloween, tell ghost stories, build fires and whatnot. They tend to leave a lot of beer bottles and cigarette butts. I don't know if they've been around recently."

"No airplane activity?"

"I think it got used a few years ago for an emergency rescue when the weather turned bad. But that's the last I know."

"Thank you, Mr. Drew." I hope I sound sincere, but all I can think about is my police training, where we were taught that criminals often insert themselves into the investigations of crimes they are involved in. *Is Mr. Drew just helpful? Is he simply bored? Or is this something more?*

Mikey takes over the logistics, separating the searchers into pairs and telling them how to use the walkie-talkies if they find anything. After a final warning to be cautious on the ice, the group divides, eyes to the snow.

❖

The search reveals nothing. Not a shred of clothing, not a carving in a tree, not a piece of hair or a shotgun shell. Nothing. It's like the whole scene's been whitewashed. But the snow isn't falling hard enough. Branden Halifax has just disappeared.

CHAPTER EIGHT

As we finish, I receive a call from Dr. Fenway. Her voice sounds enthusiastic and sweet. I duck away from Mikey to talk to her. I don't know why. I like that she just jumps right into whatever she has to say.

"Hey, I know this isn't what you want to hear, but the autopsy results from that headless body are inconclusive." It's the worst news possible.

"Shit."

"Well, I said *fuck*, but close enough. The head loss could have been caused by almost anything. He was decomposed enough and tampered with by enough wildlife that it's impossible to tell. I can't even say how clean the initial wound was. The blood on the dog looks like it's from the body, so probably not helpful, though I did send it, along with some samples from the body, for DNA testing. That'll take a few weeks at least, and who knows if they'll be able to match anything. We couldn't get a print either. None of the fingers were in the best condition."

"Inconclusive. Okay. Well, thanks for letting me know. We'll talk soon."

"I hope so!"

I disconnect as Mikey approaches.

"So?"

"Inconclusive."

"It took all that time for them to say it was inconclusive?"

"Well, they know that's not what we want to hear."

"So that's it? Now what?"

I rock back on the heels of my boots. My stomach says I'm ecstatic, nervous even. My brain knows I should be wildly disappointed with the lack of evidence. It's hard to reconcile.

"I guess we need more to go on."

"Crud. What else can we get? We have a body. If there was a weapon involved, we have a weapon. Didn't they get fingerprints?"

"Didn't take. He was falling apart. You saw how the skin came away when Dr. Fenway touched it."

"Yeah, true. But I mean, he matches the physical description. He was close to the trailer. Date of death matches…"

"That doesn't feel like a lot."

"That's a ton more than we normally have. What about an ID? Can the mom ID him?" *Good question.*

"Good call. You wanna give the morgue a ring back?" I hand him the phone. I hover nearby as he dials, trying to hear over his shoulder.

As he listens, he looks me in the eye as if he's trying to send mental notes through telepathy, then he remembers to vocalize them. Dr. Fenway okays the ID. Tonight. It'll be best if we're there. Mikey asks if she can tell us about the clothing, other than the jeans and coat we could see.

"Long johns under the jeans. White briefs. Blue and white plaid flannel. No T-shirt. No hidden jewelry. Any tattoos or piercings?"

I wouldn't have even thought about that.

"Okay." He sounds disappointed. "Thanks, Doc. See you this evening." He hangs up.

"Long johns under the jeans?"

"Yeah. The clothes are bagged for us."

"We can ask Mrs. Stanton about that, I guess."

"Can't hurt. Besides, we'll see her this evening."

I nod. It's going to be a rough night.

❖

I dread our conversation with the Stantons. We decide en route Mikey will ask about the ID. It's become obvious he's much better at that sort of thing. Mrs. Stanton opens the door with a clear look of apprehension on her face. Then she sees the dog, and it worsens.

"Officers. You find something?"

"I'm afraid so, ma'am." I am content to not say a damned thing while Mikey talks. He's even got his hat in his hand like he's in some sort of war movie come to tell the new widow the bad news. "Mind if we come in?"

"Sure."

"The dog all right?"

"That's fine." Tails waits on the threshold like a good guest until she pats her leg to welcome him. She directs us to a sofa covered in plastic. She doesn't bother to sit herself—she paces in front of an unusually large television instead. The dog follows along behind her, not interrupting.

"I'm guessing this isn't good news."

"Ma'am, we know you like to get straight to the point. We found someone in the woods that may be Lee."

"You can't tell?"

"No, ma'am."

She stops midstride and turns toward him. Mr. Stanton has appeared silently in the splintered oak doorway behind Mikey.

"Are you sure you don't want to have a seat, Mrs. Stanton?"

She looks at him quizzically, then she suddenly slips into an armchair across from us. Mikey leans in toward her, hands on his knees. "Ma'am, I'm sorry to tell you this. I really am."

Mr. Stanton is frozen in the doorway. I cough, and when Mikey looks at me, I nod toward Lee's father. Mikey inclines his head.

"Would you like to have a seat with your wife, Mr. Stanton?"

Mr. Stanton grunts and settles himself on the arm of the corduroy seat. He takes her hand in both of his in a surprisingly gentle manner. Their wedding rings click against each other.

"Mr. and Mrs. Stanton, we found a young man in the woods a couple miles from here. The dog led us to him. Now, we don't know for certain if it's Lee or not. I want to stress that. We'll need your help there. The body we found…Well…It's missing its head."

Mrs. Stanton blinks rapidly. It's the only indication she's even heard what Mikey said.

"Missing its head?"

"That's right, sir. It's not clear right now what happened. It could have been any number of things, but the…the person we have was gripping a shotgun."

Mrs. Stanton closes her eyes and squeezes her husband's hands until her knuckles turn white.

"You think Lee committed suicide."

Mikey handles the loaded statement like a champion. I can't imagine anything worse to tell parents. Their child was so miserable he chose to leave the world they so lovingly brought him into and raised him up in. It's the worst thing aside from telling them their child's missing.

"We certainly don't want to assume anything. We don't even know that the young man we found is Lee. Many people go missing in this area every year. It could be a total coincidence." He bends forward at his waist, twines his fingers together and contemplates his hands before he glances at me. "But...the labeling of boxes for loved ones... That's something we tend to see in people who have made a conscious decision to...make another choice."

Mr. Stanton disagrees with this conclusion for his son. He flares his nostrils, then glances at his wife and takes a visible deep breath as Mikey continues.

"That's why we could use your help. The person we found, he's at the—hospital—in Seward." Mikey avoids saying *morgue*, a mental note I save for later. "If you could come down, that would make a huge difference. We could rule him out if it's not Lee."

"Do we both need to be there?" Mr. Stanton looks at his wife.

"It's all right. I want to be there. I need to know."

I'm proud of Mrs. Stanton for saying so, for some reason. Mr. Stanton pats her hand as if he is too. I take over. "How does this evening sound?"

"We'll be there."

"Thank you so much. We know this is about the worst news you could receive, and we're very sorry."

Mr. Stanton just nods firmly, but Mrs. Stanton speaks. "Thank you. Always best to just know what's happening, right?"

Mikey and I nod in unison. We all stand. The dog jumps up from where he's settled at my feet, and it's only then I remember he's there.

"Oh. The dog..."

The Stantons both look at him wearily, then back to me.

"We weren't sure—"

Mrs. Stanton is obviously aggrieved by the idea. "No! I don't think—" Mr. Stanton puts a hand on her shoulder.

"Would you mind watching after him for now? If it's not Lee, then..."

"That's perfectly fine. We'll take care of him until we know something for sure."

"Thank you." Mrs. Stanton looks relieved. Tails is already standing and wagging his nub as if he's ready to go, though he doesn't know where he's going.

❖

Back in the Tank, Mikey looks restless. I think maybe he's nervous about looking at the body, but he breaks the silence.

"I'm starving. You wanna get a late lunch? Dinner? Hell, I don't even know what time it is."

As if on cue, my stomach growls loudly. "Sure. Why not?"

"Back into town?"

I nod and throw the Tank into gear. "Know of anywhere that'll allow a dog?" Ass still in the back seat, the mutt leans forward to lay his head on the center console, from where he occasionally licks my coat sleeve.

❖

We find a place called the Showdown, which I can only consider a saloon. A heavy bar runs the length of the whole place. A massive gilt-framed mirror tags right along with it so patrons can see their reflections as they hunch over on the maroon leather stools. We choose a table in the back and we each have our own tufted chaise on wheels. Both Mikey and I automatically angle our bodies so we can see the door.

"We both must be reincarnated poker players," Mikey says. The bartender eyes the dog, but the place is empty, and the waitress seems happy to see him.

"Chips for your pup?"

"Sure. Why not?" Mikey and I each order a burger and beer. It's only just after noon, but given what's ahead of us still, I feel all right about a stout. Mikey's IPA smells like a citrus nightmare. I push it away from me when it arrives.

"It smells like a goddamned Polynesian vacation."

"What, you don't want to lie on a beach drinking rum from a pineapple?"

"Sure, but there's something wrong about wafting grapefruit while talking about a decapitated man in an Alaskan bar."

"This is a meal, and we aren't talking about a decapitated man in an Alaskan bar." He grins and takes a big sip. "Mmm. Refreshing."

I shake my head, thankful for the overpowering coffee and chocolate aroma of my selection. The smell of coffee, even as just a note in my beer, seems to immediately turn my brain on full speed. My phone rings shortly after I've started my review of the facts. Must be time to update the chief.

Reception is still a little fuzzy, but better now we're in town. I tell him about the search for Branden, the inconclusive exam, and the visit with the Stantons.

"Fuck!" I picture all the other Anchorage officers turning to stare at him as he shouts. "Well, what do you and Mikey think? Is this your man? I mean, one of your men?" Mikey is leaning far enough over I'm sure he's catching most of what the chief says. I look at Mikey and cover the mouthpiece. He just blinks slowly and nods.

"Yes. We both are fairly confident they're Lee Stanton's remains. Time of death is right, and the shotgun looks like something he'd have. There weren't signs of struggle at the scene. The clothes looked like other stuff in Lee's trailer too, but we'll get to check it out more closely today when we head over to the morgue."

"Checking out the body again?"

"The Stantons are coming in to see if they can give an ID."

Chief Quint gives a low whistle. "Nice. That's quick. Good work, you and Mikey. If you could get a positive ID, that'd be great."

"Well, I'm not sure if we'll ever get—I mean, we could really stand to find the head, don't you think? Check the teeth with the dentist in town and—"

"Hell, we're lucky you found a body at all, especially given where it was. I saw the pictures the Seward lab faxed over. Hell of a good job recovering that. Maybe give the scene another quick go-over, but I wouldn't spend days. A head would be too easy for an animal to carry off or knock down the mountain..."

The thought of a moose kicking Lee Stanton's skull for it to careen off a rock and over the edge of a waterfall, smashing against everything in its path, is gruesome. Good thing those burgers haven't arrived yet. I tune back in to find the chief is still going.

"...besides which, I'm sure the family would like to know whether that's their kid or not. Let's hope they can identify a mole or something on the body this afternoon. Would sure be a help. That happens, you can go ahead and close the case."

"Yes. Here's hoping." I'm naturally skeptical, but this pessimism is based in reality. That body lay outside for several days, and it was wet. And animals. The chances of any clear marks are slim.

"Well, tell Mikey I wish you both good luck. You've done a nice job. Even nicer if you get a solve today."

"Thanks, Chief. We'll be in touch later. Oh, and hey, can we get an APB out for Branden Halifax? If he got on a plane, he could be anywhere." The chief agrees and promises to get right on it. I slam the phone on the table.

"What's wrong?"

"Nothing. He said great job."

"So, what are you taking out on that poor phone?"

"It's not anything really. He just...the chief is pushing for an ID."

"Well, we *are* fairly certain that it's Lee. Right?"

"Yes, definitely. I mean, it probably is. But we aren't one hundred percent sure."

"True?"

"I'd just rather be sure."

"I get that."

"Especially with all the people who go missing from around here. Most are men. Most dress like Lee Stanton. Plenty of locals disappear, like Branden."

He nods. "I know. Same area, around the same time of disappearance. But it doesn't fit that the body could be Branden. His tracks clearly led up the mountain, and we don't know that he would have been carrying a shotgun."

"We also don't know he *wouldn't* have been. Nobody drives around here without a gun, and we didn't find one in the truck."

"True, but he was just going out to a bar he goes to every week, and to his boss's house. I'm just having a hard time seeing it. And we have no reason to think he would have used a gun on himself."

"Yes." I lean back against the chaise leather, which creaks in response. I down the rest of the beer and am left with a frothy, rich taste. My stomach performs a jump and twist like gymnasts do in the Olympics. Maybe a heavy beer on an empty stomach wasn't the best idea. My head feels light. I ignore it. "But we know he was a party guy. What if he was picking something up from a dealer? He might take a shotgun then."

"Getting something from a dealer in a random clearing in the middle of the woods? That would be a hell of a meeting to arrange."

We both order coffees as the waitress sets a heaping plate of homemade potato chips on the table. I taste one, just to see what Tails is getting. They're amazing. I raise my eyebrows at Mikey, who then throws a handful down next to his french fries. When I toss a warm one to Tails, he jumps to grab it midair.

CHAPTER NINE

We eat in silence because the burgers travel down our throats at unhealthy speeds. Tails wags his butt impatiently, but there's no time for throwing him chips while the humans eat. When I'm finished, I settle back into my seat. Tails puts his paws on my knees and finally receives what's left of his snack. Mikey leans as far back as possible, spreads both hands over his generous belly, and groans.

"Oh, hell I hadn't realized how much I needed that."

"Me neither." We both sigh deeply. We had an early start, and with the heavy meal, I worry we'll both fall asleep. Not really. But when Mikey starts to speak, slowly, I do idly wonder if it's primarily to keep himself awake.

"Couldn't help but notice you seemed eager to take this case. When the chief assigned it to you, I mean."

I feel my muscles tense. "Yes. Maybe."

"Oh, it's a good thing! I thought it sounded like an interesting case too. Missing persons. I mean, these are tough. People either love them or hate them. Some of the officers do their best to dodge them because of the bad solve rates."

"I bet. Wouldn't want to hurt the stats." I snort and a tingle of spicy mustard reverses up my nose. I ate way too much, but I don't regret it. Tails doesn't regret his chips, either. He searches the empty plate for more. Mikey looks at me with his head tilted, saying nothing. It freaks me out. "What?"

"It's just…you shouldn't be so hard on them, you know. It seems like you want to assume the worst about the Anchorage team."

I shift in my seat uncomfortably. He's not wrong.

"It's just…" I half hope he'll see my discomfort and drop it, but he just looks at me patiently. "They don't exactly make life easy for me."

"Is being an officer easy for anybody?"

I don't know what to say. I guess I hadn't thought about it. There's a real danger in me digging too far into my own head. It doesn't tend to end well, and I plan to avoid it as long as I can. He finally relents and changes the subject just as I'm about to run for the bathroom to escape this conversation.

"I was just wondering why you were so eager to take this case on." He slides his spoon around the ketchup and mayo combo on his plate. If he's trying to act casual to relax me, it's not working. The spoon makes an irritating metallic scraping sound.

"No reason." I'm not talking about this. He lifts an eyebrow.

"Yeah? Wow. Most people get into police work because it's personal. Weird to meet somebody who is into it for the money." The money is nothing. His technique works this time, though. *Damn.*

"It's *not* about the money. I guess it *is* sort of personal. None of that *mommy and daddy got murdered by a bad man and it's my life goal to find the fucker and throw the cuffs on him* TV drama, though, if that's what you think."

He laughs. "Yeah, not for me either." I tilt my head at him in a silent prompt for more. If he wants story time, he can go first.

"I grew up in Anchorage, you know." I nod. He's mentioned it before. "I've got one hell of a big family. Four brothers, a sister, and somewhere around a dozen first cousins that are about my age." I'm silent and he continues. "Well, a bunch of the older ones, and I mean most of them, they got in with gangs."

This surprises me. He radiates good, so it's difficult to conceive others in his family aren't good too. I must unintentionally give him a bad face, because he stops pushing the red mayo and looks down.

"Well, you know, we were poor. And there weren't too many options at the time. Still aren't. There's seasonal work for a few months, but it doesn't pay enough to get you through the year, and there's a bunch of competition for any job from the traveling kids that come through in June or July."

I believe that. The part that's hard for me to picture is Mikey struggling as a kid. I've worked with hundreds of kids with super rough backgrounds, but it hadn't occurred to me to even think about Mikey's childhood. I used to sit in restaurants with my ex speculating about the histories of the people around us. I guess it's time to admit to myself I've stopped caring two shits about other people's stories since she left. That is, unless their story involves a crime I need to solve.

"So, you know, dealing drugs and stealing car radios it was."

"They ever try to get you into it?"

"I *did* get into it—the stealing, anyway. I was little so nobody thought to look at what I was doing too much. I lifted a couple of purses, food—stupid stuff." He looks embarrassed.

"Hell, if there's one population I don't rush to judge, it's kids. I bet I've seen a lot worse than anything Little Mikey was throwing down." I'm relieved when he laughs. I'm enjoying this conversation, though that could be because it's him doing the sharing and not me. "So, what changed?"

"They got caught. Two of my cousins went to jail." Tails seems to sense Mikey's sadness and goes over to him. Mikey sighs and pets him. Surefire way to make anyone feel better, a dog is.

"Worse, though…my brother—my oldest brother—he gave some drugs he'd picked up in the city to this girl he liked. He was going to keep it for himself to sell. It was worth a mint, and he didn't do any drugs himself, but he liked her a lot and she was asking, so he said he'd give her a taste of it. So, she comes around and gets it—not even the whole bag, mind you, just a little like he promised, and she's flirting with him and invites him to a friend's party that weekend. Then she goes off to, you know, do what she does. Didn't want him to see her high, maybe. Anyway, he mentions the party to a friend the next day and the friend is like *Dude, you didn't hear?*"

"Uh-oh."

"Yeah. She'd died that night. Went to a girlfriend's house to shoot up and overdosed. My brother hadn't told her how much was cool to take. I mean…You know. Not that any of it's cool to take…" He eyes me and I focus on giving a kind face and as sympathetic a smile as I can, since I don't know if I should say that I don't know what to say.

"My brother…he felt like it was his fault. And it was. So, he got out of the business. Started consulting with the cops. Couldn't be one on account of his record. They treated him okay, though, and he got to liking some of them. Brought me over to meet them once he moved away from living with the cousins and got his own place outside of Anchorage. They adopted me, sort of. Guess they could see I was the only other one in the family not wrapped up in it. They recruited me before college. Had me intern at the station for a year afterward, then training."

"Nice."

He grins proudly. "Yeah. Youngest cop to join the force yet." His face clouds over fast. "I've had to arrest a couple of them now, though. The whole force knows my family. They try to leave me off those calls. But it happens. We don't always know who we're going after." Tails floats back and forth between us now.

"That has to suck." I don't have any siblings. I've never met my cousins in Bangladesh. Still, I always dreamed what it would be like to have a huge family full of people my age. I'd never factored in the thought of having to arrest them.

"Yeah. It does."

❖

The waitress arrives to collect Mikey's empty plate.

"Can I offer you anything else? Save room for dessert maybe?"

Mikey perks up. "No, but what have you got anyway?"

"Homemade brownies with vanilla ice cream and a peanut butter pie."

Mikey's eyes go wide. He turns to me with his hands clasped together like he is pleading to his mom. I smile. "Want to split a slice of peanut butter pie?"

"I couldn't possibly fit another calorie in my body."

"Want to watch me eat a slice of peanut butter pie?"

I chuckle. "Yes. Out of sheer scientific curiosity, you understand, just to see if you explode."

Mikey looks at the waitress and blinks rapidly. "What happens if I explode?"

"We just roll you on out to sea."

"Perfect."

She leaves to get his pie. Tails watches her go but sticks by our knees. I'm still chuckling.

❖

"So, you feel like sharing?"

"No way. I said no pie for me."

"Oh, I meant the conversation we were having before the miraculous presence of pie was revealed."

"Oh." I won't avoid it now, I guess. Seems fair since he shared. Besides, Mikey doesn't seem so bad. He's a comfortable kind of person, and it might be nice to have a friend in this giant state—someone to check on me if I don't show for work or something. I rotate my coffee cup like it's no big deal, but I can't manage eye contact. I hate talking about myself.

"Well, I didn't plan on being a cop originally. I came from the Department of Child Services." He already knows this, but I don't know how else to start.

"Yeah, the chief mentioned that. Said you'd quit there and decided you wanted to be a cop."

"Something like that." The truth is, I was fired. I'm not ready for my partner to know, though. "DCS is a shit-show, so that helped my decision."

He cocks his head to the side.

"Well, I majored in social work in college. I wanted to help." I laugh, remembering how naïve I was then. Mikey's nodding. "That wasn't how it went. *At all*. The parents hated me, saw me as the bitch trying to take their kids away. The kids saw me as the bad lady taking them from their families. The kids would get bounced around, get abused by other relatives or a foster family, then they'd repeat the cycle. The kids would wind up in the hospital or in jail. Sometimes dead. So, I got out. What's the point if you can't *actually* help?"

"So, how'd you get interested in missing persons?"

I nod. "The last case I worked reopened a case I'd worked before. We call those families frequent flyers. A girl said her brother was raping her. The mother denied it, protected her son. I worked with the Seattle police, therapists, juvenile detention, and about every residential placement center for troubled kids in the state trying to keep that girl safe, and in the end, I couldn't. The judge kept ordering the girl to different residential facilities, so *she* was getting punished for being raped. Eventually, her little sister said the brother had raped her too, and that was that. My girl ran away from her placement, then the boy disappeared." He turned up dead, but that's a story for another day.

"Whoa. What about her?"

"I don't know. I couldn't find her."

"Were you close to the girl?"

"Yes." He tilts his head to the side again. "She figured out…Well, she realized we had things in common, I guess." He persists with his inquisitive stare. "She knew I was…" I have the shortest moment of decision-making, and I decide to go for it.

"She knew I was a lesbian, so she came out to me."

"Oh. Oh man. That's intense stuff." He blushes, but I see no signs of judgment. "That poor kid. To be going through all the stuff that comes with adolescence, and working through her feelings, and then having her brother assaulting her—"

The waitress returns with the peanut butter pie, seems to sense our mood, and sets the plate exactly halfway between us. She even leaves and reappears with a second fork.

"Uh-oh. I think she's trying to tell you to eat your feelings."

"I just might do it too." I'm emotionally exhausted.

He dramatically throws his arms around the plate, shielding it. "No chance in hell!"

When I laugh, he slides the plate toward me. The pie feels like silk on my tongue. Mikey and I alternate bites of the pie, sliding it across the table after each forkful. Tails's head weaves back and forth with the plate. Mikey seems to sense that I'm done with the topic of DCS and my missing girl.

"Good thing you're eating half of this, because I'm pretty sure I can feel my arteries clogging." Mikey rubs his chest.

"Great, so now we'll both have heart attacks instead of just you."

"Hey, it's always good to have company!"

"I'm beginning to think maybe it is." When the plate's empty, we both lean back in our seats. I stroke Tails's back.

"So, what do we do with him? If that's Lee, I mean? The Stantons didn't seem to want anything to do with him."

"No. Painful reminder, I'd think." Tails digs his wet, pitch-black nose into my pant leg.

"He sure seems to like you."

"He's a pretty cool dog."
"You should keep him."
"You think?"
"Why not? Take him back to Anchorage. I guarantee, you bring a dog around town, everyone will know you within a week."
I make a show of cringing. "Why would I want that?"
Mikey just grins.

❖

We have plenty of time before we're due at the morgue, so Mikey and I return to the station. I emerge from a pile of paperwork a couple hours later to find two Seward officers playing with Tails in the breakroom. Tails looks at me with huge eyes and swallows something before I can glimpse what it is, or even think to take it away.

"Hey! Did you know this dog has the worst farts any of us have ever smelled?" It's the older cop. They mock gag with accompanying noises.

"I'm guessing you're feeding him stuff that's going to make for a bad situation in my hotel room tonight." They glance at each other. The bearded officer speaks up.

"Yeah, you might want to make him sleep in the bathtub." He backs away from Tails. "Oh, hey, we meant to let you know, we were talking to some folks in town yesterday about a burglary…"

"Yes?"

"Well, some of the folks got chatting about the Halifax case and Stanton, and one of the restaurant managers mentioned he interviewed Lee Stanton about a week before he went missing."

"Interviewed him?"

"Yeah. He was hiring for a chef. Said Stanton came in to try for the position."

"How did that come up?"

"Hell, he just threw it in there all casual after the chat about the missing men. Said how sad it is people are always going missing. That's when he brought up Lee."

"Which restaurant?"

"The Bake. You know where it is?"

"No, but if it's downtown it won't be hard to find. Mikey, you want to head that way? Probably a good time to catch the manager, before the dinner rush starts." Mikey nods, already grabbing his coat.

"You mind watching Tails?"

"Love to!"

I glare at them both. "Do *not* feed him anything else." The younger officer blushes as they both nod.

❖

The hostess walks Mikey and me to the break room when we arrive, as if she's been told to expect us. We are quickly joined by the manager, a slim Native Alaskan man in a suit that looks custom tailored. Even before introductions, he offers to order us something on the house. Mikey and I remain stuffed, so we have to decline, which is sad because the place smells like toasted bread, shrimp, and cheese. Seafood paninis are still listed on the chalkboard as the lunch special.

"Mister…?"

"Alaku."

"Mr. Alaku, thanks for talking to us. One of the officers mentioned you interviewed Lee Stanton about a week before he went missing." He pulls a leatherbound notebook from a bookshelf.

"Lee came in to interview for the chef position. We're losing the man who does most evenings and weekends now, I'm afraid. He took a job in Fairbanks. Lee talked to one of the waiters about it and the waiter told him to talk to me."

"Can you tell us about your interview process with Lee? What was he like?"

"Well, normally I talk to the candidates first to make sure they're personable and can communicate well. If everything seems all right, I have them cook a few of the Bake's signature recipes. Then if *that* goes well, I have them create a dish with the ingredients we have on hand. That part's fun. The staff always likes tasting the creations… Unfortunately, he didn't get past the first part." I follow his gaze to his polished black boots.

"The man clearly knows food and cooking techniques. But something was off. He wouldn't make eye contact. He just kept looking at his hands. He spoke slowly, but he still stumbled over his words. A chef must be able to work fast and communicate efficiently. They must be confident in what they're doing. Mr. Stanton was not. He seemed very nervous."

"What did he talk about?"

"Just food. Any time I asked him about himself he deflected to food, but like I said, it was disjointed. He talked about a recipe he made for Thanksgiving, but halfway through describing that, he talked about some berries he likes to use from the mountain, then how he had always wanted to learn to cook Indian food, which of course isn't what we serve here."

"Mr. Alaku, how did Mr. Stanton react when you called off the interview?"

"Well, I was as polite as possible, of course. I told him we were looking for someone with previous restaurant experience, which is true. We are the most highly rated restaurant in town, and we must maintain our reputation. I gave him a chance because I'd love to have a local instead of an import, but he was clearly a home chef, not ready for a commercial kitchen. He looked…despondent. He didn't say much, but I got the feeling I crushed his dream. I referred him to the owner of the restaurant since he owns a bunch of places in town and might be able to help a local. I feel terrible knowing he's disappeared. Like perhaps not getting the job was the last straw."

"You had good reasons to not hire him. What happened to him wasn't your fault."

Mikey nods in affirmation. "Thank you so much for your time, Mr. Alaku."

Mr. Alaku walks us to the front of the restaurant and closes the door behind us. We're due at the hospital soon, so we head there. I ask Mikey what he thinks.

"I think he was depressed. I think we're looking at a sad case where a guy was already struggling, he got turned down for a dream job, and maybe it put him over the edge."

"Maybe."

CHAPTER TEN

The Stantons are already at the hospital when we arrive, and so is Anna. She's given Lee's parents Styrofoam cups of tea, which both clutch as if there's some elixir inside that will bring their son back. They're glued to the plastic-covered seats of the waiting room, vending machines staring down at them. Mr. Stanton stands when we enter, but he looks like he aged a decade with the effort. Mrs. Stanton doesn't move. In fact, she doesn't seem to breathe. I nod at them.

"Good evening, Mr. and Mrs. Stanton." *Best to get this over with.* "Ready?"

Anna escorts us to the viewing room and immediately approaches the place where the sheet is draped over the stump of the neck. Mikey stands near Mrs. Stanton's shoulder, and Mr. Stanton squeezes her hands in his. Anna slowly pulls the sheet down to just past the shoulders. The Stantons gasp and instinctively turn away. After they've recomposed themselves a little, Lee's mom speaks.

"I don't know how we're supposed to be able to tell if that's Lee by—by that." Mrs. Stanton's eyes are cast toward the green speckled linoleum tile.

"It's okay, Mrs. Stanton. We have however long you need. You may not be able to tell by...this area. Are there body markings or features you think might be more recognizable? More helpful for you?"

"No. I mean, he has a lot of body hair, on his chest I mean."

"Okay. I'm going to pull the sheet down to waist level." Mr. Stanton keeps his eyes on the body, which is a brighter and lighter shade of blue-green than it was, perhaps the effects of refrigeration.

There are distinct spots where the flesh is eroding away despite the cold morgue drawer. The dark chest hair stands out in deep contrast.

"That looks right." The words are promising, but Mr. Stanton sounds skeptical to my ears.

"If you're not sure, that's all right." I mean to be reassuring and hope I sound so.

"I don't feel comfortable saying that's Lee based on some chest hair, you know? And the way the skin looks…Well, I'm not sure we'd be able to tell anything anyway. Lee has a couple scars, but I don't know…"

"Where are those scars located, Mr. Stanton?"

"Well, the most obvious one is on the tip of his left ring finger. He sliced it open real good with a knife when we were making Thanksgiving dinner a few years ago. Thing was near hanging off. He wouldn't get it patched, though—that's not his way. Got a nasty scar from it."

"That would normally be a great clue, but I'm afraid in this case…" Anna carefully pulls the cloth from the left hand to show Lee's parents that confirmation of the scar won't be possible. The tips of the fingers are gone. I remember pieces of the fingers in Anna's hand.

"Oh." Something about seeing the mangled fingers seems to affect Mrs. Stanton even more than the severed head. I wouldn't have predicted that, but I suppose everyone reacts differently to things like this. "What happened to the hand?"

Anna covers it again. "It's likely animals got curious about the body. That's always a problem if someone has been outside for any time at all, I'm afraid."

Mrs. Stanton closes her eyes. "Lee would like that if that's him. He loves animals. He'd love being around fox and mink and all that kind of stuff." It's a strange thought, but also a strangely comforting one. Suddenly, Mrs. Stanton's eyes snap open again. "You don't think that dog—"

"It's impossible to say, Mrs. Stanton. But most dogs will not chew on their owner. They might paw at them, try to wake them, sometimes even lie with them. Until they start to starve themselves, of course."

The image of Tails pawing his owner, trying hard to bring him back to life, breaks my heart. I have the overwhelming urge to wrap my arms around the dog, but he's back at the police station, surely distracting the other officers from doing their paperwork. I clear my throat.

"If it helps to know, Tails was very hungry when we first found him. I don't think he would have been if he'd been doing anything like that."

Mikey and Anna nod their agreement. Mrs. Stanton nods too, and Mr. Stanton mercifully changes course. "The other scar would be a burn on his right calf. Inside, from a motorcycle."

Anna nods, pulls the sheet over the neck, then swings around to the feet, where she displays the body from the feet to the kneecaps. She gently moves the legs apart, then turns the right one slightly outward. The body looks so fragile I'm afraid it will turn to a pile of skin patches in her hands.

It's obvious any burn scar would be nearly impossible to detect, the skin is so discolored. It's especially decomposed here, perhaps because of getting wet. The top layers are gone in many places. Both legs look the same. I see traces of wool stuck in the hair of the calf. Anna notices my glance, or coincidentally answers the question I didn't ask.

"From his socks." So, they were stuck to his legs badly enough that she had to cut and peel them off. Mrs. Stanton shakes her head, and tears well ever so slightly, confusion all over her face.

"I just…I don't know. I can't tell…But that's a good thing." She looks at me. "*Right?* If it was my boy I'd know right away. Mothers are supposed to just know things like that." Mr. Stanton pulls her close to his side. I'm so relieved when Anna handles the question, which seems like a muddy slope eroding to an unhelpful place.

"No, Mrs. Stanton, that's a myth. There's no magical maternal instinct that means you should be able to pick out your son regardless of how he looks. People like to think they could because it's a comforting thought, but it's just not true. We've had mothers incorrectly identify bodies as their children before. One of them insisted the girl on this same table was her daughter. She saw scars she knew her girl had, recognized teeth, everything. She was positive. Only it turned out to not be her daughter."

Mrs. Stanton's tears dry as she listens. "How did you find out?"

"Because her daughter came back six months later. She'd met a boy on one of the cruise ships and left with him, then returned when things went badly. She'd always been a handful, and her mom was certain she'd meet a terrible end. The mother saw what she assumed she would see. Our eyes *can* deceive us." The Stantons nod slowly, in unison. "Is there anything else we should try to find?"

Mr. Stanton shakes his head. "I don't think there's much point. I can't tell if this is Lee or not. How about you, Peaches?"

Mrs. Stanton shakes her head, eyes on a drawer this body could slide back into when we're finished. "Maybe if I saw the clothes, I'd recognize something then."

Anna nods and retrieves a large Ziploc bag labeled with the case number and coordinates where the body was found. She carefully extracts a pair of heather gray long underwear, some dark easy fit jeans, white briefs washed too many times and clearly cut off the body, wool socks with holes where they've been cut away from skin, a blue flannel, and a hooded sweatshirt lined with fake sheepskin. Mrs. Stanton touches the items lightly. She shakes her head as she does so, though I'm sure she doesn't realize it.

"This could be Lee's. His shirts all look pretty much just like this one."

"Okay. What about the other items?" Mr. Stanton pulls at the leg of the jeans.

"He always wears long underwear under jeans if he's leaving the house when it's cold out. His legs get cold quick."

"Okay. And the sweatshirt?" They both shake their heads.

"If it was new, we just might not have seen it." It's hard to say if it was new, covered in mud and dried specks of blood as it is.

"So, it sounds like you're saying overall these clothes might be Lee's, but you can't be positive."

"That's right," they say almost in unison.

"Perfect. Thank you, Mr. and Mrs. Stanton. I know this is a terrible thing that no parent should have to do. It was brave of you to come in."

"So, now what? I feel like we don't know anything more than we did before."

"Well, we can still search for..." I just glance at the covered neck to finish the sentence.

Mrs. Stanton jumps in. "Oh. The head would solve it, right?"

"Yes. Even if...Well, we can do a lot with dental records."

"And if you can't find it?" Mr. Stanton seems unsure, just as I am.

"We can use a DNA sample. It's fairly new science, and to be honest, we don't know yet how reliable it is. But if we could match the sample DNA to yours, that might at least be better than nothing. It's up to you whether you'd like to try."

"You would need our DNA, Doctor?"

"If you don't mind."

"Both of ours?"

"That would be helpful. More data will give us greater faith in the results." Anna smiles. "Don't worry, it's nothing invasive. We can get DNA by rubbing a cotton swab in your mouth. We already have a blood sample from him." Anna nods toward the body.

"How fast will we know?"

"We don't have a lab to test it here, I'm afraid. His sample has already been sent away, but I'd need to send yours along. It will take them several days to process and then to see if there's a match."

"But we would know."

"It's *possible* the DNA would match. Some people find that reassuring."

The Stantons look at each other. "Can we just do it now? Give you our samples?"

"That would be great, Mr. Stanton. Then you don't need to come back. We can do that in my lab if you're ready to follow me."

They take one last look at the sheet-covered body, then Mr. Stanton takes his wife's hand. Anna holds the door for us and locks it once we're all through. I wait for Anna as the Stantons talk with Mikey. I hear Mrs. Stanton.

"I just wish I could tell. I think either way, it would be easier than not knowing. Is that bad?"

"No, ma'am. Most people feel the same way. Not knowing is the hardest thing, and we're terribly sorry you're in that position right now."

They're silent for several moments. Mrs. Stanton excuses herself to go to the bathroom, and Mr. Stanton turns to speak to me. "If that's Lee, what do you think did that to him?"

"Mr. Stanton, we don't want to speculate, and unfortunately the exam was inconclusive. But like I said, the body was found with a shotgun."

"Had it been fired?"

"Yes."

He nods. "Please don't tell my wife that."

I nod. Our secret.

As Anna collects samples from the Stantons, I retreat to her office, which has a small window high in the wall. It's started to snow again. I call Mikey over to ask him to escort the Stantons to their car. It will be slippery outside, and they're both shaken. He nods.

"I'll chat with them a little—make sure they're okay to drive." He glances at Anna as she seals the samples and thanks the Stantons. "You need to hang back?" My eyes follow Anna as she puts the samples into storage, then turns to me and Mikey.

"Yes, I'd like to speak with Dr. Fenway for a moment. Meet me at the Tank?"

One of his eyebrows goes up, but he doesn't ask questions and joins the Stantons.

❖

It's just the two of us in Anna's office, but I haven't thought through what I want to say. I just want to be in her presence for a moment. Maybe it's selfish—I'm stressed and there's something calming about her I noticed the first time we met. She turns to me with her head tilted slightly to one side and a faint smile on her bare lips.

She touches my hand with the tips of her fingers. I look down at them. No polish. Just smooth, short fingernails. Her hands belong to a piano player—long fingers and wide palms. I could stand here forever, looking at her hands in some sort of trance. It's been a long couple of days. I should be exhausted.

"It takes a lot out of you, doesn't it? Leading families through an ID? It's awful for me too, even after all these years."

"I guess so. I've only had to do it a few times. I was in DCS, and there were deaths there too. I went to funerals, but this is something totally different. I'm not sure how to get used to it."

She shakes her head, her ponytail landing over her shoulder. "You don't. And honestly, I'm not sure you'd want to. They need to know you care, and that it's hard for you too."

"You must have to do this all the time. Usually, I'm arresting people or doing check-ins. The deaths I've handled here so far were overdoses. Shitty for sure, but easy for the families to ID. Nothing like this."

She glances out at the snow. "It comes with the territory, unfortunately. The tradeoff for living in beautiful, rugged, remote Alaska is that people die in all that wildness, and when they do, it's not pretty. When I first took the job, I wasn't sure I'd be able to do it. I don't mind the gory stuff, but I wasn't sure I could be there for families viewing their dead loved one. During my internship, I had to leave the room the first few times."

"How did you get over that?" I lean against the cabinets, careful not to disturb any of her equipment on the counter.

"Well, part of me didn't. I realized how important it was for me to be there for families at what's the hardest moment of their lives." She leans against the cabinet too, so close her hip nearly touches mine. If I move my hand an inch, it will be on hers. She has created a current between us and now I can hardly resist the connection. She smiles at me and then toward the door. I move away from her. This is her office. I immediately miss her proximity.

"I should get going. Mikey is waiting."

"Was there something you wanted to ask me?"

I say nothing while my brain runs through and discards possibilities. "The DNA. Do you think the Stantons will be convinced that's Lee with a match?"

She looks out again toward the parking lot. "Police here can take a while to get on board with new science, but it may surprise you how open-minded people in Seward can be. I think they'll believe it if they want to believe it."

I nod and start toward the door. "Thank you for your help."

She touches my jacket sleeve. I swear I sense the warmth of her skin through the fabric. "There is something *I'd* like to ask *you*."

When I turn, her face is close. I smell her amber perfume again and stop myself from taking an obvious deep breath of it.

"Would you like to have dinner this weekend?" When I gape at her, she continues. "You and Mikey are putting in a lot of hours. Seems like you deserve a night off."

My brain overthinks the invitation. *She's only asking out of professional politeness.* Then I wonder if she means to invite both me and Mikey. I consider asking her to clarify, but then she might think I *want* Mikey there. I close my eyes briefly. I just need to answer her. *I can overthink this back at the hotel.*

"Yes. Absolutely yes."

She grins. "How about Saturday, at seven. The Bake?"

I nod. Then I make my escape before I say something stupid.

CHAPTER ELEVEN

In the morning we travel to the fjord at the base of the mountain where Lee's body was found. Chief Quint convinced Willington to have a team of volunteer fishermen help us drag the water. Quint knows I won't be able to let it go until we at least try to find the head. Still, no one but me seems to take the task too seriously. I get the impression they like dragging because of all the random gear they find. On this trip, one of them makes off with a nice pocketknife.

Predictably, there's no trace of Lee. It was a long shot—if he killed himself with that shotgun, there wouldn't be much to find. We may never have a firm ID.

When we return to the station, Lee's mother has asked us to come visit as soon as possible. We go straight to the Stantons' with the Tank crunching through the piling snow like a champion. It's one of those snows that refuses to fall straight, preferring to swirl in circles that make looking through the windshield a pure act of hypnotism. It is impossible to make out the road at several points. We have to stop until the wind blows in another direction and it's clear where there are trees or a sheer drop-off. I've never been so grateful for the hideous Tank and its snow tires. We arrive at the house feeling, and probably looking, as if we've been through a war. Just making it to the front door might as well be planting a victory flag atop the bodies of our enemies.

But when Mr. Stanton opens the door, he barely glances at the gust of powder that pushes over the threshold. He focuses on the dog instead. Tails trots in as if he's part of this investigation. I suppose he is. Mrs. Stanton gets right to the point.

"Did you have any luck with the dragging?"

"No, I'm afraid not. How did you know we were looking today?"

"My sister's in Seward. She called to say she saw them loading nets onto the boats. Figured you were probably looking for his head. Guess it could have been the other boy who's missing, though."

"Branden Halifax."

Her face scrunches as she tries to place the name. It comes to her. "Is that who he is?"

"Yes. Do you know him?"

"Sure. He lives round the mountain a little, doesn't he?" I nod. "He and Lee went to school together."

"Really?" Mikey and I say simultaneously.

"Yeah. They've never been good friends or anything, but they had the same teachers. Some of the same classes. Same building. Now they're both just the same, I guess." She blows out a strong huff and then coughs. There's an ashtray full of butts on the kitchen table next to a pack of Camels. She lights another cigarette.

I sit across from Mrs. Stanton. Mikey remains standing near her husband. I lean forward, inhaling the cigarette smoke that mixes with the smell of frigid air we let in.

"Mrs. Stanton, you asked us to come by. Did you have something to tell us?"

Mr. Stanton turns his head away.

Lee's mom looks down at the pine wood of the table. "The boy in the morgue. It's Lee."

"Are you sure?"

"Yes."

Mr. Stanton slowly shakes his head. He doesn't seem to notice me or my questioning look.

"You didn't seem certain when we were at the hospital..."

"I...this is going to sound real stupid." Her husband exhales sharply. She turns to him. "I know you think it's baloney and I get it." She swivels in her chair again and faces me. She lowers her voice. "It was a dream. I had a dream about Lee, and when I woke up, I just knew."

I agree with Mr. Stanton. It sounds like a pile of horseshit. Mikey, however, reassures Mrs. Stanton that stranger things have happened. I hope he's making that up.

"What do you think, Mr. Stanton?"

"I think she's having a hard time dealing with not knowing, and she's worried we'll never know exactly what happened, so this is easiest."

I watch Mrs. Stanton as Mr. Stanton speaks. She looks like she will argue, but instead she just sniffles lightly. I'd guess they've been through this argument several times before. To my own surprise, I justify Mrs. Stanton's change of heart. Wild as all this sounds, Mrs. Stanton just looks so vulnerable right now. I don't want her to think we're ganging up on her.

"It makes sense that it's him. It does. Even if the dream part is… unusual. The body was found close to Lee's trailer. The time of death was close to when he went missing. The gun and the clothes look like Lee's. And then there's the dog." I feel Tails jerk to attention under the table. "The chances of it being anyone else *are* slim."

Mr. Stanton grimaces. "I know. It does make the most sense. It's just—"

"He really wants to hope he's still out there."

❖

When we fight the weather back to the hotel, I call the hospital's evening administrator and let him know the body can be released to the Stantons whenever they happen to make it down there. I'm guessing that won't be for a few days. Taking a body home on an ATV just doesn't seem right.

❖

It's late, but I'm having trouble sleeping. I pace the hotel room to find it's six strides across and eight strides long. I knew the room was small but knowing exactly how small bothers me. Suddenly there's not enough air in the room. My breaths become short and shallow. I stop my feet and make myself inhale fully. I want to go outside, but it's so cold.

I go to the window to remind myself there is fresh air. I hold my hand to the glass. Arctic cold seeps in around the window, but I don't pull the thick gold and wine striped curtains shut. Instead, I stand wedged between the table and a stiff armchair probably no one has ever sat in. I lean over the heating and cooling unit and watch the squall as it encloses a streetlamp like a swarm of angry bees. The weather matches my anxiety.

I release a little stress by picturing it floating out the window to join the swirling snowflakes. Tails eyes me from where he's sprawled on the bed. I wonder briefly if Anna will cancel dinner, then I laugh. She won't. She lives in Seward. A blizzard here means even less than it does in Anchorage. It's a point of pride to be able to venture out in anything. But part of me hopes she will cancel anyway, because just the thought of a date makes me nervous.

A knock on the wall startles me. It's Mikey. I press my ear to the thin, wallpapered drywall.

"Yes?" I barely raise my voice.

"You want to come over? I've got granola bars."

I laugh—it's not until he mentions food that I realize I'm hungry. Maybe it accounts for the jitteriness.

"Sure. Tails invited?"

"Of course!"

❖

His room is disconcertingly similar to mine, right down to the poorly executed painting of a humpback whale tail emerging from the water. The only difference is that Mikey's clothes are lying all over the place, as are random food items. Tails immediately jumps on the bed, then rolls over to expose his belly for rubbing. Mikey obliges and the dog rolls around in delight.

"Figured you couldn't sleep."

"How'd you know?"

"You seem like one of those cops who just doesn't sleep till something's solved." He's not wrong.

"Is it Halifax?"

"It's both…I guess the Stanton case more than Halifax. Something about it just isn't sitting." I drop into the armchair, not expecting how hard it is. "Damn!"

Mikey has a good laugh. "Right? It's not even comfy for me, and I've got plenty of padding." He throws me a pillow off the bed where he's seated. I settle it under my butt and shift until it's at least moderately tolerable.

Mikey exhales through his mouth. It randomly reminds me how a very short time ago I was worried about being able to hear him snore through the wall. Which I can, but now I don't mind. There's something sort of comforting about it.

"How about we make a deal to not talk about the case? There's nothing we can do about it in the middle of the night anyway."

I laugh. He's right, of course, but that's never stopped my middle of the night worry about bills or whether I'll ever be able to afford to retire. "All right, I'll try."

He perks immediately. "I couldn't help but notice…Anna looks at you like…well…" He winks as if we share a secret. I'm embarrassed, so I stare at the carpet.

"We have a date."

"Really? *That's* why you hung back at her office!" He throws a flat pillow at me. "Lou, you sneaky dog. She's gorgeous. When is it?"

"Technically, today. I'm not ready, though." I'm surprised I'm so honest with Mikey. I don't have friends. He laughs.

"Why? You probably go on dates a lot, right?"

"How many lesbians do you think there *are* in Anchorage?"

He chuckles. "Good point. I have a terrible time finding dates, and I'm straight…Why is that, anyway?"

"I dated a fair amount in Seattle before I met my ex. It was easy to go into a bar or a coffee shop and meet someone. Not here. I don't know. Maybe it's Alaska itself."

"How so?"

"Well, the people who live here, they're independent. Otherwise, they'd move away. You have to be okay with being alone…be comfortable with yourself to live around here. And the people who aren't from here, they come here for solitude."

"Ah. So, people here are more comfortable than most with being single. They may even prefer it. That's a good point." He flops backward on the bed, nearly whacking his head on the wood frame. "But it doesn't bode well for me!"

"I'm afraid not. But you've got a sense of humor, and hell, even a woman who loves being alone can appreciate that."

"Okay, Lou, but you're changing the subject. Why aren't you feeling ready to go out with Dr. Anna?"

"I'm not interesting. I never have anything to say. The job is the only thing that's sort of unusual, and Dr. Anna deals with cops all the time, so that's my only advantage gone right out the gate."

"What? You're interesting, though."

"Me? No way! You know what my hobbies are?"

He squints as he contemplates. "Uh, no?"

"Right. Because they're work, thinking about work, and watching hockey or shitty television."

"You don't travel? Go out?" I make a face at him. He looks concerned. "Well, you must have opinions on the things you watch on TV?"

"I can tell you what sucks. But I'll also watch it anyway."

"Do you ever watch anything thought-provoking or that you have a strong reaction to?"

"Oh, I never talk about that stuff on dates."

He raises his eyebrows at me. "So, no thoughts or feelings on a date? No wonder you can't find anything to talk about!"

"I just don't like sharing is all!" I'm defensive, though it's not as bad with Mikey as it is with most people. "I'd rather just listen to the other person talk." He seems to approve of that consideration. "But then I don't know how to respond to what they've said."

He props himself up on his elbow. "And here I thought all lesbians did was talk about their deep innermost secret feelings."

I pull the pillow out from under me and throw it at him. I immediately regret my impulsiveness.

"Too bad. Now your ass just gets to be sore."

I sit on my hands. I know he's just being funny, but he's onto something. My inability to talk about feelings, or to even think through my own feelings, has been a problem in every relationship I've ever had, romantic or otherwise. If I ever went to therapy again, they'd probably make me talk about how my father laughed at me every time I expressed an emotion. It's why I don't go to therapy.

"We should practice." There's a devious sheen in his eyes.

"Practice what?"

"Practice having a conversation. Since apparently you can only talk to a hot woman if it's about a decapitated body."

"Ouch. Not sure I needed so much honesty." I laugh so he can hear I'm joking.

"Okay. I'm going to talk like I would on a date, and you'll respond. Maybe eventually we'll work you up to *leading* a conversation."

"Now that seems like a little much."

He gives me a blank stare. "Yeah. We've got our work cut out. We better eat something."

"That would be good, because I have a real knack for timing my bites so I have to awkward-pause at least twelve seconds while I chew."

"Perfect." He throws me a granola bar while he opens a bag of chips that fill the stale room with the scent of barbecue. Then he talks about a Paris-set romantic comedy.

❖

It works, sort of. Around five in the morning, I take Tails out and then wander back to my own room feeling better about seeing Anna, even as I pass out. I wake at noon planning to purchase some decent date wear. My standard off-duty running fleece and jeans are cozy, but not attractive.

At the window I can tell it's still bitterly cold. With the unnatural stillness of the air all the particles seem frozen in place, suspended and waiting for someone to walk through them and break the spell. Or try to walk through them and become trapped, frozen themselves. Maybe I can jog through them. I pat my new buddy on the head, sternly telling him to be a good dog while I'm gone.

Seward is silent. A foot or so of snow creates an uneven blanket, bunched in corners where the wind blew it into unruly folds. I try lifting my feet into the steady pace of my usual run and slip almost immediately. I thankfully manage to regain my balance before my ass hits ice. Some of the shopkeepers have shoveled the walk in front of their stores, but not all. I suppose a run will have to wait for Anchorage. I slow my pace and watch my foot placement. It's nice to focus on something so simple. There aren't many tourists around in the weather, and all the locals are used to trudging along at the same slow pace as me.

After I've selected my new outfit—straight-legged gray pants that make my butt look better than reality and a lavender cashmere turtleneck—I've got time to spare. I walk to the shore. The campground is almost empty, with just a few trucks in the parking lot. Their owners stand on the boulders that slope steeply down to the water. There are sea lions playing near the shore, with otters floating on their backs nearby, watching. Two of the otters hold hands. I heard somewhere they do this to keep from drifting apart while they sleep. They sleep for about half their lives.

A fog settles in as I watch, and the coast on the opposite shore disappears behind a white-gray mist. The shapes of the few scattered houses along the water vaporize and rematerialize like ghosts in the warped windows of a haunted house. The peaks of Mount Alice and Marathon are invisible—I only know they're there because I glanced at the map in the hotel lobby. A brochure on the front desk said the rocks that jut from the harbor are good for bird watching. Today, they're just slightly darker shapes in a sea full of suddenly foreign objects.

It's hard to believe hundreds of thousands of tourists take boats out here in the summer, binoculars in one hand and a beer in the other, looking for glaciers and enjoying the scenery. *This* sea is full of foreboding and opportunities for collision.

A hard wind comes in, sharp like a scalpel to my cheek. My eyes water and the tears freeze on my chapped lips. I wonder how long I've been standing here as I pull up my hood. Hair that has escaped my ponytail whips into my mouth, tasting of cheap hotel shampoo.

The sea lions smile despite the cold, and the otters look unfazed.

My heart wants to stay by the water. It's peaceful here with no cruise ships in the harbor, and just sea-life out and about. But I can't feel my fingers or toes, while the end of my nose feels windburned. I don't want to impersonate Rudolph the Red-Nosed Reindeer on my date, so I trek back to the hotel to rest for a few hours. As I walk uphill, pressing my teeth together against the cold, I realize I am dizzy with the past week's fatigue. I need good sleep. My jaw already hurts—a sure sign I've been grinding my teeth in my unrestful slumber.

Tails leaps into the air and throws his body at me when I open the door. I catch him by his butt. This dog is so heavy and he's wagging his ass so vehemently, it's hard to keep my grip. He covers my face in slobber. I'm about as delighted as he is until I see that ugly armchair.

"Tails!" I loosen my grip and he slides to the floor, burying his nose under one of his giant paws. I grab a handful of stuffing from a jagged slice in the cushion. "What the hell is this?" I shove the yellowed filler in his face. "Nuh-uh! No!" He whimpers though I haven't touched him. He looks so sad with his honey-colored eyes squeezed shut and his head down I don't have the heart to repeat any admonishment. I growl at him lowly, then slap my leg for him to come to me. He stares at me, keeping eye contact while he licks my hand.

"Yeah, yeah. That was a bad dog, though." He understands. I don't have the energy to re-stuff the chair, so I just throw the filler on the table. When I flop onto the bed, Tails jumps up with me and throws his legs over my stomach.

Chapter Twelve

*I*t's Lee. Or I think it's Lee—I cannot see his face. I follow him, but from an elevated height. I look at the back of his head. He wears the coat and jeans from the morgue's sanitary plastic bag. He tramps through the woods, but his hands are empty. Tails isn't there. Lee hikes up the mountain; he zigzags slightly as if disoriented. Snow swirls around him and sticks to the hood of his coat. He stumbles but catches himself against a tree trunk. He rights himself and continues, falling forward more than walking.

The stream he comes to looks gentle and halfway frozen but sounds like a crashing Icelandic waterfall. He slips on the edge and falls headfirst. There's a crunch that sounds like bone breaking, and it splits through my own head like lightning through a long-dry tree. His whole body is in the water now, his arms flailing as he tries to grip the moss-covered rocks.

I can see his face now, but it's not a real human face. It's grotesque, contorted, and melted as if he's been in a horrible fire. Somehow, I can see his face even as he slips away downstream and crashes over a waterfall. His bones crackle like lit firewood over the sharp boulders.

I bolt upright, just like in the movies. I am coated in a thick sheen of sweat; my skin and clothes cling to the sheets beneath me. Even Tails's fur sticks to me as he blinks, startled, and jolted awake from his own slumber. His eyes are huge. My heart must be going two hundred beats per minute, and I am both feverishly hot and freezing all over. Even when I remember where and who I am, I still see that melted face.

I check the alarm clock on the nightstand when my breathing

slows. I have ninety minutes to get ready. Part of me just wants to lie back down and collect myself a little more, but I can't risk falling back to sleep. Instead, I shower as Tails spies on me with his head draped over the end of the tub. He doesn't seem to mind me naked, so that's a good sign. I'm washing my hair when I hear a door slam. Mikey's returned from his Saturday. Right before I leave, I knock on his door. Mikey grins when he opens it. He agrees to watch the wily beast of Tails so he doesn't destroy any more perfectly bad armchairs.

❖

The Bake is on a quiet street that runs parallel to the main drag. The last time I was here I only saw the break room. The restaurant is beautiful, though, and I take the time to appreciate it. It's a small place, dimly lit with a bar floating like an island in the middle. A few guys sit there in work clothes and rubber boots even though it's a fabric tablecloth kind of place. A couple of them follow me with their eyes when I come in.

"Can I help you, miss?"

I spot Anna facing me all the way in the back. She smiles and waves exuberantly. When I arrive at the table, she stands to give me a hug. She is stunning in a jewel toned dress and black heels that make her some sort of Grecian column topped with a flowing red flame. Her snow boots are tucked neatly under the table.

I am speechless for what must be a full five minutes, and she chuckles. I finally manage one of my Mikey-supplied openers.

"You look amazing." I should have thought of something more original. I sound so generic. Maybe a drink will relax me. She's already ordered a glass of wine, so I request the same. I'm glad she chose white; I won't have a headache tomorrow.

"This place is so nice! It doesn't look like the other places around here." *Classic, Louisa.* I backpedal. "Not that the other restaurants aren't nice, just..."

She laughs and it rings around the restaurant like a Sunday school bell, bouncing off everyone's wineglasses.

"I know what you mean. It's because it's not designed for the tourists. And I love this place too. They make a really mean shrimp alfredo."

"Does it bite?" *Nice one.*

"It might if you ask it politely." She side-eyes me and gives me a smooth wink, then falls into a comfortable, self-possessed silence as she peruses the short menu.

I sense I need to say something, but I don't know what. My mind goes entirely blank. Maybe a compliment and the tiniest of jokes is all I've got. I see Lee's melting face in my dream, even though Anna's delicately featured, perfectly intact face is right in front of me.

"Thanks for inviting me out. I really needed a change of pace." I brush my hand in gesture, almost sending my menu sailing across the room. I grab for it just in time only to almost knock over a basket of warm bread in the process. I didn't even notice it arrive at the table. "Work has been so intense."

"It's my pleasure." Suddenly, Anna reaches through the water glasses and the basket and grabs my hand. "How about we make a deal, though, to not talk about work for the evening?"

And again, the peace that comes with Anna settles over me. I look into her eyes as she talks meal options.

"There are so many good choices, but I think I will go with the seafood macaroni and cheese." I laugh. "Are you laughing at my selection, Officer?"

"Not exactly, *Doctor.* I just remembered my college years. I lived in a house with five other women, and none of them could cook. I always associate college with boxed mac and cheese."

"Well, the Bake's offering may rid you of all those negative associations."

When the waiter comes, I choose an entrée randomly since I forgot to even glance at the choices. When he's left my wine and gone again, Anna leans forward, letting her pale cleavage spill forward under her dress. Sky blue veins contrast with her nearly translucent skin, and I try hard not to stare. She either doesn't notice or doesn't care. She also seems unaware of the couple that walks past, the woman elbowing the man for an obvious glance at her breasts. I wish I could be like that—so present in the moment I forget about other people and what they think of me.

"So, I'm dying to know more about you. Give me some puzzle pieces."

My shoulders tense. I always dread this part. I want to avoid talking about my parents and my ex, of course. I consider telling her about DCS, but I quickly decide against it. I've managed to make her laugh and I don't want to bring the mood down.

"I'm from Seattle. I lived there my whole life until last year." *Not too bad.* Especially since I'm not a natural storyteller and I never know which details to include. Thankfully, Anna's very good at asking questions and prompting for more.

"So, after all those years in Seattle, what made you want to try Alaska?"

I break eye contact, as my mind fills with my DCS case. It's amazing how fast that happens. I try to shut it out, but it won't be avoided.

"There was…the last case I worked with DCS ended badly. It was a sad situation, and I didn't handle it well. I thought leaving Seattle would make it easier to move on." She nods. My usual MO is to dance around the topic, but something tells me I can be honest with Anna about my compulsion.

"I can be obsessive with work. With puzzles, really. When I feel like I owe someone something, I try so hard to fix the problem or help them I…sometimes I…let go of myself, I guess." Anna reaches across the table and places her hand next to mine. An invitation. I take it. "It's something I usually don't talk about. It's still hard, so I'd rather not dwell on it if you don't mind."

"Of course! This is a *Choose Your Own Adventure* conversation. Where would you like to go instead?"

I smile. I loved those books as a kid. "How about Canada?"

She lifts her eyebrows three times in rapid succession. "Ooh la la! An exotic vacation."

I wonder where she developed her knack for lightening the mood. Maybe it's a skill Alaskans develop to deal with the dark and cold.

"I decided to leave Seattle and I had no plan, so after I wandered around Oregon and Washington for a while, I drove all the way through Canada in the world's crappiest sedan, all because some woman said Alaska might be desperate for cops." *Did I just imply you don't have to be qualified to work in Alaska?* Will she think I doubt *her* credentials? I am nervous again, and I open my mouth to backtrack, but my scallops arrive.

"So why did being a cop catch your interest?"

The waiter returns with Anna's dish and a wine top-up, which we both accept. I take an initial bite of my food. It's delicious, but eating when nervous has never been my strong suit.

"Excuse me while I shove all this macaroni into my face. I have absolutely no self-restraint when it comes to cheese."

My mind's juxtaposition of this clever, elegant woman and her Cookie Monster way of devouring cheese and pasta tickles me. I laugh aloud. I sip my wine and watch her. She's not a graceful eater, which somehow makes her more attractive. A piece of cheese clings to her mouth, stuck in her lipstick. So, I stare at her lips. I look down before she can notice. When Anna pauses for air, I continue.

"There was an officer I worked with a lot in Seattle. He was a really good cop, and a good person too. Kind of a friend. He let me work with him closely on that last case, even when I shouldn't have been. I got to see what it was like, having a more active role in helping people. With DCS, there was only so much I could do, you know? When I worked with him, I felt I accomplished more, I guess. I wanted that." I stop and wonder if I went on for too long. Anna leans forward and offers a bite of her mac and cheese with a nice juicy piece of lobster in it. No wonder this place has the highest ratings in town.

"You know, if you'd told young me I'd examine dead bodies for a living, I would have just made a face and told you to go away." She takes a long glance at my scallops, which I keep forgetting are there. I offer her one, then eat a bit myself. We both sit there chewing slowly. I savor the garlic sauce.

"What did young you think you'd grow up to be?"

"A writer, for sure," she quickly answers. "Even when I was a kid, I wanted to write children's books. Mystery books. I had this whole series planned about a duck who lives on a houseboat and solves crimes. I'm obsessed with houseboats. I've never lived on one, but it's my retirement plan. Cruise it all around the world."

"You'd leave Seward?"

"Yup, but I'd always come back. It's home." It seems like it would be a nice one. I've tried to picture myself settling in Anchorage before, and I can never quite do it. Seward, though…*maybe*. "Besides, my family is in Alaska. My parents are in Fairbanks. My sister's in Juneau."

"So, how did you end up in Seward?"

"Once I decided my path in med school, I decided I wanted to specialize in animal attack."

"Whoa."

"It does sound gruesome. It *is* gruesome. But it's important to understand what animal attacks look like in my line of work. If you can't distinguish between, say, a stab wound and bear claw cuts, you could send someone away for murder when really the victim just disturbed mama bear."

"Makes sense. We don't get too much of that in Anchorage, but the occasional moose injury does happen."

"Right. And the best way to learn about animal habits in Alaska is to work with the Native Alaskan communities. The Qutekcak had an elder who was state-renowned for his ability to identify animal attacks. He'd been hunting since he was a kid and he could tell you not only what kind of animal inflicted a wound, but also why, and *sometimes* he could even tell you the exact animal, if it was close enough to home. He lived about twenty miles from town, so I got permission from my professors to do some independent study with him. I started a trend too. He passed away a few years ago, but the university still sends students to learn from the Qutekcak. Probably half the MEs in the state trained in these mountains."

"And you loved it so much around here that you stayed?"

"Well, if I say *yes*, that will be half of the truth." She gives me a long look before she brazenly swipes another scallop off my plate. "There was also my first real girlfriend. She's Aleut." I don't know much about the Native Communities of the Kenai Peninsula yet, and it must show.

"People call the Native Alaskans around Seward Qutekcak, but that's the name for people from lots of different villages. They all lived separately and had different traditions, but since they tended to have close relationships and worked together a lot, they got sort of legally grouped together as Qutekcak."

"Ah, okay. Like the Tulalip in the Puget Sound. I had a kid who lived on their reservation for a while. There are people from seven different lines of ancestry. Tulalip is just the name of the place, but everyone thinks it's one tribe."

"Similar, then."

I nod so she'll go on, then wipe my mouth. Between the two of us, we've made quick work of both entrées. The waiter notices immediately and the plates disappear.

"We met while I was studying, and we got really close, really fast. College romances. You know." *That I do.*

"When I graduated, I came back here to live with her. She moved out of her family's place and down to Seward with me. It was a big deal for both of us, you know? Being *out* in a part of the state that isn't always friendly made us bond even faster."

I am slightly jealous of this woman I've never met, even though she's clearly not in the picture. I keep my rejoinder brief so as not to betray my irrational emotions.

"What happened?"

She chuckles. "Well, at one point, it felt like all we had was each other."

I frown.

"I mean, we were together because we didn't know what else to do. She had a huge falling-out with her family over me, and I think I felt I had to stay with her because of that. And it turned out she felt the same way because I'd moved to Seward for her. But it was clear, probably right after I got here, to be honest, that we didn't have all that much in common." She smiles at the memory, though it sounds painful. "Besides, she couldn't stand hearing about my work. She said it was depressing. Which it is."

"Yes, but that means it's important to be able to share it with someone."

"Precisely." She lifts her glass to me just as the waiter deposits a dessert sampler between us. We both look at him, wide-eyed.

"The manager sends his regards." He's gone before either of us responds.

"Either Mr. Alaku is glad to see me out on a date, or you talked to him." I laugh and try a cube of cheesecake.

"Can't it be both?"

CHAPTER THIRTEEN

Silence falls as we make our way through tiny tiramisus and chocolate dipped strawberries. And because I struggle with comfortable silence, and because if left without a distraction too long, my mind can go to less than pleasant places, I find myself telling Anna about my terrible dream.

"Wow. That sounds horrible."

"Yes. It was intense."

"Do you dream a lot?"

"Not really. Or at least usually I don't remember them. But once in a while I'll have a vivid one. It's usually about work."

"Oh no! Do you get paid overtime for that?"

"I'll be sure to ask the chief!" We laugh.

"These cases must be getting to you." She pauses, almost expectantly, perhaps waiting for me to go on. I stop, conflicted. I promised not to talk about the case.

"Are you sure? It's work." She nods and I wonder if my need to talk about it is that obvious. I'm disappointed in myself.

"We promised no work talk over dinner, but we've finished dinner, haven't we? If we change venues, then the rules change." Her smile reminds me of a fox. *A sexy red fox.* "What do you say we head to the hotel?" My stomach does an elegant swan dive.

"My place? It's awful."

She laughs with her head back and her slightly overlapped teeth visible. "Oh no! I know where the department puts people up. That place *is* terrible. But the Hotel is a place just a few blocks from here.

The bar there is one of Seward's great secrets. Overpriced, but I know the bartender. She'll treat us right."

"Oh! That sounds much better. Sure." She does that amazing thing where she barely even glances around and the waiter magically knows to appear with the check. Anna covers it.

"Can't have you thinking Seward is just headless people," she says. "Some of us have all our parts attached and appreciate good conversation."

❖

The Hotel is decorated in total Victorian style, which doesn't make sense for Seward. There's a lot of intricately carved wood, and the narrow steps that lead to the rooms have a maroon carpet runner. Light from gold floral chandeliers bounces off the glass of gold floral-framed mirrors. It's not my aesthetic at all.

The bar is a different story. It's tucked toward the back of the first floor and features giant leather chairs reminiscent of Ernest Hemingway. While the rest of the Hotel is overwhelmingly frilly, the bar is more like a hunting lodge. It even smells different—bourbon and cloves instead of powder and drying flowers.

Anna pulls out a heavy walnut stool at the bar. We're the only customers and it's quiet. Someone heard her, though, because there's rustling behind a pocket door before a brown-skinned woman with silver hair piled high in a bun emerges.

"Anna! Oh, how nice to see you, dear!" The woman comes around the bar and kisses Anna on both cheeks. After a moment of catching up, the older woman turns to me. "And who's this?" Her light brown eyes scan me. Anna holds out her hand like she's a delicate model presenting a masterpiece.

"Marge, this is Louisa. She's a trooper from Anchorage." She smiles slyly at me. "She's also my date for the evening."

I'm sure I turn as dark red as the plush rug under our feet.

"Louisa, this is Marge. She's something of a gay mom to me." They both laugh in unison. "Marge is the first out lesbian I met in Seward who lives here permanently. She helped me navigate the people in town so I could be comfortable to be me." Anna takes both of Marge's hands in hers. "She's been truly invaluable."

"Wow. It must be incredible to have a friend. I don't know anyone out in Anchorage."

Marge nods slowly. "Alaska can be a little intimidating if you let it be. The ideal image of femininity here is pretty much what it was in the 1920s. It can seem there's not much room for queer folks, but like I've told Anna, you'd be surprised. People here may act gruff about it when they first find out, but at the end of the day, they respect anyone who can make it here year-round." My chief said pretty much the same thing.

"Did you grow up in Seward?"

She raises her eyebrows in a sort of amused challenge. "I did. I didn't know a single other gay person. But I like to think I started a trend, because now there's seven of us!"

"We should drink to that!" Anna is ready to put the bar to use. "What have you got for us, Marge?"

"Oh, the usual. Bunch of dusty bottles of stuff nobody drinks and some fine bourbon." She turns to the bar, her face reflected in the long mirror. She flashes her teeth, a lot of gums, before she blows over the tops of the bottles. A dust powder-puff lifts around her and she sneezes. She's right. The only bottles not covered in a layer of white are the bourbons and scotches.

"Why even bother keeping the other ones around?"

"Oh, at this point it's a running joke. If a tourist comes in and orders something weird, I make a big show of blowing off the bottle for the regulars. We all get a good laugh." She laughs.

"So, which one, and how do you like it, Ms. Trooper?"

I go for an old fashioned with Anna following suit. Once we've tasted our drinks, Marge excuses herself to go do some chores around the hotel, instructing us to call out if we need anything. Once she's gone, Anna moves us to a small table nestled between two comfortable armchairs.

"So, tell me about it." She means the case.

I stare into the auburn whiskey for courage, then take a sip. The orange hits my nose and balances out the light sweetness of the sugar. The alcohol doesn't burn—it just goes down smooth. Anna patiently sips hers, then licks her lips as if the taste is a wonderful surprise. I'd bet she usually takes her whiskey neat.

"Well, you know the basics. Man goes missing. Mom calls it in after a few days. Dog finds a body in the woods, sans head and with gun. Another man goes missing around the same time from an airstrip. No word on a body nor any clues as to where he went. Mom and Dad visit the morgue." I nod to her since she was there. "Mom decides the next day that it is their son, but Dad isn't sure."

She nods. "And the theory is that it's Lee Stanton and it was a suicide."

"Right." I swirl the bourbon and bitters around a large globe of ice. Around the world in eighty-proof.

"But…"

"Yes. But."

She leans back in her chair, clutching her tumbler in both hands. "It bothers you, but you don't know why."

"Exactly." I lean back too, relieved she understands. "This dream about it has me second-guessing. Or maybe I was second-guessing already and that's why I had the dream."

"You think maybe it's not Lee?"

"I don't know. Not necessarily. Maybe it *is* Lee, but what if it wasn't a suicide? What if it was connected to Branden, the other missing man? Or what if it's *not* Lee? And with Branden, I've got nothing. Just some magically disappeared footprints, a distressed girlfriend, and a haunted airstrip."

She raises her eyebrows. "Sounds like the start of a great mystery novel. The girlfriend is Marli Lei, right?"

"Right." Anna whistles. "You know her?"

"Everybody knows everybody around here. We call her the Maiden of the Mountain." I must look shocked. "Oh, don't pretend you didn't notice she's gorgeous!"

I straighten my imaginary tie. "Well, I try to stay professional."

"Of course you do. That's why you're here with me!" We both laugh.

"So, no one's tried to convince you it's aliens yet?" I blink rapidly and she laughs. "Oh, come on now. You're in Seward! You must know this is the Bermuda Triangle of the North!" I shake my head. No tourist brochures covered that. She kicks off her heels and curls her legs into the chair, glass in lap, as if it's story time.

"Have you met AJ?"

"AJ, Branden's friend from Kolit's?" She nods. "Not yet, but Mikey and I plan to talk to him soon."

She tilts her head back into the tufted leather and chuckles at the ceiling. "Oh, he's not the one you need if you want to know about aliens—you need his mother. She's a local expert!"

Marge reemerges stealthily as Anna speaks, her low heels drowning in the carpet. "You two doing all right in here?"

"I can use a top-up, please, Marge." Anna looks at my glass. "Louisa can too." Anna stands, collects my glass, and heads to the bar. "We were just talking about the Seward aliens. If I recall, you know something about that, Marge."

I can see Marge's smile in the mirror as she talks over her shoulder. "Oh, now that I certainly do! My daddy was absolutely convinced about the aliens. He was good friends with those folks at Kolit's, and they know the most about it of anybody in town because Kolit himself used to work at the military base."

"Oh?"

"Yup. Daddy was a Navy man himself, Top Secret clearance, and he swore he saw some stuff made him think it was all true."

"What kind of stuff?"

She turns back around, our glasses full again, but shakes her head as she hands them back to Anna. "He couldn't say. Not even to me. He knew the aliens were a regular part of school gossip, and if I'd gotten hold of any juicy piece of information, I would have repeated it. So, he never told me. I suspect he told Mama, but when I asked her after he died, she only said *loose lips sink ships*. Rumor was aliens landed on the airstrips up the mountain and picked people up for experiments." Anna carefully carries the full glasses back and hands me mine.

"Would that include the abandoned airstrip by Mr. Drew?"

"Mr. Drew?" Marge scowls, then turns her face away from the mirror. I am not sure if it's purposeful. "No, he never mentioned anything about Mr. Drew."

Police work is like a good massage—you find the sore spot and you dig into it till it releases. For Marge, Mr. Drew is obviously a sore spot. I turn back to Anna.

"Do you know if Mr. Drew is involved in anything weird? Is he honest? He was the last person to see Branden."

I hear a bottle *thunk* against a shelf, and Marge suddenly leaves the room. Anna sets her glass on the table, then reconsiders and picks it up again.

"The haunted airstrip *is* Mr. Drew's. He stopped using it a while ago. I don't know why he says it's somebody else's—no one else lives on that part of the mountain." She twirls her glass, not looking at me. Her normally easy manner and fluid speech seem stilted. "The cops here seem to trust him."

"Should I ask them about his use of the airstrip?"

"*No*. No, I wouldn't. They'd have told you, right? There's probably no point." She takes a big sip, then smiles and changes the subject, but her face and Marge's behavior tell me Mikey and I need to quietly investigate Mr. Drew.

❖

It's nearly midnight by the time Anna walks me back to the hotel. I've drunk enough to feel artificially warm, but it's still pitch black and cold enough to make life miserable. I ask if she's all right to get home by herself. She assures me that it's within easy walking distance and that the route is well lit. The officer in me wants to argue about her safety, but I don't want her to think I'm questioning her judgment.

"You should come out sometime soon. I'll cook dinner."

I've had a fantastic time, and I'm already looking forward to it. Before she goes, she gives me a tight hug. She smells like maraschino cherries and maple syrup under her amber perfume. *This could be something.* I thank her for the evening and wish her a good night.

❖

I'm exhausted. It takes me a few minutes to identify why I can't fall asleep once I've washed my face and collapsed on the creaking bed. *Tails.* I press my ear to Mikey's wall. I can hear the television on low, but that doesn't mean he's awake. Sometimes it's on all night. I don't hear snoring, though, so I take my chances. He opens the door with a kid-like grin.

"And here I thought you weren't going to be coming back tonight!"

Tails jumps at me, licking any skin he can find. "Must have gone well, eh?"

"You could say that." I press my lips together, making it clear I don't plan to say anything else.

"So? Spill it, Linebach!"

"A lady doesn't kiss and tell."

"Ooh. So, there was kissing!" He makes a face I'm sure I've seen on a cartoon skunk. I feign scandalized shock. He chuckles. "So, is there to be a second date?"

"There was mention of dinner at her place."

"Nice! You'll have to be sure the case keeps us around Seward."

"Oh, I think it might." He tilts his head in a question. "Something came up about the case. I think we need to interview Mr. Drew again." He's still curious, but I wave it off. "We'll talk about it when I'm not exhausted. How about brunch tomorrow? I'll come knock when I've managed to pull myself out of bed."

"Roger that." He leans down to give Tails a hug. The dog obliges and licks his ear.

I don't remember anything after all four of Tails's furry legs are thrown over me and his big wet nose is nestled into my neck.

CHAPTER FOURTEEN

Mikey and I walk into the station prepared to do some digging on the last person to see Branden: Mr. Drew. He has a large amount of extra money for someone in construction, suspects Branden was on drugs but didn't test him, and happens to own the airstrip on which Branden's prints seem to end but didn't share that fact. I haven't set my things down, though, when Chief Willington calls me and Mikey in to tell us Whittier is on the line. After he's explained—to me—that Whittier is a town on the coast a couple of hours away, he tells us the police there have found a body. I hustle to the phone.

"Officer Linebach? This is Chief Rodriguez." I'm pleasantly surprised to hear a woman's voice.

"Yes, hello, Chief Rodriguez. I've got Officer Michael Harper here on speaker as well." She doesn't respond, so I press on. "I hear you have a body."

"I do. Young guy. Mid-twenties, maybe. Hard to pinpoint age because of some swelling and discoloration. Brown hair. Slim, about five foot nine or ten. Bush pants. Flannel. Coat. Yellow backpack, but it's empty."

"Where was he found?"

"On top of a mountain."

I pause. I want this to be Branden, but so far it sounds like it could be half the world.

"I'm sorry, but what makes you think this might be Mr. Halifax?"

"Well, the circumstances. No one new has been in town in months. No one in Whittier has seen this kid before."

"You already asked everyone in town about him?"

"Um, yes." It sounds like she's laughing. "You've never been to Whittier, huh?" I haven't. "There's nothing here. It's just a couple hundred of us in a tower." I picture some sort of castle. "So yeah, I knocked on doors already. But there's the other thing too. We found this guy on the mountain, but there aren't any footprints around him even though the snow's a good half-foot thick. No signs of camping, no sleeping bag or anything. Almost like he dropped there from a plane."

I look at Mikey. He starts packing his stuff and shoving food in his bag.

"Any ID?"

"Nope. Looks like he's been cleaned out. Only thing we found was a receipt from a store in Seward in his back pocket."

"We're heading there now. How do we get to you?"

"Follow the highway through the tunnel. You'll know it when you see it." I look to Mikey for clarification, and he waves his hand like he knows where we're going.

"We'll see you soon."

Chief Willington promises Tails will be well-fed and happy at the station, but the dog still looks like he's disappointed in me when we leave him. I feel a pang of guilt. I never would have guessed I'd bond so quickly with a dog.

The two-lane highway to Whittier must be a gorgeous drive, but we're plowing through a snowstorm, so I make my assumption based on the looming mountain shapes hemming us in on either side. Around Moose Pass the road conditions deteriorate, and we decelerate to twenty miles per hour. By the time we get to the one-lane tunnel, which is mercifully open and allowing traffic going in instead of out when we need it, it's near lunch.

❖

The Tower is obvious because it seems like the only structure in Whittier aside from some docked and covered boats in the harbor. The building reminds me of the hospital near my Seattle apartment, except its salmon color and dark gray stripe across the top makes it look like a fish with the skin still on. Each floor has a series of wide windows, and there's a spacious covered entrance on the front with windows two stories high facing the harbor. It must be a nice place to sit and watch the boats come in and out on a sunny day. There are a couple of other low buildings. One resembles a school and I swear I see a bar, but otherwise it's just mountains and a harbor.

We park next to the other SUVs outside the building. Snow is piled at least a foot deep around the entrance, and when we get inside it's bright on account of all the fluorescent lighting. The interior reminds me of my college dorm, with whiteboards on the doors. A little directory advises the church is downstairs and the health clinic is on the tenth floor. There's even a bed and breakfast at the top. A few people stop to look at us curiously.

I'm nervous. I have more than one memory of getting stuck in a similar elevator in college, and confined spaces aren't my favorite thing. I breathe deeply in and out, then distract myself by reviewing the posters for various building events as we ride to the tenth floor. There's everything from Avon parties to fishing trips.

The man who greets us at the health clinic looks how I picture a mortician, but he's dressed for the outdoors. He is lanky and wears a dark pullover with charcoal gray trousers and hiking boots. He even has giant metal frames and thick lenses. I wonder if he's also the optician. His voice is even and deep as he introduces himself as Fritz. No title is given. Behind him, a woman a couple inches shorter than me with a black bob and matching sweater rises from a waiting room chair.

"Officer Linebach?" I nod. "I'm Chief Rodriguez."

She turns to Mikey, who introduces himself. "We're sorry to have kept you waiting. The road after Moose Pass was tough."

"We never expect anyone to be on time. Usually, visitors get caught with the tunnel running the wrong way."

"Oh. Well, I hope we didn't keep you from anything."

"Not at all. It's not like we need to run back and forth across town around here. I can be almost anywhere in an elevator ride."

"So, everything is in this building?"

"Just about. Most people live here, and this is where guests stay. There's a market and a clinic. The school is connected out back and there's a pub just across the way that's also a restaurant. We try to keep everything we need close because, as you experienced in small measure, the weather here is even more inhospitable than most other places in Alaska."

"I bet. The mountains certainly are impressive, though." The clinic boasts a broad window, as I'm guessing most rooms do based on the building's exterior. A craggy formation covered in white hovers over us. It's so close I bet I could make out a person standing on its face if it was a clear day.

"They are. They are also deadly, as you might imagine, and as I believe our DB discovered. Fritz?"

The mortician-doctor-pharmacist-maybe optician Fritz walks past a partition that separates the waiting area from the rest of the clinic. We follow. The back wall is covered in shelves of medical texts and instruments, with two refrigerated drawers subtly built into the bottom. I idly wonder if two drawers have ever *not* been enough storage, and what was temporarily done with the other bodies.

Fritz opens the drawer with a quick swoop as if he's doing a magic trick. Chief Rodriguez is already wheeling over a shiny clean stainless-steel table. It's clear they're used to working together, as I suppose everyone here must be. The naked body is covered in a clear plastic bag, and Fritz and Rodriguez each grab an end while Mikey and I support the body's torso as we ease it onto the table. When Fritz unzips the bag, it is easy to see the body matches the description of Branden, even if he is violet tinted with swollen limbs.

"Why the swelling? How was he found?" Rodriguez and Fritz look at each other before Rodriguez answers the last question first.

"He was found on a mountain a few back from the one you can see out the window, but around the other side. We think he'd been outside two or three days, but it's hard to be sure. He was almost frozen solid. It's been around ten degrees up there at night this past week. We are lucky someone found him before he got covered with snow."

"Who found him?"

"A few residents choose to live outside the Tower. One of them has a house around that mountain, by the base. He's an older guy who hikes up every couple days to stay in shape. Extreme health enthusiast."

"Was he along a trail?"

She laughs. "No. There are no trails. He was in a clearing, though, so the backpack was easy to spot." Fritz reaches into a cabinet drawer and retrieves a giant plastic sack that contains a bright yellow backpack. *Not something Branden would carry.*

I dig through my bag for the photocopied, blown-up picture of Branden. I hold it near the body's face to reassure myself, trying to distinguish the swollen features. Everyone examines it as closely as I do. As I glance around, the others seem doubtful of the identification, but I resume searching the nose and brows and find similarities. Sure, the brows are thinner, but…that happens with age. And the nose is a little crooked, but…he could have gotten into a fight. Maybe *likely* to have gotten into a fight, given what he was into.

"There's a tattoo on his back." Chief Rodriguez nods to Fritz, and they flip him over.

Mikey scowls when the tattoo is visible. "That looks familiar."

"You mean from your missing person?"

"No. No, his girlfriend didn't mention tattoos. I mean, it looks familiar from, like…life." The tattoo is still distinguishable, which indicates a man familiar with hiking conditions and wearing expensive gear, like Branden—and not like Branden. The tattoo shows a sprawling tree, a young boy looking up at it as if in awe.

"It's from a children's book," Chief Rodriguez informs us, though I've already recognized the image. *The Giving Tree.* Mikey smiles a little as if he's having a positive memory. Fritz looks bored.

"You don't think your man had tattoos?"

"No—"

"It didn't come up, but he has little kids, so maybe that would make sense." I interrupt Mikey to allow hope for a positive identification while I compare the features to the picture again. Chief Rodriguez scans our faces.

"This isn't your body, is it?"

I reply quickly. "We don't want to jump to that conclusion. He's so discolored. The height's right, the build, the hair color. I'd want his girlfriend or his mother to see him." Mikey looks at me, concerned, I would guess. He is right—Marli would have mentioned any tattoos. But I need to believe this could be Branden for a bit longer. *Just a bit longer.* The thought of a third dead man within one week is making my head spin. I work best when one case has my whole focus. I don't want this to be messier than it already is. I change the subject.

"So, how could he have gotten into town?"

"Not easily. There's no train or buses. Cars and trucks come through the tunnel, and he could have hitched in, but it wasn't with any of the residents. Besides, people don't really *happen through* Whittier unless they are on a boat. A plane, though, is our working theory, like I mentioned on our call. Sightseeing copters, rescue copters, and charter planes come and go. We don't keep track unless someone's in trouble, but a plane could have landed on that mountain. There are flat bits we use for supplies when needed."

"But no one would know who'd landed there."

"No, not necessarily. I asked Mr. Williams, the health enthusiast. He'd be the most likely person to hear a plane coming or going. He said he heard an engine a few mornings ago, but he didn't see the plane. He avoids people, so he wasn't about to go poking around."

"Louisa, this man could have come off a plane dead or alive, and depending on how it was done, no one would have known."

Chief Rodriguez considers Mikey's statement, and then addresses me. "Do you have reason to believe he dropped from that plane dead?"

"If this is Branden Halifax, we have no idea what he's doing here. He was supposed to be on his way to a local bar to drink with his buddies."

"I don't think they're going to let him in looking like that!" Fritz's attempt at humor reminds me of my earlier question.

"What about this swelling?" I delicately touch the taut skin on the deceased's arm. Fritz grabs the arm, unafraid of damaging him.

"Weird, right? A lot of things can cause swelling, but we can't autopsy him here. They need to do that in Anchorage."

"Any idea what he died from?"

"Could be plain old cold. No obvious injury. If something was done to him, we sure can't tell what it was. There's a bump on the head, you see here, but that could have been a fall, or just a whack on a door frame. Anything really. Could have been asphyxiation. He's weird colors anyway, so it's hard to know."

"What do you think?"

"I think this is a body dump where someone assumed the guy wouldn't be found anytime soon."

"Is that a normal thing around here?"

"Normal? No, of course not. Unprecedented? Also no." Chief Rodriguez shrugs.

"You said you found a receipt."

"Yeah. That's part of why we thought he might be your man." Chief Rodriguez produces the receipt from the evidence bag. It's a generic white slip of crumpled paper with a convenience store name printed at the top. The date corresponds to last Thursday. The total price of $3.27 accounts for a granola bar and some sort of jerky.

Mikey has been looking out the window for the past minute or so. The snow has stopped for the moment, and the sun tries to wrestle some clouds aside to make its debut. He turns to Chief Rodriguez. "Think we could take a look at where this body was found?"

She inclines her head and grabs a parka that's laid over one of the purple chairs. "Why not? You got good boots on?" She checks our feet, looks unimpressed, and asks Fritz if he wants to join us. He agrees, citing a need to work on his tan. He then pulls on a ski mask that covers everything but his eyes.

Snow machines are the only way to get where we're going from the Tower, so I ride with Chief Rodriguez while Fritz and Mikey buddy up. The close physical proximity to someone I don't know well makes me uncomfortable, so I focus on recalling the geography facts Mikey told me about Whittier on the drive out here. It's an eerie ride uphill and south of Whittier, where the Chugach Mountains run against the Kenai Range, teetering dangerously on the edge of the Kenai Peninsula and its disappearing men. With the white mountains rolling one above the other in front of us, I have a hard time wrapping my head around the fact we're traveling on a delicate isthmus, sea encroaching on either side of this sliver of land with all its sharp edges and peaks. I picture the land splitting one day—Seward becoming part of an island to the south of Anchorage, Whittier torn apart by the effort of all the mountains slowly forcing themselves to go one way or the other, and the Tower collapsing under the weight of the avalanches.

For now, the landscape is so silent it seems it will stay this way forever. The chief points out the few named mountains. There is the low Shakespeare's Shoulder, the Bard, the Baird, and off to our right, Byron. The literary names conjure lines of delicate poetry, fragile as petals buried under compact snow. Our destination mountain is an unnamed summit on the way to the locally well-known Carpathian Peak. Chief Rodriguez stops a few times to pick out a route. Finally, she spots a tiny log house of maybe four hundred square feet. She cuts the engine to advise this is the home of Mr. Williams. We see a curtain pulled back and she waves, but no one comes out onto the miniature porch. She laughs as she restarts the engine.

"That means he's all right with us going up. He owns about half an acre of the land he's on, but in his mind, he owns the whole damned mountain—possibly most of the range."

"Well, I doubt he really has to share it."

"It's true."

We climb about four thousand feet, digging a pattern of switchbacks into the shin-high snow. There are few trees on this mountain, and those here are squat and thick. They look like padded hockey goalies hoping to stay firmly in place so that nothing can knock them over. We drive in what feels like circles for half an hour until Fritz waves an arm at something just above us. As we approach, I see a crude wooden cross maybe two feet high, its two sticks bound together with twine. Chief Rodriguez heads for it and parks the machine.

"We use these to mark where people die in case we need to find the spot later. Mr. Williams must have placed it after we took the body away."

"Good idea."

"Yeah, these have been helpful a few times."

It's helpful in this case too. Other than the wood cross, it is impossible to guess anything happened here. The fresh blanket of snow obliterates all that may be amiss—footprints, shards of clothing, everything. The land here is flat. There's a spectacular view of the surrounding peak, and my eyes find one path a plane could have taken to approach and land here. It would be easy, at least from my non-aviator perspective. Clean shot in from almost any angle. If the pilot knew the area, they could have avoided flying over Whittier. According to the chief, though, it's not easy at all.

"Pilots can fly around these mountains maybe half the week with good weather. The air currents are dangerous otherwise, and it's easy to get slammed into a stone wall. Takes someone who knows what they're doing, for sure."

"Would they have landed here in the snow?"

"With a ski plane? Sure. Why not? It's nice and level." While we chat and I take a few pictures, Mikey wanders the site. When I join him, he bemoans we couldn't bring Tails, as the dog may have scented something under the snow. It's a good point. I kick snow, imagining how Tails would dig under it.

There's a small area of low shrubs with mostly dead branches weighed down by powder. I kick around these for a while, thinking about Branden. Thinking about Marli and their kids at home without him. Thinking about Lee and the Stantons and wondering whether that headless corpse is their son or if we're all just assuming so because it's most convenient. *What was I thinking, getting into police work because I assumed it would be an opportunity to solve puzzles and wrap them up in neat little packages?* Nothing here is getting wrapped with a bow.

The snow is shallower here. I kick for the fiftieth or hundredth time and my boot comes out with its toe stained pink. I squint down, then drop to my hands and knees. The snow comes in around the tops of my boots while I dig with my gloved hands. Mikey doesn't ask what I'm doing. He just helps.

CHAPTER FIFTEEN

I hold up the culprit—a few innocuous-looking round red berries. They were frozen before I trampled them to mushy bits. Disappointing. I assumed it was blood.

Fritz comes over to examine them. He carefully takes one from my hand and turns it over between his fingers. He speaks directly to it in his bass voice.

"Well, hello! What are you doing out here?" He lifts his mask to bite into the berry and the chief lunges forward with a gasp. He spits the berry out as she watches, clearly alarmed. He smiles. "And my assumption is correct!" He proffers the punctured berry to us, while he scrubs his tongue with his teeth several times.

"Jesus Christ, Fritz!"

Mikey and I just stare. *I'm confused.*

"*This* is a baneberry. Our very bitter little friend here is the most poisonous berry in Alaska. Were I to consume enough of these, I may well go into cardiac arrest right here on this mountain." He turns to Rodriguez. "Don't worry, though, I would have found my way back to Begich Tower to haunt you." She backhands his shoulder.

"Had I eaten just this one," he rolls the berry in his gloved fingers, "the worst would be some un-kissable blistered lips and a bout of putrid diarrhea." He bounces on his heels. "Oh, and maybe some hallucinations, which by itself sounds quite lovely, but the other side effects are usually enough to stop people seeking this edible."

I turn back to the shrub. "It grows here?"

Fritz smirks. "You'd think, but nope." He stoops to rub some dead branches between his fingers. "This is not a baneberry plant at all. And even if it were, these guys would have died off at the end of summer." His knees crack as he straightens again. "They wouldn't grow here, though. We only find them in the woods. They don't like these snowy mountains."

"Well, that's good to know."

"Officer Linebach, you can't be a state trooper and not know your poisons!" I'm offended, but I don't say a word. With my inability to exhibit indifference, though, I probably don't have to. After a silence, he holds the berry back out to me and Mikey.

"All right. First lesson. Baneberries can be red or white. You of course already know to never eat a white berry in Alaska because they're pretty much *all* poisonous." He looks us in the eyes. "Well, now you know. But the red ones," he turns it over, "the red ones have this distinct little black dot. That's how you know what this guy is. That and his rather horrendous taste."

Mikey nods, and I know he will note this in his journal. "So, someone brought these here."

"They did." He collects the few I have and carefully places them in an inside pocket. "We'll bag these for you back at Begich. You said your person Branden was from Alaska, so I'd wager he'd know about these."

"We'll keep that in mind." We search the area a few more minutes, but the clouds swirl, and Fritz predicts it will snow again in half an hour, and not gently. When we're back at Begich, Fritz puts the frozen berries in a plastic container for me to take back to Seward.

"Chief Rodriguez, since Branden's family is in Seward, and since we know this body doesn't belong here, would it be possible to take the body back there?" It's unappealing to think of cruising the highway with a corpse in the back, but it must be done. She just shrugs.

"What are you driving?" Fritz produces a long Styrofoam-like coffin and starts to fill it with ice, like possibly-Branden will be part of a large tailgate. The idea of a tailgate makes my stomach growl, which seems disrespectful as we stand over a swollen and half-frozen body.

"Is there somewhere we can get something to eat before we leave? It's going to be a long drive back."

"Sure thing. There's a pub just across from Begich. The food is decent. We'll be here." Fritz is now in medical gloves and pries around inside the dead man's mouth. He smirks again as his fingers emerge from the cavity.

"You'll never guess what I found." None of us answer. It's hard to want to know.

"Blisters!" Rodriguez blinks at him. "Like he ate baneberries, of course!"

Mikey and I glance at each other.

I need to be outside. My throat is closing, and the mountains are moving to trap me here. An underground tunnel connects the building to the pub, but I walk out the front door. It's frigid out, but I stop in the parking lot to take in some deep breaths of air.

"This place reminds me of my dorm in college. Fun, maybe, but you can't do anything without somebody knowing. Which, to be fair, is good for us, in a way, I guess. Seemed easy enough for Chief Rodriguez to confirm nobody saw anything." Mikey launches into a twangy rendition of the song "Everybody Knows Everybody."

"I don't know. It does kind of have a dorm feel, I guess. It's great if you're raising kids. Or need a dog sitter."

"True. And if you go missing, someone's going to realize it fast." My brain feels like it's on fire from trying to process all of this. I shake my head to let the cold air flow into my ears, and just as I do, it starts to snow.

"What about the body?"

"Now, you see some weird stuff here in Alaska, don't get me wrong. But this? This is the weirdest stuff I've ever seen." He shakes his head slowly and pulls his hat down around his ears. "He *has* to have gotten here by plane, but why wouldn't he have flown the plane himself, if it was Branden?"

I don't acknowledge the question. All this new information is overwhelming. I need time to accept the truth of it.

The pub is quiet, but based on the surprisingly large number of seats, I bet it can get busy when the fishing boats come back in for the day. They make good fish and chips, and no wonder—the fish probably comes from about twenty yards away.

"Should we call Quint and let him know about this body?"

"No," I say quickly. A little too quickly. I've already considered the question. I backpedal. "Once we're back in Seward, and we've talked to Mr. Drew again, we'll share."

"Louisa, I don't know if that's a—"

"He may be the only person who has answers for any of this."

He sighs. "Well, let's go say our good-byes to Fritz and Rodriguez and get our guy, yeah?"

"Sure."

Neither civil servant seems surprised I'm anxious to get going despite the snowy conditions.

"That's Whittier!" Fritz exclaims. "You either love it or you can't wait to leave!" Just like when we came in, we leave in a snowstorm.

❖

Despite the late hour, we are met at the hospital by a surprising sight—multiple reporters. There are at least three news crews, all too big to be Seward-based. A crowd of Seward citizens has been attracted by the commotion. They don't even pretend to have some other reason to be here.

Mikey and I stare at each other as they rush to us, and I am unsure whether to move the vehicle or get out of it. Anna and Stan run toward us and part the crowd; Anna shoos the people with camcorders away as she arrives. I unlock the back doors to help with the body. Mikey can do whatever talking is required. I hear the Q& A as we try not to drop the container while pushing past the reporters.

"Is that the body of Branden Halifax?"

"We don't know yet. Please—we need to respect the privacy of the family in this time of sadness."

Reporters snap pictures of me, Stan, and Anna as we struggle to carry the coffin to the hospital doors. A couple of the citizen bystanders jump in and lift the center of the coffin, and we finally get into the building.

Chief Willington arrives just in time to be of no help carrying possibly-Branden inside. He also doesn't tell the reporters to fuck off. When I leave Anna to her work and return to the front of the hospital, Mikey is failing to ward off the crowd. My patience is frayed—it's been a long day and I just want some quiet to try to make sense of this. Mikey's face looks drawn and tired. Maybe that's why I finally let loose on all these unhelpful people.

"Look, I'm not sure who told all of you you could be here, but this is a hospital and a morgue, and this man has not even been identified by his family. Shame on you!" I'm breathing hard, and my pulse quickens in my chest. I'm reminded of my past panic attacks, and I know I need to rest. Soon. The faster I can get these people gone, the better. "You're invading the privacy of the dead. Get out!"

A couple of the crowd back toward the door. A young reporter with a perky ponytail is the only one brave enough to speak.

"We don't mean disrespect. We were told this might be the missing man, Branden Halifax. It's quite a story, someone being found so far away. We just…Well, we think the story is amazing and the public would like to know about the police work that led to his—"

"And if it is Branden Halifax and his family identifies him, *in peace*, then we will be happy to talk to you at the station. However, this is an active investigation, and you are actively hindering our ability to do our jobs. This man deserves respect and an examination, and his family deserves to be able to view him in their grief in private. Now out!"

The reporters and camera operators slowly retreat. Many look at me askance. Only one reporter, a squat fellow with a lot of stubble and a wide nose, hangs back and extends his hand.

"So sorry, Officer. It's just…it's just we're all very impressed. It gives people hope, you know. That a missing person can be found. I am sorry we went about it like this. Please forgive us. We thought it was okay…" He glances at Chief Willington. "Mr. Drew seemed to imply everyone already knew the body was coming."

I instantly redirect my anger at the chief, who blushes slightly. I shake the journalist's hand. "It's nice to meet you, Mister…?"

"Founders."

"Mr. Founders. I look forward to speaking with you after the case is closed."

He nods and follows his crew. When the media is gone, I intercept Chief Willington before he can head to the morgue. I should be more respectful, but I blurt my question without preamble.

"How did Mr. Drew know we were bringing the body back?"

Willington blinks rapidly a few times but answers calmly. "Mr. Drew and I have been friends for years. We happened to be having dinner when you called from Whittier. Normally I wouldn't give out information, but he would have known what was happening just by my end of the conversation, so keeping it a secret wasn't a possibility."

"Did you know he was going to tip off every news crew between here and Seattle?" Now he looks flustered, but I can't tell if he's annoyed at me, Mr. Drew, or both of us.

"No. Now that I certainly did not expect or appreciate." Willington pauses as if he might say more, then nods and exits the front doors. *How much can I trust Willington?* I don't like having to doubt him.

Anna is already busy, so Mikey accompanies me to retrieve Tails from the station. When I express my further misgivings about Mr. Drew, Mikey nods.

"Something is rotten, for sure." I stare at him, and he grimaces. "I know my concerns about Mr. Drew, but what's on your mind, Louisa?"

"Why would Mr. Drew call the media? How does it benefit him?"

"It's a good question. If he thought it was Branden and he had anything to do with it, he wouldn't want his body found, right?"

"Unless he thought whoever did his dirty work did a better job and made it look natural. Then the media would run it as some sort of sad hiking death, and he'd be off the hook...but..." I hesitate. "What if it's not Branden?" My breath escapes me as a I say it. I so want it to be Branden. *I want this to be over.*

"Louisa. You know it's not. Right?"

I dig in my heels again, and my breath returns. *I need this to be over.* "That's not for us to say. It's for the family."

He slowly shakes his head. "If Mr. Drew knows it isn't Branden because he knows where Branden is, then he's hoping the diversion will draw attention away from him. Maybe he thinks we'll drop investigating Branden to figure out who this guy is. Maybe he's right. That could give him time to...I don't know. Clean up, maybe?"

"Maybe." I shake my head fast to clear some of the clutter. It doesn't work. I need to lie down. Tails yawns as if he's an empath to my exhaustion. Mikey acknowledges our collective fatigue.

"We should take the rest of the night off, talk more about it tomorrow."

I nod and we head back to our residence after calling the morgue to say good night to Anna.

I lie in bed, waiting for the nightmares.

CHAPTER SIXTEEN

Marli Lei will come to the hospital first thing in the morning after she drops the kids with Branden's mom, who talked to me only briefly. She had no new information to add to Branden's case, but she did express her wish that Marli be the sole decision-maker for anything having to do with the investigation. In her mind, Marli was Branden's wife, even if they weren't legally married.

I still hope it is Branden, if only to give Marli some clear answers. I like Marli, and the longer it takes for us to find her partner, the less likely it is she'll ever get closure. A missing person can haunt you. I live with it every day. I don't want Marli and her kids to live with it too. But if Mikey's right and this DB is not Branden, we'll need to talk to anyone who might know his identity, starting with the convenience store clerk.

❖

It's not him. Marli knows as soon as Anna pulls back the sheet. She handles it more calmly than I've ever seen anyone handle viewing, and she is certain. As she looks at the dead man's face, the emotions play across her face in fast-forward. I catch both her relief and her disappointment. It's not her man, but she still won't sleep at night. Her initial feelings are quickly replaced with sympathy for the man whose body lies in front of us. She shakes her curls and says a low prayer for his family before she leaves to retrieve her children and return to the mountain.

We get Tails from the station before heading to the store. The mini-mart clerk is young, snaps her gum often, and quickly reveals herself to be incredibly observant with a long recall. She remembers the young man who bought a granola bar as soon as we describe him and mentions the yellow backpack he was carrying—the one that was empty in Whittier—while scratching the soft fur under Tails's chin. According to her, he had an accent and she's sure he's from the Lower 48.

"The way he talked," she adds while rubbing the soft fur between Tails's ears, "sounded like he's really smart. Like, he was trying to not use a whole lot of serious vocabulary words when we chatted, but you could tell he was holding them back. Like he was used to talking to educated people, but he didn't want to sound pretentious." She pushes some dyed black hair behind her ear. "Not that I would have cared. I like guys who are smart." With the light flush across her freckled nose, I suddenly realize why she is so nicely forthcoming and remembers so much.

"Did he tell you his name?"

"Kyle. But when he said it, he paused a little and I thought maybe it was a made-up name. He had that kind of air about him, you know? Like maybe he didn't want people knowing about him."

"Did he seem like he was into anything he shouldn't have been?"

"Nah, I don't think so really." She buries her dark purple fingernails in Tails's short fur. He doesn't seem to mind. "Just hiding out maybe. Getting away from family or something."

"Maybe. Did he tell you why he was in town? What he planned to do?" She nods, looking around to see if her manager is listening. Seems she spent quite a bit of time on the job talking to this guy.

"I saw him in here off and on for at least a couple of weeks. He was staying in town and mostly hiking, but he wanted to find a job here. He liked it. Said he was getting a little low on money, though. Asked about a job here, but this place isn't hiring."

❖

We want to follow up on the clerk's information that not-Branden was staying somewhere in town. There are plenty of hotels, hostels, and campgrounds in Seward; thankfully few are open in October. Before we speak to anyone, though, Mikey and I agree we will ask about the hiker under the guise of wanting to talk to him about Branden. People may be more forthcoming if they think that's all it is than if they know this young man has died under mysterious circumstances.

We start with the campground by the water, which is empty except for a couple of RVs with enough furniture and outdoor decorations they look semipermanent. That observation turns out to be right—one of them is the manager's vehicle. There's a sign stuck in the ground out front that says so.

When I describe Kyle to the woman who opens the RV door, she seems unimpressed.

"So, you're looking for a young twenties guy with a beard and scruffy hair and hiking clothes. I can tell you that describes just about everybody who comes 'round here looking for a tent or a caravan."

"He would have checked in late in the season, though. Maybe two weeks to a month ago." She shakes her head.

"We haven't had anybody looking to rent anything in the last month. Only folks we've had been in their own vehicles just looking for a place to hook it up. Sorry can't help you more." She doesn't seem sorry at all, so I am not sorry delaying her a little longer.

"*Sorry*, but would you mind telling us where you think a young backpacker wanting to stay cheap might stay?"

She huffs. "Probably the hostel. The one out near the grocery store. That or Land's places."

"Sorry, we're not from here. Land's places?"

She rolls her eyes. "And here I'd think Seward would have the Seward police doing this shit. Land is a guy who's got a bunch of little cabins and an old hotel on Third. The little cabins are popular with backpackers that don't want to deal with the party crowd." We don't have reason to think this guy would avoid a party, but okay. "Land's open year-round, so go get 'im."

I lean into the doorway so she can't shut us out just yet. I like to have the last word with assholes, but I can't be openly hostile, so I invoke my childhood babysitter's mantra *kill 'em with kindness*. I plaster on a candy-sweet grin and thank her profusely for her help.

"If you happen to think of anything that might be helpful, I sure hope you'll give us a call. We'd be happy to come back around and visit." She squints at me like she wants to say something even more rude, but we *are* still officers. I make her wait while I intentionally fumble for my business card. I'm just a big enough jerk to love making her stand there when she so obviously wants us to leave. When I do finally produce my card, she grabs it from my hand and slams the thin RV door, which shakes on its metal frame.

Mikey turns to me with a quizzical look, and I give him the same big plastic smile I gave her. He snorts and then covers his mouth, giggling.

❖

It takes three tries to start the Tank, as if the vehicle doesn't approve of my treatment of the campground manager. Tails watches patiently from where he's curled on the back seat. If the Tank decides to give up the ghost, we'll have to stick around Seward for a while. Between Anna's presence and the mysterious Mr. Drew, I wouldn't complain. The snow starts falling hard as we travel to the edge of town.

There's nothing street level on the outside of the hostel that indicates it is one. It's a generic, slightly run-down, chocolate-brown clapboard building with three stories and a length of icy wooden stairs leading to the main entrance on the second floor. The only thing that gives the place away is a taped-on paper notice for the buzzer next to the door: *Hostel closed for the season. Questions or booking? Call Marcus.* Marcus's number is listed.

"Well, darn."

"Not so fast." I step back on the platform. "There's a light on upstairs. I'd guess Marcus lives here year-round. He probably just doesn't have enough business this time of year to keep the place open."

"Nice." The wooden stairs continue to a final landing, so we hang on to the handrails and carefully make our way to a door painted bright orange. There's no sign on this one, but yellow light pours through the gauzy floral fabric pinned over the window. When I knock, I see a hazel eye peek through and pull back a bit. I've learned from policing in Anchorage that folks do not like to answer doors in the off season unless they know who it is.

"Hello. Marcus? Officer Linebach. Police." The door opens quickly, and we're greeted by a handsome man with a bird nest of curly brown hair and an equally avian nose.

"Hello! Sorry, I thought you might be looking for the hostel. Happens once in a while."

"No, but we'd like to ask you a few questions about someone who may have stayed in the hostel two weeks to a month or so ago."

"Oh, of course." He opens the door wide, and the smell of chai wafts out. "Please come on in and have a seat. Tea?"

"Thank you, yes." I hear Tails barking below us. I wonder if he's cold. Marcus reads my mind.

"That your dog?"

"Kind of."

"Bring him in if you like. I'm pet friendly."

Mikey is already halfway down the steps, gripping the rail, so I follow Marcus inside.

The apartment is almost hot, but it feels good right now coming in from the cold. The overall look is bohemian. There are tapestries on the walls, rugs from foreign countries on the floor, and lots of colorful throw pillows. The walls are mustard yellow and there are teal lanterns hanging from the ceiling. Marcus notices me looking at them when he returns with three mismatched mugs.

"Got those in Morocco. Anything to keep it light and bright in the winter, yes?" I nod. "I'm starting to get used to it. This'll be my eighth winter in Seward."

He sounds proud, and I can't blame him. Though the extra-long summer days were great, I've been worried about winter. Even in Seattle winter could bring my mood down, and it gets darker and colder here. I've been meaning to organize some sort of activity in Anchorage. A running group, maybe—anything to give me something to do until spring aside from sitting in my apartment watching hockey. I must remember to do that one of these days.

"I'm still trying to get through my first winter. Where are you from?"

He laughs. "Well, my parents are from Israel, but I grew up in Baltimore, Maryland."

"What brought you here?" I push aside a green throw and settle into a papasan chair. There's room on the sofa, but I haven't seen a papasan since the '80s, and the novelty is too much to pass up. I may not look quite as official with my ass sinking into the giant round cushion, but it is totally worth it.

"I managed a hostel in Baltimore, and they used to send me to other hostels to get ideas and network. They sent me to Anchorage, and I made it into a little vacation, then took the train to Seward and fell in love. And of course, I noticed that Seward didn't have a hostel, so I couldn't pass up the opportunity to run my own place." Mikey returns with Tails, who greets me with a lick on the hand and then sits at Marcus's feet. Marcus scratches under Tails's chin.

"Business must be going well if this is your eighth year."

"It is. No business in the winter, of course, but there's so much in the summer that as long as I budget, it's all A-OK. It's like a dream. I meet people from all over the world and hear about their adventures, and I get to tell them about Alaska. I can't imagine doing anything else." He laughs while he sets down his cup of chai. His laugh has a rhythmic, musical quality to it. "Though I'm sure police work is interesting too."

"About a third of the time, yeah. The rest of the time we're posting bear notices or pulling dead moose off the road," Mikey says. We settle in our chairs. I note a rolled yoga mat in a corner. Marcus's place oozes serenity. The man clearly has well-being down to a science.

"So, how can I help?"

I blink. I'd almost forgotten about business. The place is so comfortable. A light coconut fragrance is in the room, but I cannot tell where it is coming from over the spices of my drink.

"We're looking for a young man who's been hiking in this area. He came into town sometime in the past month, maybe earlier."

"Ah. What does he look like? Where did he come from? Every guest writes their hometown in the log." Marcus walks to a shelving unit that contains a record player and a few books and retrieves a leatherbound log.

"Light brown hair. Beard. Early twenties. Skinny, about five-nine with a tattoo on his back and a bright yellow backpack. He told a clerk in town his name is Kyle." He flips the log shut and his face lights up like his lanterns.

"Oh yes. I know Kyle. He didn't stay here, but I've picked him up a couple times and given him rides to Camelot."

Mikey prepares his notebook as I start the interview. "Do you remember the first time you gave him a ride?"

"Sure. It was the same week I closed the hostel. I felt bad because he was looking for a place to stay. I recommended Land's." Mikey scrawls a note. "So that would have been the second to last week in September."

"Perfect. And do you remember the last time you saw him?"

"Oh, just about a week and a half ago. Or wait. Was it longer? I feel like it was a Thursday for some reason." His tan skin forms a couple of light forehead creases as he thinks through the timeline. "Oh yes, I was heading back to Seward from a massage, so it *was* Thursday. I saw him walking toward Seward too. That yellow backpack is easy to pick out. I gave him a lift to the grocery store."

"Do you know where he was coming from?"

"Yes, he said he'd been crashing in Camelot. Didn't say where exactly, though. I guess he made a friend out there."

I glance over to see if Mikey has any questions, but he still looks down as he takes notes. "That's helpful. How many times did you give him a ride, do you think?"

"Oh, maybe four or five. I'll see him walking. Usually, he's carrying grocery bags. Talk to him for a few minutes each time."

"What do you talk about?"

"Oh, places he's been. Places he wants to hike. He asks a lot of questions about Seward. He likes it here, I think. The first time I picked him up he said he was just here for a week or two, so I laughed when I saw him the third week. That tends to happen here. I don't know what it is about Seward, but people come for a visit, and they stay forever. Like me. Guess we make up for the folks that grow up here and can't wait to move to Florida."

"So, he first came here to hike..."

"He's already hiked around Juneau and Fairbanks, and around Anchorage, but he didn't like the city. Said he'd been in Alaska since he finished his master's. Came out here as soon as he could as a present to himself." His eyes wander toward a tapestry with an elephant on it. "I asked him how long he'd had to save up to get out here, and he hemmed and hawed. Maybe he didn't want to answer. My guess is his parents footed the bill. I see that a lot with the hostelers." He laughs.

"Mister...?"

"Dahan."

"Mr. Dahan, do you know where Kyle was planning to go last time you saw him?"

"Hmm." He's quiet as he considers the question. "He didn't

mention plans to move on. Fact, he asked me if I'd be hiring soon for the hostel. I told him no, kindly, of course. The kids who work with me over the summer have done so for years. They always come back. But he was looking for a job, I'd guess he's still around? Unless he got a whim and went on his way, that is. Say, everything's okay with him, right? He's a nice kid. I hope he's not in any trouble."

"We just want to talk to him about a man who went missing last week. We think he might have some information." Mikey's face is neutral.

"Oh, I heard about them both. Stanton and Halifax. Just terrible." He looks distressed while he shakes his head slowly. "It happens around here, I'm afraid. One of the hazards of living around Seward."

"Yes, about that. We're from Anchorage and we haven't been here long, but it does seem like people go missing a lot around Seward. What's your take on why?"

"Well, if you stick around long enough, you'll hear some wild theories." We both nod and he laughs. "My theory is it's just the people Seward attracts. They are looking for wild and solitude, and both those things come with hazards. So, you're bound to see high numbers of missing and dead people. It's a shame, though. Every time it happens, it's a shame."

"It really is. Especially for the families." He nods. "Is there anything you can tell us about Kyle's personality?" His eyes wander toward a framed concert print this time.

"Sure. An easygoing kid most of the time, seems to roll with the punches, though you can get him riled over politics if you aren't careful. But he did say that when he lived in Portland, he felt stressed out all the time, like everything was moving too fast for no good reason. He's here for the same reason a lot of young kids come here—it's an escape, and they feel like it's a permanent one. Of course, sooner or later the ones who try to stay realize it's still life. You need a job and a place to live and all. Then they tend to go home."

"Every vacation has an end, I guess."

"Yes. He's sure trying to make it last, and I get the impression he's not opposed to working if it's a job he likes. When he was trying to convince me to hire him, he told me he's organized and good with people. I believe that last part, at least. He speaks well. He has a sort of charming way about him. You can tell he's educated. Said he double-majored in history and geology, so he'd be quick to learn about the area so he could talk to people about Alaska. Said he'd work long hours, take a drug test and all if need be."

"He mentioned a drug test?"

"Oh yes! Most of the people who hire seasonals around here do them, and if you're a hostel, you just have to. Sometimes the people staying in the hostel like to...live fast. I make sure my employees aren't participating in those types of extracurriculars. I test them every season."

"That makes sense. Did he say anything else about that?"

He grins widely. "He *did* volunteer he smokes weed occasionally. Asked if that would disqualify him. I said no, as long as he wasn't coming to work on it. Though I've never found weed to affect work performance, I can't have the residents thinking it's okay." He scowls. "I sure hope he won't get in trouble for me saying he smokes."

"If we arrested every Alaskan who smoked weed, most of the population would be in jail all winter." Mr. Dahan nods. "And you don't know where Kyle is staying in Camelot."

"Not exactly. I drop him off at the end of Lancelot Drive. He wants to get out at the end of the road. Says he likes to walk the rest of the way. I thought it was a little funny, but I didn't pry."

"Could he be squatting?"

"I guess it's possible. It happens. Seemed like he had some money, the way he dressed, but who knows. If he saw an opportunity, he may have taken it."

"Okay. And you don't know his last name."

"No, but if he went and stayed at Land's, Land would know. He keeps careful track. He had a kid go missing from his place a few years back, so now he makes them all sign in and out, and if they're hiking, he has them record where and when they plan to return."

"Excellent. That's a great practice, especially around here."

"It is. I've adopted it myself."

I stand, and Mikey and Tails follow suit. Tails adds a yoga stretch. Mikey and I reach for our business cards at the same time.

"Thank you. You've been very helpful. If you think of anything else, will you call us?"

"Of course. And good luck finding those men. I've never met them, but it must be awful for their families."

We thank him and then gracelessly slide back down to the street. In the car, Mikey asks if we can visit Mr. Dahan again and just make up stuff to ask him.

"His place is awesome." I get what he means. "I even trusted him. How about you?"

"Yes. He seems like he tells you the truth instead of what he thinks you want to hear. Maybe we can come back and ask him if he knows Mr. Drew." I grin wickedly.

CHAPTER SEVENTEEN

L and's Cabins and Hotel is only a few minutes away. If I was a visitor to Seward, this is where I'd want to stay. In fact, I should ask the chief about switching our accommodations. The tiny little houses are spread over a couple blocks, interspersed with Christmas-sized pines and angled away from each other to offer privacy. They're legitimate log cabins, made of Alaskan cedar, which is easy to pick out by its brilliant pale-yellow hue. It's a small reprieve from our job as I imagine how they smell inside. There are lights on in a couple of them. The hotel sits to the side; it matches the cabins but has a long row of identical doors. Some have plastic window boxes and Halloween decorations as if there are permanent residents.

We knock on the door labeled *Office*. A man opens it immediately, as if he's been waiting for us. He has peppery gray hair and a thick mustache, and he'd be well placed in a Western in his fleece-lined flannel and square-toed cowboy boots.

"Mr. Land?" He confirms with a nod.

"I'm Officer Linebach, and this is Officer Harper. Do you have a moment?" He waves us inside. I note the office is tiny and Mr. Land's desk is right next to the door. There's a small loveseat at the back of what is clearly another hotel room he's converted into his workspace. He steps over to an electric kettle and raises an eyebrow, indicating a pack of teas and instant coffees. I don't want to kill the lingering taste of chai, so I decline. Mikey does too. Land settles into a rolling office chair and just stares at us. I wonder if he will speak.

"Mr. Land, we're looking for a young man who may have been staying with you about a month ago. His name is Kyle. He's in his early twenties, light brown hair, beard? He's been in town hiking. Came in from Portland, we think."

Land nods and opens a drawer to retrieve an old black and white composition book. "Yeah, I remember him. He stayed a couple nights." His voice is surprisingly gentle. He flips a couple pages back from his bookmark and reads. "Kyle Calderon. Portland. Checked in Monday, September 20. Out Wednesday, September 22. Stayed in Cabin 3. Paid cash. No problems."

Mikey transcribes Mr. Land's words into his notebook and underlines *Calderon* several times.

"You want a copy?" Mr. Land holds up the log.

"Sure. That would be great."

He rotates his chair to a cheap white copy machine and runs one off, hands it to me.

"Mr. Land, have you seen Kyle since he checked out?"

"Nope. Hasn't come by. Not around town, either."

"Okay. Was there anything that struck you as interesting about Kyle?"

"Nope. Seen a bunch of kids like him. Runnin' from something, thinks he'll find better here."

"Okay. Did he ever indicate he was hiking in the area?"

"He asked about trails. I suggested Marathon and the Point. Told him to write it down if he was going to go do them, but he didn't." He scowls. "I don't like that. Somebody staying with me disappears, I don't want to feel like I could have prevented it."

"Makes sense. So, you weren't sad to see him go?"

"Nope."

"You know where he went?"

"No. Just checked out, thanked me. I asked if he was leaving Seward. He just said he'd found somewhere else to stay. Polite about it. Took a trail map from the holder there."

"Okay." I wait, but it's clear Land's got nothing else to say about the matter. "We're looking for Kyle to question him about a person he may know who's gone missing. If you see him, will you give us a call?"

He takes my card. "Will do." He nods as we thank him for his time and turns back to his paperwork. At the car, Mikey and I agree that we've gotten all we can from Land.

We head back to the hotel to call Chief Quint in warmth and

relative comfort. The sun is setting, and I'm looking forward to a quiet evening. Maybe I will find a movie I've already seen and fall asleep to it.

If you'd told sixteen-year-old me that one day, crashing out of boredom would be the perfect end of a day, I would have died laughing. But here we are.

❖

Mikey and I huddle around the phone on my room's rickety wooden desk while I tell Chief Quint about Kyle Calderon. He will find the parents in Portland. If he was in college there, it shouldn't be too hard. When we've finished filling him in on our hiker, I hesitate.

"What's up, Linebach?"

"There's one other thing, sir. Mr. Drew—Branden's boss? We'd like to get some more information on him. But…Mr. Drew is well-known here. He's the richest man around Seward. And we get the sense digging into him is…not done. I'm not sure people will help."

The chief understands immediately. It's his job to help navigate the politics of policing.

"All right. I'll put our Anchorage team on it, see what we can find from here. Don't tell the folks there you're looking into him yet. If need be, I can always have a word with Willington."

"Thanks, Chief. That's helpful. Uh, Willington and Mr. Drew are friends, just so you're aware."

"Ah." He pauses. "That's good to know. Stay safe, and I'll be in touch as soon as I know anything. How's Seward treating you, anyway? You okay with being there a few more days?"

I look at Mikey, who nods with a smile. "Yes, it's good. The people have been welcoming so far, for the most part. We're both okay to stay for as long as we're needed. Oh, and…is there a policy about dogs found at crime scenes?"

"You talkin' about the dog that led you to the body?"

"Well, yes. We think it's Lee Stanton's dog. The parents don't want it, and he has taken a liking to us."

"Well, since Stanton's dead, that's an ownerless dog. You got as much right to it as anybody. The medical examiner got what she needed?

"Yes. Those samples were sent *outside*."

We all understand the Alaskan reference to the Lower 48.

"Sounds like you're good to go, then. The hotel okay with it?"

"I can pay for any damage, sir, if need be."

He laughs. He knows me well enough to know I will beg forgiveness, not ask permission, and the damage I *may* need to pay for is probably already done.

"I'll look forward to meeting your dog in Anchorage." He hangs up abruptly.

❖

The phone rings immediately after I replace the receiver. Mikey raises his eyebrows; I gesture for him to sit back down in case he's unsure whether to leave or stay. There's no one calling me for personal reasons on this phone, of that, I'm sure.

I'm right. It's Willington's voice on the line. I close my eyes. *If there's another dead twenty-something year old man, I may lose it.* Instead, he asks if Mikey and I have plans for tonight. *Does he think we're a couple?* I stop my mental meanderings. It's so easy to follow my own train of thought and forget to listen to what's being said to me.

"No, sir. Do you need us?" I look at Mikey and he sits up straight, ready to go back out there if need be.

"No. Nothing official. It's just, you've been in town a few days now, and I threw you into a little bit of a mess with these missing men, so you never got a proper Seward welcome."

I'm confused as to what a proper Seward welcome is. "We're happy to help, sir. No formal welcome required." Perhaps this is an attempt to make up for the snafu with Mr. Drew.

"No, no, I insist. A top-of-the-line cruise ship is here, and we try to keep a good relationship, you know. They make an excellent buffet, so I thought maybe you and Harper might enjoy dinner on the department."

"With you, sir?"

"I'm afraid not. I'm in Moose Pass giving a training." I don't know what to say. Fortunately, Willington continues.

"It would be sort of a favor to the department, if I'm being honest. The passengers have gotten wind of the thefts, so I promised the cruise line I'd put a police presence on board while they're docked in Seward to comfort the passengers, and all. One of my officers was on board for lunch right after they arrived, but he can't be there tonight. His kid's got a school event. You would be there to eat and to be seen. The buffet really is good, though."

"Sure. At least, I'd be happy to. I can't speak for Harper."

Mikey tilts his head.

"Oh, just one of you would be fine too if you can't both make it. I know you've been pulling long hours."

"Okay. Well, thank you, sir. At least one of us will be there."

"Great. Thanks, Linebach. Just let them know it's on the department. And please do go in uniform. Sorry to spring this on you, but I promise you won't regret it."

"Thank you, sir. Good—"

"Try the coconut shrimp!" Willington hurries off.

Mikey looks at me expectantly.

"Interested in some snow crab legs on the water?" When I explain the situation, Mikey laughs.

"And it's okay if just one of us goes?"

"Yes, why? You want to go alone? That's fine, I guess."

He laughs, but his forehead wrinkles while he looks at me. "Why would you assume that? No, I'm asking because I honestly can use a night off." He shifts his position in my still ruined, but not yet reported, hotel chair. "If *you* want to take tonight off instead, then I can do it. No big deal." I realize his eyes are puffy, and he's back to slouching.

"No. I'm good. I'm bad at relaxing anyway." He smiles and looks away. I'm probably not telling him anything he hasn't already figured out for himself. "I've never been on a cruise ship. I've always kind of wondered what they are like."

"Really? They're pretty cool," he says. "It's like a whole city on the water. Restaurants, shops, bars, dance floors, gyms—everything. The food is the main attraction for a lot of people. It's an experience for sure, even if it is just for a meal. Some of them even do formal dinner attire. Depends how fancy it is."

"I think I won't have to worry about that. He wants me in uniform, so the passengers know there's an officer on board."

"Oh, that makes sense. You won't be uncomfortable eating by yourself?"

I smile. I'm getting good at eating alone. It was uncomfortable those first meals after my ex and I split. It had always been the two of us, and before her... Well, I'd managed to avoid being single since college. I've never been a big fan of my own company, and having a partner keeps me out of my head. But these days, I almost enjoy it. Besides, it's a good way to eavesdrop without anyone trying to interact with you. I'm invisible, yet I see and hear everything.

"No, I'll be fine. Can you watch Tails?" I pat Tails on the butt, and he stretches his head around to lick my hand.

"Oh, heck yeah!" Mikey pats his knee. "You wanna watch some movies, buddy?" Tails walks over and leans against Mikey's leg.

"Thanks. He obviously can't be trusted to be left alone."

Mikey isn't listening to me. He's asking Tails if he likes pepperoni or pineapple pizza best. "Maybe we'll do both!" Suddenly he jumps a little in his chair. "Hey, I just had a thought."

"No meat lovers, please. I don't want to have to walk him a zillion times tonight."

Mikey laughs. "No, I thought maybe Anna would want to join you." He looks at me. I look away. Mikey's interest in my life makes me uncomfortable. Maybe because I'm not quite comfortable with my love life. We're so different. It's weird to share so much. I've always been serious about safeguarding the line between the personal and the professional. "You like her, right?"

"Yes. Yes, I do. Definitely." My blood pressure rises as I stumble over the admission.

"Okay. You haven't really talked about her since your date. Just wanted to be sure I didn't overstep or anything."

"No, it's okay. I'm not good at talking about personal stuff, so I just kind of avoid it." I look at him, worried about offending him. "I also wonder why you're so interested in me and Anna."

He physically leans back. "Oh, geez, I'm sorry! I think maybe we're getting to be friends, and friends talk about stuff, right? I like hearing about people's relationships."

"So, you're a hopeless romantic or something?"

"Well, not hopeless, but romantic? Yeah." He straightens his back like he's expecting me to challenge him on this aspect of his personality.

"Huh. Okay. I wasn't expecting that. I've never talked to a coworker about my relationships before." I realize suddenly that I just lied, but I don't correct my statement. There was another cop who knew tiny bits about my past relationship, but only after it had failed.

"Well, I *am* probably too nosy. It's just, I haven't exactly had any epic relationships myself."

"No offense or anything, but why are you so worried about serious relationships?"

He shrugs and scratches Tails behind the ears. "My parents have this like, perfect relationship. The kind of stuff you see in movies. They were high school sweethearts. Middle school sweethearts even."

"Wow. I can't even imagine. My parents' relationship was a nightmare that mercifully ended in divorce." I laugh to make light of the situation, but there was nothing light about it.

"I think that's true for a lot of people. I grew up seeing my parents, and I've always just known that's what I wanted. The *till death do us part* stuff, a bunch of kids, the whole thing. But it seems like everybody my age is just playing the field, figuring out what they like. I already know what I'm looking for."

"And that is?"

He tilts his chin up like he's reciting memorized text. "An elementary school teacher who cooks and loves movies."

"Um, okay…that's very specific. Do you even know anyone who meets that description?"

"Well, no."

"You can no longer give me shit about my dating life." He pouts as I continue. "You've created such a restrictive idea for your future wife, no one will ever possibly be able to meet it."

His face is contemplative. "You think so?"

I laugh. "Are you kidding? *Yes.* What's the harm in just dating to see what you like and what's out there? Give somebody a chance to surprise you. Give yourself a chance to surprise…yourself, I guess. What's the worst that can happen? You fall for a high school teacher instead?" He laughs for a bit, and I join him.

"Okay. Maybe you're right." He jumps up. "I'm gonna go think about that and order this dog a pizza." He looks at me as he clips Tails's leash. "So, what's the worst that can happen if you ask Anna to go on board with you?"

I squint my eyes at him. I hate it when people use my words against me.

"Point taken. I'll see if she's interested." I lift my cell while I wave him out, but then I put it back down. There's a professional line between me and Anna, or at least perhaps there should be. *Have I already crossed it?* If she was one of my colleagues at the Anchorage station, I'd never even consider a personal relationship. *Why is this different? Because she's here?* I pick up the phone again before I give myself a migraine. I'm seriously attracted to Anna…She is so kind and smart and beautiful. I close my eyes and recall our date, at least up until the subject of airstrips and Mr. Drew. I prepared for hours for a time that ended up being almost easy. I can't ignore the quiet that settles over me when she is near. I smile. I haven't felt this sense of possibility…in a long time. Maybe it's a weak self-justification, but Anna's not part of *my* police department. There's something special about her. *We* could have something special—if she's willing, of course. If Quint ever finds out, or even gives a shit when he does, I'll cross that bridge then.

I'm betting she's still in her office, so I use the directory Willington gave me. When Anna answers, she sounds too close to the phone, like she's holding it between her ear and shoulder. There's a lot of rustling.

"Anna? Hi, it's Louisa. How are you? Sorry, are you busy?" She could be examining a body. I tense at my late recognition of bad timing. *Could there be a worse time to call?*

"Louisa. Hi! No, I'm just packing up to head home. I'm glad you called. How are you?"

I sigh my relief, and my shoulders relax. "I'm fine. Hey, would you be interested in dinner tonight on board the cruise ship? I should tell you it's kind of work-related."

She chuckles and the rustling sounds stop. "Did Willington ask you to *be a presence?*"

"How did you—"

"He has his officers go mill around the cruise ships from time to time. And I heard he's been ramping up efforts lately. I wondered if he'd recruit you and Mikey."

"He sure did. Mikey is staying in tonight with Tails, though, so I thought maybe you'd be interested in some coconut shrimp."

"There is never a moment when I am not interested in coconut shrimp. What time?"

"Seven?"

"Perfect. That'll give me time to change. Meet me at my place at a quarter till? It's on the way down to the water."

After I record her address, I pull on a cap and hop in the shower. When I'm clean and dressed, I stand in front of the bathroom mirror. I take my hair down. There's a sort of indent in the waves where my hairband always rests. I flip my head over and shake it out. Sometimes I forget what my loose hair looks like. I've never been one to spend a lot of time on a beauty regime, but I want to make an effort tonight, even if I have to be in uniform. I separate my hair into sections and brush it gently, then dig through my toiletries bag. Leave-in conditioner is the best I have, but when I finish smoothing it through the top and sides, it's made a notable difference. The dark strands are neat and orderly as they sweep over my shoulder blades. I swipe on a coat of mascara and evaluate the result. *Not bad.* My college roommates always claimed to be jealous that I don't have to wear foundation or blush. I smile at myself, but it's not entirely convincing and it feels slightly unnatural. Baby steps, I guess.

❖

Seward does such a nice job with the streetlights that walking in the dark doesn't feel the least intimidating. The snow is piled in tidy heaps again, with the sidewalks cleared and salted. Anna's house is about halfway between the hotel and the cruise ship terminal. I have passed it several times as I've worked around town, but it's set back from the road and partially obscured by a massive pine tree. I stand at the end of the driveway and look at the house for a moment. The porch light illuminates a patch of pale-yellow siding, a navy door, and white trim. The small porch must be a great place to sit with a cup of coffee and watch everyone walk to the water in the summer. There's a window box painted to match the door below a tall, arched window and a steeply pitched shingle roof. I wasn't sure how to picture Anna's house, but now that it's here in front of me, it's clear this place reflects her charming and cheerful personality. It looks like a cottage in a fairy tale.

Anna answers the doorbell immediately and ushers me inside while affixing a dangling earring to her left lobe. She wears a camel-colored turtleneck sweater dress that accentuates her shape perfectly with a hem just below her knees. The material looks so soft I want to touch it, but she walks toward the stairs.

"Sorry, can you give me just a second? I have to find my shoes!"

"No rush at all. I always thought food was a twenty-four seven option on a cruise ship anyway."

"You're not wrong! Feel free to sit, or poke around." She waves an arm toward the living room, just off the entryway where I stand. "Sorry it's kind of a mess!" She hesitates, then hugs me and plants a kiss on my cheek before she disappears up a narrow set of stairs with a dark wood banister.

The living room *is* a little disheveled, with clothes and dishes scattered. Instead of seeming messy, though, the place feels lived in and cozy. The room is small and comfortable, with a striking rug in pinks and yellows under a plush upholstered sofa. There's a wood-burning fireplace with mismatched stones forming a wide hearth. I appreciate the older aesthetic. I lived in a gargantuan new build growing up, and except for my college dorm, it's been more modern apartments ever since.

The first floor is three rooms: an eat-in kitchen with a small round table, the living room, and a room that runs the length of the back of the house that Anna seems to use as a study or reading room. Everything is on a small scale—the rooms, the doorways, the cabinets—and I like the separation of rooms. It gives a nice sense of privacy, and of mystery about what's through the next doorway. I like this cottage even more from the inside. In the study, there's a desk, but I don't spy a hint of work. Instead, there are loads of books and magazines and a few, mostly dying, potted plants. I laugh when I notice even her cacti are none too healthy.

"Don't you judge me—it's hard to keep a cactus alive in Alaska!"

I turn to her standing in the doorway. She's wearing a pair of lace-up chocolate leather boots that reach beyond the hem of her dress. They are beautiful but also flat and practical. She's added her ME badge.

"No judgments here! I don't even have any plants to kill."

"No plants? But every home needs plants, even if they are…in distress."

I gently touch an ivy spilling over the edge of a bookshelf. This one still has a lot of green in it. "You're probably right. I haven't exactly made my place in Anchorage a home yet. It was supposed to be temporary until I could get to know the city and figure out which neighborhood I want to be in."

"Well, there's still plenty of time, right?" She takes my hand and leads me through the doorway and down the short hall to the front door, stopping with me as I examine the photos lining the walls. Some are landscape photos, but one is of Anna and what I assume are her parents in front of a white cottage that looks strikingly similar to the house we're in. "My parents' house. Cute, right?"

"Is that where you grew up?"

"Yup! I go back whenever I can, which is not often enough with work. Now hurry it along, lady, I'm starving!"

I laugh, hoping I'll have more opportunities to get acquainted with Anna's house. As we head out the door, she grabs the bright orange coat I first saw her in. There are more fashionable choices hanging next to it, but I'm guessing she wants to make clear she's affiliated with the city. For some reason, Anna's coat choice makes this feel slightly less like a date. I exhale. I put the strangeness of this not-a-date date and the discernment of the professional-personal line out of mind. I've never crossed that line before, but it could easily get blurry.

CHAPTER EIGHTEEN

Fishing charters and whale watching tours depart from this section of the harbor. Most of the boats are covered, and seagulls cover their masts. As we pass through, Anna stops suddenly and squeezes my hand with her soft glove.

"Look at that!" I turn to see a group of sea lions removing a boat's cover with their heads. They're massive animals, and the boat is listing a bit to the side they've overtaken.

"Will they damage the boat, do you think?"

"Oh, they sure can. The owners try as hard as they can to keep them off. They're forever breaking off steps and anything that's not durable and well attached. They're curious things just having a rollickin' sea lion good time. I'm sure they don't mean to cause harm but, well, when you're a family of giant animals..." One of the deck covers is halfway off now, flipped back on itself as the animals try to work their way underneath it.

"Should we try to run them off?"

"You do that, you're on your own! They're usually friendly, but they're still a lot bigger than us. And besides," she grins under the white orb of a streetlight, "the boat owner is going to learn a valuable lesson about securing their property."

"Hazards of living here, I guess."

"Exactly. We don't tolerate shit from other humans, but we're pretty understanding of the animals. They were here first, right?" *True.*

The cruise ship looms ahead of us. Ships come into Anchorage's port constantly, but I've never had reason to get close. When we're ready to board, I look up, and the ocean liner towers several stories overhead. Anna and I are miniscule.

"Mikey's right! A floating city."

"That about sums it up. You love them or you hate them."

"Have you ever been on a cruise?"

"Exactly once."

I raise my eyebrows at her as a security guard glances over my badge, checking my face against the photo. He probably knows all the regular Seward officers well. "My parents wanted to go to the Bahamas, and they convinced me to come along. It was brilliant for the first three days."

"And then?"

She shrugs. "It was a little much for me. Kind of sensory overload. There's always a party or music or kids running around the pool. I guess I was more interested in just sitting on the deck staring out at the water, but the deck was always packed. You had to fight for a chair in the morning, and I'm not the fighting type."

I wrinkle my nose. "That probably wouldn't be for me either. I like my privacy."

"Me too. I recharge best when I can get away. Ideally outside, but the sofa will work in a bind."

"Sounds like me." I'm kind of surprised we're alike in that way, though.

We follow an extremely long carpeted hallway to where it ends at a glass-domed atrium ringed with real palm trees. A glittering white fountain sits at its center surrounded by potted plants and, as Anna noted, loads of running children. White Adirondack chairs sit in random groups, all of them occupied by groups of people talking. I blink against the onslaught of noise. A child barrels into my side and then takes off again, yelling.

"Welcome to dinnertime on a cruise ship."

I stand completely still, flustered. I'm overwhelmed easily by crowds. Somehow Anna knows I am unmoored. She takes my arm and guides me away from the rush. My tension eases a little, and I sigh.

"Let's find the buffet. It should be a little quieter there." She's right, thankfully. There are several dining rooms and restaurants on board, and Anna asks for directions a couple times. The buffet dining room is surprisingly quiet, with low conversations, soft classical music in the background, and the clink of chafing dish lids being put back in place.

I start toward a table against the windows before I remember why I'm there. "I guess center of the room, close to the buffet line is best. I'm supposed to be visible to the passengers."

"Good call." Anna sits her black leather clutch on a chair, and I frown. She winks. "Anyone silly enough to swipe a purse from a table an officer just claimed deserves what's coming to them."

Right. I do in fact have *Police* sewn in giant capital letters across the back of my jacket, which I carefully hang on the back of my chair. My occupation is now perfectly visible to anyone in the buffet line. I smooth my uniform and check my badge is visible.

"Ready for that shrimp?"

"Born ready."

A few people nod in my direction. Most don't say anything, but this is what Chief Willington wants. A presence. Anna travels the buffet line with me as I load my plate with one tablespoon of almost everything. She has nothing on hers but king crab legs. People greet me or occasionally ask light questions as we move along. Anna helpfully answers when they're Seward-specific. When we finally head back to our table, Anna gets to work cracking shells.

"I admire a woman who knows what she likes, but I thought you were *born ready* for coconut shrimp?"

"Oh, don't you worry. Its time will come. But life is short, and who am I to pass up crab legs as an appetizer?" She dunks a large chunk of meat in a tiny bowl of butter. "Then again, it may not have been the most elegant choice."

I laugh, going right for a shrimp, which is as divine as Willington promised. My face gives me away, because Anna immediately reaches across the table to take one off my plate. Whatever the people glancing our way think, Anna seems not to care, so I try not to care, either.

Just as soon as I've popped the biggest shrimp left on my plate in my mouth, a woman approaches our table. The large purse she clutches is partially concealed under an elaborately embroidered shawl. She scans Anna until her eyes find her badge.

"Excuse me, Officers. I'm sorry for interrupting your meal."

I choke down the shrimp as quickly as I can without accidentally killing myself. "Not at all, ma'am. What can we help you with?"

"Well, nothing I suppose. It's just that I've been hearing people say they've had things stolen, and I also heard about those young men that were chased off the ship. I just wondered if you've caught anyone yet." Anna and I glance at each other. She raises an eyebrow. I guess this is also the first she's heard about men being chased from the ship.

"Yes, ma'am. We know about the thefts and we're here to deter anyone looking to steal from the passengers. The Seward Police Department is very serious about finding them and returning any lost items. If they're recovered after you've departed, rest assured that anyone who's had belongings taken will have them mailed back to them as soon as possible."

"Well, that's good to know, I suppose." She shifts her weight on her low-heeled pumps and looks around the room. "But what about those men? They weren't supposed to be on board. I don't think the security officers are doing a very good job if they were able to get on, do you?"

"I'm sure they're doing their best, ma'am. It's a very large ship, and unfortunately that kind of thing can happen. Do you mind me asking how you heard about that?"

"Well, *everybody* is talking about it. I heard it from one of the other passengers at the hot tub. I don't know where she heard it from. Did the police catch them in town?"

"I'm afraid I'm not sure, ma'am, but I'm also on a special assignment, so I wouldn't necessarily be aware. I'll be sure to check up, though."

She scrunches her lips to one side and scowls, obviously dissatisfied. But she tells us to have a nice meal and then goes on her way, still clutching her purse to her chest as she joins a few other women before departing. Anna and I continue eating in silence until the conversation around us starts again.

"Well, that's news to me!" Anna keeps her voice low.

"Me too. Willington didn't mention anything about anyone sneaking onto the ship."

"He probably doesn't know." That's true. Cruise lines have their own security. Since they operate in international waters, they're not tied to any police department through any one country. They handle on-board crime themselves, so it can often go unreported unless it happens while the ship is docked.

"Yeah, but if they chased them off, then they chased them into Seward. They should have notified the department, right?"

She makes a face at her final crab leg as if it did something wrong, then she cracks it open. The waiter immediately whisks the plate of empty shells away. We both stand, ready for another round. As we get back in line, I quietly suggest we seek out the ship's security director.

"Any idea where the security offices might be on this monster?" I'm surprised she's asking me.

"No clue, but sounds like a fun scavenger hunt."

"Could be a lot of walking. Better load up on more protein." She clinks her fresh plate against mine like it's a champagne glass. There are pros and cons to being comfortable enough with Anna to eat in front of her. I usually get so nervous I waste food. Instead, by the time we head off to explore, I need to unbutton my pants. Since that's not possible, I place a hand over my stomach and sigh as I stand.

"Now you see why I wore this stretchy dress." Anna rubs her own stomach.

"You are a wise woman, Dr. Fenway. Here I thought you picked it because it's so flattering."

She strikes a pose before we leave the dining room.

❖

I am disoriented by the ship with its long passages, all with the same carpet. We walk the ship's decks first, guessing the offices to be in a place easy for the passengers to find. That turns out not to be the case. It's much easier to locate a security officer patrolling the deck. When we do, he leads us to a small office in the ship's interior. He peers through the small round window in the door before showing us in. There's barely room for four people.

"Sir, this is Officer Linebach and Dr. Fenway from Seward."

A tall, dark-skinned man with close-cut hair and heavily muscled biceps shakes our hands. "Pleasure to meet you, and thank you for dining on board. I requested the additional police presence. The passengers have been nervous."

"The pleasure is all ours." He indicates a bench built into the wall, and Anna and I sit facing him as he settles in behind his desk.

"We wanted to speak with you about something a passenger mentioned. We were aware of the thefts, of course, but a woman told us a couple of men were chased off the ship. Is that true?"

He nods slowly. "It is, but I didn't know the passengers were aware of it. That's unfortunate. We try to involve them in security matters only when necessary. They are here to relax and have a nice vacation, not to worry about their safety." He presses the tips of his fingers together in front of him.

"Did you alert the Seward Police Department?"

He sits up a little straighter. "No. It wasn't necessary per the cruise line's protocol."

"Even though you chased criminals into Seward's territory?"

"Well, for one, we don't know they were criminals. No, they should not have been on board because they were not paying passengers, but they were not caught with anything, and the complaints about them could well have been gossip."

"The complaints about them?"

He looks confused. "The passenger who told you about this didn't mention why they were chased off?"

"No."

"Ah." He relaxes into his chair. "A cook brought to my attention one of the men was trying to sell drugs to the kitchen staff. Whether it's true or not, I don't know because we didn't catch them and no one confessed to having bought drugs, assuming anyone did. Still, I have no reason to think the cook would lie."

"How did you know they weren't passengers?"

"We didn't. We just had a description of them. When one of the security officers approached them and asked their names, they took off."

"To where?"

"Back the way they came, I suppose. Over the edge."

"You mean into the water?" Anna chimes in.

"That's right. The officer certainly wasn't expecting that. They pencil dived into the water and swam to a boat anchored close by. Took off in it, away from town. That's why I didn't alert the Seward department. They weren't headed to Seward."

"I'm guessing they were wearing wet suits?"

"Baggy clothing, layers, so it's possible. My guess is they snuck on by boat too, and if that's how they planned to leave, wet suits would certainly make the event more survivable."

"You think they climbed the side of the ship to get on?"

"It's unlikely but not entirely impossible. There are ways to do it using some of the rigging that supports the lifeboats if a person knows boats well and isn't scared of getting caught in ropes. There's an officer at each entrance and they check tickets for anyone coming on, so their getting on the traditional way doesn't seem likely."

"So, you don't know how long they were on the ship."

"I'm afraid not."

"How did the cook describe the men? Did it match your officer's description?"

He nods and waits as I retrieve a small flip pad from my back pocket and borrow a pen from his desk.

"Two men, mid-20s to mid-30s, similar build. Around five foot ten. Both Caucasian, both with brown hair. One with a short beard and the other with stubble, one thinner than the other, but both somewhat muscular. So, in other words, accurate but not exactly helpful." He's certainly right about that. The description can fit Lee, Branden, or Kyle—not to mention unknown numbers of young men in the area.

"And when was this?"

"The first night we docked in Seward. Just over a week ago."

Anna looks at me. I'm confused too. And possibly thinking the same thing. "But I thought the ship just came into port a couple mornings ago."

"Came *back* to port. This tour is a Land and Sea." I shake my head to show I don't understand, and he continues. "The ship does several types of tours, but these passengers paid for a Land and Sea package. We departed from Seattle, cruised to Alaska via Juneau, then came into port here in Seward eight days ago. We stayed a night, and the passengers disembarked the next morning for the start of the land portion of their tour, which takes them up to Denali and back down through Valdez. While they're doing that, the captain takes us to Anchorage. Ship gets cleaned and repaired, a few of the crew changes off, we all get a few days of leave, then we come back to meet the passengers here in

Seward. They get a couple days to enjoy the town, do some sled dog tours, walk around on the glaciers, then we head back to Seattle."

I lean back and my back hits hard against the wall. I wish I had some time to think about what he's saying before asking more questions, but I have a feeling it will be hard to get answers once they've left early tomorrow morning.

"So, is it possible these two could have gotten on in Anchorage?"

He looks at me with a steady gaze, then blinks slowly. "The thought had occurred to me. I would hope not. I like to think my officers are as concerned about security when the passengers aren't on board as when they are, but sometimes things can be a little more relaxed when we're on leave."

"Could they have traveled from Anchorage to here without anyone noticing?"

"There are plenty of places to hide. So yes."

"Is there any way to know for sure?"

He sighs deeply. "Officer Linebach, I have reviewed the footage of every camera on this ship. Whoever these men were, they were good at avoiding those cameras until they were chased off."

"Do the cameras cover everything?"

He raises his eyebrows. "That would certainly make my job much easier, but no. The ship is too big to have everything covered by cameras, and it makes guests uncomfortable to have them right outside their rooms, so they are limited around the guest quarters. These men weren't exactly hanging out in the lounge or the pool areas, where there's plenty of coverage."

I'm beginning to think he isn't going to be able to help us until I remember the picture of Branden still tucked into my wallet. I slide it across his desk.

"Who is this?"

"Branden Halifax. He's been missing from Seward for several days now. He meets the description of your intruders. Any chance the officer that chased them off could look, just in case?"

He turns in his chair to speak into his walkie-talkie. Anna and I glance at each other. I shoot her a quick smile. Unfortunately, the officer who joins us is not entirely sure.

"They were both wearing hats, so I can't say about the hair. One of them, though…" He taps his finger on the picture laying on the desk. "One of them could have been this guy. But with a little bit of a beard. The other one, I think he was a little too skinny to be him. Unless he'd lost a bunch of weight. Even then, too narrow in the shoulders, I think."

I step outside with Anna to call the Seward PD and ask them to send a picture of Lee Stanton to the ship's security office. They'll run a physical copy over because it's easier than dealing with the technology.

Anna and I stand out on the deck while we wait. The moon is a perfect white slice in an onyx sky. The lights of Seward cast a slight orangey glow to one side, so we face away from it, out toward the tiny islands dotting the coast. Something large splashes in the water.

"Whale?"

"I sure hope so. I love knowing they're around." We listen to the silence. "You know, the Native Alaskans associate them with power." She's looking out at the water, but I'm looking at how that perfect slice of moon illuminates her profile.

"I can understand why."

"Have you done a whale watching tour yet?"

"Oddly, no. You know they have them in Seattle and Anchorage, but it's one of those things I always say I should do and never actually get around to doing." She leans against me so briefly no one else would notice. But I notice, and I enjoy the touch for the second it lasts.

"We should go. You don't mind boats, right?"

"I love being on boats, and I will certainly take you up on that." We look toward the stars in silence.

"When do you think you'll go back to Anchorage?"

I sigh. "Hopefully not until these cases are closed, but I guess it'll depend on whether the chief needs us for anything else before then."

"Well, I hope it's not too soon. Though even if it is, at least you're not too far away."

She leaves that open-ended, but the fact we could visit each other doesn't need to be spoken out loud. It's something I'll need to think about more once these cases are closed. I cannot mentally juggle multiple missing men, the idea of going back to Anchorage, whatever we might jump into there, *and* the idea of distance-dating, or whatever this is or will be. Sure, a few hours don't seem like much, but I already know the trip is long, and can guess it would be grueling in winter. I stop myself before I can get any more anxious about it.

Thankfully, we spy a slightly lost-looking young man with a manilla envelope. Anna waves him over. Rahul is a high school student who sometimes does odd jobs for the department. He delivers the envelope to Anna, then rushes off. When we show the picture of Lee to the officer, he shakes his head.

"I don't think so, but it's hard to say. He looks like the other dude you showed me." He stares at the picture. "I mean, yeah—either of them could be the bigger one."

"But you don't think it was both of these two together." He shakes his head firmly.

"No. One of the two was a lot thinner than the other one. His jacket seams didn't sit right. His shoulders were narrow. His pants seemed too big. Like somebody who's been on a diet but hasn't gotten new clothes yet." *Or someone who's lost weight due to a drug habit.* He seems certain, and again I feel my nice tidy ending to these cases slipping away. Anna tries to reassure me as we walk back to her place.

"If one of them was Branden, that's a serious breakthrough, Louisa! That opens a whole new line of possibilities, don't you think?" I stare at my shoes, deep in thought. "And if the other person wasn't Lee, then that means there's someone out there who was with Branden not long before he died, and they might be able to answer a lot of questions."

At that, I look up. "That's true. If it was someone else from Seward, they'd likely be a known someone. They couldn't be that hard to find, right?" The irony strikes me immediately. Now it's Anna's turn to stare off into space, except her gaze seems fixed on a point far in front of us.

"What are you thinking?"

"I was just…" She shakes her loose hair. "The body from Whittier. He matches the description too, but he's thinner. He has narrow shoulders. He was wearing hiking clothes that looked a little too big. What if he lost weight hiking? He'd match the officer's description of the second man."

I stop in my tracks to look at her. I lean forward to kiss her so suddenly that my nose crashes into hers. We both laugh at the clumsiness of it. I try again and gently take her face in my hands, kissing her softly.

"Why aren't you an officer again?"

"Doesn't pay well enough."

On her porch, Anna gives me a long hug. I am not sure she will invite me in, and she doesn't seem sure either. I certainly won't be the one to suggest it. It's an awkward moment.

"I have a long day tomorrow, but how about if you come by on Sunday? I'll make you dinner and then maybe we can walk to the Point, out near the old fort."

"I would absolutely love that." I linger on the porch until she's safely locked inside her cottage again.

I don't rush back to the hotel. There's a lot to think about, and I think best while I'm moving. As I pass the houses on Anna's street, indoor lights blink off. It's late. But I suspect I won't sleep any time soon.

CHAPTER NINETEEN

Mikey and I travel to Camelot to try to determine where Kyle stayed. I updated Mikey on what Anna and I learned when I picked up Tails last night. He looks energized and ready to get some answers this morning. Relaxing last night clearly did him good. I got maybe three hours of sleep.

We go house by house, heading deeper into the neighborhood. Eventually, we come to a partially finished house. The walls and the roof are complete, but the windows aren't set in; there are thick layers of plastic secured over the frames. The porch is still under construction, with only the steps finished. Something about the place feels off and the plastic flap has already been torn from the door opening, so we step in.

This is where Kyle was staying. There are empty crushed cans in one corner of the room, a pile of dirty clothes and a stack of clean ones in other corners. There's a trash bag with paper plates and plastic utensils in it. There are some groceries gathered. Mikey pokes through them.

"This milk is expired by a few days and the bread's gone moldy. So, he's been gone at least three, maybe four days. Adds up for the body, right?"

"Sounds right to me." As he checks out the downstairs, I climb to the lofted area that will most likely be a bedroom. There's a sleeping bag laid neatly under a window, and a book is open facedown next to it. In the corner of the room, there are more books in a pile. One bound in red leather with gold lettering catches my eye. It's certainly different from the other cheap paperbacks. *Robinson Crusoe*. I flip through the volume; every new chapter has a detailed, full-color illustration from the story. Something about it triggers a memory, but I can't quite access the details. I hear the book title said aloud, and recently. And then I hear Chief Willington's voice. But why the hell would he talk about *Robinson Crusoe?* I go back downstairs to Mikey, flipping the pages of the book. He glances my way.

"What have you got there?"

"*Robinson Crusoe.* Wasn't Chief Willington talking about this book for some reason?"

He purses his lips and blows out some air. "Beats me. I don't remember writing anything about that down."

"Probably because it didn't seem relevant. He was just complaining, I think. It wasn't long after we got here. He was talking about…" I turn my brain over to piece together what Willington was saying when he mentioned it. "Cruise ships! But why did it come around to…Oh! The things that went missing from the cruise ship! He said some jewelry, but also some guy's special copy of *Robinson Crusoe.*"

Mikey blinks. "How the hell did you remember all that?"

"I tend to replay conversations over in my head." He raises his eyebrows. "So, if Kyle has this book, more than likely Kyle stole it, right?"

"Right. You said he mentioned jewelry too. You didn't come across any of that by chance, did you?"

"No, but he probably wouldn't leave those things in a house with no locks."

"Maybe." He reaches for the book and thumbs through it delicately. "What a strange thing to steal. It may be valuable, but only in a specialized market. The other stuff would be easy to pawn."

"He can't be dumb enough to steal it off a ship and pawn it in the same town." Mikey hands the book back and I tuck it under my arm. "Let's take it back with us. Between this and what we know about those men being chased off the ship, I think we have enough to present to Chief Willington."

"Sure seems that way to me." I head back upstairs and sweep my eyes around the mostly empty room one more time. I'm interested in the other books; maybe they were nabbed as cruise ship souvenirs too. I pick up the open novel, and when I do, a slip of yellow notepad paper

falls from the pages of *The Stand*. There's an appointment scrawled in tiny cursive. *Mr. Drew. Tuesday. 6 p.m. 907-431-2927*
I immediately yell for Mikey.

❖

When we tell Chief Willington about the book we found in Camelot and the cruise ship incident, he claps my shoulder hard.

"Damn, I ought to have Anchorage send troopers out all the time! You find me a missing person *and* you solve my cruise ship burglaries? You ever consider transferring?"

I can't tell if he's joking.

❖

Mr. Stanton invites me and Mikey to Lee's funeral. They will pick up the body from the morgue this morning and plan to bury it early this evening, despite the frozen ground. They're going to bury him at the top of the mountain, above his trailer and the tree line, in a spot with a view of the harbor and the fjords beyond.

I promise we'll be there, even while a stone turns over repeatedly in my stomach, growing larger with each turn until it's a boulder pressing against the bottom of my throat, threatening to cut my air supply. I still don't feel right about Mrs. Stanton's ID, but there's no way I can argue with it. He was their son. I never even saw the man alive. My mind floods with images of them lowering those remains into the ground, without the head, and without one hundred percent certainty it's him. In my mind, the box goes into the ground over and over. I begin to sweat. A panic attack is coming. I need to get out of the building.

I am so out of control of the situation with both the Stantons and Branden. I can't take the stale air of the station—the smoke-stained walls close around me, the stripes of the wallpaper make me dizzy as the peeling ceiling drops lower to my head. As soon as the call ends, I rush Tails outside under the pretense of a potty break. The frozen air shocks my lungs into working again.

I've been outside for minutes, folded over myself on a gray bench, when Mikey rushes out to me, furiously rubbing his ungloved hands together. I pull myself together as best I can. I make a point of never letting other people see my panic attacks. They might think I'm not capable of doing my job. Thankfully, Mikey gives me a new focus.

"Quint just called with a number for Kyle Calderon's parents in Portland. He's still working on—" He shifts his eyes around. There is no one else nearby, but he comes close to sit and whisper anyway. "He's still working on Mr. Drew, but he thought we'd want to talk to the Calderons while we wait." Anything that's *not* thinking about Lee Stanton's headless burial is good, so Tails and I follow Mikey back into the oppressive warmth of the station.

❖

"Hello?" Mrs. Calderon sounds hostile, and the shuffle of papers with clanging dishes give a sure impression she's busy. The background noises stop after I officially introduce myself and ask if her son is Kyle.

"Mrs. Calderon, when is the last time anyone in your family talked to Kyle?"

Her tone changes from irritated to concerned in seconds. "Not since his graduation party at the end of May. Why? What's happened?" I can hear her panic rise. "Is he in trouble?" Maybe I should have let Mikey handle this one. I consider handing the phone to him—he's already leaned over the receiver—but I decide against it. It wouldn't be fair to make him handle all the difficult conversations.

"Can you describe your son for me, please?"

She snorts. "You've never seen him and you're calling me about him?" I don't answer the implied question. "He has brown hair, usually a beard. Five foot nine and too skinny, in my opinion. He's got a scar on his right knee from a bike accident when he was a kid and a tattoo of *The Giving Tree* across his back."

My heart drops into my stomach. I nod to Mikey. He closes his eyes. I should be relieved this man, at least, will get a certain ID. But first I have to do the worst job a police officer ever has to do. I can't bring myself to say those words yet. So, I stall.

"Mrs. Calderon, can you give me any information on why your son's been in Alaska?"

"He's staying with friends in Anchorage. Are you going to tell me what this is about or are you going to keep asking me stupid questions?"

"Both, I'm afraid." I consider delivering the news now, but as soon as I do, any further information from her will be lost. "Do you know who these friends are?"

"No. He doesn't tell me things like that."

I inhale deeply and intentionally exhale softly for as long as I can. I glance at Mikey. He nods slowly. I soften my voice to sympathetic.

"Mrs. Calderon, I'm afraid I have some news." I hear the sharp intake of breath. "We can't make any definitive conclusions yet…"

She's already heaving, but between gasps she hisses, "Oh, just spit it out!" I don't take her abruptness personally.

"A young man was found in Whittier, Alaska. He matches your description of Kyle, and he's given the name Kyle Calderon at a hotel here in Seward. He's…" My throat squeezes shut, and I'm going to cough or choke, but through my own discomfort, I hear Mrs. Calderon wheezing, trying to catch her breath. She needs to hear what I'm having trouble saying, so I force myself to voice the words. "I'm afraid he is dead." I close my eyes against a vision of her breakdown just as she begins to scream. Then there's a shuffling noise and a man's voice on the line.

"Hello? Who *is* this?" After confirming I am speaking to Mr. Calderon, I re-explain. Thirty seconds pass before I hear his voice again.

"Kyle is supposed to come home on a Saturday morning flight. I'm planning to pick him up. His job starts Monday. I can give you his flight number if that helps."

I say it does and he goes off to find the information. Of course, it doesn't help anything, but he needs the moment away from the phone where he feels like he's being helpful. I can use the time too. After he's given me the information, I ask when he can get out to Seward. He assures me they can be here first thing tomorrow.

"Mr. Calderon, does Kyle have any…history…of getting into trouble?"

Mikey shakes his head. I guess he would have waited on that. I sigh, disappointed in myself for trying to steer the conversation back to territory that's comfortable for me.

More time passes before Mr. Calderon answers. His voice sounds muffled. "No. He never gets into any sort of trouble. But he is a free spirit, I suppose, and sometimes he launches into his...adventures... without fully knowing how to prepare. Is that what happened? Did he go out hiking and...?"

"We're not sure yet, Mr. Calderon." The Calderons are grieving. We can speak of the suspected foul play and the need for an autopsy when they are here and the ID is confirmed.

"I see." His voice is almost a whisper.

"Mr. Calderon, you mentioned hiking. Does your son have hiking experience?"

"Some. He's hiked Utah and Arizona for a few days at a time. But Alaska is different. He must not have..." I hear sobbing in the background. "Did he...was he hiking when this happened?"

"This person......well, he was found on a mountain in a remote town. We don't know how he came to be there, but the people who met him here said he hiked all over the state, so that's possible."

"He hasn't been in Anchorage?"

"My understanding is he may have been for a while, but he explored a lot of the state before he got to Whittier."

He asks my name, thanks me, and assures me he'll be in Seward as soon as possible before he hangs up. Mikey's eyes look misty. I'm having trouble seeing clearly too.

I call Anna to warn her tomorrow will be a rough day. And there's still this evening to endure.

❖

The funeral is just a few family members and Lee's coworkers from the snow machine shop. Everyone is dressed in work clothes and parkas except Mikey and me. We are still in uniform. We meet at the Stantons' house and follow them up the mountain to the burial site. The body is in a simple plywood box bungeed to a larger snow machine. Mikey told me lots of Alaskans don't like a full formal funeral—they'd rather just be cremated or buried quickly.

Tails is with us. Lee's mom pets his head and tears up a little as he trots beside us.

The wind makes it difficult for the pallbearers—all the men

present—to get the body up the mountain. It's about a quarter mile to the burial site, and the wind barrels straight into our faces. Lee's dad helps carry for a short time before a coworker takes his place, joining Mikey, Lee's cousin, and three other friends from work. Nobody speaks on the way, and even Tails's energy is subdued. His forehead wrinkles as if he's worried.

There's already a hole, though it's lightly lined with fresh snow. It can't have been an easy dig. It's only a few inches larger than the coffin's dimensions. Wordlessly, the pallbearers lower the box into the ground with a pulley system. My stomach sinks with the box as I picture the headless body inside. The thought makes me nauseous. I squeeze my eyes closed to steady myself. In the brief blackness, I see Lee Stanton, shivering, cut up and injured, rubbing his hands over a fire, head still on.

Mrs. Stanton says a few words and reads a Bible verse, but her words are a flat monotone. Everyone has their heads bowed respectfully, even Tails, though his nub wags slowly. I stroke his head to keep from running down the mountain to the Tank and driving straight back to Anchorage.

The whole event lasts maybe twenty minutes, and most of that is the guys throwing dirt on the grave with pre-placed shovels. It's over. Mr. Stanton grabs his wife's hand, and they thank us for finding their son. It's a terrible moment. There's something humbling about a couple that has experienced the worst thing parents can—the death of their child—and can still manage to be thankful someone found his dead body.

Mikey says his good-byes to Mrs. Stanton. I nod since I cannot speak. She's not crying, and I can't even swallow around the lump in my throat for fear of choking. Mr. Stanton rubs his wife's back as he walks her back downhill, away from the homemade cross that marks where the headless body lies.

It's not until they've gone, and the shop guys have silently slipped off into the swirling snow, that I find the will to move. And then it's only because Mikey taps me on the shoulder, concern on his face.

"You okay, Louisa?"

"I don't know."

"Yeah. I get it. But there's nothing we can do here. Let's leave him be now."

We navigate our way back to the Tank, Tails sticking so close he frequently bumps his warm body against my leg.

❖

Back at the hotel, I barely remember to say good night to Mikey. He makes me look him straight in the eye and tell him I'm okay. I do, but it's like looking at someone in a dream when your subconscious hasn't fully reconstructed their face.

I fall on the bed clothed. I don't brush my teeth or complete any of the rest of my bedtime routine. Tails does a lap around the bed. I don't move. He curls next to me, wide awake. I haven't fed him, but he doesn't whine.

I haven't cried, but perhaps he senses I've had enough tears for one evening.

CHAPTER TWENTY

Something is outside the door. There's scratching—like fingernails scraping—down the cheap wood. The door never opens, but suddenly there's Lee. Lee with half his face blown off. The eye that remains stares blankly ahead. On the other side, shards of skin hang coated in dried blood. He walks toward the bed, and pieces of flesh and clumps of hair fall soundlessly to the ground. He doesn't notice.

His expression changes. It's not neutral. It's not anger, though I deserve anger. I wish it were anger, I know how to run from anger, but I don't know how to react to Lee's sadness. He wants me to understand something, but he cannot speak. He doesn't have a mouth anymore.

The light of day does not come soon enough. Everything is fuzzy and spins slightly. I'm not sure whether I slept, so the feeling of waking from a bender and hallucinations makes some sense. Tails is wide awake and taps his nose against his bowl.

As soon as I hear movement on the other side of the wall, I call Mikey to ask when he'll be ready to leave. If the Calderons took an overnight to Anchorage, it's possible they caught a charter at sunrise. I don't want to keep them waiting.

❖

The Calderons are not at the hospital when we arrive, but the media is back. And they have company. There are thirty-five extra people beyond the reporters, camera crews, and townies I recognize from the other evening.

"Who are these people?" I whisper to Mikey without looking at him, but I don't know what makes me think he would know. I watch him shake his head out of the corner of my eye. Part of me wants to turn back around. *I don't have the energy for this.*

We try to go around the crowd, but the reporters are on us. They all ask variations of the same question at the same time. *"Who is the body in the morgue?"* I ignore them and instead turn to a civilian with a scarf wrapped halfway around her face.

"I'm sorry, but are you and these other folks all reporters?" I already know the answer, but she helps exactly how I hope she will.

"My name's Glenna Johnson, from Nanwalek. I'm here—" She turns to the other plain-clothes people and motions at them with a wave of her hand. "I think a lot of us traveled here because we want to know if the body you found is a person we're looking for." I am confused, and obviously so, because she continues. "My husband Tom has been missing for weeks now. His description would be the same as Branden Halifax's—about five foot ten with thin, brown hair and a beard—so if it's not him, maybe it's my Tom." Her lip trembles a little, then stops.

They do not know about the tattoo. Maybe I should tell them, but they've come all this way. I can't bring myself to kill their hope so quickly.

"Ma'am, I'm sorry, but the body here has only been deceased a few days. I—"

"Oh, that's okay! He was the type to try to survive outside. It could be he was living off the land and just recently died." She sounds almost joyful. I turn to address all of them, cameras flashing in my face, making them all vague ghost-like outlines.

"Are you all here hoping the man we have is someone you're missing?" They all nod enthusiastically, then many talk at the same time, trying to tell me the name of their person and their story. I have no idea what to tell them, nor how. I look at Mikey. He nods at me and steps forward.

"We appreciate you coming out. This must be a difficult day for you. We know how few people are found, and to have this sliver of hope is a beautiful thing. We truly appreciate it." Some of them smile at him. None of them interrupt.

"We believe we know who the man is we have inside. We contacted his family and they confirmed he is indeed missing. They are on their way now, and their plane should arrive any moment." That's a lie. They may not even arrive today given the weather.

"When they arrive, we ask for your respect and patience. Please let them try to identify their son in peace and privacy. If for some reason this person is not who we think he is, *then* we will discuss further details."

An elderly man in a wheelchair speaks. A woman stands behind him. I don't envy them navigating a chair around Alaska in this weather. "But since they're not here yet, can't we view the body to see if it's any of ours?"

"I'm afraid not, sir. I'm sure you understand this is a very sad time and this process must be orderly. How long has your person been missing?"

"Four months. But if he was in the snow, then the body might—"

Mikey holds up his hand. "I completely understand, but you see, all of you have had at least a little time to cope with the disappearance of your person. The parents who are on their way...They just found out late yesterday. Do you remember how it felt those first few days?" All their faces cloud in near unison. Some of them tear up. "Would you have wanted to see your loved one with a crowd of other people?" Some of them look down. Others shake their heads. "Right. It's very private. Even though you're all grieving, it's still a private thing. So, here's my suggestion. This is a rare occurrence, so many people gathered with missing loved ones who can understand and relate to each other. Why don't you all stay for a bit—there are some great restaurants downtown. Get to know each other a little. Break bread together. And as soon as we have an update, we'll send officers around to let you know what's happening. Or you can call me if you'd rather."

He walks around the crowd distributing his business card. It's a bold move, and I don't offer mine. I'm already having visions of grief-stricken parents and wives calling me in the middle of the night. Besides, I'm certain my hands would shake if they weren't stuffed into my pockets. My nerves are on edge. I just want to hide.

"We can't wait here at the hospital so we're here if it's not who you think it is?"

"I'm afraid not, ma'am. It's a tiny hospital and it would be impossible to not make it even more cramped and uncomfortable for the parents who are about to arrive, never mind the hospital workers and their patients."

The woman who asked nods and turns to a man standing next to her. A dozen side conversations ensue. They're planning where they should go to wait. They mill around, unsure. Some look at me, maybe because I spoke first. I clear my throat.

"We suggest the Showdown on the main drag. They have a very good peanut butter pie. If you tell them the police department recommended them, they'll treat you right." They will too. All the local businesses do.

They disperse in a few separate groups.

❖

Anna is inside, of course. When I see her, I nearly fall into her. Mikey is still a little behind me, so she lets me lean my head against hers for a moment. She doesn't even ask what's wrong until I've composed myself enough to stand upright.

"There's a crowd outside."

"I wondered what was going on. One of the interns mentioned dozens of people in the parking lot."

"They're all missing a loved one who looks like Kyle Calderon. Or reporters."

Her eyes get big. "That's a first. I've had a few cases where a couple families showed hoping it was someone they loved, but that many people can't all be from around here."

"No, I believe a lot of them traveled in."

"That's extraordinary. I mean, I know it's overwhelming and it won't make your job any easier. But it's kind of remarkable too, don't you think?"

"I'm having trouble thinking anything right now. I didn't sleep." I rub the back of my hand over my eyes in circles. She places her hand on my shoulder. I look past her. She must have arrived very early, because she already has the body on the table covered with a white sheet. Mikey comes in, and we have only a few moments of comfortable, peaceful silence before the Calderons arrive.

❖

The Calderons don't take long to officially ID their son, after which the chief sends a car to take them wherever they want to go. As soon as they've gone, Mikey's phone rings. It's one of the people from the crowd this morning, wondering whether the body was who we thought it was. The caller is at the Showdown but informs Mikey another group went to the restaurant across the street, and a few others talked about going to one of the waterfront places. We decide to split up to go have those conversations.

I hang back for a few minutes to talk to Anna while Mikey heads to the Showdown. But we don't speak. She just hugs me. I want to be able to say that it's all I need, but even as I breathe in the amber smell of her hair and enjoy the warmth of her pressed against me, I'm conflicted. My head swims with all the possible scenarios of how Kyle came to be on top of a mountain. Why Branden's footsteps disappear on an airstrip. How Kyle ended up with either Lee or Branden on a cruise ship. I know Anna is trying to comfort me and I appreciate it so much, but I want so badly to sit with all the evidence and go over it again and again until I see whatever it is I'm missing.

I welcome Anna's hands as they rub my back. It feels good, but I realize if I'm not careful, Anna could distract me from my cases through no fault of her own. It's happened before. In my last DCS case, I tried so hard to keep my ex happy, I missed details I should have seen. If I had just stayed focused, maybe it would have ended differently.

Anna is talking. I ironically haven't been paying attention.

"I'll speak with the Calderons about the autopsy. Don't worry about it, okay? You should try to get some rest."

Rest. *That's funny.* I just nod and wander out the door.

❖

They're gathered in a group of fifteen or so at a restaurant with views of the docked boats. None of them watch the sea lions and otters play. They all lean slightly in toward each other around a heavy log table lacquered to a high, dark shine. There are a few plates of mussels and scallops between them at random intervals along the table, but no one eats. Their tones are so quiet I can't hear them until I'm almost on top of them. A teenage boy on the end spots me. He stands, and the rest fall silent. Several of them stand too.

"Officer." The man in the wheelchair placed on the end nearest me says my title as a simple greeting. But I hear it as a question. They're waiting.

I sit on the bench seat of the next table, facing the group. Their faces are expectant, hopeful, almost happy. I wish I didn't have to take that away. I close my eyes briefly to center myself and to summon my courage.

"The family has positively identified the body. I'm so sorry." They take it well. No one shouts or curses. No one looks angry. A few of them shut their eyes. Many squeeze hands with the person seated or standing on either side of them. They are bonded, as family and strangers, experiencing the same disappointment and hurt all over again. An elderly woman with tears welled in her eyes is the first to thank me, and then they all do. None of them move as I stand to go, but I'm compelled to sit again. They've come all this way, and I can't just dash their hopes and run away. *What would Mikey say?* I think of his beautiful words and calm phrasing, then dismiss the thought. Words are not me. I'd think myself in circles trying to come up with the right line.

"Well, you're all here because you are looking for someone, and you think they could have wandered far from home. I'm guessing most of you reported in your hometowns, so we wouldn't have information about your people here in Seward, or in Anchorage, where I'm from. How about if you tell me your stories so I can have that information in case anyone shows up?" It's the right thing to say, and I know it by the collective exhale. They all start to speak at once, then all stop to look at each other. They somehow silently determine the man in the wheelchair will go first, and they look to him.

"My name is Stanley Gussido, and this is my wife, Lena. We're looking for our son." His wife doesn't speak, just nods as he tells their story. Based on the tears muddying her eyeliner, I'd guess he is able to keep the more even tone as he tells me about the drug-addicted son who came home to recover, but who ran away because he thought his parents judged him every time he relapsed. They've been searching for Marty for four months. The police spent a couple of weeks looking, but no one had seen him and there was no reason to believe he wanted to be found.

It's only when he's finished that I think to pull out my notebook and jot some basic notes. When I ask if they happen to have a picture of their son, Mrs. Gussido pulls a stack of at least ten 3x5 shots of Marty from her purse and hands me one. The son stands between them, smiling in a graduation robe. They've carefully circled him in red marker.

Mr. Gussido nods to the next person, a young woman who looks about Kyle and Branden's age. She keeps her story concise and sticks to the facts. Her brother is the missing person. He went out backcountry camping with his friends. They were "going hunting," which usually meant they were going to drink and let the animals pass them by. His friends returned, but he didn't. They said they'd woken up in the morning to find him gone. She has no evidence to say that's not what happened, though she sets her mouth sternly when she says so. She has pictures too, all different ones. There's something about the one she gives me; I know she took it. Maybe it's the delicate way she handles it. Her brother is smiling over his shoulder, hand on the leash of a dog just out of the picture as they walk through the woods. He's been gone for ten months.

They're all like this. The circumstances vary wildly, but the stories of the people they've left behind are the same. Suspicion about what happened. Police searches truncated by weather and a lack of clues. The overall feeling that maybe the missing just didn't want to be found. The families searching endlessly. The lack of peace. The cruel and razor-sharp hope.

My eyes burn, and my cheeks feel swollen. My throat feels like I have strep. I flip my notepad shut. There's one page for each of them, and now there are seven photos tucked between its pages. As they leave, all of them waiting until all the stories are finished, they shake my hand in turn. I give each of them my card. It feels deeply impersonal compared to what they've given me.

CHAPTER TWENTY-ONE

Mikey doesn't tell me about his conversations with the families in the morning, and I don't tell him about mine, or how I didn't sleep at all last night. We just go right back to the Halifax case. I, at least, am anxious to get my mind on something more concrete.

While Mikey pours his to-go cup of hotel coffee, I flip open my wallet and look at the photocopy of the yellow notepad paper we found in Camelot. I rifle through my *buy ten get one free* punch cards until I find the crisp white business card with green lettering. It's the one Mr. Drew gave us when we first visited him. The phone number on it isn't the same as the one on the paper. I must look disappointed because Mikey asks what's up.

"I thought this number was Mr. Drew's, but it's not."

"Well, the area code's right for this area. The station probably keeps a list of phone numbers for folks outside of town so they can do winter check-ins." I raise an eyebrow. "Rural Alaskans look out for each other." Makes sense. It would be hard for folks on the mountain to get supplies in the winter—they could easily starve without the right resources.

I borrow the reception phone and call the station to see if they have such a list. They do. I listen to some crackling hold music while they find the right number for me. When the desk attendant returns, she tells me it's the phone number for Branden and Marli Lei Halifax. *Jackpot.*

So now we have a paper in Kyle's possession with Mr. Drew's name and Branden's phone number—a solid link between the three. This is obviously the lead we need, but we have to approach it delicately.

Going to Mr. Drew first isn't wise—we need more before we revisit him. We'll have to go back to Marli eventually, but she won't appreciate us trying to connect her boyfriend to a thief. We decide Branden's friends might be the best option. If they can explain the connection between Kyle and Branden, that might be our best chance of figuring out both men's fates.

It's a little bit of a drive out to Kolit's, and my thoughts wander back to my meeting at the restaurant. Even though it's frigid out, I ask Mikey if he minds cracking the windows. He obliges, and we both breathe in deep lungfuls of the cold air. I try to relieve the nausea of hearing all those stories. Everywhere I look I imagine bodies under the snow, in crevasses and streams, hanging from trees and lying decayed in abandoned buildings.

Kolit's Hole has a *Twin Peaks* vibe. It's a seemingly random compilation of extremely rough-cut wooden buildings. I'd bet almost all were built with hand tools. They cling to the side of the mountain as if they might fall off and tumble their way down into the fjords.

A combination mud and stone road runs through the middle of the clump of houses. The bar is at the end, which means Eliyah is the log cabin two doors down. AJ should be easy enough to find; the hardware store occupies the same building as the bar. We decide to start there.

The Tank is the only vehicle parked in front of the place. The door pulls open easily, but it's silent inside. I don't know why I expected to find the bar and the hardware shops occupying separate sides of the building, but that's not the case. We walk into rows of wrenches and gardening gloves, as well as an endcap of random tourist stuff—Alaska sweatshirts and decorative-handled knives that advertise as carved by Native Alaskans, but somehow all look assembly-line identical. There's a musty, sawdusty smell as if someone does woodwork indoors. The ceilings are low, and the paint peels badly all around. Not exactly the kind of place I'd want to drink in, but there's the bar, right in the back of the shop. One row of liquor is lined up neatly along the long wooden slab countertop made for slamming glasses. There are a couple guys at the end on swiveling stools with pleather green seat cushions. Given the lack of cars outside, I'm guessing these are locals. One of the men spots us.

"Help you with anything?" He yells the length of the building. When we don't answer, he sets down his pint glass, sloshing amber-colored beer over the side, and hurries toward us, a slight limp slowing his pace. He's done a rough job of shaving—there's still some stubble around his neck, and he's nicked himself in a few places. I notice the laugh lines around his brown eyes and wonder if he's a bit older than Branden or if he's just been out in the sun without a hat more often.

"I'm Officer Linebach, and this is Officer Harper." He grabs my extended hand with enthusiasm. His nails are rough to my skin.

"Oh, right. I heard you would be around. I'm AJ. You're here about Branden."

"That's right."

"Well, that's Eliyah at the bar." The other man is in a leather bomber jacket and has a round, bearded face and a light brown complexion. He nods at me. "We're both good friends of Branden, so we're happy to help any way we can. You want a drink or anything?"

"I'm afraid we can't drink on the job, but I'd take some coffee if you've got some."

Mikey nods in agreement.

"Sure thing! Have a seat." AJ moves briskly around the bar and slaps down a couple of coasters. The guy clearly takes pride in the place.

"So, you own the hardware store. You run the bar too?"

"I own it, yes. Inherited the hardware store from my pop, but it's hard to make enough sales to make a living round here, so I added the bar in. Did the trick! Whole town does its drinking here. No need to go down to Seward." He warms a pot of pre-brewed coffee as he talks. I wonder how many times it's been reheated.

"Clever," Mikey says.

"Yeah. It's been a great business! And you know, when I did it I was just thinking about the profits, but it's been great for the town. Keeps everybody sociable in the winter, you know? We can get isolated here when it starts snowing serious."

Eliyah nods slowly and agreeably at everything AJ says. *Could be Eliyah's a little high.* AJ continues.

"People get depressed and all, during the dark time. Used to be people would sit in their houses by themselves and drink. Now, they at least can come round here and drink together, talk it out and all. Keeps everyone up to date with each other."

"Makes sense. So, everyone in the area comes around here?"

"Oh, yeah. There's the folks who live in Kolit's, then there's folks like Mr. Drew and all that live a few miles out." I carefully avoid a look at Mikey. "They come around too, most weekends."

"Mr. Drew comes in sometimes?"

"Oh yeah, most every weekend! Isn't that funny? Man's probably got the best stocked bar in Alaska right there in his own house and he comes in here." He beams like it's a winning testament to his entrepreneurship. "You met Mr. Drew yet? He's a good dude."

"We have met him, yes. We talked to him out at his place."

Eliyah throws his eyebrows in the air and whistles at a high pitch. "Wheeew! So, you saw that bar yourself. Quite a place, right?"

Mikey laughs roundly. "It's definitely something."

Eliyah nods. "He's done a lot for this area. Brings in a lot of money, and he likes to use locals for his work. That's why he comes in here—find folks to do odd jobs. Sometimes it's about the only thing saves us in the winter."

"Shut up, Eli." AJ smacks at Eliyah with a dishcloth. "He comes in here because I make a mean gin and tonic."

"You even *have* tonic?"

"It's my business, don't tell me how to run it!" Eliyah just shakes his head while AJ pours our coffee. It smells burnt. Good thing I like it that way.

"What does Mr. Drew do, again? We know Branden worked with him in construction."

"Yeah, construction for sure," AJ says. "He builds most everything in the whole area, and he fixes everything whether he built it or not. He's got some other side businesses too, stuff he does in the winter. I know he flies in supplies and does deliveries and whatnot."

"And he helps put up a lot of the businesses in Seward," Eliyah chimes in. "Guess he, like, buys a stake in them or whatever. Lot of those little shops and restaurants there couldn't have got started without the extra cash. Hell, he's technically the owner on most of them."

"He sounds very important around here. You said he does supplies and deliveries in the winter. So, he's got planes?"

"Yeah, I think he's got a few of them, and a couple different airstrips. Not sure if he owns them all, but he uses a bunch of them.

That's a good business he's got going. He flies stuff all over the place, gives an awful lot of pilots work. That's why Branden got his pilot's license—so he could fly for Mr. Drew."

"When Mr. Drew comes in here, who does he usually talk to?" Eliyah speaks this time.

"Oh, we all try to talk to Mr. Drew! He offers the best-paying jobs around here, so soon as he sits down, it's sort of a competition to see who's going to get to sit next to him." He laughs.

"I'm guessing you've tried to get that seat yourself?" Mikey uses his talent for making everything seem casual and innocuous.

"Yeah, but it doesn't usually pan out. I don't have a pilot's license."

"It's true, he just hitches a ride whenever he needs one."

"Shut up. I pay you in booze!" Eliyah nods to the bottles on the shelf.

"You pay me in cheap crap I gotta pour into fancy bottles so the guys won't notice how bad it is."

I choke back my laugh. They bicker like an old couple. Then again, they've probably spent so much time together up here they might as well be. I turn back to AJ.

"How about you? Do you ever try to get jobs?"

"Oh absolutely! Hell, it's worked a few times. Oh, sorry. I cuss more than I ought to." Mikey waves it off with a chuckle. "He's given me a few really good gigs."

"Like what?"

"Oh, private contract jobs. I do some woodwork, building furniture and all. He's had me build some stuff for his place and a lot of the shops he works with, you know." He looks at his hands, which are thoroughly calloused around the beds and tips.

"Anything else?"

"Just the woodworking gigs and errand runs. That's it."

"What kind of errands?" Mikey leans forward.

"I drop off cash for people in Seward when he doesn't feel like going."

"Cash for what?"

"I don't know. Never thought to ask."

"Does anyone ever give you anything for him?"

AJ looks at Mikey as if for affirmation he needs to answer my question. I don't get the impression he *wants* to lie to me. Something about the set of his eyes and the open body posture says he's an honest person, and I like to think I have a good eye for that. I'm betting he's just loyal. He looks me in the eye when he speaks.

"Yeah. Occasionally the people I drop off checks to give me padded envelopes."

"Any idea what's in there?"

"No. I really can't tell you. I never asked." He puts his hands up as if to say, *Search me, that's all I've got.* I believe him.

"So, you're both close with Branden."

"Branden and I've known each other forever." Eliyah answers first. "Least since middle school. He's a real good person. See him every weekend in the cold months. He used to come round the bar a lot more often, but since he got with Marli—well, you know." He gives this information good-naturedly and with no eye roll. He's not jealous of Marli Lei.

"Well, having kids will do that."

"They're sweethearts too." He swirls the remnants of his beer around in his glass. "That's why we were all surprised when we heard Branden was missing. Heck, people disappear all the time around here, usually because they don't want to be found. But Branden? He wouldn't do that. He loves those kids, and he loves Marli."

"So, you think whatever happened to him was some sort of accident?"

"Yeah. Definitely. Branden...He can be a little, I don't know. Maybe reckless? I don't really want to say that. It makes it sound like he takes risks a lot on purpose, and it's not really like that. He just...he doesn't always think things through."

"Can you give us an example?"

"Eh, I don't know. He just...just stupid stuff. Like he always overestimates how long he can run the boat on the gas he has. He's gotten himself stranded a bunch of times." Eliyah turns to AJ and grins. "He's gotten all of us stranded like that before."

"Eliyah, AJ, if Branden wrecked his car a few miles from home, what do you think he'd do?" They both scowl, but they don't look to each other for confirmation before they almost simultaneously respond to my question.

"He'd try to walk home," Eliyah says.

"He'd just leave the car and walk back to the house," AJ says. Mikey nods.

"It looked that way when we found the truck. There were footprints leading away from it. But they lead to the airstrip, then stop. Any thoughts on that?"

"It's weird." Eliyah nods adamantly as AJ speaks—it's obvious they've had this conversation, mulling it over. "I can't think of any reason he would have been going out there. He would have gone to Mr. Drew's for sure, pick up his check and all, but he wouldn't have had any reason to go past Drew's, or to the airstrip. That's just…bizarre."

I look at Mikey again, and he nods. "We should let you know we are aware Branden was into some drugs." They both lean back on their stools, frowning and probably concerned. "It's okay. It's not a big deal. We're only interested in drugs if it might explain what happened to Branden."

They both look skeptical. Finally, AJ nods. "Yeah. He did like to do some stuff every once in a while, on the weekend. Nothing too bad, I don't think. Not like, heroin or whatever. Just some pills. Maybe some weed. Coke if it was around."

"Did he usually buy from people around here?"

"I think so. We didn't really talk about it much. He'd just kind of show up with it."

"Had he started hanging around with anyone new or different?"

AJ scrunches his face and looks at Eliyah. "What was that hitchhiking kid's name? Didn't you meet him at the house?" *Yes.* This is where I wanted us to get.

"Oh, yeah. Yeah. Hang on, it'll come to me…" Eliyah fiddles with a stray long hair in his beard.

I wink at Mikey, whose pen is ready.

"Kyle! The kid's name was Kyle." He snaps back to it and remembers Mikey and I are there. He explains. "Branden picked up this hitchhiker a couple weeks ago. He's hiking around Alaska or something, I guess. Branden had him up to his place. They were having some beers and he invited me over."

My heart's beating hummingbird-fast and I swear I can hear Mikey's from several feet away. He's sweating when I glance at him. "Was Marli there?"

"Nah, she was out in town with the kids. The baby needed some stuff, I think. She wanted to get down there before the snow got bad."

"So, what can you tell us about Kyle?"

"Eh, he seemed all right, I guess. Probably twenty-four? Twenty-five? Brown hair, scraggly. Real excited about being in Alaska, I can tell you that. He was kind of wired. Drugs maybe, but maybe not. Got the impression that's just sort of how he is. Excited about life."

"Did he tell you where he's from?" I hardly hide my excitement. *This has to be our Kyle.*

"I asked. He was sort of cagey about it, but he eventually mentioned Portland. I laughed at him. He did not like that, I don't think." He laughs as he explains. "I been to Portland once. Not my kind of town. People there think they're rugged mountain men." His grin reveals a broken tooth right in the top middle. "Anyway, real rugged mountain men who enjoy a spiced latte when they're done with their three-mile hike in their designer boots."

Mikey chuckles and I laugh. "He didn't say much of anything about it after that. I asked if he'd been in college. He just said *yeah* and changed the subject. Wouldn't say a thing about his family. Just raised his beer and said he was shaking all that off now—starting over with his life by seeing the world. Something about really getting out there in it. You know. The usual."

"Did he say how long he was planning to stay around here? Or, hell, how he even ended up out here? It's far out from Seward."

"Hitchhiked. Said it was too touristy down there, so he waited around the hardware store till he met a local—that happened to be Branden. Asked Branden to show him somewhere that was *real* Alaska. So, Branden brought him here. He said he liked it. Said he'd come drink with us that weekend. You know—weekend when Branden didn't show. Branden wanted to help the kid out—even offered to introduce him to Mr. Drew, see if he could get him a job."

I concentrate on controlling my breathing. "So, Branden was supposed to pick him up again and bring him here?"

"I guess so."

I'm anxious to get back to the station. Kyle Calderon is clearly Branden's hitchhiker, and being able to connect the two, especially around a common theme of drugs, gives us a lot more avenues than we've had so far with Branden Halifax. Plus, it's more likely it was the two of them stealing from the cruise ship passengers. I'm already considering my excuse for why we need to go when I remember we intended to talk to someone else out here in Kolit's.

"AJ, would it be possible for us to talk to your mom?"

He laughs in surprise. "My mom? Oh, shit—am I in trouble?"

"Yeah, and nope." Per his usual, Mikey sounds nice and casual.

"Mind if I ask why?"

"Oh, it's nothing bad. Promise." I force my version of a Mikey chuckle. "A few folks now have mentioned some interesting theories about the airstrip where Branden's footprints stop, and we hear your mom might know something about that."

AJ's eyeroll is exaggerated and Eliyah bursts out laughing so enthusiastically I think the buttons on his flannel might pop as he lolls back on his stool. "Jesus! Not the aliens—"

"Yes, the aliens, I'm afraid." Mikey plays up the stern cop face.

"Well, it's her favorite topic, so I hope you've got plenty of time."

I look at Mikey and crack a smile. "Well, *I* didn't have any big plans for the night. You?"

"Nope! Just so happens I've got no hot dates!"

AJ and Eliyah laugh. "Well then, have at her. I'll walk you over. He throws a dishrag at Eliyah. "You mind?" Eliyah catches it but makes no move to head behind the bar—just nods into his beer.

As we walk the couple hundred yards down the street, I ask AJ a question that's been nagging me the past couple days.

"Hey, don't take this the wrong way, but I've noticed nobody but Marli seems too bothered about Branden disappearing."

AJ looks thoughtful as he steps over the raised cracks in the makeshift sidewalk. "Oh, it's not that. We're plenty upset about it. Hell, it's about the only thing anybody talks about. We really like Branden and we're worried for Marli and those kids. It's just...I don't know. You live around here long enough, you get to know a lot of people who disappear."

"Do *you* know a lot of people who've disappeared?"

"Yeah. Five or six. Mainly men who've come through town. And my brother."

"Oh wow. I'm so sorry."

"It's all right. That was a long time ago." AJ lets out a long sigh. "Damn. Twenty-seven years ago, now."

"What happened, if you don't mind?"

"Oh yeah, it's okay. We lived out on the way to Anchorage then. You would have passed by the place when you drove out here if you went along the coast. Anyway, when I was a kid, my little brother liked to play out by the water. No big deal. We all did. But if you got too far from the house and went down along the water headed south, you'd hit the mudflats."

I can guess where this story is going. The mudflats are stretches of sandy beach that look stable, but can easily become like quicksand, trapping a person. Tourists often see animal prints on them and assume it's all right to walk there. What they don't know is that animals often get stuck themselves. I've gotten quite a few calls to the mudflats already, most ending badly.

"My brother...we think he wandered and got himself stuck. Then the tide came in."

"Oh no—"

"Yeah. There were footprints that led there. About his size. Then nothing."

"He was never recovered?"

"Nah. But it seemed straightforward at least. It made us all feel a lot better to know that, more than likely, that's what happened." He pauses outside the door of the place he shares with his mom. "Not like this stuff with Branden. This doesn't seem straightforward." He turns toward me and looks me directly in the eye. His stare is almost disconcerting. "I just hope, no matter what happened, Marli doesn't always have to wonder—that she feels like she knows what happened to him."

I think I understand.

❖

AJ lives in the upstairs apartment, and his mom is on the first floor. AJ just walks us straight into her place, past the landscape oil paintings in pine frames hung on spruce logs. The whole apartment smells like an evergreen forest with a hint of cinnamon coming from the back. It makes me want to curl up with one of the fleece throws flung across the sofa and take a nice long nap. Preferably with Tails, who's probably eating junk food at the station. When we arrive, AJ's mother is in the kitchen, which is separated in the back of the house. And she doesn't seem surprised in the least to see us.

"Aah," she says, stirring a large pot of a cinnamon-scented liquid, "there you are! I made something to drink." She ladles an auburn liquid into three blue speckled camp mugs that are already on the counter. *How did she know three people would be visiting?*

"Oh, I'm all right, Ma. Thanks, though." AJ pecks his mother on the cheek. Her face crinkles when she smiles.

"Nonsense. It's good for you." She fills one mug halfway, then tips in a splash of bourbon. She hands the steaming cup to her son. She hands the other mugs—no bourbon—to me and Mikey. AJ drinks his while he introduces us, then he excuses himself to return to the bar.

"Mrs. Butler, we're interested in the airstrip—the one Branden Halifax's truck was found next to. Given the rumors we've heard, sounds like some strange things happen there. We've been told you keep an eye on what goes on around here."

She pats the silver-white bun on top of her head. The hair is still thick, and it falls out of place the more she pats it. She eyes us with mischief, then motions for us to sit on the reclining sofa.

"Oh. Well, that's Mr. Drew's strip. Mr. Drew himself supposedly hasn't used it since the early '90s, you know. But I wouldn't say it's out of use…"

"So, who used it after the '90s?" She seems *very* happy I asked. I belatedly feel as if I have been lured into a trap.

"Well, *the guests*, of course. That's where they pick up the young men they take." She says it matter-of-factly, like we're talking about what happened on last week's episode of *The Golden Girls* over a spot of tea. This tea happens to be spiked. Mikey redirects the conversation.

"How many people do you know who've gone missing from around here?"

"Oh, since I was a kid, probably thirty, thirty-five. Not all from Seward, of course, but I read the papers for the whole peninsula."

"Do you remember anything about the other people who went missing, Mrs. Butler?"

She pats her hair again while she looks at Mikey. I hide a smirk behind my fist. *I think she's flirting with him.*

"Well, it so happens I *do* know quite a lot about the people who've gone missing. At least the ones from around Seward. There was

Caroline, who went missing when I was a kid, and then there was that young man Patrick a few years later. And that was just after Mr. Drew came into town and all his guys started to go missing. First there was that awful young man, George. He was trouble and I'm not sure anyone missed him at all. And—"

"Excuse me—I'm sorry, Mrs. Butler. Did you say the young men started to go missing when Mr. Drew moved here?" I check to make sure Mikey's scribing.

"Well, no one else will mention this, but after Mr. Drew moved here, the disappearances happened a lot more frequently, and it was mostly young men in their twenties or early thirties."

"Were they people who knew Mr. Drew?"

"Yes. All of them would have known Mr. Drew. Fact, pretty much all of them worked for him in one or another of his businesses."

"Mrs. Butler, are you saying you think Mr. Drew has something to do with the disappearances of the young men?" Mikey leans forward as he asks his question.

"Well, of course I do! It can't be a coincidence, can it? The number of missing persons goes up by the dozens and they all know *him*? My goodness, anyone who can't see the connection has their eyes closed. He's clearly the one who delivers them to the aliens."

I blink rapidly. She looks my way and I pretend I have something in my eye. Thank goodness Mikey covers me.

"Why would he do that?"

"Well, you're the police, I suppose that's what you have to find out, right?"

Mikey seems momentarily at a loss, so I ask a more practical question. "Mrs. Butler, have you seen aircraft taking off from the airstrip near his house?"

"I have. They come in the middle of the night. But they still must have lights, you know, so I see them. At two or three in the morning, they land for a few minutes, then take off again. Like they're picking something up."

"So, you think the planes are picking people up from Mr. Drew?"

"Yes. I think they have an agreement where he supplies them, and they leave him alone. Maybe they help him. Don't you think it's weird *he's* never disappeared? All alone on that mountain? He'd be the first person they'd go after, and yet they don't."

I squeeze my eyes and rub the spot where the bridge of my nose meets my head. "Well, I think that's about all we need, Mrs. Butler. Should be enough for us to get started." On what is unclear, but she seems satisfied because she nods. I am so relieved Mikey got us moving. "If we need anything else, we'll call in on you, all right?" I hold my breath, but thank everything, he doesn't give her a business card. "And thank you again for the drinks. That was just great."

She walks us to the door and fills us in on town gossip the whole way.

CHAPTER TWENTY-TWO

When we're safely back in the Tank, I look at Mikey and he bursts out laughing. His mirth escalates until he's howling, cackling so hard he grabs his side and falls over the arm rest. I can't help it—I smile too.

"My God!" The corners of his eyes are wet as he gasps. "My good Lord. If only the chief could have heard—"

"She was killing me. Possibly literally. My brain may be rotting as we speak."

"She is a character, that's for sure. Your facial expressions were priceless. I could have died laughing just looking at *you!*"

"I'm pretty sure she would have kept us there for days if she could have." I turn to him with a serious expression and my eyes wide. "That's where the men went!"

His face falls in sudden confusion. "Wait. What?"

"They didn't die or get abducted by aliens. AJ's mom invited them over for spiked tea and just *talked* them to death! She must have them buried in the basement. I bet that's why she lives on the first floor…"

Mikey's laughing all over again. Suddenly he grabs for the door handle. "Well, we better go back in there and do a search!"

I slap at his hand screaming "No!" and "Stop!" As we pull away, he's still recovering, wiping the tears from his eyes.

"Well, that was certainly a way to spend the evening." Mikey genuinely sounds like it was the most fun he's had in a long time.

"That it was. Possibly a waste of time, but definitely a way to spend the evening."

"Oh, I don't know about that. Her theories on Mr. Drew are pretty compelling."

I can't even tell if he's serious or not. "Hang on. Are you kidding right now? The aliens?"

"If a bunch of men really did go missing after he moved here, that's grounds for us to keep talking to him, isn't it?"

Clear grounds, but I'm amazed Mikey's on board with this line of thinking.

"Yes, it is. And those will be easy numbers to find." The pieces start to develop a picture. "Hey, what if he's having them run drugs? That would explain the padded envelopes and the cash, and why they so frequently disappear. It would also explain what the cook on the cruise ship said. If that was Branden and Kyle on board, they were attempting to sell to the kitchen, and apparently at least Kyle was stealing while at it."

Mikey turns to me, bobbing his head happily. "Dang. That's why I like working with you. You take a theory and run full tilt."

I do some sort of awkward laugh and break eye contact as quickly as possible. I've never known how to take a compliment.

When we reach the station, the officers are gone. There's a woman at the desk with multiple telephones. She wears a blue sweater, gray slacks, and no badge. I don't know her position, but she seems to be in charge of the place once everyone else goes home. I ask about Tails, and he emerges from underneath her desk, stretching dramatically.

"He's been fast asleep under there since nine thirty. Must be his bedtime."

"Hopefully he wasn't too much trouble." The dog sits in front of me, ready for ear scratching.

"None at all. He's a pleasure. The guys even stayed late to play with him."

"Well, thanks a lot. And hey, do you do any record pulling, by chance? Would we need to wait until tomorrow if we needed a little bit of information?"

She snorts. "I've been around here for so long they've had me do just about every odd job you could imagine *plus* dispatch. Only thing I won't do is make the coffee. That's my line."

"Understandable. You make it once and it's on you forever." I learned that lesson the hard way. "Would you mind finding out what year Mr. Drew moved to the area when you get a chance?"

"Oh, I'm pretty sure it was when I was ten or eleven, so right about 1985."

"Uh, wow. That's some recall—"

"My dad changed careers to run fishing tours for him since tourism was picking up. He's smelled like fish ever since." She laughs.

At least her dad is still alive. That's more than can be said about a lot of men who work for Mr. Drew.

We need those numbers, but I don't want to tip off Willington. I turn toward the door, but then act like I've just remembered something totally unrelated. I turn back.

"Oh, and if you could, we also need statistics on the number of missing persons who've disappeared from the Kenai area in the last thirty years." That should give us good grounds to compare who went missing before and after Mr. Drew moved here. She jots down my request.

"Oh hey, an autopsy report came in for you just a few minutes ago. Didn't know if you'd want to hold it for tomorrow."

I rush to her so fast she backs away from me. "I'd like it now, please."

She flips open a file on her desk and produces it. Mikey leans over my shoulder to read. *Kyle Calderon. Cause of death: Cardiac arrest caused by poisoning.* There's a lot I need Anna to interpret, but the examiner has written in the notes section. *Deceased young, so cardiac unusual. Likely cause is poisoning by baneberries in large quantity.* The examiner's contact information is at the end of the report, but we have all the confirmation we need—at least concerned with *how* he died.

Now for the why.

❖

Before we head out for the day, I review the stats pulled overnight. They confirm what AJ's mother stated—not about the aliens, of course, but about the dramatic increase in people going missing after Mr. Drew's arrival. There were missing persons cases before; a couple kids, a woman, a couple older men. Those continue after he arrives, but the number of missing men aged eighteen to forty starts climbing the year after he gets here by just one, then averages out to four per year after that. Some years there's none, but one year seven men in the age range go missing. It's incredible to me no one has drawn the correlation before. Or they have, and they think it's better to ignore it. Maybe it's no coincidence Mr. Drew is good friends with Chief Willington.

I need more information from Marli, and not just about Mr. Drew. I want to know if she was aware of Kyle. He was in her house. If he and Branden were dealing drugs or stealing together, she had to have known something about it.

Because of the heavy snow, it takes us about three times as long to get to Marli as it did the last time we visited. Other than that, nothing seems to have changed. Marli wears her bathrobe over some fleece leggings and a turtleneck sweater, and she still looks exhausted. The puffy bags under her eyes are beginning to take on a semi-permanent look, as if they might have been tattooed.

The kids are awake this time. The girl Alicia sits at the table, coloring well outside of the lines, while Marli bounces the baby on her hip. I get the impression it's to comfort herself more than the child. When we enter the kitchen, Marli asks her daughter to take the coloring to her room, and the pajama-clad girl gets up to do so without complaint. She stops to look at me and Mikey. Her hazel eyes are huge and significantly older than a child's eyes should be. She doesn't say anything but touches her lip with her finger. I crouch and hold out my hand.

"It's nice to meet you. I'm Louisa."

She just blinks at me, then stretches her hand out in slow motion. "Hi. I'm Alicia," she says while we shake. She keeps her eyes on mine as she goes off to her room, crayons falling from her hands. She waves as she closes the door. I smile, almost wishing she could stay in the room with us. I've always found children easier to talk to than adults, and I'm never more confident than when I'm helping a kid understand something.

Marli again offers coffee or tea, and again we both choose coffee. She puts the baby in a bassinet and moves it close to her, pours our cups and then wraps her hands around a steaming mug. Her hair is down, and curly ends graze the rim of her cup. She looks on the verge of sleep, but when we ask how she's doing, she just quirks the corners of her mouth up slightly and says she's fine. She hasn't seen any of Branden's friends, and she hasn't been keeping up with the news. No one has visited her.

"It's okay, though. People don't know how to talk to you when something like this happens. They care. I know they do. But what do they say? *Hey, sorry your boyfriend's been missing for a week. How about this weather?* It's easier to just stay away. And with me being up here, it's easy anyway."

"You must feel isolated, though. Have you had anyone to talk to about all this?"

She shrugs. "I call my mom sometimes. I've talked to Branden's mom, but she's so shaken *she* has a hard time even talking about it. I have a sister I talk to. But not really. I could, I guess. There's a lot of people in town who've had family members go missing. I just feel like, I don't know. Even if that's happened to a lot of people, it's never the same. It's not a shared experience. It's something you deal with alone."

"Do you feel like you're dealing with it all right?"

"Yes. No? I guess as well as anyone does. There's just nothing I can do. That's the thing. I have all this anxiety in me," she rests her hand on her diaphragm, "but there's just nothing *at all* I can do. I can't even go looking for him because of the kids, so I just take the anxiety and I clean, or I play peek-a-boo." She takes the baby's pinkie and waves it around. "But it's too intense. Sometimes she cries because I guess I'm scary. There's just so much worry and sadness…and anger built up. It feels…"

"Manic?" Mikey supplies the word, and she nods emphatically. "Are you sleeping?"

"No. Oh, no. Not since the day I realized he was gone." I'm glad Mikey's good at the emotional stuff, but I'm pretty sure if we continue *Psychology with Mikey*, we'll be here all day.

"Marli, what do you know about Branden's relationship with his boss?"

She tilts her head. "Mr. Drew?" When I nod, she jumps up to get another mug of coffee. She does it fast enough, she stumbles and has to grasp the chair's back. I recognize that symptom of insomnia, feeling slightly off balance. But I am also certain she's put her back to me on purpose. *Curious.* Her facial expression must show something she doesn't want me to see. She speaks with her back to us over the sound of pouring liquid.

"He really likes Mr. Drew." She pauses. "*Liked* Mr. Drew." Suddenly she turns toward us, her face vulnerable and open. "I don't know if I should use the past tense or the present tense. I wish I knew how to talk about him! How to think about him." I'm silent, and Mikey steps in.

"What do you think? When you think about Branden, in your stomach, in your heart, do you feel like he's alive?"

She resumes pouring her coffee, then takes our mugs and tops them off. I wonder if she even heard, but then she almost-whispers her answer into the steam.

"I don't want to say it out loud."

"It's all right. You're not going to say anything surprising to us, and we're not here to judge."

My foot taps a staccato rhythm under the table. I am annoyed with Mikey, maybe irrationally so, for pursuing a *conversation* that doesn't help us move the investigation along. I take some deep breaths in, and blow them out softly, but it doesn't help. All it does is make me realize I'm getting anxious.

This time, Mikey doesn't notice my anxiety. He's too busy listening to Marli.

"I feel like he's gone. I've felt that way since the day he disappeared. Like—this is going to sound silly to you, I'm sure—I feel like his energy just isn't in this world anymore."

"That doesn't sound silly at all. It's like walking into a house and knowing it's empty before you even look around. It's intuition."

"I guess so. But I'm supposed to hope, right? I'm supposed to be the grieving girlfriend who looks for him forever and just waits and waits."

Mikey speaks so slowly I find myself wanting to reach down his throat and pull the words out. My heart is thumping away in my chest. We're on to something and I don't want to waste time that could be used to find Branden.

"Marli, there's no right way for you to act. You're in an extremely unique situation. There's no good way to handle it. There's no grace in a thing like that. You just stumble through the days until it starts to get a little more bearable. And you pretend it's okay until it starts to *be* just a little bit okay." She reaches her hand out to touch Mikey's arm, and Mikey, having silent permission, covers her hand with his. "Don't worry about how you should react or what you should think. If you feel like he's not here, then I'm going to bet he's not here."

A tiny drop of moisture forms near the inner crease of Marli's left eye. She doesn't bother wiping it away. I wonder if it's an illusion—something caused by getting too close to the mug—her last bit of steam running out.

"Marli, did Branden's relationship to Mr. Drew seem unusual to you?"

"Unusual?" Her brows are furrowed.

"Yes. Did he ever hang with Mr. Drew outside of work? Did Mr. Drew call him at odd times? Did Branden ever take the phone elsewhere when Mr. Drew called?" She squints. I can't tell if she's being defensive or trying to remember.

"I don't think so? I mean, sometimes Mr. Drew would call late at night. But there were building emergencies and Branden would go help if, you know, the snow collapsed something."

Maybe Marli believed that, but I'm not buying it. Everything in Alaska is built to withstand snow. I keep pressing her.

"Did Branden ever leave town on business for Mr. Drew?"

"Of course. Mr. Drew's company builds all over the state. Sometimes he was gone for a week or more."

"Are you sure he was doing building jobs?"

She sits up straighter. "What else would he have been doing?"

I don't answer and instead fire back with another question of my own, trying to catch her by surprise—a technique that tends to work with people who are hiding something. "Marli, did you ever have any reason to think Branden was running drugs for Mr. Drew?"

She grabs the table, then leans back in her chair, gasping as if the wind's been knocked out of her. It takes several moments for her to recover.

"Drugs? For Mr. Drew?"

"That's right." I'm leaning forward and my heart is racing. I avoid looking at Mikey.

"No? I mean, I don't think so." I can see her chest heaving. "Like I said, Branden...liked to *take* something once in a while, but he would never *deal*."

"How can you be sure?"

She's agitated, her foot twitches rapidly. She won't make eye contact with me anymore and looks around the room.

"Because Branden would never endanger us. Me...the kids. He wouldn't have done that." She talks faster now. "And he didn't need the money. Mr. Drew paid him good money to work construction. We've never needed anything. He even has an insurance policy."

Now I know she's just trying to steer me away from this conversation. She told us before that she takes side work to supplement their income. *What is she trying so hard to avoid?*

"What if there was a faster way than construction to make sure you had what you needed? What if Mr. Drew pressured him? Don't you think Branden would have done it?" I'm following my own obsessive train of thought and I can't stop myself. *I've never been able to stop myself.*

She stands abruptly, both hands making a hollow smack on the table. "No. No! Branden wouldn't have. I know he wouldn't have. And if he would have, he would have told me first. We made decisions together."

I'm suddenly standing too. "Then how are you so sure he's dead? If he wasn't doing anything questionable, how can you know?"

"I just..." She looks at Mikey and her eyes almost plead for his interference. "I don't know. I *just know*. That's all."

Mikey stands too and walks to her side, places a hand on her shoulder, and looks at me as if I'm the enemy. I know I should stop myself, but I can't. *I need to know.* My voice is raised.

"Branden's footprints disappear at an airstrip. Branden running drugs for Mr. Drew explains everything. It would explain his hurry to get there and meet whoever was flying in on time. If it was a legitimate business exchange, there would have been a log of the flight and a record of the shipment." It makes so much sense. I want Marli to see it, to stop turning a blind eye.

"I just don't know." She falls into her chair as she speaks, defeated. She looks hurt, as if I've betrayed her.

Mikey's eyebrows are low, and he's not amused. The air suddenly abandons me. The muscles in my face pull, twist, the corners of my mouth rise and fall, my tongue forms words and then loses them. I can't continue.

"Louisa, maybe we should be going."

I look Marli straight in her eyes. I see pure hurt. I've fucked up. Badly. Any trust I built with Marli is now gone, all because I'm so anxious to make the connections and solve what happened to Branden that I've forgotten *she's* a victim in this situation. My chest feels constricted, like someone's rolled a massive stone onto it. I flare my nostrils, trying to take in more air. My heart beats erratically in my chest. I don't know what to do. I've attacked Marli. I need to get out of this house. I need fresh air. I can't form words, so I just nod to Mikey while I maintain eye contact with Ms. Lei.

Mikey starts toward the door. Marli goes with him to hold it open. In the doorway, I stop and turn deliberately toward her. There's nothing I can say, but I have to try anyway.

"Marli…" She shakes her head almost imperceptibly. *It's useless.* "If anything comes up." She just nods in silence.

Mikey wordlessly gets into the driver's seat of the Tank. I sink into the passenger's side like a child. I can't look at him. My head sinks onto my knees.

"Fuck." I try to breathe deeply, the way a therapist told me to years ago. "Fuck. Fuck. Fuck. We didn't even get to Kyle…" Mikey hasn't started the car yet. He's looking at me, and I wish he wasn't. I put the window all the way down and stick my head out.

"I fucked it up." I gasp the words out, my breathing still irregular. The silence is a thousand needles in my limbs. I can't look up. After what feels like at least five minutes, he speaks.

"What was that in there?" His voice no longer sounds like my partner's voice.

I shake my head between my hands. I don't know how to explain, but I owe him the effort.

"I just thought…I just kept thinking that we *have to* give her some sort of answer. Even if she thought he was dealing drugs. That's better than just thinking he's disappeared out in the wilderness forever, right?" I find the courage to look him in the eyes. He's cloudy, like I'm seeing him through fog. "Wouldn't you rather think…"

He shakes his head slowly. "No one wants to think that of someone they love." His words come out slowly, like they're pouring out of his mouth in a thick maple syrup. "If Branden was dealing drugs, that wouldn't just mean he was breaking the law. Clearly Marli could forgive that. But it would also mean he was lying to her. That he was betraying her and the kids. That he was putting them in danger, and for what? For a little extra cash?" He sets his face firmly in conclusion. "*No*. I wouldn't want to think that. I'd rather think the person I loved had fallen into a crevasse or been carried away by a bear than to think they'd been lying to me all along."

He looks at me, then he starts the Tank. The roar of the engine is embarrassingly deafening. I know Marli can hear it, and she knows somehow what this conversation has been. I can't stand the thought of it.

"It got away from me. I wanted to give her closure, or I thought I did. But I want to give myself closure too, and I just...I let my need be more important. I lost track of where she is and what she needs." Mikey sits perfectly still, staring at me. I can't stand it. "Just drive."

He doesn't say anything. He just puts his foot on the gas and starts us, painfully slow, around the mountain.

We travel in complete silence. I keep my hands over my face for most of it. The Tank slides a little and I feel the brakes catch, skidding, beneath us. I finally do look up to realize we're not on the road that leads back to town.

"Where are we going?" My question is childish and helpless in the cold air, and I hate myself for sounding young and weak.

"We're going to Mr. Drew's."

"*Why?*"

"Because clearly there was something going on with him and Branden and possibly Kyle we need to know about. And he's the appropriate person to ask about it."

My face flushes hot. "No. Please just let's go back to the station. Let's just forget about it for today, okay? We don't need to..."

He comes to a slow stop in the middle of the road. The Tank veers slightly to one side as he eases it into silence.

"Louisa, just because you approached it wrong, that doesn't mean you aren't right."

"But Marli couldn't tell us anything."

"No. She wouldn't want to believe it herself. Still, the theory makes sense."

"You think he was dealing for Mr. Drew?"

He scowls, and I see a future police chief. "I think it's the best theory we have. And like I told Marli, you shouldn't ignore your intuition. It means something." He turns to look at me full on. "Louisa, I trust you enough to follow your leads and to keep us on the right path, which you do. You need to trust me to know how to deal with people." I stare at the center console. He's right, and I need to apologize, but it's foreign territory for me. He's waiting for me to say something. I force myself to look him in the eye.

"I overstepped at Marli's. I know you were getting around to it. It's just...I'm so used to working by myself and having to handle everything. I'm the problem-solving person. That's what I do. I'm not good at people's feelings." Oddly, it's not so hard to say once it starts coming out. It helps Mikey isn't looking standoffish. He's just listening. "But you *are* good at people's feelings, and I should have been patient and let you do it your way. I'm sorry."

Mikey just nods. "I get you're used to flying solo. But that's the thing about working with a partner—if one person's strategy doesn't work, you can use another's." He looks up the road toward Mr. Drew's gate. "And right now, I think we're going to need your strategy."

I'm still off-kilter and exhausted. I just want to go back to the hotel, but I can't stop our arrival at the gate of Mr. Drew's estate.

CHAPTER TWENTY-THREE

I need to collect myself, play certain, and be the lead detective on a missing persons case. I have the distinct impression Mr. Drew was expecting us. He sounded almost pleasant when we buzzed at the gate.

He sits in the living room with what appears to be an old fashioned. The smell of beef, peppers, and onion permeates the room. Mr. Drew puts his argyle-socked feet on the coffee table.

"You're just in time for dinner, Officers. I know it's past work hours for you, so do feel free to join me for some chili. It should be ready soon. Can I get you a drink in the meantime?"

I'm not playing this game. "No. We're fine. I'm going to get right to the point, if you don't mind." My words come out stone cold. He leans forward and deliberately sets his drink on the table, placing his feet back on the skin rug.

"All right then."

I prepare to execute the strategy Mikey and I planned before we buzzed into the gate. It's a gamble, but if Mr. Drew bites, it will be worth it. I lock eyes with him.

"Tell us about Kyle Calderon." It comes out with more authority and confidence than even I thought I had.

He leans back in his chair. "Well, I admire how you get straight to the point, Mrs. Linebach."

"*Officer* Linebach."

He makes a point of checking my left ring finger. "Oh, I see. So sorry." It takes everything I've got to ignore the intended slight. Mikey grimaces silently. "I met Mr. Calderon once. Branden Halifax brought him here to talk about a construction job. I did not hire him, and that's the only time I've seen him. I'm sorry, was I supposed to tell you about that when you asked about Branden before? I had no idea Kyle could be of help in his disappearance, or you can be sure I would have." He smiles smugly. He thinks he has the upper hand.

"When was this?"

"Oh, I'd say maybe a few weeks before Branden went missing. My planner is on that shelf, so if you have time, I can find the exact day." He crosses the room to retrieve a leatherbound book.

"Please do." Mikey and I watch him like bald eagles surveying the ground for rodents. Drew flips the rough-edged pages of his planner. I can see a lot of scrawled writing that is totally illegible from where I sit. We wait for a couple of long minutes.

"Ah, here it is. We'd set the meeting for a Tuesday evening. Branden finished work at five and was going to have dinner, then pick Kyle up and come out here. I remember they were about ten minutes late."

"Walk us through that conversation."

"Yes. I even have notes on it." He flips to the back of the book and finds the right page. "Branden didn't stay in the room for most of the chat. It was a job interview, after all, so he didn't want to intrude, I'm sure."

"What did he do instead?"

"Went over to the bar and poured himself a drink. I heard the television come on. He was watching a game, maybe? Kyle and I were in my office."

I stop myself from checking Mikey to be sure he's taking notes. Of course he is. "How long did you and Kyle talk?"

"Not long. Maybe half an hour? Could have been forty-five minutes, I guess." I look at him, prompting. "He wanted a job with the construction company. I asked him about his work experience."

"And he said?"

"Well, he said a whole lot of nothing. Just talked about what he studied in college and turns out he really didn't want to talk about that either because I'm sure he realized I don't care about what he's read in books. I wanted to know he could show up on time, that he could do solid work and get along with the crew."

"So, he didn't have any work experience," Mikey states.

Mr. Drew looks at Mikey and laughs. "Hell no. You know how those college kids are. They'll talk you in circles to tell you they don't have a practical bone in their body. And get this," he leans toward Mikey, "he wanted me to put him in charge of a crew!" Mikey forces a smile. "Can you imagine? Thought he had some leadership skills or something." He leans back. "As if workers who've been doing the job for a decade are about to listen to a college kid who's never worked a day in his life." He clearly prefers to talk to Mikey, so I butt back in, making sure he stays uncomfortable.

"So, your impression of Kyle Calderon was not positive."

He laughs and winks. "I guess you could say that. Yes, that's a fair summary there, Officer."

"Why do you think Branden brought him to you?"

His face is serious for a second. "Well, that I can't say I know."

"You said Branden was a model employee. He knew what the job entailed and what you looked for in your crew, right?"

"That's true."

"Then why would he bring you this kid, who he surely knew couldn't cut it, to interview for a job in construction? It's not like Kyle looked like he could lift a ton." I lean so far forward in my seat that I worry I'll lose my balance.

He looks at Mikey, who stays silent. "I can't say. I really don't know." He scratches at a spot above his ear. "I guess we all lose our judgment sometimes. Maybe he owed the kid a favor or something."

"Why would he owe a hitchhiking college kid a favor?"

"Well, I can't know, now, can I? I was just speculating." More scratching as he shifts in his chair.

"Are there any other jobs Branden thought you might be able to offer Kyle?"

"Well, I run a lot of businesses. Some of my restaurants were hiring waiters and cooks. I don't know...I have a housekeeping business that works with a lot of the hotels in town. Maybe he wanted to wash sheets." He leans back again. "But somehow I don't think a kid with such a *mighty* education," he snarls his derision, "is going to want to make minimum wage washing linens. Do you?"

I breathe in and out slowly to keep myself calm.

"Mr. Drew, Kyle sounds like a drifter who didn't know what to do with his life. This doesn't sound like someone who was looking to commit to a career in Alaska. We would imagine he was looking for some sort of temporary or freelance work. Construction, maybe since that's project based. Do you hire for any other"—I strive for an even and neutral voice—"*temporary* jobs? Contract gigs maybe, where he could just work a few days or weeks and get paid right away?"

Mr. Drew eyes me carefully from beneath his sparse eyelashes. He turns his head slowly to the right, perhaps so he can see me and Mikey at the same time. "What are you implying, Officer Linebach?"

Mikey dips his toe in. "Well, she has a good point there, Mr. Drew. Given what we know of Kyle's personality, temporary work would make sense. I'm sure she's asking if you ever hire kids to run errands around town, take the laundry to the hotels, run the ATV from the grocery store to the restaurants in winter when they run out of supplies, things like that."

Mr. Drew's words come out so slowly, each one seems screened. "Why yes, your partner is right. I do sometimes hire people to run errands like that. But I didn't even mention that possibility to Kyle. Even with errand boys I ask for references. Usually, the business owners in town recommend high school or college kids they know, because *I* need to know they're reliable. If I have a boy run tools out to a work site, I can't worry he's going to run off and pawn them. They need to be trustworthy. I had no reason to trust Kyle. And I already have plenty of errand boys. I didn't need to take a chance on him."

I'm not buying any of this. It would be the easiest thing in the world to catch a kid pawning Mr. Drew's tools when every shop owner in town knows Mr. Drew's company. And if Mr. Drew is running what I think he's running, there could be huge benefits in having a revolving door of new faces to make the exchanges. If he's hiring out-of-towners for his dirtier errands, no one will connect them to him, and if something goes wrong… Well, they're disposable. I make thick, deliberate lines in my notepad with my pen because I don't know what else to do. I can't come right out and accuse him knowing he'll run and tell Willington. Mikey must see that I'm not going to say anything else because he takes over.

"Mr. Drew, when you ended the conversation with Kyle, did you make it clear you weren't hiring him, or did you leave it open, like *I'll get in touch* or something like that?"

Mr. Drew's face relaxes as he turns to my partner. "I made it quite clear that I didn't have any positions for him, and that he should come back once he had some solid work experience and references. If he was still in Alaska by then." After a long pause, he pushes up out of his chair, looking upstairs. "Is that all you need from me? I need to get ready for an appointment." He hasn't taken a step before I stop him.

"Not quite." He sits back down, his eyes locked on me. "We have evidence Kyle was stealing from the cruise ship passengers. He kept little souvenirs for himself, but he was surely giving most of what he stole to someone else. Who might he have been working with in Seward? Any ideas?"

Mr. Drew leans back and smiles like I've lobbed the easiest pitch in the world. "No one in their right mind. No local messes with the cruise ships. We may not like them, but they make the town a lot of money, and if they stopped coming to Seward because they were getting robbed, we'd all lose out."

"So, the Seward locals would run anyone involved with cruise ship crimes out of town?"

He laughs. "Before they even knew what happened. People around here don't tolerate anything that messes with the local economy. We'll gripe about outsiders, but we certainly recognize how valuable they are." I'm certain Mr. Drew recognizes their value as an expendable workforce, but I also think he may be telling the truth this time. I can't see Mr. Drew putting someone up to the petty and easily caught crime of cruise ship theft. Though I can see him quickly having a person who did it dealt with if he found out about it. Mr. Drew rises again like he's going to brush us off. I stand and get close.

"Don't you want to know why we're asking you about Kyle Calderon?"

He looks flustered, his eyes flitting away from me and to the skin rug. "Well, of course I had wondered."

"He's dead." I watch his expression carefully. His face doesn't cloud or fall like it normally does when you tell someone that somebody they've met has died. His face stays exactly the same except that he forces his mouth into a frown. His eyes are the same. So are his eyebrows.

"Oh, that's terrible to hear. What happened?"

"He was murdered." I sense Mikey's glance at me, but I don't look at him. *Now* Mr. Drew's face falls. I see a mix of anger, annoyance, and frustration.

"Wow. When? Here in Seward?"

"In Whittier."

He whistles. "That sort of thing never happens there." He's looking at me as if I may be making it up, suddenly skeptical when it's too late for that.

"We don't believe he died in Whittier. We and the police there believe he was killed and dropped from a plane. The berries he was poisoned with don't grow in Whittier."

Mikey sits perfectly still as I speak. I'm almost positive he's not breathing. I force myself to sit again and look relaxed as I proceed. "Kyle Calderon was poisoned by someone who knew the native plants of Alaska, who wanted to make it look like an unfortunate hiking accident if Kyle's body happened to be found. Someone who had access to a plane and pilots and knew Whittier well enough to drop him on a mountaintop."

"Well, that all sounds very suspicious."

"Yes, it does." I change tactics, sensing he's about where I want him. "Mr. Drew, I'm going to ask Mikey to close his notepad so this can be off the books."

Mikey obediently closes his notebook and shoves it into his back pocket.

"We know that some of your businesses aren't legitimate." Mr. Drew raises his eyebrow as he reluctantly sits. "Not everyone in town may be as friendly with you as you think. And that's fine. We don't care. That's for the Seward police to deal with. We're here for missing persons. That's our only concern. But if Kyle was working with you and he's been murdered, we need to know what your connection with him was, as much for your protection as for our knowledge."

He looks as if he's considering saying something, but instead he just picks up his drink and takes a sip. He's certainly got emotional control down. I could probably take lessons from him. There's another long break in our meeting.

"I'm afraid I can't help you, Officer Linebach. I understand people tend to be suspicious of those with money, especially here in Alaska. We're under a microscope, we're investigated constantly, and I have to consider that at all times. That's why I know the police chief well. I know the officers. You'll find they've never had an issue with me." He and I stare at each other, the air between us completely still. Mikey's voice startles me.

"Mr. Drew. We understand that you are under constant scrutiny. We do. And we're not here to try to get you investigated. But Kyle Calderon is dead. His parents are in Anchorage with the body. Journalists have already taken an interest in the case. The press is bound to be on us—on all of us. Branden Halifax is still missing, and eventually the public is going to know the link between the two of them. We have the paper where Kyle wrote the details of his interview with you. It has Branden's name and phone number on it too. They're going to ask questions about you and Branden. People in Seward have to trust the police just like they have to trust you."

Something about that seems to stick with Mr. Drew. He breathes in deeply and nods slowly at Mikey, then shifts his glance to me, examining my face. I wonder how it looks to him—bags under the eyes, lids red from rubbing, hair probably totally disheveled.

"That's a difficult position—for both of you." He leans toward us, placing his elbows on his knees and clasping his hands together. He spends a little more time staring at us, weighing something. *Or trying to look the part.* Finally, he leans back again, spreading his arms wide and hooking them behind the couch.

"I'm going to come clean with you about something. I admire what you're trying to do here, and I'm impressed by your work. Especially you, Officer." He looks at me. "So, here's the truth. I fired Branden Halifax. Just after he brought Kyle here and right before he disappeared, I fired him." Mikey instinctively breaks out the notepad, stops, looks at me, then Mr. Drew. "It's all right. There's no need for it to be a secret. I only kept it from you for Marli's sake, but it's only fair for her to know. He'd brought me this unqualified, strung-out kid for no apparent reason. It was so strange I thought I'd better drug-test Branden. And he failed. Meth, it seems. When he came to pick up his check, I fired him."

It's a good story. "But that doesn't explain what happened to Kyle, or why Branden went to the airstrip."

He shakes his head slowly. "Kyle…I just don't know. No idea. Branden, though. He used to fly out of that airstrip to pick up supplies for me. There was a plane he always flew—a little maroon and white one with skis. I believe he was looking for that plane. Maybe he wanted to steal it. I don't know. It was out back of the house, so he didn't find it. How he disappeared from there is anyone's guess. But that might be why he went to that runway." There's a moment where he knows he should stop, but like all liars, he's so impressed with his own ability to weave a story that he keeps going.

"Then again, Branden was very familiar with the terrain of Alaska, including Whittier. He's picked up guys from there for me before. He knew the native plant life. He could fly a plane. Maybe he had something to do with Kyle." He shrugs dramatically. "But I suppose we'll never know, will we?" He smiles. "Unless Branden shows up, that is."

And that's all the confirmation I need that Branden Halifax is dead. Mr. Drew would not pin Kyle's death on him if there was a chance Branden could refute him. Mikey's eyes are wide.

"I want, though, if you don't mind, for Marli to know that Branden was not a bad person. I never thought he was. Him failing the drug test, that doesn't mean anything about how I felt about Branden. He was a good man. He just adored his family. That's why I didn't want Marli to know. But the two of you, you're trying to do your job, and I get that. I'm sorry I kept it from you."

We all let his words hang in the air.

The maid thankfully breaks the silence. The chili is done.

❖

Mikey calls Chief Quint on the way back to the hotel, filling him in on the conversation. From the sounds of his end of the conversation, the chief is saying little.

Mikey uses the chief's silence to do some thinking out loud. "What if Mr. Drew really fired Branden because he'd gotten into these cruise ship burglaries with Kyle? Why else would he be hanging around with him and keeping it secret from Marli? And if he was on drugs, why did his tox report come out clean?…Yeah, I don't know. Maybe Mr. Drew found out and had them both gotten rid of because they were putting the town at risk with the cruise ships." As he explores his own theory, he gets more excited. "Or maybe he was afraid Branden and Kyle would get caught and rat him out…Well, I don't think Mr. Drew would get his hands dirty. He'd have somebody else do it." He's going down a rabbit hole and seems to catch himself; he looks at me like he's surprised I'm there. "Actually, Chief, maybe you should be talking to Louisa about this." He hands the phone to me.

The chief doesn't even say hello. He just asks how plausible I think Mikey's theory is. Not like I've had much time to think about it.

"I like it. It tracks with what we know about how Mr. Drew masterminds things. He's a criminal, I'm totally sure, but he has a lot to protect. He'd have every reason to want Branden and Kyle out of the picture if they were messing up his game with the cruise ships and stealing from them instead of just dealing drugs, which I think is what we've got going here."

"So, you think he would have hired someone to kill both of them."

That doesn't feel quite right. Branden would have been a huge loss to his operation, since he was a pilot. He knew his terrain. Branden knew the wilds of Alaska, right down to the berries he took Marli foraging for. An idea starts to percolate.

"What if he had Branden kill Kyle as a way of making things right, but then he killed Branden because he was afraid he'd talk?"

The chief is silent. Then, "I like your theories, Linebach, but I'll warn you, if Mr. Drew is as powerful in town as he seems, Willington isn't going to like you investigating him."

"Will you?"

Chief Quint doesn't say anything for a long time. "I'll look forward to seeing you two back here soon. Excellent work, Linebach."

Chapter Twenty-Four

As we head through town to the station the next morning, I notice a familiar figure rushing toward us with her head down against the snow. I tell Mikey to pull over. He asks why, then he sees Marli too. I need to apologize to her for being such an ass. We hurry to get out of the car before she walks past us.

"Oh, Officers!" She loses her balance but rights herself on Mikey's arm. "Sorry. This ice is something, isn't it?"

"That's all right. Are you okay?" Mikey puts his hand out to steady her. "I'm surprised to see you in town."

"Yeah." It's obvious she's been crying when she looks at Mikey. She doesn't make eye contact with me. "I left the kids with Branden's mom so I could come down. I needed a little time to myself. And I wanted to see…"

"How are things going, Marli?"

"Actually, I was going to come by the station and see you, so I guess it's just as well you're here."

"We're free if you want to pop in somewhere and have a chat." I try to sound as friendly as possible, so she knows I'm not going to accost her again.

"Sure. That would be great." She actually smiles at me. I would be pissed if I was her. She's clearly the bigger person in this situation.

"Maybe the coffee place would be a little more inviting than the station." She's been through enough. She deserves to be as comfortable as possible.

"Yeah. Definitely. I've gotta move the truck so I don't get a ticket." She laughs. "Oh, I guess it's okay, huh, since I'm talking to you?"

"Somehow, I think you'll be fine." Mikey laughs along with her.

One of the two coffee shops that stay open all year is just a few doors down. Marli walks alongside us, her tall waterproof boots floating beneath a shin-length puffer coat.

"Marli, I wanted…I need to apologize for the way I talked to you yesterday. I'm really sorry." Maybe I should stop there, but I have the compulsive need to explain myself. "I wasn't frustrated with you. I'm frustrated with myself. I really thought we could find Branden, and it bothers me we haven't. I hate feeling helpless, is all."

She stops and turns to me. "It's all right. I appreciate you care. You wouldn't have gotten so worked up if you weren't serious about finding him. I'd rather have someone who can be…*abrupt* than someone who just goes through the motions and doesn't get invested."

A weight lifts from my shoulders. It's amazing how gracefully she's accepted my explanation. I like Marli. I've hated feeling like I made this worse for her than it already is.

When we get into the coffee shop, Marli excuses herself to the bathroom, giving Mikey and me time to worry about what she's going to tell us. When she returns, her tear-creased makeup is gone, and she looks almost refreshed. The waitress sets her mug down and she wraps her hands delicately around it.

"Okay. So, I'm sure you wonder why I wanted to talk to you."

"Have to admit, we do," Mikey says.

"Will you promise not to judge me?"

"Of course." I nod along with him.

"I wanted to let you know that it's okay if you need to stop looking for Branden."

I was hoping she was going to remember some other connection between Branden and Mr. Drew, or at least tell us about something Branden was involved in that might lead to his disappearance. This is not what I was expecting at all.

"Why's that?" It's the only thing I can fumble out of my mouth.

"Okay. This is the part where I need you to not judge me." Mikey and I both lean forward because she lowers her voice even though we're the only customers in the shop. "I went to see a psychic." Mikey does a nice job remaining neutral. She clearly notices my eyebrow darting up before I can stop it. "That's not a thing I'd normally do. In fact, I've never been to one before. It's just, Branden's mother thought it was a good idea. She knows the woman and sees her once in a while, I guess, so she recommended her after our…after our conversation." She glances at me so quickly that I barely catch it.

"Who is this *psychic*?" I barely keep the sarcasm out of my tone.

"She's just down the street above that little art gallery. She's been in town forever, but you have to know about her to find her. She doesn't have a sign."

"So, Branden's mother recommended her, and you went to visit. Couldn't hurt, right?" Mikey's taken back over.

"Right. I mean, I've been kind of desperate. Anything that could help…" A pang of guilt stabs me in the side. It's possible I drove her to take such a ridiculous step. "Anyway, she knew a lot. A lot of things about Branden it seemed she shouldn't know."

"Like what?"

"She knew he went missing near a runway."

"Well, everyone who was part of the search knew that. She could have heard it through someone in town."

Mikey narrows his eyes at me. "I know. That's true. But other things. Personal things. Like, things only I would know since I'm his girlfriend." She blushes.

"Ah. No need to say more. So, it's safe to say you feel she has some credibility?"

"Right. Not that I think she can see everything that's ever happened to him or anything, but…she seemed to have a sense of things. Maybe she was just reading *me*, I don't know." She crosses her legs carefully.

"Maybe, but who knows? A lot of people around Anchorage visit psychics. Some of them are obviously frauds, but some of them…I don't know. Hell, the police used to consult with them every once in a while too."

"Really?"

"Yeah. Haven't heard about it being done for a while, but it has been done."

"Oh. Well, that makes me feel a little less nuts, at least." She laughs into her mug.

"So, what did the psychic tell you?"

"She told me a lot about our lives so far, I guess to let me see she could *see* certain things, so I'd believe her. Then she told me he loved me and the kids, and he had been thinking about us at the end."

"She thinks he's dead."

"Yeah. She felt like his soul was gone from the world."

"Did she have any insight into how it might have happened?"

"She knew he crashed the truck, and I hadn't told her. But I guess she could have known from the search party. Anyway, she said there was a man there when it happened, that he killed him and watched him die. She said when she pictured it, they were in some sort of shelter. They weren't out in the snow. She said the police already found where it happened, but he was taken away so you couldn't find him."

"Whoa. Like in a plane?"

"She didn't say that, but it makes sense maybe, right? If someone killed him in a plane..."

Mikey just nods.

"She said..." She looks at the cup and pauses. I can almost believe the illusion of the moisture in her eyes being from the rising steam. Mikey scoots his chair closer to her.

"She said it will be five years."

"What will be five years?" His voice is so quiet, I barely hear him.

"It will be five years before we find him."

I gasp at the balls of a psychic who would tell a grieving woman that. "Jesus Christ." I immediately cover my mouth, but Marli doesn't react. "Oh, Marli, I'm sorry. That must have been terrible to hear." She is crying.

"It was..." She wipes her nose on a tiny paper napkin. "But at the same time, I don't know. I kind of want to believe her. Even if it's five years, that means that for now...for now, I can stop looking and hoping he'll come home."

We all lean back in our seats simultaneously. I have no idea how to process this. Mikey is the first one to speak after a long silence.

"Did she say anything about why he was killed, or how?"

"No. Just that the person who did it would never face a jury."

I think about Mr. Drew and the maroon and white plane. Mikey leans forward and looks her in the eye.

"Marli, what do you want us to do now? We're happy to keep looking. That's our job. But his mother has deferred to your wishes, so it's in your hands. We don't want to keep going if it's making things worse for you."

I stare at him. How is putting this decision to Marli Lei even an option?

"I know. And I appreciate that. But I think..." She wipes away the tears and looks straight ahead, resolved. "I think I want to stop searching. If the psychic is right, maybe in five years' time..." She shakes her head as if she's trying to clear away a thought or a fly in her hair. "Even if she isn't right about that, *I* think he's gone. And if I keep looking, it's just going to keep me in...I don't know."

"That's all right. You don't have to explain." Mikey pats her back. "We can stop the search if that's what you want."

"I do. But what happens then? From your end?"

They both look at me. I stammer for a few seconds before I can speak. It's incomprehensible we would stop looking.

"His name would go into the missing persons file with his picture and all the information about when he disappeared and where. That way, if someone learns something new later, we can go back to the file and pick right back up where we left off."

"Good. Okay. That's good to know." She downs the rest of her drink. "I should go. I need to pick up the kids, and I know Branden's mom is anxious to know what the psychic said."

"All right. But even though we're going to stop looking for now, if you ever need anything at all, Officer Linebach and I are always just a phone call away. Anchorage isn't too far. We could be here in half a day."

I blink rapidly to clear my vision, in hopes it will clear my head. Everything is going too fast.

"I know. Thank you." She looks at me. "Thank you, both of you, for everything you've done. I know this must seem impossible. I can't even imagine doing your jobs. But you've tried really hard, and I know it must keep you up at night too." We both nod and look at our feet. Visions of my nightmares flash through my head. "I just want you to know I appreciate it."

"It's no problem at all." Mikey shakes her hand, then she stands. I stand with her to shake her hand and wish her luck. And then she's gone.

I'm in shock, I think. Mikey shakes his head slowly, staring at the solid oak door through which Marli just departed. The gust of cold wind that replaced her when she left still hovers around us. I shiver. Mikey sighs.

"Damn. I think that could have really gone somewhere if we had found a body."

"What do you mean *could have gone* somewhere? We're not going to stop looking."

"Louisa, Marli just asked us to." Mikey is really pissing me off.

I put my coffee cup down hard enough the waitress comes over to sheepishly offer me a refill. I silently focus on the table even while she tips the last of the pot into my cup, stopping just after the grounds splatter into the brown liquid. *That's poetic.* After she's back at the counter, I stare Mikey down.

"This isn't only about a missing person. It's about Mr. Drew and Kyle and whatever's going on with drugs in this town. If Mr. Drew got Branden killed having him run drugs, don't you want to know? Don't you want to know if he got Kyle killed, or all those other dozens of men who've gone missing? He needs to be in jail if this is all on him, and you and I both know that it is." My voice is a whisper, but my pulse is so fast. I worry I'm about to have a panic attack.

"Louisa, we have to respect Marli's wishes as far as searching for Branden is concerned, and with no body and no concrete evidence Mr. Drew is in the drug trade, we can't start a criminal investigation into him. You know that."

"But you and I both know Mr. Drew is behind this!"

"I agree with you, Louisa, I really do, but so what if he is? W—"

"*So?* What do you mean, *so?* That's our job, Mikey. Find these missing people. We came here to find two people, and we've only found one headless body who we're not even sure belongs to the person we're saying it does, and one body we weren't even looking for."

He draws his head back and looks at me like he's never seen me before. "Whoa. What? You seriously don't think that's Lee the Stantons buried?"

"No. Yes. Maybe. I'm saying we don't know for sure. We're guessing. And if it does happen to be Lee, that's just a coincidence that happened to work in our favor. That case isn't closed because of good police work, it's closed because we happened to find a body that sort of lined up with someone we were looking for. You want to let a grieving woman call off a search. How on earth can you be satisfied with that?"

"I mean…" He looks vaguely ashamed. "I really wish we could be positive too, but that's the best we had. And hell, it's better than folks down here normally get."

"So, telling a parent we think maybe that's their son without a head is better than telling them we don't know where their son is?" My hands shake as I fumble for the keys to the Tank and slap some bills on the table.

"I'm just saying that we do this job to make people feel safer and give them some closure when something goes wrong. And we did that. The Stantons have closure now." He's rushing to keep up with me as I force the door open against the wind. He doesn't even look to see if anyone else is on the sidewalk. "They buried the person they believe is their son, and if they're satisfied with that, I think we should be satisfied with that."

I take a few breaths in, then out, closing my eyes before I answer. I try to keep my tone even.

"It's not our job to make people *feel* safe. It's our job to *make* people safe. Period. Their feelings don't have anything to do with it. We're supposed to solve cases with facts."

He doesn't respond, which is smart. When I'm fired up like this, there's nothing anyone can say that won't just get them yelled at more. He must sense it, because he sits and stares at me in silence while I blast the heat, trying to warm the Tank enough to drive. As my fingers thaw, he speaks.

"Louisa, we're not part of whatever game folks are playing here. The people in town won't tell us a thing about it, and Mr. Drew's clearly been covering his tracks for decades now. The chief here isn't going to let us investigate Mr. Drew. We both know that." He turns around in his seat so he's facing me.

"Look, we'll give Chief Willington the stats we have on the missing people. We'll tell him we suspect Mr. Drew is having the guys run drugs. We'll tell him about the note we found at Kyle's. We'll tell him everything. But he has to decide from there. We came here to find a missing person. You found him. We happened to get called into another one. His girlfriend just asked us to stop looking. Hell, we even got asked to ID a random body in the middle of nowhere and managed to do that too! Things don't wrap up in neat little packages. Missing persons are messy. Let giving three families closure be enough."

I want to challenge him, but I don't. If I open my mouth, I might cry. He continues.

"You've given the Stanton family something most people with missing children never get. They got to have a funeral. They get to sleep at night believing their son isn't out there freezing, wandering around a mountain, wondering why no one has found him. Because we did find him. You found him, Louisa."

He's waiting for me to say something. I want to say that just because families usually don't get answers, that doesn't mean it's okay to give the wrong answer. That Marli deserves to know where Branden is regardless of what some phony psychic told her. That maybe he *is* actually wandering around a mountain wondering why no one has come to find him. I want to say so much, but there's no point. It can't change anything. Because we're wandering a dark state the size of a country searching an inhospitable wilderness for people who sometimes don't want to be found.

I have to say something, but I don't know what, so I just spit out the dreams I've been having. Mikey doesn't question me, or even look alarmed.

"Yeah, I've been having those too. Well, not the same exactly, of course, but the same theme. They're out there, trying to tell us something I can't quite understand. I wake up feeling totally useless." He looks me straight in the eye. "But we're *not* useless. All cops feel like that sometimes, but we keep going because it's our job."

I press back in the seat. "I felt like this in DCS. No matter how hard I tried or how much I did, I could never help. This feels like that."

"Well, I guess it is, sort of. People get themselves into dangerous situations where they need someone to step in and help. You're there because somebody wasn't able to help themselves, so you can't blame yourself if things end badly for them. Things were bad before you got here."

"Yes, but with our cases, it's not their fault."

"We don't know that. If Lee killed himself, even if he thought he had a good reason, he still owns that. He chose it. Branden, who knows? Maybe he was caught up in drugs. I don't think he stumbled onto that airstrip totally sober or innocent. He made choices that led him there. Just like Kyle made choices that led to him being in Whittier."

"But Marli didn't make that choice. Neither did Lee's parents."

"No. They didn't. That's true. They got the shit end of this deal."
The air rushes out of me. My head hurts. I solve problems for other people. That's what I do. I don't know how to reconcile Mikey's understanding of missing persons work with that, but I know I'm going to have to. I can't let myself fall off the deep end like I did in my last job.

"You look tired."

"I am. I'm *so* tired right now."

"Let's go see Tails." I start up the Tank.

CHAPTER TWENTY-FIVE

The next day we are outside Chief Willington's office with our files in hand before he even arrives. When he sees us, he stops midstride. "Officers. Good morning." He unlocks the door and waves us in. "Congratulations on the Calderon solve. Case closed yesterday. Natural causes. What a shame. Kids come out here hiking, don't know what they're doing. Must have thought he was some sort of Chris McCandless." He *tsks* his disapproval as he sits at his desk.

"Actually, sir, we don't believe he died of natural causes. He was poisoned by baneberries, which weren't growing anywhere near his body. We believe he was poisoned elsewhere and dropped in Whittier, where he most likely wouldn't have been found if it weren't for a hermit with a health agenda."

Mikey stands ramrod straight, hands clasped behind his back as I speak. I told him he didn't have to come with me, that there was no use jeopardizing both our careers, but he insisted. The chief swivels in his chair a bit and whistles.

"Well, that's a hell of a claim, Officer. And who would want to kill a college boy hitchhiking around the wilds?" He raises his eyebrows at me.

"We believe he was pulled into a drug-running scheme by Branden Halifax. We found a note with Branden's phone number. They had arranged a meeting. The two of them also match the description of two men chased off the cruise ship for trying to sell drugs to the staff."

"So, you think Branden killed him over some drug deal, then disappeared out of guilt or something?"

"We don't know if Branden killed him and was then killed himself, or if they were both killed by a third party. But we do believe the drug scheme they were involved in is widespread." I pull out the statistics for missing people and place it on his desk. He glances at it and nods.

"You've been doing a lot more than looking for bodies."

"Yes."

He slows his speech like some people do when they're talking to someone they don't think speaks the language well. "But you were only sent here to look for bodies."

"Yes."

He appraises me. *Maybe he'll throw us out.* He gets up to check outside the door before he returns to his seat. There's no one else in the station.

"Let's get to it, shall we? You figured out the missing men began in earnest when Mr. Drew arrived."

"You know." It's a statement. Of course he knows.

He laughs. "I certainly know. It's my town, after all."

"And you've done nothing because Mr. Drew is your friend."

"Oh, no—no. There you are wrong, Officer." His face is dead serious. "No one is Mr. Drew's friend. He may keep this town running and food on our tables, but he is no one's friend."

"And the drugs?"

"We haven't found any hard evidence to link them to him. We know drugs come out of Seward and disperse on cruise ships, to other towns, but they never quite come back to Mr. Drew. There's always some kid from out of town to take the fall. Never seems to tie back to the locals. They never get caught with anything, though they do have a habit of turning up missing."

"And you're okay with this?"

"No. I don't want our folk here getting hurt. But I also realize that, should anything…happen to Mr. Drew, most of the people in town would be without work, and many are not skilled in tourism. They'd be beat out of jobs by the seasonals. That would be a real shame, wouldn't it? It would just be one big souvenir shop without the locals."

"So, you won't follow up on this evidence we're giving you."

He pyramids his fingers and then leans over his desk. "Here's what I'll tell you, Officer. Between the three of us. Any evidence you have will be carefully protected and maintained so that if the situation in Seward ever changes and the people wish to live…*different* lives, even with another police chief, the records will be there for follow-up. Unless, of course, there is concrete evidence in that file?"

I can't say anything because I know there's not. Besides, if I do say anything, it will most likely get me fired.

Mikey thanks Chief Willington for his time and assures him we've been happy to help out, but seeing as how our cases are all closed, Chief Quint wants us back in Anchorage. Mikey quickly ushers me out of the building and directly into the Tank. I grind my teeth so hard, my jaw hurts. He pulls into the hotel parking lot but doesn't get out of the car. He turns to me.

"Louisa, I think you might as well let it out."

I scream. I scream as loud as I can for as long as I have breath. People on the street could hear me if there were any. Maybe people in the hotel can hear me through the Tank's thick walls. I don't care. Mikey just sits there with me, unflinching.

❖

I'm packed in less than five minutes. Turns out Mikey wasn't lying, though I hoped he was. Chief Quint does want us back in Anchorage. He talked to Mikey this morning. There's a major bust going down and it's all hands on deck. He warned Mikey personally because his cousin is involved. I'm ready to go as soon as I'm packed. I don't want to be in this town anymore if I can't get to the bottom of what's going on here. I hear Mikey's phone ring, so I take Tails out and give Mikey time for whatever conversation he's having. When I get back a few minutes later, he knocks on my door.

"Hey, you okay with leaving after lunch?"

"What? I thought we were leaving now."

"Yeah. Sorry. I got a phone call and I've gotta...I've got an appointment."

"An appointment?"

"Yeah...Chief Willington wants to meet with me, just to wrap some things up, I guess. Paperwork maybe? You know. Case closure stuff." Mikey could stand to take some lessons in lying from Mr. Drew.

"Why didn't he ask me?"

"I don't know. He asked me specifically...Maybe he figures you're pissed at him. I mean, your face was obvious."

"Okay. Go do whatever he wants you to do." I shut the door before he's even turned away. I hear Mikey sigh. It's a few seconds before his footsteps proceed down the walkway. I sit on the bed, betrayed. I wonder how I'm going to kill five hours.

I need to get out of the room. I consider walking down to the water one last time. But when I get out to the parking lot, I see the Tank. I assumed Mikey would take it, but it's there with a note flapping against the windshield. I read Mikey's cursive. *I thought you might want to go see Anna.*

Anna. We were supposed to have dinner at her place. Maybe I can catch her before she gets to the hospital.

❖

Almost all the lights are on in Anna's house, pouring pale, warm light out onto the still-dark street. Winter is setting in. I park across the street and turn off the ignition. I can see a silhouette in the kitchen. Her shape comes and goes as she gets blocked by doorways and partial walls. I think I hear strains of music, but it could be drifting from a boat out on the water. It could be inside my head. There's a moment when she bends to reach down, maybe to pull something out of a cabinet. When she stands again, she turns toward the road such that the light falls on her face. She looks content framed by the bright yellow of her home, like she's standing in a patch of sunshine while the snow falls around without being able to touch her.

I realize I can't knock on her door. If she invites me in, I'll want to stay in Seward forever. I can't stay in Seward another day. I can't work for Chief Willington or the police force here and ignore Mr. Drew. *And what else would I do? Sell fake native hunting knives?* So, I make the easy choice. I do what I always do. Instead of dealing with complicated emotions, I drive away.

The sun tries to rise somewhere, but gray clouds force it back into an inept position. The snow blows toward me in a hypnotic funnel. I lean forward in the seat, squinting even with the wipers on high, but I look away occasionally so I don't go into a trance. Halfway there, I realize I'm going to the airstrip.

The spot where Branden ran his truck into the bank is hard to identify. I pass it and recognize after half a mile I've gone too far. I park where he was parked, where his footsteps marked the snow, which is much deeper now. Somehow, I clamber up the bank the same way he did, the snow past my knees. It's a brand-new landscape. The trees are ominous, towering as if they've grown centuries in the week or so since we searched for Branden. The ground is a blank slate, entire boulders invisible. There's no chance of finding anything in this, but its newness has a strange allure. I keep moving toward the tree line.

I don't know how long it takes to reach the pines because the light doesn't change through the snow. It would be impossible to pick out the long landing strip without its obvious lack of underbrush and trees. It's a sheer expanse of shimmering, crystalized snow for hundreds of feet in front of me. There's nothing here, and I don't know what I expected. I kick at the powder, which flies up and showers down, settling into place. It doesn't mind my disturbance at all.

I'm on my knees, digging with my gloved hands into the deep snow, which has been gusted into mounds by the wind. As I dig, the snow collapses onto my hands, into the hole, and covers my progress. I grunt and scream at it, flinging it to the sides until I can see the yellow markings of the runway. They don't tell me a goddamned thing. There's no blood. No berries. No body. No Branden I can present to Marli, frozen but otherwise looking exactly like the man who walked out of her house so recently. I move forward a couple feet and dig again like a wild animal. Wild animals may be nearby. I don't care. I dig and dig and move forward. I dig to the paint and move forward again, digging. *Dig.* Digging. *Digging.*

I'm near the end of the runway. My legs are weak from walking through waist-high snow. There's nothing here and the tiny frozen flakes come so fast. I squint and it still gets in my eyes. I don't care. I dig. But there's nothing. No blood. No berries. No Branden.

My arms hurt and my fingers are so numb. I can't feel them now. The snow won't move anymore. I need to take a break. I settle back onto my heels, and the snow stains the seat of my pants. My whole lower body is cold. The snow spins, the clouds spin, the trees spin. People and animals come in and out of my view. Branden moving across the snow. Kyle, purple and poisoned. Lee, with half his head. Bears and moose and eagles. I close my eyes.

When I open them again, the snow falls slower. I can barely see the sun overhead. My body is numb. Everything is still and solid, as if I could walk across the two feet of snow and not make a dent. *Why am I here?* I try to stand, but I can't feel my legs. I place my gloved palms flat on the snow and try to push up, but my arms sink. I push up. I stand, teetering. I move in slow motion. I see the tree line below me, but it seems forever away. *What did I think I would find here?* It makes no sense now.

My new goal is the tree line. There's nothing in my lungs, in my stomach, in my muscles. I can't feel. I'm moving a ghost.

Much later, I'm at the pines. My sweat freezes in place. There's the road, the Tank. I can't feel my fingers, so I track their progress into my pockets. If there's metal there, it's the same temperature as my limbs. The idea of being stuck here overtakes my breath. I panic. My throat is closing.

I can't be here.

I stop, close my eyes, and breathe in and out. Deep breaths.

Keep trying. I feel again. The sharp end of a key pokes my finger. I drop my keys three times, then hold them in both hands. I manage to unlock and then fall into the Tank.

Somehow, I arrive at the hotel. I don't remember the drive. I spill onto the pavement. When I get to my door, it's bewildering. I can't open the door. I can't remember how to open the door. I stare at it, then let my head drop against it. I hear whining on the other side, but I cannot get to Tails.

There's a loud noise.

"Louisa? Jesus Christ!" It's Mikey. I must look bad. He rushes to me with his arms spread out. *What's he doing?* He bear-hugs me, rubbing my arms so quickly a little bit of warmth generates.

"Where's your key?" I just look at him. "Hang on." He disappears in the direction of check-in and then returns to open the door. He peels my wet and frozen coat off and puts all the blankets from the bed around me. He even wraps a towel around my head like a turban.

I suddenly feel like an idiot. Tails jumps on the bed to thoroughly lick my face. His breath is warm, so I let him continue. Mikey squats next to me and just looks at me until I speak.

"I couldn't." My voice is just a rasp. I clear my throat and try again. Mikey leaps to his feet and starts the coffee maker. "I couldn't find anything."

"You went looking for Branden."

"Yeah."

He shakes his head, but he looks sad more than anything. "I should have known you would. I should have gone with you."

"No. I had to do it myself."

"That could have been really bad."

"I know."

He thankfully doesn't say anything else about it. He just checks my fingers for frostbite, runs hot water in the bathtub, and tells me to get in to get properly warm. He'll come back with food. He instructs Tails to take care of me.

Tails looks at him and then at me like he fully understands.

I don't know how long I'm in the bath, but I am slowly able to make out the room more clearly. Tails stands on the white tile with his head over the tub rim, licking at the water. As soon as my eyes open, he licks my nose. I breathe in, trying to draw all the air in the room into my lungs. I look into the overhead light.

There's a knock on the door.

"Just me," Mikey yells. "I've got food whenever you're ready."

I scarf a massive portion of fish and chips. Then I ask if our cases are officially closed. Mikey nods but doesn't make eye contact.

Still lying, I see.

I let Mikey drive back to Anchorage. It's not like me, but I'm exhausted. We stop for coffee twice. We don't talk much. He turns on the radio occasionally, only to turn it off when it turns to static.

❖

When I arrive at work the next morning, Chief Quint claps me on the shoulder and congratulates me.

"Extraordinary work, Linebach!" His voice is at a volume for all the gathered officers to hear. The department has a scheduled briefing in a few minutes. He lowers his voice.

"Hang back after."

I listen to the briefing in a total haze. I couldn't repeat back most of what the chief says, but I'm familiar with the gang we're going after, and I know the neighborhoods he's circling on the giant map pulled down on the conference room wall. The rest of the guys are quiet, maybe pissed about being here on a Saturday. I think I catch sidelong glances my way.

When the meeting breaks up, a few officers smack Mikey on the back.

"Nice job, man."

"Heard you found a couple bodies."

"Two out of three ain't bad!"

I wince at the jovial tone of that *compliment*. Mikey points at me and starts to say something, but they're already gone, gathering their bags and coats from their desks.

"Wanna ride together?"

It's then that it hits me we're not partners anymore. Not on this case. We're back to being just two cops in the same station. *Who else would I even ride with?*

"Sure. I've gotta talk to Quint first, but I'll meet you out there."

Chief Quint is powering down the projector and seems surprised to see me even though he asked me to stay.

"Louisa." He repeats his clap to my shoulder. "I just wanted to congratulate you again." He looks at me expectantly until I utter a dull thanks.

"I also wanted to say," and now he looks less jovial, "I know how frustrated you must be. I'm frustrated. I investigated this Mr. Drew as much as I could, and he looks shady as hell, but he seems untouchable. I wish I could send folks to do more, but without concrete evidence…"

"Yeah. Yes, Willington said the same thing."

"Well, anyway, it's a tough break. That's the worst part about police work—knowing someone's up to something and not being able to do anything about it. But you did a great job, you and Mikey. Really, you did. I know he learned a lot. I'm sure you will move up the ranks in no time."

"Sure." I sling my bag over my shoulder. I'm ready to end this conversation.

"All right." He fumbles over what to say next and settles on a "Go get 'em" that leaves me feeling like a middle schooler being ushered into a sporting event. I leave Tails with reception. When I get to the parking lot, Mikey leans against a Land Rover that is distinctly *not* the Tank.

❖

The bust goes all right, by paperwork standards. We arrest over a dozen people, Mikey's cousin included, and seize over fifty bags of product. When we get back to the station and finish the debrief, the other officers gather around Mikey at the back of the conference room. I'm the only one who immediately sits to document my notes. I hear muffled laughter and watch the group briefly. Mikey's face is bright red. They all grab their things and start to leave together with Mikey at the center of the crowd. He breaks off as he reaches my desk on the way to the door.

"Hey, Linebach, the guys want to take—*us* out for a drink to celebrate the work we did in Seward. What do you say?" I notice the almost imperceptible adjustment. He indicates the other men. They are still smiling, but it now looks forced. I'm sure we all know I'm not going.

"Nah, it's cool. I'm pretty tired. Besides, Tails needs fed."

"You sure? We won't stay out long, promise. We can find somewhere else Tails can come too."

A couple of the others look at him, then nod slowly.

"It's all right. Have a good time, though. I'll see you tomorrow."

Mikey turns to the other officers. "Hey, I'll meet you there in fifteen, yeah?"

They shrug and leave. I hear "Nice work" muttered to me as a couple of the guys pat Tails. He leans his head forward for more and gets scratched behind the ears too. I briefly resent Tails for wanting them to pet him. Mikey waits for the door to close before he turns to me. Whatever he's going to say is not something I will want to hear.

"I wanted to let you know…Chief Willington offered me a job in Seward."

"A job? Seriously?"

"Yeah. I'm going to tell Quint tomorrow. I was going to turn it down, but we got back here and I arrested my cousin. My family's going to hate me for it, and I'm sick of having to do that. Just like I'm sick of watching people overdose and just cleaning up the mess and telling their families. If I was in Seward—well, you know how it would be. Petty tourist crimes and lost hikers and all. And missing persons."

I stare at him. I want to hit him and beg him not to go because he's the only friend I have, but I don't do either of those things. He waits for me to say something, but I don't. I can't think of what to say.

"I'm sorry. I really am. Working with you on those cases was great. Honestly, I think he probably would have hired both of us, but…"

"But he knows I'd keep going after Mr. Drew." Mikey doesn't comment. "And he knows you won't pursue Mr. Drew if he asks you not to."

"Come on, Louisa, that's not fair."

"Am I wrong?"

He doesn't say anything for a long time. When he does, he speaks slowly. "Maybe you're right. I can't say I know what Willington is looking for. I can only say being in Seward is something I want." He exhales. "Willington won't be around forever. He says he's got another five years in him, if that. While Willington's my chief, you know I have to play by his rules, but after…" He places his hands lightly on my shoulders, and I stand straight so he immediately pulls them back. "I promise, Louisa, as soon as he leaves, Mr. Drew is fair game."

"Sure." I don't want to talk to him anymore. I feel betrayed. And undermined. And overlooked and controlled. I'm boxed in. And I've lost my only friend. I can't believe this. *How dare he take that job? I should have been offered a position in Seward, even if I wouldn't take it.* Mikey may want to go, but that's not the point. I need to get out of this building. I need to go home with Tails and just be alone. I turn away.

"Well, congratulations. I hope you like it better down there."

"Hey, Louisa, you know, it's not far away. You could come visit. I'd love to see you. I bet Anna would too."

I just nod. I already know I won't visit Seward. I know I won't be able to see Willington and not say something I'll regret. I know I won't be able to go just to see Mikey and Anna. I cannot ignore what's going on there and I'm amazed Mikey can. So can Anna, for that matter. There's a moment when I know this isn't how I want to leave it, but instead of saying a real good-bye, I move toward my desk. Mikey starts toward the door. Tails moves to follow him but stops after he glances back at me.

As soon as Mikey's gone, I gather my things. Tails leans forward, straightens his front legs, and lowers his head to the floor in his tired yoga stretch. I confirm Mikey has left the parking lot before we leave the building.

"You're right, buddy. Time to go home." As I switch off the lights, I tell myself that tomorrow, once I've had some rest, I'll call Anna and explain why I didn't show for dinner, and why I can't visit her in Seward. I wonder if she'll want to visit Anchorage, or me.

CHAPTER TWENTY-SIX

June 2009

The phone snaps me from a dream about faces emerging from the snow, their features just below a fine layer of ice, fingernails clawing to try to break the surface, trying to dig out. I grab at my cell automatically, clawing the air like the fingers in my dreams.

It's Senior Special Agent Mensel, aka my contact in my new role as Special Liaison to the FBI. I sit up straight and put my hand over the phone as I clear my voice.

"Sir?"

"Linebach. Sorry to call so early, but it's important."

"Not a problem, sir."

"Any chance you can get to Seward?"

"Of course, sir. What's going on in Seward?"

"They had a bad fire in all those mountains around Alice. They found something during cleanup. A bone. I don't have all the details, but they seemed to think it could be connected to something much bigger, some case you worked before. Chief Harper requested you specifically. It's already cleared with Quint." By which he means he's not asking *if* I can go; he's telling me I'm going. I don't mind at all. I love my new role, so I'm eager to jump on anything the FBI hands me.

Still, it will be strange working with Mikey Harper again. I haven't really seen him in the five years since he moved to join the Seward force. It was the talk of the whole Anchorage team when Willington personally named Mikey chief while announcing his own retirement.

One of the Seward officers who'd minded Tails when we were in Seward had already moved to the Lower 48, and the evening dispatcher apparently insisted she would never surrender her days to the force, but there was enough bitterness about Mikey's promotion on the part of the remaining senior officer that he promptly transferred to Juneau. Mikey becoming the chief riled me a bit too—especially because that was before I was appointed FBI Liaison. When he visits Anchorage, he always stops by headquarters or calls, but I always find some excuse why I can't talk long. But if Mikey has something related to the Lee Stanton and Branden Halifax case, we have much to discuss. I need to get off this phone so I can hop in the shower and get there.

"I can leave here in an hour."

"Thanks, Linebach. Harper got you a room at a new hotel by the water." I record the address he gives me. Not that it should be hard to find.

"Thanks. I'll update you as soon as I can."

I hang up and glance around the room for my bag. The place is messy—there are clothes, dog toys, and dust everywhere, with food going bad in the refrigerator. There are no plants for me to kill, and it smells stale. It's just a place to sleep and store my things. *Why have I never moved?* I ask myself almost every day, and I recognize my *I'm busy* answer for the pile of horseshit it is. The new role comes with extra pay, so I can easily relocate. I'm sure Tails would love a place with a yard, though he certainly doesn't complain.

At least he gets to go on morning runs with me, and he's often with me when I'm on duty. I got him trained with the drug sniffing dogs and the dogs we use for tracking missing people, which he's got a real talent for. He also fulfilled Mikey's prediction of helping me make some friends. My relationships with the other officers got a whole lot better once we had Tails to bond over.

It didn't hurt I also found solid evidence that Rippy harassed women. I expected his being fired would make me an outcast, but it turns out everyone was delighted to have him gone.

"Prepare yourself, bud." I pat Tails's head, where a few white hairs spring up between his ears. "We're headed back to your homeland." He goes to the door and sits as if he understands me.

I shower fast and throw my hair up, leaving my white forelock uncontained as I've taken to doing. I theorize people will respect me more or find me more approachable if they can see I'm graying, but it doesn't seem to be working so far. I've made a couple casual acquaintances around Anchorage, even gone on a few dates, but even with the great new job, I'm still struggling in the social arena. I joined a triathlon group to get me through the winter, so I spent the dark days swimming, riding, and pounding miles indoors, making casual conversation. Still, as soon as the weather warmed and we'd done our mini-Ironman, the group dispersed. Thank goodness for Tails. The need to take care of something other than myself gave me a focus I didn't realize I was missing. When I wasn't exercising, I filled my winter days teaching him tricks and helping him practice his tracking skills in the snow. I came to love being outside in the semi-dark, snow to my knees, watching that dog sniff out whatever I'd hidden for him.

Still, I sometimes wonder if I made a mistake by not trying to get on at the Seward station with Mikey. As much as I love my work with the FBI, I haven't gotten close to anyone here yet, and even though I wasn't there long, I miss Seward more often than I care to admit. My therapist—my FBI-mandated therapist—urged me to go there just to visit, to see what happens and how I feel. But I'm not good at admitting when I've made a mistake, and I've already fucked things up with Anna. Or, I've really been meaning to, but the liaison work has kept me busy. I keep telling the therapist I'll do it soon. She'd be delighted to know I'm headed there now. It will give me a chance to have the live, in-person conversation I've been wanting with Anna. As I dress, our penultimate phone conversation plays over in my head.

"I'm trying here, Louisa. I think you and I could have something great. I don't understand why you're so resistant. Just come down. I'll cook you that dinner. Nothing has to happen. I just want to see you."

"I know. I'm sorry I'm being an asshole to you. You deserve a lot better. It's just that I know myself. I can't be in Seward and not try to finish what I started there. If you and I are together, that could come back on you. Mr. Drew could retaliate on you, and on Mikey too. It's best if I just stay away."

I thought about inviting her to Anchorage, but I knew I'd totally fall for her, and then what would I do? She wouldn't move here—she loves Seward. And I couldn't go there. I can't do any version of long-distance. I know this about myself. The next—the last—time we talked, she told me she had started seeing someone. I never called again.

I toss some things in my overnight bag, clip the leash on Tails, and grab the bright orange parka with *Seward* on it that Willington gave me after Anna suggested it. I try not to think about what I'll say to Mikey and Anna when I get there. What is there to say? *"Sorry. I was a jerk who couldn't handle her own shit. I'm working on it. I promise."*

As I pull out of the driveway, I remember I planned to follow up on a kidnapping case today. The trial starts soon, and we collected DNA evidence to help put the perpetrator away. The lab should have it back by now. I'm excited how widely accepted DNA matching is becoming as evidence. It adds a layer of certainty. The department started working with the scientific crime lab on some of our cases a few months ago, and there have already been some great results. I hope they have a good result for me in this case too. I dial with one hand while I drive. Tails stares at me from the passenger seat. I scowl at him.

"You just concentrate on the road, okay? I know what I'm doing." He turns and stares out the windshield at the beautiful day ahead of us.

"Diaz? Hey, this is Linebach. I was just calling to see if you've got anything for me."

"Hey, Linebach! Good to hear from you. I was just getting ready to call you. You're gonna like what I've got."

"A match?" I accelerate in my excitement. Tails looks at me again.

"Yes, it's a match."

"You're a rock star, Diaz. You're willing to testify, right?"

"You bet. You give me the details and I'll be there. You'll be around today to get the paperwork?"

"No. I'm on my way to Seward to work an old case. New evidence." I glance at Tails, who still stares at me. The exchange reminds me of the time his sample was collected for testing. Anna had taken samples from Lee's body too. *Hmm.* And then those samples disappeared into thin air.

"Hey, Diaz, I've got a random question for you."

"Shoot."

"There was a case five years ago, in Seward. A missing man. Lee Stanton. We collected DNA from his body and sent it off for testing. I'm not sure where it was going at the time, but we never heard anything back. I know it's a long shot, but is there any chance of tracking the results down?"

"Whew, you sure are asking something there. But if it was an Alaskan case, it should be in our databases. We've been around a

long time, even if the departments weren't using us for all that much."
He's a little jaded on that particular point, and rightly so. He and his
colleagues insisted DNA could be a game-changer for law enforcement
years before everyone else got on board. Even now, a lot of officers
don't collect DNA like they're supposed to. "Let me check it out and
give you a call back, all right?"

"Sure thing. Thanks. I'll swing by as soon as I'm back."

"Sounds good, Linebach. Drive safe."

❖

Seward in June is a different universe than Seward in late October.
The streets are packed with tourists in sweatshirts with *Alaska* on them
because they only packed T-shirts, not realizing it would still be cool,
especially out on the water. I get stuck behind a line of massive tour
buses unloading senior citizens with eight pieces of luggage each. There
are even a couple off-brand taxis. The crowds don't seem to mind the
layer of smoke that hangs in the air, or the smell of burnt cedar and
flambéed pine sap. I head straight to the station.

It's mostly empty. Everyone must be out cleaning up from the fire.
I turn to leave when the door to the back office opens. I turn back and
briefly expect to see Chief Willington. Mikey emerges. A grin spreads
across his face.

"Louisa!" The grin somehow grows when he sees Tails. Mikey
drops to one knee and opens his arms. I drop the leash and Tails runs
straight for him. Before I know it, Tails is on his back while Mikey
gives his belly a vigorous scratch. I give them a minute to catch up.

"So, you're running the show now?"

"Guess you could say it that way. Willington was going to wait,
but his mom's not doing well, so he went a year early to take care of her.
I sure was surprised when he appointed me."

"I was kind of curious about that, honestly. Wasn't there another
officer who'd been here a while?"

He glances around to make sure no one else is present. "There
was, but it turns out he had some…*connections* that would have made
him unsuitable for chief. Willington was doing him a favor overlooking
them when he was here. He left immediately. Got a rec from Willington,
from what I heard."

I raise my eyebrows. I was right to be suspicious of the former Seward chief. "How's it been going so far?" I want to ask about Mr. Drew, but I bite my tongue.

"Honestly? It's been pretty great. I can't really complain. It's a good team here, and I like knowing everybody in town. I don't think I've paid for a meal or a haircut since I arrived."

I smile. Now I appreciate the situation with his family in Anchorage was rough, and I'm glad Mikey's happy. He deserves it.

"So how have you been, *Liaison* Linebach?" I just shrug and he looks worried. "Working with the FBI. That's awesome. They obviously saw your talent for missing persons, and they always need that. Bet you're glad you didn't try to stay."

I watch him watch me carefully. He's clearly waiting for a response, but I give him nothing. Not yet. I can't say I am glad I made that choice, but I'm not ready to share my uncertainty with him. Mikey changes his approach.

"Is Anchorage treating you all right?"

"I guess so. The job is good. I like the work a lot. Otherwise, it's kind of the same. I work a ton, so I haven't gotten to know a lot of people outside the department. Haven't even moved. It's just kind of work, run with Tails, crash on the couch. Maybe a drink with Boggs every once in a while." He looks confused, so I explain. "He asked me out again when I got back, so I told him I'm gay. Turns out he was all right with just having a friend." He nods. I'm not sure when to begin talking about what's changed and what hasn't in any meaningful way, but I think it's all right since there's an immediate situation to address.

"Tell me about this bone you found."

His eyes brighten as if I've handed him a present. He motions to a couple office chairs and we sit. Tails launches into Mikey's lap. There goes all that professionalism he's been learning. Some people think dogs have short memories, but the way Tails licks Mikey's face says otherwise. Mikey takes it in stride and wipes a sleeve across his cheek once Tails settles down.

"So, there was the fire, you know. Tons of wood burned, thousands of acres, all the way up the mountains. No one got hurt, thank God, but we've been cleaning up for days and we're finding all kinds of random things. We were working on the mountains around Alice, and one of my team finds this bone. We check out the area, and there's other stuff.

A belt buckle with initials, some coins, a broken lighter. It's mostly volunteers helping, and of course they're not equipped to process a crime scene, which I think we need to treat it as. So, I wanted you out here to work with me on it. I want us to go over that place with a fine-tooth comb and see what else we find."

"What were the initials on the belt buckle?"

"*LS.* And you'll never believe what was tucked into the back side of it." He tells Tails to get down and, once the dog has removed himself from his lap, reaches into his back pocket and pulls out a plastic slipcase. He gingerly removes something from it and hands it to me.

It's a picture of Marli and her kids, singed around the edges, but clear just the same. I flip it over. On the back, in large, blocky letters, someone has written *I'm sorry.*

❖

We bring a couple fire specialists with us. One of them complains the whole ride about how he's supposed to be off. He won't last long around here. It hurts to look at the mountains blackened with sharp, burnt-out stumps sticking through like acupuncturist's needles on a charred face. Mikey drives like he's done this route a thousand times. Maybe he has. He parks the Jeep where the road ends and Tails jumps from the open back. We'll hike from here. Mikey sends his colleagues in another direction. There's another part of the mountain he wants searched—they're still looking for the fire's cause, and this mountain seems to be where it began.

Mikey doesn't huff and puff like he used to. His face isn't quite as round anymore, and there are a few lines visible under his eyes. It suits him. Seward's been good to Mikey, and I feel proud for him. He inhales deeply.

"Shame to see it like this, isn't it?"

I agree. It smells like campfire. We chat as we hike, and eventually I find the courage to ask about Anna.

"She's still in town, still our medical examiner. I see her a lot. We get lunch together regularly." He looks at me. "You're wondering if she's still seeing that children's book author."

"Is that her job? Anna just told me she had started seeing someone the last time we talked. I didn't want to know the details."

"Yeah. She was here on a book tour. That's how they met. She was only around for a few weeks, though, here and then in Anchorage. They tried to keep it going long distance, but she had no intention of ever settling in Alaska, and you know Anna has no intention of ever leaving. Especially since her dad died."

"Shit! I didn't know."

"Well, you stopped calling."

I look at my feet. "I know. I need to apologize to her. I just…my priorities were kind of a mess. All I could think about was…"

"I get it. But it really hurt her feelings." He slaps my back as we walk. "But hey, second chances, right?"

"Let's start with whether she'll even talk to me." I change the subject and ask about Mr. Drew.

"Funny thing about that."

"Oh?"

"Soon as Willington retired, Mr. Drew started laying low. Sold off a lot of his businesses. And you'll never believe what happened then…"

"Young men stopped going missing."

He laughs. "Well, not quite. This is still the peninsula. But there are a lot fewer disappearances, and there are more clear-cut suicides and lone ranger deaths. Nothing like Halifax. Or Calderon."

Mikey stops just below the tree line, snapping me from my thoughts. There's a lot of debris here. A blackened baby eagle lies in the snow with its eyes open and beak up. I try not to look at it. Mikey turns in the other direction to indicate where they found the bone and the belt buckle. He kicks a pile of downed wood that's organized into a pile. Most of it comes apart at the touch of his boot.

"We think someone had a fire going here. For a while maybe. Like they were camping."

We split up and search the immediate area but find nothing new. He asks my opinion when we come back together. "So, what do you think, *Liaison*?"

"Are there any streams or falls near here?"

"There was a stream, but it's dry and covered in ash now." He walks me around a couple darkened boulders to the dried-up creek bed.

"Let's follow this for a while. If anything made it to the water, it would have flowed downstream." Tails jumps into the crevice with us and runs along just in front, stopping periodically to sniff something that we then investigate. When we've walked sharply downhill for long enough that my knees start to tell me about it, Tails picks something up and trots toward me. He holds it delicately between his teeth and releases it as soon as I've grabbed it.

"Bone!" I practically run to Mikey. It's brittle, blackened, and impossible to identify as animal or human. Mikey swings off his backpack and procures a plastic bag, wherein he drops the bone. He then calls his colleagues over with a jovial cry.

"Hey, we've got bones!"

His announcement coincides with my accidental step on what could be a femur. It cracks. Tails comes to sniff, and Mikey promptly bags that one too. There are three other bones of varying sizes in the immediate vicinity. Two of them could be human ribs. They're fragile, but they're intact. It's possible they've been covered in snow or cold water for years. When the fire specialists rejoin us, we spread out to cover a broader perimeter. Maybe more of a body floated downstream, and an animal got to it, scattering the bones.

Some people would call it luck that my eye catches the blackened skull against the charred spruce trunks. It's fragile enough that when I tentatively tap it with my gloved finger, the bone at the back of the skull begins to cave inward.

"Careful. It looks like the molars are still there. We can use them for ID." I caution the tech preparing to bag it. He grunts and lifts the thing roughly, dropping it to the bottom of the large plastic sack and ignoring my glare. Mikey whistles long and low.

"Nice find, Lou."

We search for another half an hour, but nothing. The two fire investigators get back to their jobs, and we take the bones and skull to town. When Mikey calls Anna on the way to the hospital, I stay silent. I'm sure I'm starting to breathe heavily. When he hangs up, Mikey turns to me.

"She'll be happy to see you. Promise." I grimace at him, and he just laughs.

❖

Anna wraps me in a tight hug as soon as I set foot in her office. After an initial paralyzing shock wears off, I wrap my arms around her and squeeze back, inhaling her familiar amber scent. As I disengage, I lightly touch the blunt edge of her now shoulder-length and stylish waved bob. She pulls away from me but doesn't let go, keeping her hands on my shoulders. Tails wriggles in between us and she laughs.

"You look great!" We both speak at the same time, and then we laugh together. At least from my perspective, there's no lie. She wears glasses now—tortoise-shelled and cat-eyed—and they suit her perfectly, as does the new haircut.

She releases one hand to touch my white forelock. "Oh, I like this. Très chic!" Her eyes leave me long enough to register Mikey, and she turns toward him. I can't stop staring at her.

"Chief, you have presents for me?"

Mikey sets his pack on an examining table and gently lifts out the bags with the bones. "We found these all pretty close together. We weren't sure if they were human or animal, until Louisa found…" He pulls out the skull and she claps her hands. "This."

She carefully takes the bag from him, examining it through the clear barrier. "Ooh. There are teeth intact. That's just perfect! May I?"

"You're the woman for the job."

She slides the skull from the plastic and carries it to an adjustable light. She turns the skull so delicately it seems she barely touches it.

"Well, the fire has definitely done its thing, hasn't it?" She turns it a few more times, looks at the base of it. "But I can tell you this—I'd guess this has been out there for a long time. This person wasn't killed in the fire." She slowly removes the other bones. "Hmm. Ribs. Did you find anything else in the area that might give us a clue about what this person was doing?"

"Campfire remnants upstream. Some coins. A belt buckle." Her eyebrows rise. "It's in the evidence room, but the initials on it are *LS*. A picture was slipped under the metal in the back of the holder." He reaches into his pocket and gives her the picture he showed me. Her eyes are huge as she looks at me.

My mind runs so many scenarios at once I cannot articulate any of them, but the one it keeps coming back to is that this skull and bones must be Branden Halifax's. If he had possessions of Lee Stanton, then they were linked. And maybe Kyle Calderon can somehow be definitively linked too.

"I think we need the old files," I say. I should have stopped by the station for my old notes before getting on the road. I step into the hallway to call Chief Quint at the Anchorage office and request my old files for the Branden Halifax case. I also want my Lee Stanton file. After just a minute, I hear, "Got 'em."

"The bulk of the files and my notes are here. Let me get someone to scan and send them over," Mikey says. It seems we've silently agreed to use Anna's office as our war room while we work through our new clues. He makes a similar call to his station. He already got the files pulled from cold storage.

Mikey's files come through first. To our delight, there's a list of Halifax's last known physicians and his dentist. Anna calls the still-practicing dentist right away. He keeps his old files, he assures us, and he's happy to have them sent over. My stomach flutters with butterflies. I can't remember the last time I've felt this good. It's dizzying, the prospect of finally getting some answers for Marli Lei.

My email notification dings. My Stanton file comes through. It's almost a full copy of the Seward file. Anchorage has scanned the documents in reverse chronological order, so the most basic information is first. It's a helpful reminder of things I probably should have forgotten but haven't. I spend a few minutes reviewing my notes with Mikey, who has the record of childhood doctors and dentists, his work records, police records, and school addresses. It feels like decades ago we worked these cases, although I dream about them regularly. As we rehash the old details, my phone rings.

"Linebach, hey it's Diaz. Hey, I tracked that DNA for you. Turns out it *was* tested, though it landed in Seattle, and they didn't get around to it until a year after Dr. Fenway sent it."

Anna and Mikey both look at me expectantly. Tails raises his nub and stands perfectly still. He's great at sensing tension in a room.

"Dr. Fenway and Chief Harper are here. I'm putting you on speaker. Tell me."

"It says here the test was meant to confirm that the DNA belonged to a Lee Stanton. Dr. Fenway also later submitted DNA from his parents. Is that right?"

"Right."

"The results were negative. The sample from the body was not a match to the DNA from Mr. and Mrs. Stanton."

I nearly drop the phone. I open and close my mouth a few times but say nothing. Anna and Mikey's faces reflect the same shock I feel.

"Are you still there, Linebach?"

"Yeah. Yes, we're still here. You're sure?"

"That's what the results say, and it's a good lab. Always has been. I'd be inclined to trust the results, though there's always a margin for error."

"Thank you, Diaz."

"Can I ask what—?"

"I'll fill you in as soon as I'm back in Anchorage. It's a long story." I disconnect the call before he can even say good-bye. Anna and Mikey both lean toward me. I feel faint. I reach out for a wall and find nothing. Anna rushes over and throws an arm around my back. I lean into her.

"Holy hell." Mikey stands frozen in place. His face is ashen. *Maybe he will join me in passing out.* The implications of the results hit me in phases. I sink slowly to a crouch. Anna comes down with me, arm still around me.

We identified the wrong body. The Stantons buried that headless corpse thinking it was their son, and it wasn't. And now we have no idea who it was. I turn abruptly, searching for a trash can. I'm going to be sick. I think about my therapist, the techniques she taught me for dealing with panic attacks.

I lean back against the cool wall, then close my eyes. I intentionally slow my breathing. Inhale through the nose. Exhale through the mouth. Inhale through the nose. Exhale. Meditate. *I'm safe. This is just a physical response to stress. I'm safe.* I breathe intentionally until my heart slows. Mikey and Anna don't rush me. They just stay with me, silent. After I've opened my eyes, Anna puts a hand on my shoulder.

"It's all right, Louisa. They didn't tell us. We couldn't have known."

I shake my head slowly. "Why didn't I ever think to call?"

"*You* wouldn't have even known where to call. *I* was the one who sent the kit, remember? They never responded. I just assumed it had joined the backlog. I didn't even think to—" She stops abruptly and stares into space.

"Whoa. Whoa!" Mikey holds his hands up to both of us. Tails runs to him and sits. "This is not anybody's fault. DNA testing wasn't part of the regular routine, and we had every reason to believe that was Lee Stanton. His parents identified him. He was near Lee's trailer with the right approximate TOD. Usually that's enough."

I don't know what to do or say next. *Where do we even start?* I roll my shoulders a few times, trying to relax the tension in my upper body. The movement helps me think.

"Is there a dentist listed in that file?" It takes me a moment to realize I'm the person holding the materials now. I find the medical sheet.

"Dr. Finley. It says Lee's last visit was when he was seventeen years old."

"Okay," Mikey says. "So, all adult teeth. Let's grab the dental records if we can. Anna, is Finley still around? I've never heard of him."

"No, but Branden Halifax's dentist took over most of his patients, so there's a chance he has Lee Stanton's files. Let's call back to get the additional request in."

We don't talk while we wait for the files to be scanned over. *What is there to say?* I suspect that, like me, they're inside their own heads, processing and lamenting time lost.

CHAPTER TWENTY-SEVEN

The dentist does have Finley's old files, and the next day, Anna comes by the station to let me and Mikey know, in the privacy of Mikey's office, that the skull is Lee Stanton's. My mind is reeling. I know now that the decapitated body isn't his, and yet I keep wondering how his body and his head could have gotten so far separated. I stop myself from asking the question aloud.

I suggest the next step be a visit to the Stantons. It will not be an easy conversation, but they need to know the person they buried is not their son—that their son is here, or at least his head is. Anna believes the bones at the campsite are probably his, especially if his parents can recognize the belt buckle. I excuse myself back to the hotel so I can mentally prepare for what I'm guessing will be the worst conversation I'll ever have, which will be followed by another awful one. We have to ask Marli Lei to test her children's DNA. Perhaps the already buried headless body is a match to her long-lost boyfriend.

Anna calls as soon as I've gotten out of the tub, which is where I prefer to do my thinking with some nice Epsom salts if I'm not running these days.

"Are you okay?"

"I don't really know how to answer that. All I can tell you is I wish I'd brought my therapist with me. It's just...I don't know how to process this. This case was always messy, but Jesus." She doesn't rush to say anything while I think through it. "I wonder if it's why I kept having nightmares about Lee and Branden. Maybe my subconscious knew all along."

"Maybe. Your instincts told you the body wasn't Lee Stanton five years ago, and you were right. You're so focused...maybe your brain just couldn't force that thought out."

"I should have listened to it."

"And done what? Told the Stantons they were wrong?" She has a good point. We're both silent. I'd like company and a drink, but I want to take her out when I'm in a good head space, not while I'm a confused mess. I say as much to Anna.

"Well, I'd normally take *confused mess* Louisa, thank you very much, but I'm headed to Homer. Their ME had to fly back to the Lower 48 for an emergency. I'm covering his autopsies tomorrow, but I'll be back here just as soon as I'm finished. Maybe then I can finally cook you that dinner, if you still want?"

"I very much still want." *Especially after I have time to compose myself.*

"Perfect. I'll give you a call as soon as I'm back in town."

"Be safe in Homer, okay?"

"Of course."

I exhale a long breath. My muscles still twitch as they relax from the bath. I pat the edge of the bed and Tails jumps up. I lift the covers for him, and we burrow under together, my nose pressed into the top of his head.

I don't have nightmares, only blindingly white dreams about deep snow.

❖

The Stantons live in the same remote house far up the mountain, but when we visit them this time, it's Mr. Stanton who opens the door. His wife is nowhere to be seen, though her coat still hangs on a hook in the kitchen. When he sees us, Mr. Stanton hushes us immediately and asks us to step outside. Thankfully the weather is nice.

"Sorry about that. My wife is asleep, and I don't want to bother her."

"Is everything all right, Mr. Stanton?"

"Sure. Yeah sure. It's just, the wife's got cancer and it's not good." He lowers his voice so much that we both have to lean in to hear. "To be honest, that radiation's the thing keepin' her alive. She don't know I'm using the money Lee left to pay for it." He looks at his wedding ring, "Well, I guess it ain't ever gonna feel like the right time to let her go." He smiles weakly.

I remember my mother's long-ago struggle and offer my empathy. Mikey's face furrows deeply as he says he's sorry too.

"Lee left you some money?"

"Oh, yeah, Chief…" He's quiet for a moment, maybe remembering. "After the funeral, the wife couldn't stand to go through those boxes he'd left us, so we put them in the cellar for a long time. Wasn't till near a year later we took them out and sorted them. There was this clock in there, and when I opened it to get it running, a wad of cash fell out."

"Whoa. Isn't that something! Had he gotten an inheritance?"

"Nope, not from any of the family at least. Figured he'd been saving or something. Don't know what he would have been saving for, but Lee was always private." He wrinkles his forehead, but he doesn't dwell on it. "So, what can I help you with?"

I take a deep breath in, feeling even worse about having to give him this news now I know Mrs. Stanton is sick. It's helpful to have Mikey here at least. I look at him to steady myself.

"Mr. Stanton, I'm afraid we have something to tell you that's going to be…not pleasant. And I'm so sorry. I want to say that first. I really am."

His facial expression is that of a man who can't really be surprised anymore. "All right."

"You know about the fires, of course."

"Yeah. We were damned lucky they didn't reach us."

"Right. Well, there's been a major cleanup effort, and we're looking for what caused the fire."

"Sure."

I keep hoping he'll latch on to this topic, steer the course of the conversation elsewhere, but of course he doesn't.

"Well, in that effort, we found some human remains." It sounds so impersonal. "They prompted us to look back at the old files… From when Lee went missing, and also from when Branden Halifax disappeared. And we…" I look at Mikey, who's following along, nodding supportively. "You remember we swabbed you and your wife for DNA?"

"I remember."

"Well, apparently the lab ran the DNA and got a result a year later, but it was never reported. It just got lost in the shuffle."

Mr. Stanton looks at me steadily. "It's not Lee that we buried."

I can't help my long sigh of relief that I don't have to be the one to say it. "No, it's not."

He sinks back against the wall of his home, breathing out heavily and producing a cigarette from his pocket. "I should have known."

"Why do you say that? There was nothing to indicate it wasn't Lee."

He waves his hand toward the house. "She convinced herself that it was because it was easier. But I, I never really was certain."

"I'm so sorry."

"We buried someone who's not our son."

"Yes. It seems that way."

"So, Lee's back to being missing."

"No. No. We found Lee. He was in the fire zone."

He stands straight again. "You kiddin' me?"

"No, sir. We found his skull and bones. Matched dental records. He died before the fire, but it's him."

"Good God."

Mikey speaks up. "Mr. Stanton, there was a campfire set up, to keep warm or cook maybe. Right next to it, there was a belt buckle."

He slowly leans toward us. "What kind of buckle?"

"Rectangular metal, simple. It has *LS* in a nice script. Was that something Lee owned?"

"Hang on." He abruptly turns and goes back into the house. I look at Mikey, unsure. He shakes his head. Mr. Stanton reappears.

"All these years, I never even knew he had it. The belt buckle was his grandfather's, who he's named after. I had it in my closet for years after my dad died. I never realized it was gone. Hell, I woulda just given it to Lee if he'd asked." He seems unable to stop shaking his head slowly. I intentionally take very deep, slow breaths.

"Mr. Stanton...I am sorry, but we're going to need to exhume the body buried five years ago." He gazes at me like I'm talking from underwater. "We know now that he's not Lee, which means he is someone else's child."

His face softens a little with that. "Okay." He drops his cigarette butt, steps on it with the tip of his boot even though he's already smoked it to its cherry. "Yes, his family will want to bury him somewhere they see fit."

He rises slowly. "I have to ask something of you. I think y'all owe me this."

We both wait. I'm not sure there's anything we *don't* owe him.

"Don't you tell my wife. Do what you need to do, and get me Lee's remains, but she isn't to know about this. That woman's been through enough and she's dying. She thought she buried her son five years ago." His face is surprisingly tender. The thought of losing her must weigh more heavily on him than he lets on. "She found closure after that. Took her a lot of years and a lot of praying, and the stress on her...Having to dig that boy up and bury our broken apart son...well, she couldn't take it."

He shakes his head, pulls out another cigarette. "I'll do it. 'Course I will, for the other family, so they can bury their kin. But I'm not doing that to my Peaches. I just thank God she doesn't visit the grave like she used. She would notice right away. Can't get out there anymore, though."

I look at Mikey and nod, and he nods in reply.

"All right, Mr. Stanton. Can we ask you one last thing?"

"Yeah."

"Do you happen to have something with Lee's handwriting on it? Nothing important—just notes, a shopping list, a planner, anything like that?" Mikey raises an eyebrow at me, but I ignore it.

"Can I ask why?"

"We want to be sure Lee's file is complete before we close it. We'd like to have a handwriting sample if we can."

"Sure." He turns back to the house and soon reemerges with a note he hands to me. Mikey reads it over my shoulder. "Lee left this on our door a few weeks before he died. His ma has been keeping it with her things. She's gotten a lot more sentimental since he's been gone." In awkward block letters is written *Pops, just wondered if I could borrow the deep fryer. I'm home if you want to run it by. Lee.*

I carefully tuck it into my interior pocket. "That'll do. I'll return it when we see you. Thank you, Mr. Stanton." I shake his hand. "And I'm so sorry to hear about Mrs. Stanton. She's been brave through so much, and it seems unfair for her to have to go through cancer too. It's good she has you looking after her."

Mr. Stanton just nods and goes inside.

We get inside the car, but as soon as Mikey asks how I'm doing, I let myself cry a little for the Stantons. For me, it's not just sadness for what they've lost, though—it's the relief of finally knowing they can bury their son.

❖

On Sunday mornings, Mr. Stanton takes his fading wife to Primrose so she can go to church with her sister. He doesn't stay. He's not religious, and she likes to spend time with her family before he picks her up in the evening. He tells us this would be the best time to exchange remains. We meet him at the gravesite. He doesn't have to remind us where it is. We bring Lee's skull and the bones in a plain wooden box.

When we arrive at the overlook, Mr. Stanton is already there with a couple of shovels and the professional-grade digger Mikey arranged. We have plastic ready to wrap the entire coffin for direct transport to the hospital. I don't even want to think about Anna opening it. She's tough, but I know it will be awful.

Mikey and I both offer to run the digger, but Mr. Stanton insists on doing it himself. When he gets close to the box, we turn to the shovels. We're all sweating by the time we lift the box from the ground. We carry it, between the three of us, to the truck Mikey's brought from the station. When it's wrapped and settled securely in, I retrieve the much smaller box from the front seat and give it to Mr. Stanton, who carries it back to the open hole in the ground. He insists he wants to see. When he lifts the lid, there's the skull. He picks it up and holds it in front of him, but he doesn't say anything. He just stares into the eye sockets, glances at the teeth, nods, and places it back. Then he lowers the box into the ground. All the open space around it makes what remains of Lee Stanton seem lost and small there.

Mr. Stanton says a couple words, then a couple of lines from the Bible. He looks uncomfortable, but he assures us Mrs. Stanton would want them said and he's gotta do it right for her. When he's finished, we throw a few shovels' worth of soil on top, then he backfills the plot with the digger. I am glad Mrs. Stanton cannot visit her son. The grave is obviously fresh, and the earth smells wet, like earthworms recently dug up.

Before we part ways, I apologize again to Mr. Stanton. I could apologize forever and never feel better. If he was angry, or if he was upset, it would help. He doesn't seem to be anything. He just looks at me.

"You know, it never did set right with me that he would have shot himself." I can only blink at him. "This…the way this was, out in the woods with a fire, out there in the wilderness, living off the land. Now, that would have been our Lee. He wouldn't have taken the coward's way. He let nature have him." And he walks away.

"We didn't ask him about the picture of Branden's family in the belt buckle."

"I don't think we need to, do you?"

"But we don't know if Lee or Branden wrote on it. Who it is changes everything."

I reach into my interior pocket and produce the picture Mikey handed over to me, as well as the note we collected from Mr. Stanton. "Look at the *orr* sequence." I point at it. "This *s* here. The *y*." The handwriting is the same. "Remember the picture Marli showed us that Branden had written on the back of? About her not going home with the wrong guy?"

Mikey's expression changes to one of excitement. "When we talk to her, we can look at it again."

"Exactly."

Excepting my goodwill to Mikey when he drops me off, I am silent the entire trip down mountain. I'm too preoccupied considering what it means for Lee to have written *I'm sorry* on a picture of Branden's family.

Chapter Twenty-Eight

We visit Marli Lei in the morning. We need to collect DNA to test against the headless body that's now safely at the morgue, awaiting Anna's return. I've called ahead, so the children aren't surprised to see two police officers at their door. Alicia at nine still has the serious eyes she had as a younger child. She doesn't remember us. The younger girl seems curious but doesn't say much.

Marli looks much the same. She's gained a few pounds and more muscle, perhaps from doing the house and property maintenance herself now. The house has had some repairs both inside and out, and there's what looks to be a fresh coat of peach paint on the walls. There are no pictures of Marli and other men. In fact, there's still a picture of Branden fastened to the refrigerator with a magnet. It's the one of him holding the fish. She offers us tea or coffee, and we accept coffee. There's something calming about the sameness. I don't let myself get comfortable, though. I pace as Mikey subtly removes the picture from the fridge and flips it over. As Marli goes to the table, she sees him.

"The reason you're here. It's about him, right?"

Mikey and I both go to the table with our mugs. Mikey remains standing while I sit with Marli. The girls are around the table too, eating cereal from big ceramic bowls.

"It is." I glance at the children.

"It's all right. He's their father. It's okay for them to know." I nod respectfully. Marli is silent for a moment. "You found him, didn't you?"

"We believe we have."

She inhales audibly. "What happened?"

"Before I tell you, I just want to say that I'm so, so sorry. It—"

"Did you kill him?"

"What?" Her face is so intense I can't tell what she means by her question. "No, of course not."

"Then it's not your fault." Mikey's eyebrows are up. This is a different Marli, even while she looks the same. "I'm sorry, I didn't mean for that to sound harsh. But I've wrestled a lot with that myself, wanting to blame myself for Branden disappearing. Or for stopping the search for him. I've had to come to terms with the fact that whatever happened to him wasn't my fault. And it's not your fault either."

"No, but..." I put both of my palms on the table. "There was a fire recently, in the area around Mount Alice." Marli and the girls all nod. Fires around here affect everyone. "During the cleanup, a man's remains were discovered. We were able to find out whose remains they are with dental records." Marli gasps. "Which means that the person we thought was already buried is actually...someone else. We...*unburied* him so we can figure out who he is."

"So does that mean the buried-unburied man could be our dad?" There's an edge of happiness in Alicia's voice. I don't know if it's because she's thinking like a detective and actively putting pieces together, or if she's excited that she'll finally know where her father is, even if it's a confirmation he's gone for good.

"That's exactly what we're thinking, Miss Alicia. You'd make an excellent officer." She smiles at me. "But we can't know for sure if it's your dad unless we can match DNA."

"How do you do that?"

"We need the DNA of somebody related to him so we can compare it to the body."

The younger girl looks terrified. "You need Mom's DNA?"

I turn to her. "No, your mom wouldn't work because she wasn't *related* to your dad."

"Because they weren't married?"

"No. No, that wouldn't matter." I smile. "Because your mom and your dad don't have the same parents or the same grandparents. DNA travels in the blood from the parents, so your mom and your dad don't share the same DNA."

"Oh, okay."

"But both of *you* have the same parents. One of your parents is your mom, and the other parent is your dad. So, you both share your mom's and your dad's DNA, and you can help us." The youngest girl is wide-eyed, but Alicia puts her chin up.

"You can take my DNA if you need to."

I quickly cover my smile with a hand, and I see Mikey feign interest in anything behind him. Her face says she believes we may have to maim or kill her to get it. I clear my throat.

"Thank you, Miss Alicia. It's simple and it does not hurt at all. We just wiggle a long Q-Tip in your mouth."

She looks almost offended. "That's it?"

"Yes, that's it. The cotton picks up the skin inside your cheek, and we can see your DNA in that. It'll be sent away to a lab where the DNA from the man who may be your dad is too. The scientists there will be able to tell if you and the man who died are related."

"Wow!"

"It *is* cool, isn't it?"

"That easy, huh?" Marli says. Mikey assures her.

"How are you feeling, Ms. Lei?" I have to ask.

"Surprisingly okay. I've had five years of knowing he was gone. It would be nice to be able to bury him." Again, I wish she was angry, but she seems all right. "How soon will we know?"

"We'll let you know as soon as we hear something." I hope Diaz can turn it around in a couple days.

She nods and collects our empty mugs, a subconscious signal it's time for us to leave. I would be anxious to be alone with my family and my thoughts. I hope Marli will tell the kids the best stories she knows about their dad. Mikey has a field test kit in his bag. He shows it to Alicia and explains again how it works.

"Are you ready, Miss Alicia?"

Alicia opens her mouth wide. I smile at her act of faith and bravery, but I'm a little choked up. She reminds me of the kids in Seattle, before it all went downhill. Mikey swabs both her cheeks, then carefully places the sample in the plastic collection bag.

We thank Alicia Halifax, thank Marli Lei, and thank all of them for being so understanding. We assure them we'll be back soon. We emerge into the blinding sunlight of a June day, where the air is warm and the mountain smells like wildflowers.

It feels like an injustice.

❖

Anna calls as we're driving back into town. She's just arrived, but instead of going home she's at the morgue to collect hair from the body. "Would you mind sending it to Scientific care of Dr. Diaz? He and I are working together on another case, and I know he can turn it around fast if you let him know it's for me."

"Sure thing. I'll send it off ASAP and STAT. And hey, are you feeling up to coming over tonight? No pressure, I promise. I'll cook and we can talk about anything you want, work or not."

Just talking to her on the phone soothes my nerves. I don't hesitate. "That sounds amazing. Honestly, I'd be happy with just your company and a frozen pizza, so no pressure to cook. Can I bring anything?"

"Just yourself, and Tails of course." He'll enjoy the attention from Anna almost as much as I will. Who wouldn't? "How does six sound?"

"I'll be there. Promise."

"I'm holding you to that!"

I smile as we end the call. When I look at Mikey, he just smirks.

"Shut up."

"Good to have you back in Seward, Lou."

"It's good to be back."

❖

At the hotel, I call my FBI contact with an update. He asks for a full explanation of the Halifax and Lee cases. I launch into a rundown that includes the Kyle Calderon case. My attempt to be concise makes my head spin. I need to rewind and clarify frequently. There's a long silence after I've explained my theory that connects Mr. Drew to at least two of these men. I can almost feel tension crackling through my cell phone.

"Linebach, I'm going to send you some files. I want you to review them closely. They're about Mr. Drew. Given what you've just relayed to me, I'm considering keeping you in Seward for a while."

"For how long?"

"My inclination is to say as long as it takes, and that could be a while. I know you were keen to get to Mr. Drew while you were in

Seward before. It's time I come clean with you. That's part of why I recruited you as a liaison." I'm glad he cannot see my mouth open in surprise. "We've had an eye on him for years but were roadblocked every time we tried to connect his Anchorage activities to situations in Seward."

"Well, the former chief here was a friend of his."

"Yes. That situation was...unfortunate. Now that it's Harper, has the situation changed?"

"Absolutely. Mi—Chief Harper will assist in any way he can."

"Do you believe he can be discreet?"

"Yes, sir."

"All right. You call me as soon as that DNA is back. Don't say anything about this conversation to anyone."

"Yes, sir."

This is it. This is what I'm supposed to do—stay in Seward and nab Mr. Drew once and for all. My heart rate climbs. I notice immediately and exhale, then inhale. I wish I could confide in Mikey and Anna. I'll have to watch what I drink while I'm with her this evening.

I head into town to buy some extra clothes. I have a date, and it sounds like I'll be here for a while. I may as well take the opportunity to round out my wardrobe.

❖

I stand outside the door with Tails for a moment before I knock, cradling a bottle of Johnnie Walker Blue in one arm. Normally I'd never dream of buying a two-hundred-dollar bottle of scotch, but of all the appropriate occasions, this seems like one for so many reasons. My feelings are all at odds with one another. I'm still reeling from the misidentification of Lee Stanton, but now it looks like these cases may finally get some real closure. I still feel horribly guilty over how I treated Anna and Mikey, but now I have the chance to make things right. And I may have a chance to pursue the man I've been wanting to go after for five years.

Part of me is cautious. If I stay here chasing Mr. Drew, will I ever want to go back to Anchorage? Could I convince the boss to let me stay permanently? I shake my head. My therapist and I outlined a technique to manage my obsessive thoughts. *Weigh whether they can be useful in the moment. If not, acknowledge that obsessive thoughts are occurring, write them down, and then consciously let them go.*

I open my notepad and write *what if Seward?* I then focus my attention on what my senses experience right now. I hear Anna singing on the other side of the door in the eat-in kitchen. It's an old jazz staple, and she's amazingly off-key. I cover my laugh in case she can hear me. I knock lightly. When she answers, a wall of spices hits my nose.

"What smells like my childhood in here?" I remove my wool peacoat.

"Oh good! Hopefully that means I did something right! I'm trying lamb korma for the first time." She looks absolutely charming with a dish towel flung over the shoulder of her breezy jersey knit dress. The house is warm, and I'm glad I went with a thin blouse.

"Did I tell you it's one of my favorite dishes?"

"No, but I'm certainly glad to hear it! And what is this?" She takes the bottle of scotch out of my hand as I unclip Tails's leash. He sits in anticipation of a head scratching, which Anna delivers while admiring the bottle.

"Whoa. Now, this scotch puts a lot of pressure on my cooking!"

"Oh no, I didn't mean—"

She chuckles. "It's okay. At least we know we'll have something delicious tonight either way." The table is already set, and it seems she's just finished cooking. She turns to ladle the creamy sauce and meat into bowls already full of white rice.

"Don't worry, Tails, I thought about you too!" She pulls a bowl of rice and unseasoned lamb out of the refrigerator.

"As if he's not spoiled enough!"

She sets the bowl on the floor, and he just looks at her. I give him the command to eat.

"You've got him well trained!"

"I realized fast that if he and I were going to be living in five hundred square feet together, he had better learn to be polite. Besides, he works with the public all the time, so he's got to mind his manners."

Tails promptly drops rice all over the floor. Anna sets our bowls on the round table, and as we sit, I notice the bouquet of fresh flowers.

"Irises and roses. My favorites. They remind me of Anneke," I say. Anna waggles her eyebrows at me, like she assumes Anneke is or was a romantic interest. I laugh and clarify. "She was a woman my mother hired to help around the house when I was maybe four or five, but she sort of raised me. She had a farm outside of Seattle, and sometimes she'd take me there if Mom was hosting some big event at the house and didn't want me underfoot. She grew irises and roses, and I always associate their smell with her." *I should call Anneke.* I refocus so I can pay attention to Anna.

"Aw, then I'm extra glad I went with that combination. It's my favorite. And you'll need to tell me more about Anneke. She sounds sweet." Anna picks up the wine bottle, then pauses. "I didn't know what wine goes with korma, so I got a pinot grigio. But since you've brought scotch, what do you say we break convention and have that with dinner instead?"

"That's the best plan I've heard all day." There's no need to tell her red goes with lamb. She pulls the scotch off the counter and pours us each a full three fingers.

"Do you want to tell me about your day? Or would you rather not?"

Tails seems to know that we're settling into a conversation, because he sniffs the bowl one last time to be sure no rice remains, lets out a loud sigh, and curls himself into a ball under the table.

I tell her how I feel about the Stanton/Halifax case and my hopes for how things will resolve. I can't tell her what I've learned about the FBI's interest in Mr. Drew, but I do drop a hint there might be a reason for me to stay in Seward, at least for a while. She claps, and then clasps my hands across the table.

"Would you like that? Staying in Seward?" She leans forward and looks into my eyes. I squeeze her hands, rubbing my thumbs over her smooth skin as I answer.

"Yes. There is nothing I would like more in the world." We sit there holding hands for a minute, just smiling at each other before I laughingly remind her that her food is probably getting cold. She lets go of me and takes a bite. I load my fork with lamb as I continue. "I realized after I left, I was letting the job affect me in ways that weren't healthy. But it took me a while to learn how to cope with the highs and lows. Therapy helped." Anna has stopped chewing. She's listening to what I'm saying, so I continue.

"My…intensity was a problem when I worked DCS too. I got so…" Her face contorts as she drops her spoon. "Anna? Anna, are you okay?" Anna raises her hand to her mouth. Her eyes get wide as she jumps out of her chair and runs to the sink. *Oh my God. Is she choking?* I'm on my feet immediately, ready to help, but she's already doubled over the sink. She holds a hand behind her to stop me as she spits food into the sink and flips on the garbage disposal. She wipes her mouth with a dish towel, then turns around.

"Don't eat it!"

It takes me a second to register she's fine. "What?"

"Don't eat the food! It's terrible!" She wipes the corner of her eyes and starts laughing.

"The korma?"

"Yes! No! It can't even be called korma. It smells great, but…I don't know what I did wrong. It's a monstrosity!" Just watching her try to catch her breath between words from laughing so hard makes me laugh too. Our laugh-fest goes on for several moments before it diminishes to giggle-bursts. Finally, it's quiet and we both catch our breath.

"Okay, now I *have to* try it!" I make a break for the table.

"Noooooo!" She howls behind me, close on my heels. I've got the spoon in my mouth before she can stop me. I laugh and run to the sink so I can spit it out in safety. Anna is crying next to me. "I told you!"

"I'm an officer of the law, ma'am. I require verifiable facts." I rinse my mouth with water from the sink.

"I am *so* sorry! I have no idea what happened!" I still taste something foul on the end of my tongue, so I swish with more water. "Are you okay? Did I kill you?"

"No, no—no need to take me to your office just yet. I think I'll recover." I move back to the table. "Nothing a little alcohol won't fix."

She laughs and lifts her own glass. "What do you say we order a pizza and perform a culinary postmortem while we wait?"

We top off our glasses and Anna orders us a Hawaiian. As we sip, we poke around the korma with our utensils, trying to determine the cause of death.

"You know, I have some great curry recipes. I could take you to the Indian grocer sometime and get you stocked up. Teach you some dishes?"

She turns her head to the side and gives me side-eye. "That sounds an awful lot like a date."

"I very much hope so." She smiles. I glance at her for a moment, trying to read how she's feeling, then move my chair close to her, hoping my assessment is right. I lean over to lightly kiss the corner of Anna's mouth, and she takes my hand.

"Anna, I'm really sorry."

"Oh, it's okay. You don't have to—"

"No, I do. I was a serious asshole to you. The way I left here was inexcusable. Nothing that happened was your fault. You at least deserved an explanation."

"I think I understand. You were feeling conflicted by wanting to be here, but also wanting to pursue Mr. Drew, and not being able to do so."

"Yes, that's part of it. But I think too I was just scared of being with you. I'd recently broken up with a live-in girlfriend of six years, and I had fucked that relationship up royally. I was scared I wasn't ready and that I'd screw it up again." She doesn't interject or try to make excuses for me, which I appreciate. I have her full attention as I speak.

"Rhaina left me because I was in a really bad place emotionally and psychologically, and I refused to acknowledge it or get any help. If I had tried even a little bit, she would have stuck with me. She was a good person. But I wouldn't do it. I shut her out completely and let myself spiral."

"Was that when you left DCS?"

"I was *fired* from DCS because I went off the rails trying to help a child who was no longer under my jurisdiction. I neglected all my other cases; I stopped coming into the office—hell, I crossed state lines to find her even after I'd been fired. I intentionally misled the police into thinking I was still her caseworker."

"That must have been a hard time."

"It was horrible. Not to mention that I'd moved my mother in with me because she was dying."

"I'm so sorry." She clasps my hand in both of hers.

"My relationship with my mom was complicated, and it hurt my relationship with Rhaina. I know now there were things I should have done differently. After you and I stopped talking...I mean, after I stopped talking to you..." Anna acknowledges my correction. "I realized I was just making the same mistakes. I started seeing a therapist. She's really helped…Or, she would say, she's helped me help myself."

"I'm so glad. Mine's been invaluable."

"You have a therapist? You always seem to handle things so well."

"Well, yup, because I learned how from an expert. Some of the things I see in a workday require talking through, though."

"That makes sense. I guess I was so stuck in my own head that I couldn't see how I was affecting the people around me."

"What matters is you're recognizing that everyone needs a little help."

I lean back in my chair as weight falls from my shoulders. "Thank you for being so understanding. It's nice to be able to talk to you and not feel judged. I hadn't realized how exhausting it was trying to come off like I had everything together when I was really feeling such complicated, sometimes pretty nasty emotions." We finish our glasses of scotch, and she pours us more. "I'm sorry your relationship didn't work out, by the way."

"Oh, don't be. She's a lovely woman, very sweet. But she didn't want to move to Alaska, and she felt like she was too old to raise kids. It was better to realize early on what we wanted was incompatible. I learned a lot from her, but breaking up was for the best."

The doorbell rings, and I silently curse the delivery person for interrupting the conversation, even as my stomach growls. Anna places the pizza on the table, then makes a face.

"Well, now that I've ruined our fancy dinner, how do you feel about going full-on relax and eating in front of the TV? I could have sworn I heard some big game was on tonight…"

I stare at her in surprise. "Since when did you start watching hockey?" She shrugs and urges me to follow her into the living room.

"I may have checked it out just to see what all the fuss was about." I settle on the sofa while she turns on the TV and flips channels. She finds the Stanley Cup final.

"So, do you have a team?"

"I think I'll cheer for the Penguins. Who doesn't like a Penguin, right?"

I make a show of throwing my hands up as I jump to my feet. "Well, it's been fun, but I've gotta—" She laughs and catches me in a tight embrace, which I pretend to try breaking free from. "If I'd known you were going to end up a Pittsburgh fan, I never would have mentioned hockey at all."

"You get back here, lady. There's a pizza to eat, and you need to help me understand the rules of this game. Like how can *icing* be a penalty? Aren't they supposed to play it on the ice?"

I laugh. I give up the fake struggle and let her lead me back onto the sofa, where she drops a slice of pizza on her plate, pulls her legs up and curls against my side. The puck drops.

For once, I'm not worried about who wins. Just being here with Anna, feeling her pressed into me, is all I need right now. I don't know where this will go, or if it will go anywhere at all. But even if we decide to just be friends, this moment with her is perfect exactly as it is. As if she shares my thoughts, she nuzzles her head into my neck and her hair tickles my cheek. I press my nose into her hair and kiss it.

"Okay, so the first thing to understand about hockey is that even though their mascot may be a penguin, the Pittsburgh Penguins are the enemy..."

By the time the Penguins defeat the Red Wings and skate their laps with the Stanley Cup, we are sleepy and silly with scotch and wrapped tightly in each other's arms.

"You can't drive back to the hotel. You've been drinking," Anna mumbles directly into my neck, where her head is nestled.

"It certainly wouldn't look great for the FBI to get pulled over for a DUI."

"No, it wouldn't. Besides, Tails is tired."

I laugh. Tails may be sprawled flat on his side, but the eye I can see is wide open, on guard in this new location. As soon as he sees me look at him, he sits up, ready for action. Anna notices and laughs, her excuse blown.

"Too bad. I was going to suggest we get ready for bed."

I hesitate. "Anna, we've both been drinking. I don't..."

She smiles and runs her hand over my back. "I know. I just thought it might be nice to sleep next to each other." She watches me as I smile in relief. I've rushed things in the past. I don't want to make that mistake with her. She moves her fingertips to the thin sleeves of my blouse.

"You can even borrow a T-shirt and some shorts."

"Good idea. Then you can comfort me over the loss of the Red Wings."

She chuckles as she opens the back door for Tails, who seems to realize we're here for the night. When he comes back in, he settles on the rug facing the door.

Anna takes my hand and leads me upstairs.

CHAPTER TWENTY-NINE

I'm back at my hotel the next morning, full of the pancakes Anna and I made together with no culinary disasters. I'm feeling unusually good. I hadn't realized how little I touch other people in Anchorage. It was good to just fall asleep with Anna pressed against me and to wake with her arm thrown over me. As soon as I've showered, not wanting to wash away the lingering smell of amber perfume, I settle on the bed with my laptop to review the files the boss sent. Tails lies next to me with his chin on my arm. I guess he's reading too.

"Looks like this might be the next big assignment, buddy."

There are hundreds of pages, including reports on a dozen missing men tied to Mr. Drew. The men's pictures and physical descriptions are eerily familiar. The phone has probably been ringing for a while before I realize it and pick up. I glance at the clock; it's already midafternoon.

"Hello?"

"Linebach? Diaz. Got a result for you."

"Already?"

"Dr. Fenway sent it overnight and said you needed it STAT. Figured I better not make an FBI Liaison wait."

"Well, I'm impressed."

"Me too. That's the fastest I've ever turned it around. You've got a match. The sample from the body matches the sample from the daughter."

"So, the body is Branden Halifax. Shit."

"You were going to fill me in on this one as soon as you were back around. That going to be any time soon, or am I going to have to wait?"

"No, you did me a huge favor running the samples so fast. Settle in, this one's a wild ride."

While I fill Diaz in on everything I can disclose, I brush my hair and grab a granola bar out of my bag. I end the conversation with him while driving to the station. Mikey is thankfully in his office. Everyone else in the station stares as Tails and I go straight in. This can't wait.

"The body is Branden Halifax."

"Well, good afternoon to you, Liaison Linebach!" Mikey fishes a treat out of his desk drawer for Tails. "We figured it might be, so that is good-ish news, right? I'm guessing Anna couldn't determine anything new about cause of death?"

"No, but I keep thinking about what Marli's psychic said about the man there watching him die. His family's picture is in Lee Stanton's belt buckle with *I'm sorry* written on it. The fact that Lee knew Branden from childhood. They're connected. I want to understand how."

"Can you think of any reason Lee Stanton might have had to kill Branden Halifax?"

"They went to the same school, right? Maybe there was some tension between them? But if he had some secret beef with him, why wait so long to kill him? And he regretted it. Maybe he regretted it so much he couldn't stand to go home and live with himself. Why would you do a thing you regret that much?"

Mikey shrugs. "A lot of money?" Mikey stands and paces as he works through his thoughts out loud. "He was about to lose his job at the snow machine shop, right?" He's been reading back through the files.

"Right. That's why he went to the Bake, but he was turned down."

"Right."

I open the Lee Stanton file and flip through the attachments for a long time before I find notes from the interview with the restaurant manager. They're in Mikey's neat handwriting, so legible, unlike mine. And there it is. One of the last lines is *mana told Lee talk to owner about job.*

"Mikey? Who owns the Bake?"

"I don't know, but I know who would. Call this number." I dial, and the woman who handles the department at night answers. She doesn't even need to research the question.

"Well, the manager started the Bake but he didn't have the

money, so Mr. Drew fronted it to him. I'm not sure if it would be in the manager's name or Mr. Drew's."

Mikey's staring at me with eyes so wide I'm surprised they don't fall out. "Mr. Drew."

I nod. "Mikey, you're the chief now. How do you feel about having a conversation?"

"I'm feeling good, Lou. Think we should call Anna and let her know we need to pick up the body? It belongs to Marli now. We can go talk with her, and then I think it's time we revisit the most fully stocked bar in town."

❖

Anna lays Branden's remains in a simple wooden box. It's not a casket, but it's enough that Marli can bury Branden as is if she wants or transfer him to something of her choosing. Mikey and I don't really talk on the way. Marli smiles when she opens the door. When we tell her and the girls that the body is Branden, the youngest cries and the oldest looks right through us. Marli just nods repeatedly.

"Marli, in the time that's passed, has anything new occurred to you about what could have caused Branden's death?"

She shrugs. "I *have* thought about it, of course. I keep wanting to believe maybe it was just a bear that got the best of him." She laughs. "But what the psychic said about a man watching him die...someone killed him...I've thought about it. I've gotten angry thinking about it, thinking about whether it was someone he knew. But in the end, it doesn't matter. Maybe Branden was doing things I wouldn't have liked. Maybe it was just bad luck. I don't know. But the more I think about it, the more I doubt my Branden, and there's no sense in that. I loved him. He loved me. He was the love of my life, and that's all I need to know, at least in this world."

I can't argue with her logic. I give Mikey a slow blink, and he nods so slightly that Marli doesn't even notice. And there it is. We've agreed that even if we find evidence Lee killed Branden, Marli will not know if we can prevent it.

We place the body in the cellar. Marli assures us Branden's family will help bury him. She thanks us for bringing Branden back to her, even if it was a little late, and she invites us to the funeral, except she calls it a *celebration*. As she opens the door to see us out, she laughs. Mikey looks at her inquisitively.

"The psychic was right, wasn't she? We found him, five years later." She laughs again. "But I guess he was here with me, right on the other side of the mountain, all along."

❖

Mr. Drew has fortified his defenses since I was last here. He's enclosed the entire perimeter of his house with decorative, but obviously functional, eight-foot-tall iron fencing, and the gate that blocks the road to his house is an upgraded, taller version with razor wire on top. I notice several cameras and motion-detecting floodlights. When I turn to Mikey with my silent questions, he just reflects my raised eyebrows and smirks.

Mr. Drew is not delighted to see us. There's no longer a maid, or she's not around. He opens the door wearing jeans and a sherpa-lined sweatshirt. His hair is shorter than it was and significantly white. There are purple bags under his eyes that weren't there before, and his skin is paler, as if he's been venturing out less. He doesn't leave the doorway nor invite us in.

"To what do I owe the pleasure, Officers?" He looks Mikey up and down before he adds, "I'm sorry, *Chief* Harper and Officer Linebach." I have no reason to play nice with Mr. Drew.

"Lee Stanton came to visit you right before he was found dead five years ago." I smile as sickeningly sweet as I can manage. "We thought you might have a story to tell us about that."

He blinks multiple times before he opens the door fully and proceeds to the living room. He reclines in his leather armchair, props his feet on the coffee table, and drapes his arms over the sides of the rests. I think I'm supposed to believe he's totally relaxed. I take a seat on the sofa, settling in for a nice long chat. The fan above us whirls silently at a good clip, pushing cool air from the twenty-foot-high cedar ceiling. Mr. Drew says nothing.

"You remember Lee Stanton, don't you, Mr. Drew? He went missing at the same time as Branden Halifax and Kyle Calderon? Made to look like a suicide?"

One sparse, graying eyebrow rises, but Mr. Drew remains silent.

"Some new evidence has come to our attention regarding those three deaths, and it shows a clear link between them. And that link," I lean forward with my elbows poised on my casually parted trouser legs, "is you." He peruses me slowly in the way a man does to make a woman feel self-conscious. I grin and don't change my posture. I see his clear disappointment when he realizes his usual intimidation technique isn't working.

"How so?"

"Well, Mr. Drew, it might interest you to know we have evidence that Lee Stanton killed Branden Halifax, and that he visited you just before he did. Somehow, he came away from that meeting with a nice wad of cash." I deliberately prop my chin on my fist, ready to hear some good fiction. "Now what might that have been for?"

"Lee Stanton never came here."

"Oh. Then he met you somewhere else?"

"No. I never met Lee Stanton."

"How interesting! In the decades you've lived here, with so few people in Seward, and even fewer people living on this mountain, you never met Lee Stanton, who lived nearby his whole life." He twitches slightly. I lean even further forward. It's good to see him squirm.

"I'm sure he and I have crossed paths before. I remember his picture in the paper looked vaguely familiar. But I don't remember ever having had any meaningful interaction with Lee Stanton." He sets his jaw like this is his final word. I raise the corner of my mouth and wink like we're in on the same joke together.

"Come on now, Mr. Drew. An able-bodied young man like Lee who knew machine repair and clearly could have used a little extra money? You never thought to ask him to work for you, even just on contract? Seems like a missed opportunity on your part. We know how much you like employing the locals."

His nostrils flare. He's lost some of his ability to keep his composure. "It's possible that at some point I asked him to fix something for me. It would have been long before he went missing. If that happened, he likely said no."

"Likely, hmm? Seems far-fetched, but okay." I act like I'm thinking for a minute, like an idea has just come to mind. "Oh, but this should be easy enough, right? You surely keep records of all the payments you make for your businesses and who you make them to, don't you? You'd have a record of paying Lee Stanton if he did some work for you."

"I do keep records of every business transaction. You are welcome to those books if you think they would be helpful." Now he's speaking confidently again. "But I can assure you that you won't find Lee Stanton's name in there."

"And what about people you pay for personal services? Are they in there too?"

"I don't know what you're implying."

"Oh, just people like barbers, folks who do repairs on your house, your personal vehicles, things like that. Any records of those?"

"No. Do you keep records of who you pay to cut your hair?"

I smile. "What did Lee Stanton want when he came to visit you?"

"I don't know why you think he visited me, but he didn't."

"Well, it's just that one of your restaurant managers told us he arranged that meeting." A stretch, but he did at least suggest Lee talk to Mr. Drew. "Lee wanted a job at the restaurant and the manager couldn't hire him. Lee asked if he knew of any other work available, and it seems your name came up. So, he visited you and then poof!" I make a dramatic explosion gesture with my hands. "Suddenly, he has thousands of dollars to give to his parents before he dies."

Mr. Drew breathes harder, and the lines in his forehead are deeper. He turns deliberately to Mikey. "Chief Harper, I don't know what this charade is supposed to be about, but do you have any evidence at all that Lee Stanton spoke with me before he died?"

"Only if your restaurant manager is an honest man." Mikey has his neutral tone perfected. I smile broadly but control my desire to laugh. "I'm assuming you only go into business with honest men. Is that right?"

Mr. Drew dodges the question. "Why are you asking about Lee Stanton? My understanding was that you ruled his death a suicide. Are you saying now that that's not the case?"

"Oh, we believe Lee made the choice to go out into the woods on his own, knowing of course what his ending would be, but we believe that whatever you paid him to do drove him to it, either out of guilt or out of fear that you'd do to him what you had him do to Branden Halifax."

"You think I paid someone to kill Branden?"

"With the evidence we have, we wouldn't be doing our jobs if we didn't explore that possibility."

"Why would I want to kill Branden Halifax? He was one of my best employees."

I make a show of looking surprised. "But I thought you said you'd fired him for a dirty drug screen. You were suspicious because he'd brought Kyle Calderon here. Is that what makes a model employee?"

He stumbles over the first few words. "I, I mean before *that*, of course. Up until then, he had been a model employee. If he could have gotten clean, I'm sure I would have rehired him."

"Even though you knew he and Kyle were involved with the cruise ship robberies?"

"Well, no, then I wouldn't have hired him back. Crimes like that are damaging to our community."

"So, if, theoretically, you had known he was involved in that, you would have tried to get him to stop."

"Of course."

"If you'd fired him already, how might you have done that?" I lean back as I wait for his response. Mikey continues to take his meticulous notes.

"Well, I don't know. I never had to think about it. But you're aware that I am friends with Chief Willington. I suppose I would have told him."

"Ah. And he would have arrested Branden."

"I'd think so."

"That would have been too bad for Marli and the kids." I shake my head dramatically. "Real shame, having Seward earn a reputation for thieves like that. At least it never came to that, right?"

He doesn't answer. "Chief Harper, if we're going to sit around and speculate about what might have happened if Branden hadn't died, then I'm afraid I'll have to excuse myself. I have other things to do."

"Sure, sure. We wouldn't want to keep you from it."

Mikey stands, brushes off his pant legs as if sitting in Mr. Drew's house has made him dirty. He smiles at me, and I stand, but I don't walk to the door. I just look at Mr. Drew. Mikey turns on his heel, hiking boots squeaking loudly on the floor as he turns back.

"Oh, by the way, we thought this might interest you." He reaches into his interior coat pocket and produces the picture of Marli and the kids, still protected with plastic. He hands it to Mr. Drew.

"Marli…Okay?"

"Oh no, flip it over. That's where it gets interesting."

As he reads the words written there, his face whitens three shades. His hands tremble, and he hands the picture back.

"I don't know why this would interest me."

Mikey shrugs. "Just because that's Lee Stanton's handwriting and it was found with his possessions." His tone is casual, light-hearted, even. "Well, thanks for your time!"

Before Mr. Drew can say anything or even move, we're out the door. We both keep our composure until we're off his grounds, knowing there are cameras watching us.

When I call my boss to report on what we've found, he tells me to share everything he sent to me with Mikey. Chief Harper is not to mention it to anyone else, but this is now a full-blown investigation. I'll be staying in Seward for the foreseeable future. When I tell Mikey, he hugs me so hard he lifts me off the ground. I can't wait to tell Anna.

CHAPTER THIRTY

Mikey and I immediately get to work to firmly link Lee, Branden, and Mr. Drew. Though we add a lot to Mr. Drew's file, we need more. After our visit to Mr. Drew, Mikey and I are both now certain he's ordering murders. After a conversation with Chief Quint about how drugs are moving around Anchorage, he's also convinced that Mr. Drew has refocused his trade on supplying Anchorage and its cruise ships instead of Seward. The further from him the drugs end up, the better. But we both know Mr. Drew is still in the game.

❖

The sun shines in an oversaturated blue sky as Anna, Mikey, and I arrive at Marli's house a few days later. The yard is covered in trucks and SUVs, with a few four-wheelers thrown in the mix. Marli surprises all of us with hugs as we walk in. She offers us homemade lemonade and then ushers us through the crowded kitchen and out the back door.

The backyard is covered in many familiar faces—AJ and his mom, Eliyah, most of the volunteers who helped search for Branden years ago, the coffee shop waitress, and the police department's night dispatch all mill around drinking and laughing. We meet some new faces and learn again just how small Seward is when we see the employee from the snow machine shop and Mr. Alaku in attendance. Marli even introduces us to her psychic, who smiles with self-satisfaction. Notably absent is Mr. Drew. Shortly after we arrive, a reporter and a photographer show up. Marli seems to have known they were coming, and she ushers them around the yard, urging them to talk to the people who were closest to Branden. Mikey speaks to them briefly, but I turn away when I see him gesturing toward me. I'm happy to let him be the face of the investigation. Besides, I work with the FBI now, and they don't like drawing attention to themselves most of the time. Anna puts her hand on my arm and smiles. It's comforting to have her here. There are folding tables set up with flower arrangements on each one, and platters of vegetables and dips that don't appear store bought.

"I'm going to say hi to some people. Do you want me to introduce you since you'll be here for a while?" She smiles just like she's done every time my residence in Seward has come up.

"Soon, but can we wait on it?"

"Of course." She touches my arm discreetly, then heads off. I wander over to a vegetable garden with bright red and orange tomatoes. *Marli has been keeping herself busy.* A puppy sprints by, chased by Marli's youngest and some of her friends.

After about twenty minutes where Mikey and Anna mingle and I watch the crowd, pretending to examine the growing carrots and radishes, Marli clinks a glass and moves to the tree line, where the simple wooden box Anna put the skeleton in is laid next to a pre-dug hole in the ground. She smiles at the crowd, which falls respectfully silent. Anna and Mikey wander back to my side.

Marli thanks everyone for being there, and for being part of Branden's life. I study my feet. I never knew the man—never even saw him alive. *I'm part of Branden's death.* She thanks his friends and family for making his brief time wonderful, and then she tells stories about Branden's many adventures, most of which involve near accidents and funny mishaps. She reassures us that if Branden were here, he'd use this as a perfect opportunity to get drunk and convince everyone to race the four-wheelers up the mountain to see who could get the highest up. She tells stories about Branden and the kids. Alicia sniffles, but the youngest just watches wide-eyed.

She invites Branden's friends and his mother to talk about him. Eliyah recounts the particularly harrowing story of Branden getting them stranded on a boat. After the laughter has died down, Marli turns serious.

"Lastly…" She turns to us. I am already blushing. "I'd like to thank Dr. Fenway, Chief Harper, and Officer Linebach. They didn't know Branden in life, but they brought him back to us in death. And even though he wasn't their friend or family or coworker, they searched for him as if he had been. Chief Harper, you've been a good friend to me and the kids, and I believe you would have been a good friend to Branden too. Dr. Fenway, your care handling my Branden's remains has been touching. Officer Linebach, I know it was hard for you to stop searching for him five years ago, but you did.

"It took guts to right the mistake about his body, but you did that too, and now we can put Branden to rest. I am one of the few people in Alaska who can say their missing loved one came back to them, and that's because of you. Thank you." I smile as much as I can through my warm face and hot throat. Her smile is genuine. "I hope you'll stay a part of our little community, because we could use more people like you."

"Hear, hear!" The crowd claps, and a few people shout. Mikey turns to me, clapping hard and grinning. I, of course, am relieved when the attention turns to the box behind Marli.

The burial is fast, and everyone takes turns throwing dirt onto the box. As they throw their handful, each person says something quietly to Branden.

"I'm sorry." It's the only thing I can say.

Mikey and I leave immediately afterward. They'll all want to drink, and we will just make everyone self-conscious. Anna opts to stay for a while. The townspeople are, after all, her friends of many years. Marli hugs us again before we leave, and Alicia makes a point of telling us good-bye.

❖

A week later, I am formally assigned the task of uncovering enough on Mr. Drew for the FBI to have sufficient grounds to bring him in. Tails and I spend the day browsing a real estate catalog, then driving by the places that look nice. It's a nice distraction from the fact I don't know how to start investigating the wealthiest, most well-connected man in this area. Mikey can help me, but only in the way of supplying resources and occasional human effort. With the cruise ships and the tourists, plus the increasing Seward population, he has his hands full.

We've checked out the exterior of the last house on our list and are headed back to the hotel, the sun still high in the sky, when I spot the trailhead that climbs Mount Marathon. I turn to Tails. "Wanna go for a little walk?" Tails shakes his back end in excitement. It's not a long climb, and the wildflowers plus the fine layer of snow at the top make the view especially picturesque.

Not far from the summit, I turn to look back at the tree line and find all of Seward and the harbor laid before me. There are almost no boats tied up—they're out enjoying a cloudless turquoise sky and water that resembles a sheet of slate blue marble from where I stand. Tails tilts his head when I sit on the ground. I never sit on hikes. He promptly comes to sit next to me, though, his face pointed toward Seward too.

"The answer is down there, buddy. I just have to figure out how to get to it. And he'll know I'm looking." My mind turns over. In an ideal scenario, how would I get him? Should I talk to everyone who's ever worked for Mr. Drew? No, I don't believe they'll tell me anything I don't already know. What I need to understand to catch him is how the operation works. How does he recruit these men? Where do they go to deliver? If one of them needs to be a *missing person*, how does Mr. Drew recruit someone to kill them, or does he manage it himself? The men who run drugs for him will never tell me—he'd kill them. He's clever enough I'm not sure I can trick him into telling me, either.

As the train rolls into the Seward station and the cabs slowly travel across the little town, I realize I need to be able to watch Mr. Drew. Closely. Without him knowing I'm there. I take that idea, turn it over, and give myself permission to follow it down the rabbit hole. How could it be done? What would I need?

By the time I stand back up, wiping the earth from the seat of my hiking pants, I know what I need from Mikey. He and Anna will be the only people who can know. As far as the rest of Seward is concerned, I'll be leaving in just a couple days. I'll need to make a show of my good-bye, so Mr. Drew believes I've returned to Anchorage. And then I'll be free to watch and wait as long as necessary. I'll catch him in the act. It's the only way.

I slap my hand against my thigh, and Tails turns to follow me down the mountain. Before we go, I turn my face to the summit of Mount Marathon, wild and beautiful and slightly foreboding even in summer. A breeze blows and the fine white powder catches, uncovering the bones of those who are not found. The flakes circle between rock peaks, trapped, until they settle, covering them again.

About the Author

Bailey Bridgewater is a nomadic grant writer and author who travels the US and Canada with her senior dog. She spends her time hiking, exploring new cities, kayaking, and convincing herself that she doesn't need directions because she's not lost. In a new city, she will quickly seek out a good coffee shop, a bookstore, an amazing garden, and a long hiking trail.

Books Available From Bold Strokes Books

A Talent Ignited by Suzanne Lenoir. When Evelyne is abducted and Annika believes she has been abandoned, they must risk everything to find each other again. (978-1-63679-483-9)

All Things Beautiful by Alaina Erdell. Casey Norford only planned to learn to paint like her mentor, Leighton Vaughn, not sleep with her. (978-1-63679-479-2)

An Atlas to Forever by Krystina Rivers. Can Atlas, a difficult dog Ellie inherits after the death of her best friend, help the busy hopeless romantic find forever love with commitment-phobic animal behaviorist Hayden Brandt? (978-1-63679-451-8)

Bait and Witch by Clifford Mae Henderson. When Zeddi gets an unexpected inheritance from her client Mags, she discovers that Mags served as high priestess to a dwindling coven of old witches—who are positive that Mags was murdered. Zeddi owes it to her to uncover the truth. (978-1-63679-535-5)

Buried Secrets by Sheri Lewis Wohl. Tuesday and Addie, along with Tuesday's dog, Tripper, struggle to solve a twenty-five-year-old mystery while searching for love and redemption along the way. (978-1-63679-396-2)

Come Find Me in the Midnight Sun by Bailey Bridgewater. In Alaska, disappearing is the easy part. When two men go missing, state trooper Louisa Linebach must solve the case, and when she thinks she's coming close, she's wrong. (978-1-63679-566-9)

Death on the Water by CJ Birch. The Ocean Summit's authorities have ruled a death on board its inaugural cruise as a suicide, but Claire suspects murder, and with the help of Assistant Cruise Director Moira, Claire conducts her own investigation. (978-1-63679-497-6)

Living For You by Jenny Frame. Can Sera Debrek face real and personal demons to help save the world from darkness and open her heart to love? (978-1-63679-491-4)

Ride with Me by Jenna Jarvis. When Lucy's vacation to find herself becomes Emma's chance to remember herself, they realize that everything they're looking for might already be sitting right next to them—if they're willing to reach for it. (978-1-63679-499-0)

Rivals for Love by Ali Vali. Brooks Boseman's brother Curtis is getting married, and Brooks needs to be at the engagement party. Only she can't possibly go, not with Curtis set to marry the secret love of her youth, Fallon Goodwin. (978-1-63679-384-9)

Whiskey and Wine by Kelly and Tana Fireside. Winemaker Tessa Williams and sex toy shop owner Lace Reynolds are both used to taking risks, but will they be willing to put their friendship on the line if it gives them a shot at finding forever love? (978-1-63679-531-7)

Hands of the Morri by Heather K O'Malley. Discovering she is a Lost Sister and growing acquainted with her new body, Asche learns how to be a warrior and commune with the Goddess the Hands serve, the Morri. (978-1-63679-465-5)

I Know About You by Erin Kaste. With her stalker inching closer to the truth, Cary Smith is forced to face the past she's tried desperately to forget. (978-1-63679-513-3)

Mate of Her Own by Elena Abbott. When Heather McKenna finally confronts the family who cursed her, her werewolf is shocked to discover her one true mate, and that's only the beginning. (978-1-63679-481-5)

Pumpkin Spice by Tagan Shepard. For Nicki, new love is making this pumpkin spice season sweeter than expected. (978-1-63679-388-7)

Sweat Equity by Aurora Rey. When cheesemaker Sy Travino takes a job in rural Vermont and hires contractor Maddie Barrow to rehab a house she buys sight unseen, they both wind up with a lot more than they bargained for. (978-1-63679-487-7)

Taking the Plunge by Amanda Radley. When Regina Avery meets model Grace Holland—the most beautiful woman she's ever seen—she doesn't have a clue how to flirt, date, or hold on to a relationship. But Regina must take the plunge with Grace and hope she manages to swim. (978-1-63679-400-6)

We Met in a Bar by Claire Forsythe. Wealthy nightclub owner Erica turns undercover bartender on a mission to catch a thief where she meets no-strings, no-commitments Charlie, who couldn't be further from Erica's type. Right? (978-1-63679-521-8)

Western Blue by Suzie Clarke. Step back in time to this historic western filled with heroism, loyalty, friendship, and love. The odds are against this unlikely group—but never underestimate women who have nothing to lose. (978-1-63679-095-4)

Windswept by Patricia Evans. The windswept shores of the Scottish Highlands weave magic for two people convinced they'd never fall in love again. (978-1-63679-382-5)

A Calculated Risk by Cari Hunter. Detective Jo Shaw doesn't need complications, but the stabbing of a young woman brings plenty of those, and Jo will have to risk everything if she's going to make it through the case alive. (978-1-63679-477-8)

An Independent Woman by Kit Meredith. Alex and Rebecca's attraction won't stop smoldering, despite their reluctance to act on it and incompatible poly relationship styles. (978-1-63679-553-9)

Cherish by Kris Bryant. Josie and Olivia cherish the time spent together, but when the summer ends and their temporary romance melts into the real deal, reality gets complicated. (978-1-63679-567-6)

Cold Case Heat by Mary P. Burns. Sydney Hansen receives a threat in a very cold murder case that sends her to the police for help, where she finds more than justice with Detective Gale Sterling. (978-1-63679-374-0)

Proximity by Jordan Meadows. Joan really likes Ellie, but being alone with her could turn deadly unless she can keep her dangerous powers under control. (978-1-63679-476-1)

Sweet Spot by Kimberly Cooper Griffin. Pro surfer Shia Turning will have to take a chance if she wants to find the sweet spot. (978-1-63679-418-1)

The Haunting of Oak Springs by Crin Claxton. Ghosts and the past haunt the supernatural detective in a race to save the lesbians of Oak Springs farm. (978-1-63679-432-7)

Transitory by J.M. Redmann. The cops blow it off as a customer surprised by what was under the dress, but PI Micky Knight knows they're wrong—she either makes it her case or lets a murderer go free to kill again. (978-1-63679-251-4)

Unexpectedly Yours by Toni Logan. A private resort on a tropical island, a feisty old chief, and a kleptomaniac pet pig bring Suzanne and Allie together for unexpected love. (978-1-63679-160-9)

Crush by Ana Hartnett Reichardt. Josie Sanchez worked for years for the opportunity to create her own wine label, and nothing will stand in her way. Not even Mac, the owner's annoyingly beautiful niece Josie's forced to hire as her harvest intern. (978-1-63679-330-6)

Decadence by Ronica Black, Renee Roman & Piper Jordan. You are cordially invited to Decadence, Las Vegas's most talked about invitation-only Masquerade Ball. Come for the entertainment and stay for the erotic indulgence. We guarantee it'll be a party that lives up to its name. (978-1-63679-361-0)

Gimmicks and Glamour by Lauren Melissa Ellzey. Ashly has learned to hide her Sight, but as she speeds toward high school graduation she must protect the classmates she claims to hate from an evil that no one else sees. (978-1-63679-401-3)

Heart of Stone by Sam Ledel. Princess Keeva Glantor meets Maeve, a gorgon forced to live alone thanks to a decades-old lie, and together the two women battle forces they formerly thought to be good in the hopes of leading lives they can finally call their own. (978-1-63679-407-5)

Peaches and Cream by Georgia Beers. Adley Purcell is living her dreams owning Get the Scoop ice cream shop until national dessert chain Sweet Heaven opens less than two blocks away and Adley has to compete with the far too heavenly Sabrina James. (978-1-63679-412-9)

The Only Fish in the Sea by Angie Williams. Will love overcome years of bitter rivalry for the daughters of two crab fishing families in this queer modern-day spin on Romeo and Juliet? (978-1-63679-444-0)